Origin:
The Nameless
Celestial

Aaron R. Allen

Published by
Melange Books, LLC
White Bear Lake, MN 55110
www.melange-books.com

Origin: The Nameless Celestial ~ Copyright © 2015 by Aaron R. Allen

ISBN: 978-1-68046-102-2

Cover Art Design: by Aaron R. Allen and Ronald Conley
Cover Art Layout: Caroline Andrus

I dedicate this book to my loving daughter, Abigail.

For Lindsay, whose "raptor walk" makes me laugh endlessly. You're the "beautifullest."

For Keltyn, your indifference to just about everything takes focus and dedication.

Thanks, Bill. I don't know if any of this would have been possible without your invaluable lessons. I also have no idea how you put up with me!

For Mom and Dad, thanks for teaching me that you have to forge your own path.

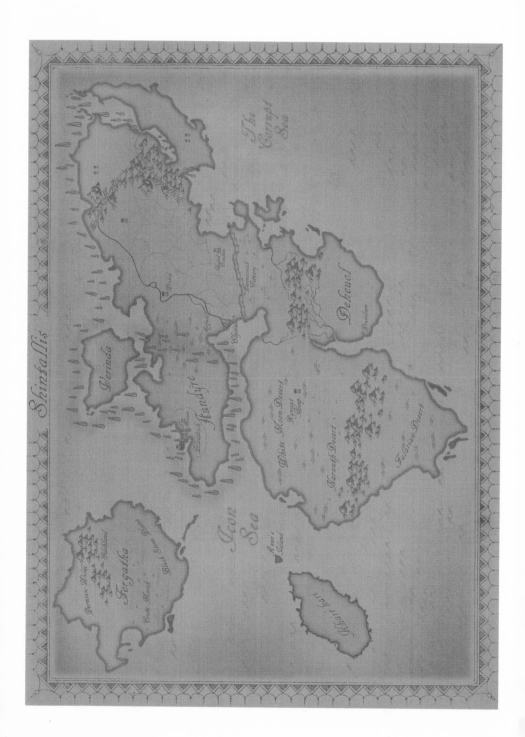

Chapter 1
~ The Bone Skipper ~

The airship lifted from the ground and took to the skies. Cahan Devlin felt a distant rumble as the central energy chamber churned to increase speed. He grabbed onto the notched handhold above where he sat. He felt a tremor in his jaw when the airship jolted him forward, but focused his thoughts on his men. Most of them had fought in several battles, shoulder-to-shoulder with him. He didn't linger on the fact some would not make the return home. He found when he thought too much about getting everyone home, the death toll was even higher. Even though it was just semi-demons they were to face, casualties were the only constant in battle.

As Cahan rose, he noticed a bleak detachment scrawled upon the faces of his men, their eyes distant and cold. They seemed wholly focused on the violence ahead and were probably unwilling to mutter even a sentence. He knew his men were just getting in the proper mindset for their mission. Some of them busied themselves by mending armor and sharpening swords.

A brush of warm air from the corner of the passenger chamber drew his attention. A spellcrafter plied a heat spell to dry out socks and boots spread out in a perfect line along the wall. A red incandescence traced the lines of his face.

The oval-shaped passenger chamber, located in the belly of the airship, met the standard no-frills approach of most Verindian military vessels. Cahan heard a slight echo, which reverberated off the alloy-lined hold as he walked. He continued to a covered window and used the concealment crank to open it. He wanted to look outside because he did not like confined areas. A biting coldness came off the window. He often took comfort in the cold. He placed his fingertips against the cool glass for a moment. Then, with his index finger, he drew the runic symbol for the goddess Valese.

Just ahead lay Blasstock, the site of their mission. Though they needed to pass the spellcrafted barrier that protected this land—for the most part,

1

anyway—their ship's ingress rune would ensure them passage. All airborne vessels required a rune, whereas humans could simply walk in on foot—if they could survive the savage demons on the other side of the barrier.

These lands were designated as a human colony by the demon-inhabited capital city of Protos, though they had once fallen heir to the wandering dogmatists of a long-dead order. The wind-blistered settlement had stood for a century near the foot of the barrier. Many humans had migrated here due largely to the need for airship workers. The constructors of these vessels had built their workshops upon Blasstock's unencumbered land, choosing the location because of the large selection of workers and the safety the barrier provided.

According to Cahan's superior officer, that safety had evaporated as throngs of Amalgam incendiary forces had routinely laid nocturnal siege to Blasstock and her human citizens. Amalgam, as they were commonly called by demons and humans alike, were born of two worlds: part human and part demon. They were often hired as mercenaries by other invading creatures, ones strictly attuned to the spellcrafted barrier and unable to pass its limits. The Amalgam's distant human lineage allowed passage between the opposing nations, freeing them to spread the seeds of conflict as their masters saw fit.

Cahan knew there was always a loophole whenever spellcraft was involved. He didn't understand why they couldn't simply fix the mistake. He supposed they would have to take the barrier down to fix it, which would allow all manner of feral demons into human lands, and eventually Protos. If that happened, it would be akin to setting loose a plague of locusts—if the locusts were ten feet tall and craved human flesh. He guessed that the powers that be could accept casualties here and there at the hands of the Amalgam.

As they closed in, Cahan watched the energy of the barrier envelop the entire vessel, transforming from a barely perceptible white to a cerulean blue. The cold that he had just felt evaporated into warmth. He watched the runic symbol he had just drawn slowly soften and fade away. Each district's unique rune turned the barrier a different color upon entry. He remembered that Protos's rune caused a brilliant emerald green.

As they delved deeper into Blasstock, Cahan felt a grim silence that pervaded over the rolling hills of the territory. It still truly looked like an archaic land inhabited by superstitious beasts. Decaying vistas held carved obelisks of long-dead demons hailing from a blood-mired bygone era. Rough, irregular stones littered large swaths of land, whose concentric orientation was cradled by earth bled of its former decadence. To the casual observer, the panorama of oddly placed stone resembled ancient grave markers, tirelessly carved for the billowing giants of old. Cahan knew that to cling to this idea was to ignore the inherent evil of these lands and the vague shrieking of the spectral hills that seemed to snake its way through the joints of the airship. Cahan felt uneasy. Corrupted lands such as these had a certain measure of sentience. The parasitic earth often fed on fallen warriors during times of bloodshed, eventually digesting the entire body slowly over long periods of time.

A faint tug jarred the airship. Cahan's men went about their business, unfazed. They needed this time to focus. He wondered if he should check it out. He decided to turn his thoughts to the mission.

He had read in his reports that the insurrection of the Amalgam had grown more and more violent, inciting murderous savagery and causing the enemy to grow emboldened. The tempest winds gathering in malevolent wisps of gray gave credence to this. Many considered this to be one of the dread omens of Shabaris, the Dead Caller, an ancient and thought-to-be-dead evil.

As they pushed closer to a decayed glen, he saw the grayish energy. It rose from the hills above and rippled outward, only to be carried away by the howling wind. He didn't expect to see such a thing before they had arrived at their destination. Why didn't the capital city, Protos, intervene and massacre the Amalgam with their gargantuan dragonoid soldiers? He decided to let that go for now. He had obsessed over the politics of the capital city for months. This made his mission all the more important because he didn't want the chaos to spread to Verinda.

Cahan faltered as the chamber shifted more fiercely. However unlikely, it felt as though they had run into something. There were no other airships scheduled in the territory, as he had viewed an itinerary of travel just before they had disembarked. He again grabbed a handhold and looked to his men.

"Tell the pilot to slow down while I go topside," Cahan ordered.

He reached the topside hatch and quickly churned the crank to open it. He stepped out on the deck and felt the air push at him violently. The wind whistled in his ears. He quickly surveyed the area. There were no other vessels in sight.

As he explored the deck, he began to think about how he had gotten here. He thought of how alien the lands and inhabitants of his last mission looked to his eyes. Their way of life was so antiquated compared to the place he called home. He almost pitied them. He tilted his head down for a moment and felt a deep sense of sentimentality. His mind flipped through images of his old stomping grounds, as if he were paging through an old travel guide. He wondered if he would ever smell the salty wind near the crystal-green bluffs of Mire Headland, or gaze at the red skyline as dusk faded into blackness, making room for a congregation of beaming stars. The seer he had met before he came to Verinda had peered into his mind and showed him what she said was his future. He had seen the moments before his death, in which he was holding an archaic dagger.

A gust of wind brushed over him. The wind sifted through his hair, tossing strands of brown into his mouth. He unconsciously moved them away. Despite the howling current, being topside was almost peaceful. The wind seemed to be his only companion at the moment. There was a blissful nothingness here. He wondered why he didn't do this more often. He had very few peaceful moments as of late, and he could tell this moment was about to be shattered. A familiar scent permeated his nostrils—a scent of a singular creature that often inhabited corrupted lands. Cahan hoped there would only be one of them.

He hunched down and eased his way across the deck. He drew his basledar dagger from the back of his belt and considered wielding his sword, but decided it would be hard to use with the gusting winds pushing against his every movement. He often felt there was a metaphorical wind determined to impede him, a darkness within him that could not be sated.

He came to the edge of the railing and made sure that he had the proper footing. He did not want to fall into one of the passenger reliefs or collide against a spellcraft-infused cannon turret. He winced at the shrill whistling sound of the creature's tymbal organ. He despised insects—even the human-like ones in Protos.

Cahan carefully lay flat on his stomach. The wind whistled harshly as it brushed over the top of his dragon-bone armor. The peace he had felt earlier had vanished as disgust slowly scratched its way into his mind, ripping and tearing at him. All that remained was a mixture of anxiety and the overwhelming urge to kill the creature festering on the side of the airship. He figured the Amalgam had driven these insects out of the corrupted forest and forced an early migration. This one was probably left behind, or too injured to join the rest of the swarm. Just as likely, it was about to enter its metamorphosis.

Cahan peered over the edge. He saw large, membranous wings flapping in the wind with branching trails of hideous blue veins just beneath the surface. The creature suddenly shifted, and revealed its midsection of translucent, smooth scales with occasional black spots that almost looked like charred dermis. Its large, globular eyes had thousands of cylindrical hairs protruding from them. Cahan did not like the look of the creature's long, rust-colored mandibles. They looked like hunting daggers with serrated edges.

Cahan watched in horror as the creature butted its head against the portside of the vessel. Yellowish insect blood oozed down the larboard. The sharp odor of an acidic substance wafted upward—a result of using its head as a battering ram. It was attempting to burrow its way in by secreting an acidic gas that was normally expelled when the creature was attacked. This "bone skipper" must have scented fetid flesh somewhere, unless the corruption of these lands had somehow driven it from hunting decomposing flesh to that of the living. The corrupted lands and the insects were likely vying for the same food source.

He had to do something quickly. He did not want to get a bunch of his men out here fighting this creature and risking casualties before the mission had even started. At best, it would be an unwelcome distraction at a time when they needed to keep their focus on what was to come. He looked to the cannon turrets mounted near him and got an idea. Cahan silently sheathed his dagger. The cannons were not linked to the secondary energy chamber at the moment, so they could not be fired. A quick solution was needed.

He waited a few agonizing moments for the creature to bash its head again. He heard only metal scraping and the subtle stirring of the tymbal organ. It was like the last bit of air being pushed out of the bellows of chanter pipes. The creature hissed violently before it once more bashed its head against the vessel. A faint vibration skittered through the cold alloy beneath Cahan's body. Cahan climbed down to a recess on the portside—uncomfortably close to the creature—barely avoiding detection. Only a few feet of metal separated Cahan from the bone skipper. He heard the insect buzzing once more, and its acidic fumes filled his nostrils. He tightly clamped his hand to his mouth to stave off a coughing fit. He wasn't sure how much more punishment the ship could take.

Just outside the recess was the copper coil that stemmed from the energy chamber and carried its raw power to the cannon turret mounted on the deck. To use the cannon, Cahan would have to move the coil, which was normally done via a switch inside on the lowermost deck, to the tubing junction and complete the pathway that led to the cannon's spellcraft receptor. Since this was not an aerial combat mission, the pathway was switched off to avoid draining the chamber.

Cahan heard the tymbal organ of the creature stir once more and the accompanying hideous shrill which filled him with dread. He was hesitant to stick his hand out there. He didn't want the creature to slice it off with its pincers. Cahan quickly swatted his hand at the coil, only to feel it partially move. He realized that he would have to hang halfway out of the recess and use more elbow grease than a quick swipe would allow. He knew full well that the bone skipper would see him. He would have to move quickly to the cannon and get a shot off. It would be a race between the two of them.

The flapping sound of the bone skipper's membranous, vein-filled wings assaulted his ears. He thought about the moment of peace the creature had stolen. He closed his eyes, focused on the whipping wind, and wondered if the death vision he had seen was wrong. He asked himself if this creature was moments away from feasting on his flesh. That would definitely make the seer wrong.

With his eyes still shut tight, Cahan grabbed some nearby piping so that he could swing his body over and move the coil to the junction. He bit his bottom lip and slowly opened his eyes. A flash of his death vision again invaded his consciousness. He shook his head to rid himself of the seer's supposed truth. Quickly, Cahan flung his body and reached for the coil. Insect shrieking immediately burst from the direction of the bone skipper, but he could not see if it was moving toward him. He felt as though it was almost on his back as shivers shot up his spine.

Cahan slid the coil to the junction just as the bone skipper's dagger-like pincer scraped against his armor.

"Shit!" Cahan screamed.

He quickly climbed topside as he once again felt the pincer, but this time it scraped the bottom of his right boot. He tucked and rolled back onto the alloy deck and sprinted for the cannon turret. He flung himself into the gunner seat, cranked the rolling lever, and whirled it around to the bone skipper's direction.

He saw it in full view for a split second. Even in that second, he noticed how the creature's bulbous black eyes stared coldly at him. The bone skipper extended its wings and lunged at Cahan. Cahan fired a radiant blast of fire spellcraft right below its head, onto where he guessed its chest was. The bone skipper launched a good distance back and fell to the deck, wings limp. It hadn't seemed like a fully charged blast, but it appeared to do the trick. He figured he should finish the job with one more blast for good measure. He grabbed the turret handle and squeezed the recessed trigger, but nothing came out. He hurled curses into the swirling wind. The coil must have not stayed in place because the switch from the inside did not lock it in position.

Cahan unsheathed his dagger again and went to check on the inert beast. He approached slowly. Suddenly, the large insect convulsed wildly as if in the throes of death. The bone skipper was limp and still, wings splayed out. Its translucent scales turned a darker, grayish color. Cahan intended to check on the insect and cast it over the port side.

When he laid a hand on one of the creature's disgusting, membranous wings, it did not stir. Cahan crouched and began to push the bone skipper's limp body toward the edge.

"Everything okay, Chief Ranger?" a crewman called. "Shit! What the hell is that? Is that a Forgathan?"

"No, it's a bone skipper," Cahan replied. "Just a carrion eater. It was butting its damn head against the ship."

"No shit?" After a pause, he yelled, "Cahan!" The crewman's eyes looked past him and widened.

As Cahan turned around, the bone skipper rose up. From its translucent skin sprouted bristly hairs—like those of a moth—all over its body. The hairs were a drab gray, like the metallic sheen of the deck, and even emerged from its membranous wings. The wings slightly differed. Within the gray, lines of red, orange, and green bristles mixed in a pattern that looked like large eyes on the edges.

The pattern and colors of the creature filled Cahan with an indescribable urge to kill. He plunged his dagger deep into the creature's abdomen, a venomous hatred erupting within him. The bone skipper sprang forward and wrapped its wings around Cahan. Cahan felt helpless and trapped, as if he were in some sort of cocoon. He fell backward, wriggling violently until he hit the deck, headfirst. Cahan still had his knife in his hand, but it was pinned in because of the bristly cocoon. He also felt an odd powdery substance caked on the wings. This filled him with even more rage. He needed space. He needed out—now.

His head ached from the fall. He half-wished acidic fumes would expel from him as his blurry vision came into focus. The insect seemed intent on squeezing the life out of him. Fortunately, his armor protected him—though the heat and insect stench weren't helping his anxiety. Cahan turned his wrist slowly, stuck the point of the knife through the wing, and began to cut upward. The bone skipper immediately spread its wings and hissed violently. Cahan breathed a sigh of relief as the howling current filtered through. The creature kept Cahan pinned with its bristly legs. As he glanced up at the bone skipper, it looked as though the eye patterns on its wings were staring at him. The green, which had sprouted forth earlier, now metamorphosed into a deep burgundy.

The bone skipper thrust its head toward Cahan. Its pincers were inches from his face. He caught the creature's right pincer and gripped it tightly just as it was about to swipe at him with its knife-like mandibles. Blood dripped from his hand onto his face as he pushed as hard as he could muster. After he had pushed the creature's head back a good distance, he turned his wrist and snapped the pincer off. As its head fell toward him, he thrust the dagger between the bone skipper's eyes and cut downward. Yellowish insect blood, brain matter, and bits of cartilage poured from the opening. Cahan pushed the creature's carcass off him and attempted to wipe the insect grime from his face.

"Do you mind?" Cahan asked the crewman, who was biting the skin of his thumb nervously. "Get me a damn towel or something!"

7

"Yes, sire." The crewman headed toward the lower deck. Then he stopped and turned back to Cahan. After a slight pause, he said hesitantly, "I also came up to tell you we will be landing soon."

"Fantastic!" he yelled out sarcastically.

Chapter 2
~ The Siege at Blasstock ~

Just beyond an outcropping of looming monoliths, Cahan huddled, grim and distracted, beneath the dense cover of tree brush. As he waited for the local militia, flashes of broken memories fired in his mind. He soon submerged himself in his thoughts and lost awareness of his surroundings. His death vision was now more lucid. He saw dark, misty flashes of himself clutching a dagger with a gnarled wooden handle. In the vision, he trudged forward with a trancelike evenness blanketing his face. "Chief Ranger," a soldier said, breaking Cahan out of his troubling vision. "I think I see the Rattock infantry approaching."

Cahan led the Verindian forces for this particular mission. Over time, he had learned that he was somewhat of an enigma to the rest of the Verindian rangers, since he had transferred from a scarcely known neighboring island off the coast of Verinda proper. Prior to his arrival, the region had not produced any rangers, spellcrafters, or soldiers of any sort. In fact, the island specialized in domestic trades, exporting fish and crops to the other human colonies. The island was almost exclusively known by human importers, a fact that seemed convenient to most.

Cahan looked down on the soldiers, who mostly stood a foot or two shorter. He kept his well-developed physique hidden under compact forged plate armor, which had been wrought with expertly hewn scales of black dragon-bone and tightly fastened to rings of onyx metal. The black metal was known for its lightness and resilience to heavy blows, as well as its ability to be imbued with spellcraft. Searing red lines stretched across the back of his armor, a remnant of the arcane dragon from which it was forged. Ever defiant to military custom, Cahan grew his hair longer than the standard.

An officer of the Rattock Demon Eaters lurched toward Cahan. The man seemed fragile and not cut out for military life, though Cahan held that opinion of most men. The man made eye contact for a moment before looking away. Cahan hated those who were too timid, at least during wartime. He felt sure they would retreat at the first sign of blood on the battlefield.

"Ranger Devlin?" The officer sounded cross.

Cahan thought to himself that his reputation, once again, had preceded him. Other militia forces often treated him with this caustic behavior, but he'd assumed it was out of jealousy for his talents on the battlefield. The best way to react, in Cahan's mind, was with biting sarcasm. The Demon Eaters had never actually fought full-blooded demons—just half-breeds. He figured that this fact should be pointed out.

"It's Chief Ranger Devlin, but you can call me Cahan."

The officer nodded and opened his mouth to respond.

"I prefer Cahan," Cahan interrupted. "What do you prefer, Demon Eater?" His sarcasm earned him a chuckle from his men. "How does demon taste, anyway?"

Though embarrassed by the remark, Cahan noticed that the officer wanted to respond. However, in Cahan's mind, just because he wanted to say something didn't mean he should, so Cahan continued. "Now that the Rattock have arrived, it's time for our appraisal. We're right on the brink of uncovering one of the key Amalgam military leaders, the one who's been organizing the strikes in this region. They'll not be expecting a preemptive attack, as the local volunteer military has been overcome at every turn."

Embarrassment and red anger once again washed over the Rattock officer's face. It was normally ill-mannered to speak poorly of the hosting forces, but Cahan did not often bother with pleasantries.

"I would not say 'overcome', Cahan," the officer said through a tight scowl, his pride visibly shaken.

"Then why are we here? Should we take leave back to Verinda?"

The Demon Eaters looked around anxiously. Cahan could tell the rest of them knew that even the word "overcome" was being gracious. According to Cahan's reports, they were barely surviving each battle; most of them seemed relieved to have the help of his militia throng.

One of the other Rattock officers raised his hand and asked for permission to speak. Cahan granted his request with a flick of his wrist and forefinger.

"We are happy to have you here, Chief Ranger," the officer said in a cajoling tone. "Please continue. I speak for most of us. We need as much assistance as Verinda can spare."

"The Amalgam are weaker during the daylight hours," Cahan insisted. "We attack in the morning, just as their strength decreases."

"Nightfall will give us better cover," the paramount Rattock officer argued.

"You've been fighting them at night?" Cahan yelled. "They see at night like we see in the day. It's no wonder your necks have been slit at every turn!" He paused to take a calming breath. "Observation is as much a key to winning battles as strength. Use your damn heads! Night will not provide cover against these stinking animals. If you had spent just a little time watching your enemy, there would be more of you standing here today."

The Rattock lowered their heads, and a silence came over them. Cahan could tell their thoughts were on the compatriots they had needlessly lost. He decided to break the silence, as he knew that soldiers shouldn't go into battle with a heavy heart.

"I want to see killers," Cahan ordered. "Nothing but victory should be on your lips. Kill two Amalgam for each comrade you have lost."

He ordered the assemblage of soldiers to advance toward the enemy's stronghold.

* * * *

Alban, a newly recruited Rattock Demon Eater, had never seen a real battle with semi-demons. He tentatively moved forward as his group crept amongst the cover of dead autumn-colored brush. Shafts of morning sun peered through tree cover and partially illuminated swaths of dead foliage with grotesque tree veins crawling outward. He stopped with them when they came across a corrupted scar in the land, which served as their marker of separation.

Just beyond the horizon of perished growth, an early tide of sunbeams laid bare a large, slightly raised, treeless area, surmounted by a prodigiously carved, uneven stone structure. The joints of the structure seeped yellowish mucus. The sight of the decayed area around the edifice waxed horrifically in Alban's mind, and the scent of carrion buffeted his senses. As he beheld the alien landscape, his mind began to wander. What had he gotten himself into? He didn't belong here.

Alban and his cohorts broke east to flank the Amalgam skulking in the deformed uprising of oak that neighbored the bleak edifice. He watched as the chief ranger's large group parted; half of the group broke west of the forested area and fanned out northward, where a few run-down structures stood—likely honeycombed with insects and blood worms. The remaining men lingered at the swath of scarred land.

Alban was partnered with an infantryman who had joined at the same time as he had—but for the life of him, he could not remember his name. He thought about asking him, but since they could both be dead in mere moments, he decided that he would be better off not knowing. He remembered the man being squeamish at the Rattock Recruiting House—and nothing had changed. In his mind, he had even nicknamed him Squeamish.

Once Alban and the man he called Squeamish reached their post, he spied two hairless Amalgam speaking in their choking, sloppy dialect, which he found abhorrent. Alban armed his crossbow and slowly brought the weapon into position, fixing his gaze upon the Amalgam Incendiary. His finger danced around the trigger for a moment, and his breathing intensified. He expelled a breath and clenched his teeth as he pulled the trigger.

The bolt cut through the wind and pierced the unwitting creature in the neck, which caused its brown, viscous blood to gush out and fall upon the corrupted soil of the forest. It was not long on the black, gritty soil. The sanguine stains were immediately drunk into the preternatural swath of earth. As the Incendiary knelt, coughing and gasping for air, Alban watched one of his cohorts sneak up behind the now-alert companion of the dying Amalgam. With a thrusting blur of white metal, the other Amalgam fell to the leaf-littered ground. Alban heard the gut-wrenching sound of the corrupted soil as it fed on the Amalgam.

Alban looked down at the ground and checked the bottoms of his boots. It was frightening to him to be standing on a living entity that hoped for his demise so it could be fed.

Alban suddenly heard the faint sound of arrows being loosed upon the wind. The archers of his militia stretched their bow strings and showered poisonous arrows upon the Amalgam, driving them back toward the decrepit structures. This was the remaining groups' signal to begin with their phase of the stratagem.

Alban and Squeamish plodded north where two rounded trees formed a ponderous archway in the grotesque forest. Tree husks, black and bent, looked down threateningly at them. Sounds of dying Amalgam rang out in the otherwise silent forest. Alban then heard the sound of a blade being drawn from a scabbard, followed by snaps and snarls. The Amalgam were obviously riled into a demonic fervor by the haunting echoes of their comrades' deaths. Through a sliver of space in the dead brush that concealed him, Alban saw his enemies' sunken eyes blaze yellow as they darted around the whispering corpses of worm-eaten woods. Their patchy, pinkish skin grew unnaturally and hideously taut around their mouths and cheekbones. He assumed it was some sort of carnal response to the conflict.

This all seemed too real to Alban. His only thought was that he could die at any moment.

Alban turned to his partner and put a shaky hand on his shoulder. "We have to do something. We have to kill these Amalgam."

Squeamish nodded. The two of them drew their blades and stole quietly toward the snapping and hissing half-demons. The taller of the two Amalgams snorted loudly. Alban could tell that this time, it was different. It was not simply menacing—it had caught scent of them.

They took cover behind a thicket. Silent, horrific moments passed, and Alban's mind raced with heart-pounding anxiety.

A sword plunged through the thicket and grazed Alban's shoulder, and a white-hot pain awakened his senses. In that moment, Alban heard opposing voices in his head. One told him to run; the other told him to grit his teeth and fight. Not being one to back down from a battle, he gritted his teeth.

Alban and Squeamish rose to their feet. The tall Amalgam hurled a small dagger toward Alban. The crimson metal dagger pierced his armor and went deep into his thigh. As warm blood slithered down his leg, he felt the unnatural earth below him vibrate with its ever-present thirst.

Alban looked down at the weapon and saw that it was a stolen knightly dagger. He had no idea why the make of the dagger mattered at this moment. He faltered and fell to his knees.

Squeamish ran toward one of the Amalgam and swung wildly to give Alban a moment to recover.

"Stop!" Alban yelled. "They will kill you!"

Alban pulled out his winding crank, and his hands shook violently as he loaded his crossbow. All he could think about was the amount of time it was taking to load the damn thing. "Finally!" he exclaimed as he finished, then scanned the area for Squeamish. For a moment, he did not see where they had gone. Red metal flashed out of the corner of his eye. When he focused on the battle, Alban was surprised how far ahead their swordfight had taken them. He made his way toward them as fast as his wounded leg would allow.

Alban got a good glimpse of the fight ahead. The Amalgam bared its teeth at Squeamish and raised its shining crimson blade.

"Shit!" Alban yelled out, then raised his crossbow, and aimed it at the Amalgam. He squeezed the trigger and loosed his last poisonous bolt, which sunk into the spoiled skin of the semi-demon's upper arm.

With a roar, the Amalgam tore the bolt out. It stared at the pointed piece of wood for a moment, then began to writhe in agony, its jaw flexing, and its head shaking involuntarily. Alban moved closer until he could see its bloodshot eyes and the trails of sweat beading down its grotesque face. Blood dripped from its lips as it unconsciously bit down and opened its mouth at irregular intervals. Its veins bulged and turned a pulsating purplish blue, while its eyes crusted over with hideous yellow mucus, flecked with solid coral-like bits. Finally, its mouth frothed with a mixture of blood and a gray, gelatinous compound, and the Amalgam buckled and fell to the corrupted soil. To Alban, the corruption sounded as if it hissed with delight.

The other Amalgam growled and spat. The creature arrogantly raised its hand and beckoned Squeamish. He attempted a panicky thrust toward its belly, but the Amalgam blocked his overextended lunge and landed a strike to his ribcage.

Squeamish cried out in pain and backpedaled sharply away from the overpowering semi-demon.

Alban tried to ignore the pain as he approached the Amalgam. His leg was moist with blood, and he could not feel his foot. He was almost there; he was not sure if he should take the time to load his crossbow or keep moving forward. Without any poisonous bolts left, he would have to land a shot to a vital area and kill the creature. Alban decided to keep moving—the crossbow was too much of a risk.

Alban heard the Amalgam release an inhuman growl. He kept his eyes focused on the creature as it charged toward his partner. Squeamish swung high toward the Amalgam's head, but the creature anticipated this and dropped low. The Amalgam swung elegantly at Squeamish's legs, and sliced cleanly through. With a look of shock, he fell to the corrupted earth. Blood poured from the stumps that were once his legs. The corruption feasted with a horrifying lapping sound as the soldier Alban knew only as Squeamish anguished.

Alban finally reached the semi-demon that had just cut down his friend. Its back was turned to him as it stood over its conquest. The lapping sound of the corruption was canceling out the sound of his footsteps, and he took full advantage.

When Alban reached the demon, he drew the dagger from his thigh, not caring if he would be able to stop the bleeding, and plunged it into the back of the Amalgam's neck. Alban circled around so that he could stand before the creature and see its face as it died. The tip of the dagger protruded from the front of the Amalgam's neck. With satisfaction, he pushed the Amalgam backward to feed the corrupted earth.

Alban knelt down before his partner. Squeamish's pupils were enlarged and fixed skyward. Sweat streamed down his forehead. Alban always thought death would be like a door shutting and locking away any semblance of light. Yet, a patch of speckled sunlight had slithered through the corrupted forest's long-reaching branches and blanketed his friend's face at the very moment he was losing his grip on life.

"What is your name?" Alban said.

Squeamish smiled. Alban could tell he was struggling to get words out.

"Alban…"

"Yes?"

"No, my name is Alban, too."

"How the fuck did I forget your name? You have the same damn name as me."

The both of them laughed for a moment until the squeamish—and heroic— Alban died.

* * * *

Cahan and his men gathered at the south entrance of the foreboding cyclopean structure. A black-haired human conjuror by the name of Bardon pressed his bony, long-fingered hand against the cold, uneven stone. He wore Verindian wizard's armor, which was a fusion of locking-scale armor on top that gave way to robes woven with strands of enchanted onyx metal from the waist down.

"The room is clear of Amalgam," Bardon said in a hushed tone.

Cahan produced three transparent spheres containing eluvium, an amber-colored substance, from a waterproof satchel draped over his shoulder. The orbs emitted a faint humming sound. Cahan carefully placed the spheres where the hinges and bolted lock would be on the other side of the stone gateway. The spheres affixed to the surface of the small opening where the door stood flush to the wall, as if it were attached by some sort of magnetic attraction. The amber-colored substance inside the spheres seeped out of their clear housings, deliberately oozing through the space between the door and the wall, as if it possessed a sort of consciousness. The eluvium enveloped the hinges and lock and began to weaken them.

Bardon grabbed Cahan's arm.

"A sentry approaches," he said urgently.

Cahan grabbed both sides of the door, cramming his fingers into the openings, bearing the weight of the slab.

"How long until it's here?"

"Moments."

Cahan grunted as he tightened his grip on the large rectangle of stone.

"Where is he now?" Cahan whispered.

"Just to the left of the door, sniffing," Bardon said quietly.

"I need you to disperse the sound from this entire area and put up a sound barrier—"

Bardon quickly conducted the spell, eliminating all sound.

"Don't worry, I can read lips," Cahan mouthed, cutoff mid-sentence from Bardon's sound barrier.

Bardon chuckled at the sight of Cahan's mouth moving silently; his matted tangle of curly black hair jiggled like molded gelatin. Cahan shook his head at the spellcrafter's inappropriate comedic timing.

Cahan peered beyond the gap in the doorway. The amber material had done its worst. Cahan charged forward, shouldering the stone door, and smashed it into the unwary Amalgam sentry. Cahan locked eyes with his men as they waited

15

several breathless moments, hoping the sound barrier had prevailed. Since the group was not surrounded by a throng of Amalgam, Cahan concluded the sound barrier was still operative. He signaled the men to keep moving.

Cahan cautiously gazed into the attached room of refuse and blood stains. A few Amalgam filed into the corridor. Cahan rested his back against the concealing wall next to the yawning stone doorway. The Amalgam had a single gruesome eye centered in the middle of their faces, resting above asymmetrical, seeping nasal slits, which were eerily punctuated by a pronounced under bite. The creatures moved strangely, due to the lack of sight on the periphery. They ambled with measured steps, as they swayed side to side with their bizarre erratic gait. The sad gaping-mouthed creatures' primary function seemed to be masonry. In unison, the one-eyed Amalgam raised their hammers, clutching at strange, half-crafted stone idols.

Cahan turned to Bardon and mouthed the words, "They can hear each other, right?"

"Yes?" Bardon mouthed with a shrug.

Cahan looked at Bardon angrily. "What the hell do you mean 'yes'?" Cahan mouthed as he shrugged his shoulders in a mocking imitation.

"In concept, yes they should." Bardon shrugged again, unfazed.

The single-eyed creatures began to toil away at their decadent, hideous statues. However, as they struck hammer to chisel, they appeared puzzled. Some swings had sound while others did not. The creatures began to wave their hands at each other, shambling about the room. Some of their odd, repellent dialect aired, while other words came out as muffled silence.

Cahan shot Bardon a sardonic look before he charged into the room, gray saber drawn. A streak of cobalt crept down toward the blade's base until it reached an embossed spider creature, basking in its blue gleam. He ducked as one of the Amalgam cyclops swung its hammer at his head. Cahan sliced low with his blade, cutting through the mangled-looking creature's thigh. One of the accompanying mouth-breathing Amalgam swung its hammer just as Cahan cleaved the leg of his cohort. Cahan spun away from the strike, bringing his blade around to slice through the attacker's arm. Rancid, brown blood spattered the walls as the Amalgam fell to the ground, their misshapen mouths agape in silent screams. A black, amaranthine-tinged projectile surged past Cahan, crushing the remaining Amalgam into the seeping demonic stone wall with violence. The lifeless Amalgam fell to the ground, their mangled-looking bodies broken and bloodied.

Speechless, Cahan stared at the bold display of spellcraft before him. He traced the smoldering path back to the grinning human conjurer. He had never seen a human produce such a blast. There was rumor of a human witch, deemed a heretic, that could produce conjurations of such a magnitude, but never one so seemingly young and male.

Cahan looked back at the corpses young, gaunt Bardon had laid to waste. Their normally stout Amalgam physiques were piles of bone and patchy flesh. Their necks had been snapped so forcefully that vertebrae protruded through the skin. Cahan stared at Bardon for a moment in bewilderment.

"What?" Bardon mouthed, as if being scolded by his mother.

The other soldiers, clad in locking scale armor, filed quickly into the room. Cahan could see they were just as bewildered as he when they saw the scene. The group, especially Declan, Cahan's second-in-command, seemed disappointed that the fight had ended prematurely.

Cahan attempted to speak to see if the sound barrier was still intact. The prevailing silence answered his question, though he heard other Amalgam gestating in the stone edifice. Cahan surmised that some of the Amalgam's lapping sounds were canceled because Bardon, the source of the conjuration, was nearby.

Declan furtively approached the chief ranger with a scrawled-on piece of parchment. Declan thrust the note and a writing lash in Cahan's hand. Cahan turned away from Bardon's direction to read the note.

Where did you find this man? If he is a man at all.

The truth was, Bardon had been forced into his company, which made him even more suspicious. Cahan wrote quickly on the parchment and returned it to Declan.

Be sure to keep an eye out.

The group moved forward to a large dual door of brindle wood with a bisecting line of metal cutting across and around the periphery. It led to a large, open room, most likely full of Incendiaries.

Chapter 3
~ The Cyclopean Titan ~

"Bardon," Cahan said, expecting no sound as he moved closer to the door. When he heard his own voice, he was puzzled. "Has the barrier worn off?"

"No, it simply does not reach this far," Bardon whispered. "I can attempt to push it farther out, if necessary."

Cahan nodded his head and gave an impatient gesture.

Bardon closed his eyes for a moment and raised his hand. His hand began to shake. A muted rumbling filled Cahan's ears and snapped away into nothingness. Cahan rubbed his ear for a moment and shook his head. He felt like he had a temporary case of vertigo.

Cahan again produced a clear spheroid housing of eluvium and pinned it to the door's center crease. On the opposite side of the door, he saw a large rectangular slab of brindle wood that barred entry through the crease. He only let the eluvium do its work for a few moments, then impatiently aimed a kick, heel first, at the brindle, breaking the slab of metallic wood. The doors to the large room flung open to a dimly lit cyclopean expanse of bestial horror.

Cahan quickly took in the disgusting living quarters of these creatures. Several impromptu rotting wood partitions stood tottering in the hideous space with leering creatures darting in and out of them. Boarded-up, round-headed windows were centered on each wall, just above the hastily raised dividers. The ceiling was clearly bound by that of spellcrafted masonry, as a barely perceptible glow traced the lines of the callused stone joints.

Thanks to Bardon's sound barrier, only the Amalgam that were facing the door were aware intruders were in their midst. Cahan turned to Bardon to give him an order, but it seemed as though Bardon had read his mind. With a grimace, Bardon extended the sound barrier to the Incendiaries so they could not audibly warn one another. Beads of sweat trailed down his brow as the exertion of maintaining the spell sapped more of his strength. The Verindian soldiers fanned out to meet their opponents.

The Amalgam screamed muted rants to their cohorts in an attempt to warn them, which resulted in comically confused anger. Even in the midst of battle, this amused Cahan. He was surprised by how fast the creatures turned on each other. The Amalgam were at each other's throats because of the chaos the sound barrier caused. Some struck their comrades with fists while others stabbed, maimed, and killed.

The movement of a titan-sized Amalgam caught Cahan's eye. The creature had set its sights on one of his men that had just bashed the skull of an Amalgam sentry. He sized up the giant; the creature possessed a mace the size of a wood imp sheathed to its Gronxth-hide armor. Cahan moved to intercept the large, lumbering creature, whose long gait seemed almost insurmountable to Cahan as he attempted to cover the large expanse of stone and muted chaos, ducking silent swords, maces, and spellcraft. The battle was surreal without the aid of sound. He could not hear the horde of semi-demons clamoring around him. At any moment, a creature could lunge from behind and dig its claws into him. Yet he felt energized by the soundless battle's inherent danger, and it invigorated his stride.

Before him, the elephantine Amalgam raised its mace above its head and swung downward, crushing the Verindian beneath its awesome force. Cahan's mouth dropped open. He wasn't fast enough. The sight of his soldier smashed beyond recognition angered him to his core.

Drenched in human pulp, the mace began to glow as Cahan finally drew into the titan's radius. The Amalgam looked at the mace in dismay and gazed beyond Cahan, scanning the room thoroughly. A nearby sword-wielding ranger attempted to lunge forward and impale the creature through the ribcage, but the titan kicked him in the chest without looking, sending him sailing backward.

* * * *

Across the stone expanse, Bardon found himself surrounded by a group of Amalgam that had emerged from the decaying partitions on the northern side of the decaying stone edifice. Bardon produced his staff for the first time in this mission. He normally preferred handcrafted magic, which was primal in its power, but not sustainable for long periods of time. Spellcraft conducted through a focal point like a staff allowed for longer use and permitted the user to mimic the attributes of certain manmade objects.

Bardon turned toward a charging Amalgam and raised his black, metallic staff, crowned with the sculpted head of a mountain dragon. The cylindrical staff emitted a burst of cool sapphire, which seemed to evaporate in the next moment. The smoky smell of spellcraft emission filled Bardon's nostrils. As the angry venom of battle rose in his chest, his eyes blazed the same blue as his spellcraft.

19

Suddenly, the conjuration reappeared before the Amalgam, mimicking the attributes of a rapier, slicing into its midsection. By this time, two other Amalgam had raced toward him.

Bardon tightened his grip on his staff and held it in front of his attackers, his eyes blazing silver. The spoiled-skinned Amalgam swung their blades of crimson in unison, which clanged against something unseen. Not trusting their eyes, the creatures swung once more. At the moment of impact, a silver light shone in the shape of a shield. Bardon saw the reflection of the light envelop their hideous, patchy faces. One of the Amalgam coughed, probably from the smoke of the spellcraft. Bardon remembered what it felt like the first time he ingested the smoke. It had coated his lungs and throat to the point that it was painful to breathe.

The Amalgam continued to strike the spellcrafted shield, which was superior in some ways to a traditional shield, because the force projected against it was wholly absorbed by the magic and not transferred to its user. Bardon pushed forward and grabbed the arm of his nearest attacker. A fiery red illuminated beneath the flaky skin of the creature, and it began to immolate in a convulsion of agony. The creature stretched its arms upward, only to crumble to the stone in a pile of ash and teeth.

Bardon smiled. He had wanted try that spell for some time. He was determined to be a killer on the battlefield, just as Cahan had said, and he felt a certain measure of deviousness.

The other Amalgam began to back up in fear of Bardon, while still swinging wildly. Bardon's hand began to blaze once more, as it did when he had smelted the creatures' cohort into nothingness. He was reviewing the new spell in the back of his mind when he realized this spellcraft smelled like volcano ash. The Amalgam took a few measured paces backward, which quickly turned into a desperate sprint. Bardon's eyes shifted to a blazing sapphire once more, and he sent a blue-tinged projectile after the retreating creature. The blade-shaped spellcraft cleaved the air, slicing off a significant portion of the Amalgam's calf muscle.

The Amalgam fell chin-first to the stone beneath, sliding a good distance forward. Bardon reached the Amalgam in a flash, leaving a trail of black energy, and turned the beast onto its back. He put his hands on the Amalgam's eyes and mouth. Black energy radiated from Bardon's eyes, down his arms, and flowed into the downed Amalgam. The energy coursed through its body, as if rummaging around its innards. It thrashed in agony. A moment passed before the black energy exploded from the Amalgam's stomach in a rain of viscous brown blood and smoldering organs.

Bardon felt a prickle on the back of his neck. He turned and saw that Declan had stabbed an Amalgam in the back behind him. Declan yanked his dagger from the Amalgam and shifted to his right to stab another with a clockwise turn of his blade, grinning fiendishly. Bardon raised his staff and sent a blue blaze at Declan, who raised his arms defensively. As the fire reached him, it parted to avoid impact. The fire merged again behind him and blanketed an approaching Amalgam, reducing it to ash. Declan appeared to be shaken by the near immolation, and Bardon stood at the ready when another group of Amalgam advanced.

* * * *

Cahan stood before the titan figure that had reduced one of his soldiers to human pulp. His hearing returned as Bardon's spell waned, and the sounds intensified the creature's menacing presence. Its hot, wet breath continued to fume venom from its mouth. It looked down at Cahan with a perturbed squint, as if he were a mere distraction, and bellowed with bared blackened teeth. Its singular eye rapidly moved back and forth in a demonic fervor, over stimulated by its surroundings. Cahan guessed the giant did not know who it wanted to tear into first. He decided to make himself a target and moved closer. It bit its lip and sent the mace crashing down toward him. He dodged to the Amalgam's right, avoiding the crushing blow.

Cahan was impressed by the creature. The strike was so powerful that a large section of the spellcrafted stonework collapsed, as the barely perceptible glow that once illuminated the joints of the stone dissipated in the force's wake. Cahan saw dark, corrupted soil begin to surface through the cracks in the floor. He figured the corrupted earth was no longer impeded by the spellcrafted masonry and sought a target.

Cahan sullenly dusted himself off and stood before the titan, just out of its considerable reach. Its strength seemed like a force of nature to Cahan, unyielding and merciless. This made him all the more motivated to kill the giant, in as grisly a fashion as possible. The fact that he might die in this fight exhilarated him and spurred his unique creativity in battle.

The titan bellowed in Cahan's direction. Cahan realized he must have gained some measure of respect for the Cyclops even to acknowledge his existence. He dashed toward the beast, as if he were going to unleash a foolhardy frontal assault on a much larger opponent, but when he drew within arm's length, he leapt to the giant's periphery, just outside its limited field of vision. It shifted its body toward Cahan, but could not act fast enough. Cahan's sword arced toward it in a flash of steel, but its flesh remained unscathed.

Such a blow would have normally resulted in a bloody dismemberment, but its skin was so thick and porous that it acted like a natural armor that could absorb virtually any indirect strike hurled at it. Cahan knew the strengths and weaknesses of these creatures were as random as their ancestry, aside from their nocturnal nature. He remained unmoved by the sword's failure to slay the titan and grew even more determined to succeed.

The frustrated giant responded by sweeping its mace in broad strokes, continuing its attempt to crush him. Feverishly, the giant swung again and again, its face red with anger and exhaustion as Cahan dodged everything thrown at him. The giant gripped its mace with seething anger, and Cahan heard its teeth grind. He could tell that the Amalgam let anger take hold and fuel him, a tactic that he regularly relied upon in battle. The beast feigned a horizontal swipe, and Cahan flinched. Suddenly, the oversized Amalgam brought its weapon overhead. Astonished, Cahan moved backward into the area the creature had crushed into rubble moments before. Cahan faltered on the broken stone just long enough for the giant to lunge and grasp him. It gripped Cahan's shoulder tightly and began to bring Cahan head first toward a wide, gaping mouth full of black mucus and sharp, decaying teeth. The stench of rot billowed around him.

The titan began to squeeze harder, but Cahan's body was resilient. He used the short pause as an opportunity to drive his sword through the Amalgam's forearm with all his might. The creature dropped him with a loud, guttural burst emanating from its mouth.

Cahan realized that he had to end this fight quickly. His compatriots needed his support, as they were engulfed with Amalgam on all sides. Cahan glanced at Declan and Bardon and saw that they needed their flank covered, as well as distance from the sword-wielding creatures that were surrounding them.

Cahan stood before the giant. "You fat, ugly, one-eyed shit," he taunted while slyly grasping for a sphere of eluvium.

The idiot giant roared again, ignoring the sword still impaled in his arm. Enraged, the wet-mouthed creature charged him. Cahan stood his ground, waiting for the right moment. He narrowly avoided a sweep of the giant's mace and grabbed the leather armor strap hanging loosely from its shoulder, simultaneously vaulting over the giant. Cahan spun in midair over his slovenly attacker while maintaining his grip on the leather strap. He landed feet first against the creature's back, crawled to its massive right shoulder, and plunged the amber sphere into its yellowish, dripping eye. He leapt off while pulling his sword from its forearm.

The dumb monstrosity covered its eye and hurled a spit-filled bellow that echoed madly against the cyclopean stone edifice. It took a few labored steps as the compound coursed through its system. Its veins bulged and its chest heaved, while its arms groped awkwardly. A visible blackness came over the titan, and it began to decay before the audience of warriors; its body seemed to cannibalize itself, withering inward like rotting vegetation. The husk of the giant fell in a mass of decay and viscous bile.

Cahan sheathed his sword and sprinted in long strides toward Declan and Bardon. His mind raced with anxiety. He could not let another one of his men die. As an Amalgam prepared to thrust its sword into Declan's back, Cahan knocked the creature to the ground, and it lost hold of its weapon. Cahan rolled with the momentum of his lunge until he was on top of the Amalgam with his knee pressed into its diaphragm. Barely able to breathe, it struggled and grasped at Cahan's throat. Cahan wrapped his arm behind the elbow joint of the Amalgam and arched his back. Cahan felt the creature's bones splinter. He rose to take on the next Amalgam.

Out of the corner of his eye, he saw Declan plunge his dagger into the neck of the downed Amalgam. Cahan felt a hand on his shoulder and turned to see Bardon with a raised staff.

"Draw your blade!"

Cahan drew his blade and watched as Bardon's eyes blazed blue. He engulfed Cahan's spiderclad blade in energy. Cahan looked at his blade in amusement. Waves of blue energy surrounded the spider, as if by design. Cahan began to cut through the Amalgam Incendiaries as though he were slicing through water. His enchanted sword left blue-gray trails of light that illuminated the carnage he had left in his wake. The energy swirled and lingered within his enemies' open wounds.

Cahan thought that Bardon looked like a child with a new toy in the battlefield as he burned through enemies with an immolation spell. He also seemed to enjoy collapsing the spellcrafted ceiling upon a large cluster of Incendiaries, laughing deviously at his own cleverness. Declan used the shadows of the room to his advantage and stealthily disemboweled several of the spoiled-skinned creatures.

Before long, Cahan noticed that more and more Amalgam were retreating. They exited through the large doors behind a partition to a grass field behind the structure, just as he had planned. Cahan followed the mass exodus of Amalgam and saw that the Rattock had accomplished their part. Many of the Amalgam lay dead on the ground, while others quickly turned to the opposite side of the grassy field, only to see yet another throng of soldiers—those who had fought near the derelict structures. The crushing blow was Cahan's signal to release a final volley of poisonous arrows.

Chapter 4
~ Suspicions ~

Bardon and several other Verindian soldiers had separated the surviving Amalgam in lines that stretched across a large, grassy area. Far off to the west side of the line of prisoners, Bardon broke away from the others and pried the giant Amalgam's mace from an Incendiary, who had picked it up in the ensuing skirmish.

He began a spell. A yellow burst of light warmed his face as he focused sharply on the mace. In the midst of his conjuration, he heard footsteps behind him.

"What are you doing?" Cahan asked.

"Nothing," Bardon replied awkwardly.

Bardon watched Cahan, hoping to glean something from the suspicious chief ranger. Cahan looked at Bardon with an untrusting face, nervously flexing his jaw. The man's jaw was pronounced, almost cubic, which terminated into a thick, well-defined chin. His triangular nose rested above a thin-lipped mouth. Beneath the face that Cahan presented to the world, Bardon noticed his black eyes held a dark anger in them, as though he were always contemplating something dire.

Cahan furrowed his brow and grabbed the duffle draped over Bardon's shoulder. He quickly checked it, only to find his various wizards' tools and some clothing. Bardon, amused by his new militia lord's distrust, decided to play up the drama of the moment and glared at Cahan.

"I've never seen a human cast spellcraft as you do," Cahan said half accusingly.

"And I have never seen a human with the strength you so freely brandish," Bardon retorted in defiance. "That stone door you used to crush that sentry must have weighed as much as five men."

Bardon walked in lockstep with Cahan back toward the staging area for the Amalgam prisoners, arguing the whole way.

"All Verindian soldiers are given potions to increase strength and stamina," Cahan replied defensively.

Bardon threw his head back and chuckled, his gelatin-like hair jiggling with his deep belly laugh. "That is your explanation? You have to think of something better, at least something more believable than that, Cahan. Your strength is beyond mere potions. You speak very strangely—and do not tell me about your little island." He counted each accusation on his fingers. "I may not know what you are—but there is one thing you are not, and that is normal."

"If you see a large mace, just let me know," Cahan said as he walked away. "I'm curious about it."

* * * *

Cahan looked at Declan as he walked toward him. He'd clearly been eavesdropping, and his blue eyes nervously darted around in different directions, occasionally returning to Cahan's face.

"Is he a demon, Cahan?" Declan probed.

"Easy, Declan," Cahan said, somewhat shaken from the interaction with Bardon. "He's as run-of-the-mill as you or me."

A Verindian soldier fervently waved Cahan and Declan toward the Amalgam staging area. To his side, an older, bent Amalgam sat slipshod among his fellow captives. From the make of his ceramic armor, he appeared to be a higher rank than the others. Cahan hurried toward the old soldier.

The taciturn Amalgam placidly glanced up at him. The sagging lines of his face seemed blanketed in apathy, and his dead eyes were extinguished of any fire they may have held in the creature's youth.

Cahan peered thoughtfully at the rank, open stronghold they had just conquered. He decided to hold the broken leader's interrogation in private so that the Amalgam would not put up any superficial airs of non-cooperation. In the room, with others around, the Amalgam was forced to keep up his placid facade. Cahan grabbed the restrained leader by his shoulders in an effort to shake some emotion into the barren creature.

"Are there more Amalgam encampments?" Cahan asked.

The heavy wooden doors of the enclosure suddenly slammed against the stone wall, and echoes rang out in the horrifying edifice, startling two rangers nearby. Cahan fixed his gaze upon the Rattock soldier who had just entered, still red-faced by all the commotion he had caused. Cahan recognized the meaning of this interruption. In the past, whenever he had detained any notable enemy combatant, Protos routinely interceded. Cahan's angry eyes tightened as he crossed his arms. He tried to bury his anger within as he clinched his fists under his arms.

"We have direct orders from the Ministry of Information to transport the Incendiaries to the capital," he said, waving a piece of parchment.

Cahan turned away from the bothersome Rattock soldier. As he drew in breath to speak, the young militia member interrupted again.

"It says in the communication not to question the Incendiaries," he said.

"Get him the fuck out of here!" Cahan ordered.

Both of Cahan's soldiers escorted the annoying Rattock out of the echoing stone chamber and closed the door behind him.

The Amalgam leader leaned its head closer to Cahan. "I have information," it said, morbidly frightened. "Do not take me to the Ministry citadel."

"The citadel is no longer," one of the Verindian soldiers began. He was silenced by a sharp look from Cahan.

Cahan stalked over to the outspoken soldier and forced him out into the hallway. "It doesn't know that the citadel is no longer in use," Cahan said angrily. "He was about to lose his shit!" Cahan hated when others spoke out of turn—or spoke in general.

A voice echoed into the room. "I know you think that the citadel is not in use, but many of my soldiers are imprisoned there."

Cahan walked back into the room. His mind whirled with a sudden, inexplicable anxiety. His company had captured many Incendiaries, and he had obsessed for months about where the Protosians were housing these war criminals if the citadel had truly been decommissioned. The Ministry of Information, or MOI, routinely ignored his inquiries.

His curiosity overtook him. The old, bent Amalgam's accusation had a ring of truth to it, but why would Protos lie about shutting down the citadel?

"Go on," Cahan said.

"Before Anaymous changed allegiances, he used us to regularly raid the mines of Dunnavisch Estuary—"

"Wait... What? Anaymous, one of the three scions of the Incendiary movement, suddenly changed allegiances?"

"Yes," it said with glassy-eyed emotion. It was the first real emotion the creature had shown.

"Allegiance to what side?" Cahan demanded, parsing his words carefully.

"He wants a seat at the Protosian Assembly of Districts," the leader said in its choking drawl. "He thinks Incendiary ways are antiquated and should remain in the bygone era, dead and out of use."

Three booming knocks thundered against the wooden outer doors of the room. Cahan's head snapped to the source of the sound. There were three more knocks. Cahan carefully strode to the door to open it, more out of curiosity than anything else. He peeled away the barring restraint from the doors.

As the aperture yawned, a towering figure stood before him, eclipsing Cahan in shadow. The towering presence was a Fenthom soldier of Protos, accompanied by two more of his kind, plus a Rattock officer. Fenthom were the descendants of the various breeds of dragon that had reigned for millions of years before Shintallis was called by its present name. The known breeds were plains, mountain, marsh, and desert dragons. According to Cahan's studies, one dragon breed, said still to stalk prey in the marshes of the Dunnavisch Estuary and Forgatha, even shared common characteristics with plant life.

The Fenthom were anthropomorphic, unlike their four-legged ancestors. Some Fenthom were finer-featured in the face than others, more closely resembling humans or Venerites than dragons, aside from their scaly flesh. Their forbearers still donned the familiar snout and well-formed hands with curved talons. Some could breathe fire, with the aid of minerals, while others were able to spew a toxic, acidic substance.

The eclipsing Fenthom was clearly a plains dragon descendant, easily identified by the nose slits, grayish skin tone, and the almost simian nature of his facial features. Plains Fenthom were large and scaly. From a side profile, it was plain to see what his snout would have looked like, had the mutation of the pre-bygone era dragons not taken place. There was a hint of protrusion and then a sheer flatness where the nose slits and mouth dwelt.

Cahan noticed the Fenthom wore a fine suit of Gargoylian armor, crafted from alloys smelted in the Gargoyle Priory. The fine lines of the armor trimmed the muscular features of the high-ranking soldier. The pauldrons of the armor cut outward in an almost trapezoidal shape and looked sharp to the touch. The torso armor culminated into a triangular contour, outlining the creature's immense back with customized slits that allowed the spikes lining his spine and serpent like tail to peek out of the armor.

"We are here for the incendiary magnate minor," the Fenthom growled in a bristling tone. His tail sliced the air as he whipped it back and forth behind him.

A magnate minor was just a few steps down from the Presidium, the ruling class of the Amalgam. He thought to himself that the old, cantankerous creature surely had more information, especially about the infamous demon known as Anaymous and his supposed defection.

"I'm the lord of this militia throng," Cahan said as he grasped the Fenthom's forearm in greeting. "Chief Ranger Cahan Devlin."

"Lieutenant General Graan," he growled, shaking Cahan's hand away. A red glint resonated in his eyes.

Cahan put on a faux charming smile and yielded to the towering dragon descendant. He knew he had gained the reputation of constant defiance over the years, so he understood why his men seemed somewhat surprised and gave him confused looks when he acquiesced without argument. Cahan had even overheard discussions among his men that accused him of reveling in breaking the law, because he often went outside of mission parameters.

The Rattock, Verindian, and Fenthom contingent marched to their respective airships, which were nestled together in a grassy, open area. Cahan looked up at the lofty Graan and made a last-ditch attempt to gain access to the loose-tongued Amalgam.

"We can transfer the prisoner in our airship. It would probably be a good idea to separate the magnate from his soldiers," Cahan said as he gestured toward the Amalgam prisoners filing into the Protosian vessel.

Graan studied Cahan, considering his suggestion.

"That would not be advisable, Lieutenant General Graan," a whiny-voiced Rattock officer said.

"Why is that, officer?" Graan inquired.

"This ranger has a long history of insubordination. It is a wonder he has not been discharged of service." The glassy-eyed officer leered at Cahan. "If he wants the magnate, then it is to satisfy his own ends."

"The magnate will board our vessel," Graan growled with a dismissive tone, washing his hands of the matter.

Cahan retreated from the argument and grabbed Declan by the shoulder. Cahan towed him to the foot of their airship, where Bardon, now dressed in a black wizard's robe, was standing.

"Even the Rattock and the Protosians know you cannot be trusted," Bardon said with a hearty chuckle.

"Funny," Cahan shot back. "Now listen. I'm going to need your help."

Chapter 5
~ The Drunken Stowaway ~

Cahan looked at his devious charge with anger, as the twig of a conjurer openly defied him.

"Why would I help the likes of you?" Bardon questioned defiantly.

"I'm still the lord of this militia throng. I can make it a direct mandate." Cahan sneered, looking down at the wizard, both figuratively and literally.

"I must admit, Chief Ranger, I am curious as to what you are. You know, being a scholarly spellcrafter and all. I will help you, if you give me insight into your physiology."

Cahan glanced over to Declan, wondering how he might react to what Bardon had said. The lines of Declan's pock-marked face seemed to convulse unnaturally as his reddish, dry flesh crinkled in bewilderment at the wizard's audacious comments.

"If you don't want to tell me the real reason why you're helping, that's fine." Cahan clutched Bardon's shoulder with his immense strength and pulled him closer. "So long as you aren't a spy or some sort of fuckin' turncoat." He pushed the words out beyond his clenching teeth. Cahan suddenly released the conjuror from his grasp, as if he had snapped out of a trance.

"Understood, sire," Bardon said with a slight bow of his head, rubbing his shoulder. "I wish I had kept my armor on," Bardon added under his breath.

"Declan, I need you to take command of the company—temporarily," Cahan said as he dismissed him to the Verindian vessel. "Keep 'em in line."

Declan took his leave without comment, which troubled Cahan somewhat. He quickly refocused his attention on getting to the magnate. If the magnate was locked away in the Ministry citadel, he would never be heard from again.

Cahan and Bardon stole their way to the least visible side of the Protosian air vessel, where a knotted cluster of decaying trees provided ample cover.

Cahan marveled at the ship, a shining testament to human engineering and demonic wizardry. Cahan had read about this vessel in the various wartime journals released to soldiers during extended combat missions. The brilliant silver vessel housed six decks, crew quarters, and captain's chambers. While some airships copied the architecture of sea-bearing vessels, this one did not. It was designed for the open, beckoning heavens. Instead of an outward arching hull, the vessel was somewhat cylindrical and terminated into a triangular point at the ship's bow.

The stern of the vessel was wide and rectangular, and the flat topside had a polished alloy deck with recesses for passengers to strap into for high speeds. Large cannons were also mounted topside, fueled by a secondary energy chamber, which was separate from the propulsion system. Propulsion ducts were located on the level underbelly and on the sides of the ship for pinpoint turns. The ship itself was fueled by drawing in the energy that was contained in all objects and the energy that floated disjointedly in the atmosphere. Another oft-used energy source was water. This was in contrast to other self-manufactured vessels propelled by eluvium. This sort of propulsion was considered dangerous, however, due to the prospect of leakage, which could result in the slow disintegration of the entire vessel. Cahan had actually been on a few eluvium-based vessels. On one occasion, he had to abandon ship due to leakage. It was a memory that haunted him, as several crewmen were liquefied into piles of cauterized flesh.

Cahan looked to Bardon questioningly and gestured to the high-reaching cargo hatch. "Can you will that hatch to open, Bardon?"

"Yes, but will you be able to reach it?"

"Just get it open."

It was apparent that the thick metal hatch only opened from one side. Bardon focused in on the opening. There was a slight click, and the door creased. Bardon handed Cahan a polished cerulean stone.

"What is this?"

"It is a defero stone. They are quite rare, said to be from beyond the reaches of Shintallis, so do not lose it. It allows me to peer through and around the holder's periphery. It also allows communication on both ends between two beings. It is the best option for those who are not fluent in one of the telepathic languages." Bardon paused and looked at Cahan. "One last thing. The communication between stones works at a great distance, but it does have limits."

A small dagger appeared in Bardon's right hand. He pricked his index finger and held it over the stone. With a clenched fist, he squeezed droplets of blood onto the stone's smooth surface, which absorbed the droplets with a branding of concentric lines.

"It is now linked to my mind," Bardon advised. "Lesser magic can be passed through this focal point of energy, as well. Sound barriers will not work through the stone. They are not a lesser magic."

"Tell the men I will be accompanying the Protosians on their vessel," Cahan instructed Bardon.

"Do you want me to tell them you are a stowaway?" Bardon chuckled as his sarcastic wit reared its head once more.

"No, asshole, don't tell them that," Cahan said with a half-smile.

* * * *

Cahan sprinted as fast as his legs would take him, which he knew was faster than most. He took cover behind an outcropping of blue clindra rock and scanned the area before he sprinted toward the now-opened hatch. He easily bounded up the distance, twice his height.

He grabbed the hatch by his fingertips and planted his feet against the side of the metallic vessel. He pried open the hatch and snaked his way through the aperture.

Cahan attempted to close the hatch, but the frame wing of the hinge had broken while supporting his weight. He heard the distinct sound of human footsteps rounding the corner. He wrapped his fingers around the defero stone and closed his eyes in thought. A blue light trickled out of the stone and encapsulated the hatch and the broken hinge. The hinge rustled for a moment until the opening was magically sealed. Cahan moved away from sight as a Rattock infantryman passed by. Once safe from prying eyes, Cahan made his way back to the small door and inspected the hinge. It looked as though it had been melted shut, preventing escape from the area.

He began to search for another way out of the freight chamber other than the space, which opened to an area heavily inhabited by Rattock. The oval area was composed of brindle wood, which could only be cut by means of spellcraft. Cahan again held the stone in his hand and concentrated.

Bardon replied with a spell. A pulpy crimson fluid began to encrust his hand. He looked for a cloth in the hold and found a large, moth-eaten rag. He placed the rag against a panel in the hold to help muffle the sound of his fist hitting the brindle wood. As he wielded his fist upward, his hand made contact with the hard surface. The pulpy fluid sparked and made a hole in the shape of his clenched fist. Cahan smelled the subtle, smoky discharge of the spellcraft and fanned the area with his hand. He noticed that the fluid went cleanly through the rag and panel, leaving a charred opening. Cahan repeated the process until the hole was big enough for him to climb.

With the last few strikes, an anger erupted within him. More frequently, Cahan had brief run-ins with an all-consuming, deep-seated hatred that was completely irrational. He paused and shook his head, forcing the malevolence back down inside him without too much difficulty—this time.

Cahan stuffed the well-used rag in his satchel, not wanting to leave behind any evidence of his presence. The newly improvised breach opened up to a hollow area of alloy and removable panels, just above where the next deck would be. The crawl space was just large enough for Cahan to squeeze through. As he climbed upward, his broad shoulders brushed the sides of the crawl space. Cahan, as a rule, avoided small spaces. As a boy, he had been locked in a small airship compartment for an extended period of time. Recently, this long-held phobia had become one of the many triggers that pushed his anger to the forefront.

Once Cahan was fully inside the metallic hollow, he could better smell the bubbling substance that had encrusted his hand. He peered down to see that the viscous compound was restoring the breach he had created. As the substance crystallized, it began an odd metamorphosis. Mucus-like red bubbles snapped and transmogrified into a brown color. What looked like wood grains emerged to the surface of the spellcrafted concoction, matching the wood paneling next to it. The newly formed brindle-like substance hardened, thus sealing the breach. Cahan was completely closed in. The malevolence began to overtake his brain, like a needle pricking the inside of his skull.

In his mind, he went back in time to his childhood. He could see the detail of the cargo hold. The smell of unfinished fáyn'dear wood filled his nostrils. His palm was numb and splintered from pounding the walls of the confined area. He even remembered the folded position of his legs as he sat there, waiting in terror. He had to keep climbing.

He briefly entertained the notion of breaking back through spellcrafted faux wood, so he would once again be in an open area where the air was fresh and not metallic. Each time he gained a hold on the curvature of the metallic hollow, he grasped it with unreasonable rage, digging his fingers in and grinding his teeth. He tried to focus on the coldness of his metallic surroundings. Somehow, the cool metal soothed him, however fleetingly. As he caught his breath, he realized that he needed to get out before he fully lost grasp of his emotions.

Cahan hastened his ascent to find himself in a polished, tan brindle wood-lined hallway with large red runners fastened to the metallic structure of the vessel. He inhaled and exhaled slowly for a moment, trying to soothe the havoc ensnaring his mind. There were several illumine orbs bearing a gothic motif ensconced in the walls at regular intervals down the length of the hallway. Cahan had seen these lights before and knew he had to be careful, as the orbs were set ablaze whenever in close proximity to crew members—or anyone for that matter, including stowaways. He would have to crawl chin-to-deck to avoid detection.

Cahan felt a tremor as the oscillation of the ship's central energy chamber under his feet roared to life, and realized the vessel would soon begin its ascent. He palmed the defero stone tightly and asked Bardon if they were also about to begin their withdrawal. Bardon communicated that the men were in disarray and not remotely close to departure. The thunderous vibrations of Cahan's thoughts quaked through the mental connection, ordering Bardon to get everyone in order. He would soon need his talents via the stone and did not want to risk a break in the link between them due to the space separating the airships.

Illumine orbs suddenly blazed at the end of the hall as a blanketing white light smothered the shadows in the corridor. Footsteps echoed rhythmically against the wooden deck. From the sound of the footsteps, another human was headed toward him. Cahan slinked into the nearest room and huddled behind a large aeronautic cabinet filled with airship logs and instruments.

As the cadenced sound of combat boots grew louder, Cahan sprang toward the doorway. He grabbed the man by his shoulder and hurled him into the room. The soldier looked up at him from his position on the floor. Cahan glared at the man with his back to the door, bolting it behind him, never breaking eye contact.

"Chief Ranger?" the Rattock cried. "What are you doing here?"

"Shut up!" Cahan scowled. "I have a very important question. How you answer this question will determine whether or not you'll still have the ability to draw breath moments from now." He paused to let his statement sink in. Cahan turned to the aeronautical cabinet and pulled out an antique-looking sextant. "This will go through your eye and into your brain. Do we have an understanding?" he asked, looking pointedly at the Rattock.

The Rattock nodded worriedly as he bit his lip and rubbed his injured shoulder. Cahan began to walk toward the Rattock, holding the sextant in front of his face.

"Where is the Amalgam magnate?" Cahan asked purposefully.

"The magnate is in the lowermost deck, in the holding area!" the Rattock blurted.

Cahan continued toward him.

"What?" the Rattock cried. "I told you what you wanted to know!"

Cahan reached into his satchel and produced a sealed cylinder of a whitish bubbling liquid. The Rattock tentatively lowered his arms from his defensive posture.

"Drink this," Cahan ordered.

"What is it?"

"It won't kill you."

The Rattock glanced from the liquid to Cahan again with a look of worried hesitation.

"Now!" Cahan clenched his teeth. His seething anger and the odd liquid bubbled up simultaneously. He sensed the lurking malevolence begin to take hold.

The Rattock took the malodorous bubbling liquid from Cahan and drank it swiftly with a sour look of disgust. A moment passed before the soldier lapsed into a deep slumber. The unconscious Rattock would eventually raise questions once discovered, so he had no choice but to use this type of potion. The potion would erase almost a week of the Rattock's memory. He wouldn't even remember his mission. Cahan hoped the Protosians would not piece together his infiltration too quickly.

Cahan looked around the office and saw a jug of apple ale next to a set of historical codex on the bookshelf before him. He lifted the soldier, placed him under the desk near the aeronautical cabinet, and grabbed the jug. Cahan sloshed it up and down in his hand. It was almost full. He muttered quiet curses. No one would believe the soldier had been drinking if the jug was that full. He looked for a place to dump some of the booze out, but if they found where he dumped the ale, that, too, could raise suspicion and give credence to the Rattock's forthcoming denial. Cahan raised the jug and began to down a significant portion of the strong, full-bodied alcohol. He doused the Rattock with some, as well, so he would reek of it.

Slightly tipsy, Cahan made his way back out to the brindle-surfaced hallway and headed toward the energy chamber, stooping, ducking, and bumping his head because of the alcohol. He finally made his way out of the sight of the mostly human crew. Once Cahan entered the central energy chamber, he scanned the components of the phosphorescent subterfuge that crackled with energy at the central artery of the room. The glow of the chamber appeared even more remarkable when inebriated.

Alloy pipes of Gargoylian construction jutted out of the clear housing of the hissing, sapphire-tinged energy, which led to the circular, oscillating hollow that tamed the energy before dispersing it into the propulsion ventricles. The atmospheric intake leading to the chamber's core also served as a detection system for pirates. Pirates used eluvium-based energy chambers in their vessels, which dispersed a byproduct into the atmosphere. This byproduct was identified when absorbed into the ship's intake, which then would sound an alert for the crew.

Cahan began disassembling the intake as carefully as he could, given the swirling in his head, so that the ship could still bring in the needed energy. Periodically, Cahan lost his train of thought, forgetting what parts he needed, and proceeded to fumble with the parts, rumbling about on the floor as the chamber hummed like a Protosian hornbill. Finally, Cahan attached a spare pipe to the intake, pulled out the defero stone, and grasped it tightly.

Chapter 6
~ Pirates over Blasstock ~

Bardon felt a slight tremor in his pocket, resonating from his defero stone. He concentrated, but could only pick up subtle vibrations. The stone heated his palm with each tonal pulse that came through it. Defero stones, a rare and expensive instrument of spellcraft, allowed for artificial telepathy through a focal point. Both natural and artificial telepathy emitted tonal markers that allowed the brain intuitively to translate the vibrations coming from another mind. There were too many markers missing from Cahan's communication. The ship needed to be closer to his locale. He rose and walked to the cockpit of the Verindian vessel.

"Do you think we can speed up a touch?" Bardon asked the pilot.

"You in a hurry, spellcrafter?" he said in a spiteful tone.

Bardon could tell by the fierce-looking pilot's tone that he was one of the many humans that hated those gifted with spellcrafter abilities. Bardon met many people with this attitude. They believed spellcraft should be left to demons and humans should not toil with what they considered an "unnatural power."

"Return to the passenger chamber," the pilot said in his odd, undulating accent.

"I can tell from your accent you are from Dranda town, are you not?" Bardon said politely.

"Yes, what of it?" he growled.

"Nothing... but it is just easier to control the mind when you know personal details," Bardon said with a devious smile. He clutched the nape of the pilot's neck, fingers ablaze. The bones in his hand shone through his skin, as if a fire burned within his hand.

The pilot's eyes widened as he resisted Bardon's influence for a moment before settling down into a trancelike state.

Bardon returned to the passenger chamber, sat down, and casually crossed his legs, stroking his chin. He chewed on the nail of his index finger as he willed the pilot to commit more energy to the aft propulsion ducts. The pilot complied by pushing the corresponding notched wooden and alloy lever forward. A surge rattled throughout the passenger chamber and pushed a few soldiers near Bardon forward.

Memories from the pilot flashed in Bardon's mind every so often. He shared a vision of the portly, red-haired pilot, dressed in women's clothing. Bardon chuckled out loud. A few of his fellow passengers looked at him with questioning glances.

As the ship sped forward, Bardon felt the harsh tones of Cahan's mind, which translated as yelling. Cahan was explaining his scheme that was to take place in the energy chamber. Bardon paused for a moment of brief contemplation, then tilted his head to the side with a slight smile.

"Are you drunk, Cahan?" he asked, trying to contain his amusement. "This really is not the time for such debauchery."

Cahan drunkenly hurled flagrant curses through the connection. Even Bardon was somewhat embarrassed at the words Cahan brandished. Ultimately, Bardon withdrew from his chastisement and told Cahan to commence.

* * * *

Cahan reached in his satchel and held up his last bit of eluvium while tightly clutching the defero stone. The eluvium began to float upward toward the newly attached pipe, now molded into place with the use of Bardon's spellcraft. The amber material began to seep out of the clear housing through a minute hole in its surface. Once the liquid touched the air, it began to turn into a noxious gas. Cahan covered his face with the dingy rag he had used in the freight chamber.

A loud, piercing bell rang out throughout the ship, followed by numerous sets of pounding footsteps. Cahan heard men yelling about pirates in the distance. He ran out into the passageway, knowing he could blend in during the confusion. He walked toward the railway descending to the lowermost deck. The screech of the bells, as well as Cahan's abnormally fast metabolism, lifted his drunken haze. Cahan peered around the corner and saw only one sentry guarding the Amalgam magnate. He walked toward the holding chamber in full view of the sentry.

"What the hell are you doing here?" the sentry yelled as he approached Cahan. He timidly raised his crossbow.

Cahan grabbed the smaller man by the throat and heaved him toward the wall. He checked the sentry to ensure he was unconscious and forced the gurgling sleeping potion down the sentry's gullet. Cahan pilfered the cell key from his belt.

He heard stirring in the room just beyond the rectangular doorway in front of him. Cahan slipped the key in the lock and creaked the door open. The magnate minor stood centered in the room behind bars with long, dangling chains stemming from his wrists and ankles that were attached to a metal ring braced to the floor. Cahan went back to the unconscious guard and hoisted him up over his shoulder. He set the guard down in the room with himself and the magnate.

Cahan locked eyes with the magnate. "I need to know more," he said almost pleadingly.

"You broke into a Protosian vessel to speak with me?" The semi-demon laughed uproariously, chains rattling.

"Did Anaymous really defect from the Incendiary ranks?"

"Yes, but there is much more to this than that."

"Explain."

"I will need some assurances before I 'explain,' drunkard," the magnate said, all traces of the previous humor gone.

"What do you want?" Cahan asked impatiently, deciding to ignore the comment about his lack of sobriety.

"As I said before, keep me from the citadel. Set me free."

"You have my word, demon."

"How can you so assuredly guarantee such a thing?" the "higher-bred" Amalgam asked.

"We're running out of time," Cahan said. "As far as I know, you have no other avenues of escape. I'm offering to free you from your captors. Don't be stupid."

"Stupid?" His jaw tightened at Cahan's blatant offense. "Freedom from my captors? Are you not one of my captors? If memory serves, you led the attack on my brigade, unprovoked."

"Unprovoked?" Cahan repeated with incredulity. "Are you daft? Your throngs have been laying siege to Blasstock for months." For a brief moment, Cahan's anger flared more deeply than it ever had before. He fleetingly thought about wrapping the magnate's chains around his neck and squeezing. Painful pulsations gripped his brain, and he felt, for the slightest moment, that killing was the only thing that could take it away. He walked over to the Amalgam, hands shaking, and pulled himself out of the hate to find the old, bent demon still blathering.

"What business do Verindians have in Blasstock?" the Amalgam spat venomously. "Blasstock, or Anashra, its true name, was demon land for centuries, even before your race huddled in the mud and cowered in their caves."

"The last time I checked, the Amalgam have human lineage, too," Cahan said as the blurring lines of hatred began to fade away.

"That lineage has all but been erased. Our people no longer lay down with humans," he said with distaste.

Cahan studied the grotesque features of the magnate. Why would anyone 'lay down' with an Amalgam in the first place? The thought made him slightly cringe.

"We don't have much time, Amalgam. Do you want your freedom or not?"

The Amalgam defiantly exhaled and bit the scabby flesh of his bottom lip. His eyes raked across Cahan's face.

"The encampments, the sieges, the increased activities of Incendiary throngs, are all part of a common plot. A new presence has inserted itself among our ranks, overtaken our presidium." He exhaled again, wetting his dry lips.

"Do you know who or what this presence is?" Cahan asked.

"No one knows, save for the Presidium itself. I am too far removed from the power structure to know."

"And what of Anaymous? His defection is substantial. Other throngs may follow suit."

"Anaymous has been contemplating defection for a long time. He wants to join the Protosians, said he had a way to do it. Something about commerce." The Amalgam spat the last word out, as if it were a curse word. "He shunned our ways. He plans to sojourn to the capital and plead his case. He may already be en route."

"Where would he be?" Cahan asked, not expecting an answer.

"There is an abandoned manor near the Veldt mountain range. Most likely, he would be there."

Cahan was shocked that the Amalgam coughed up the information he had asked for so easily. Cahan consciously kept his face schooled to conceal his shock as he realized the magnate had probably given him the information out of his disapproval of Anaymous's aims. He studied the magnate again, looking for any sign of deception. He had a knack for identifying liars and their telltale signs of dishonesty. Liars were always best at spotting their own kind, and none of the signs was present on the semi-demon's repulsive face. Not an indirect glance, shaking hands, or a nervous tick. The creature stared at him with glassy-eyed honesty. He decided to see if the magnate might divulge anything about their strategy.

"So your chief mission is to create unrest amongst the human settlements?" Cahan asked.

The magnate nodded.

"Why?"

"It is simple, human. To set the Protosians off balance. If we create enough chaos, they will involve themselves, as always. This also has the added benefit of exposing them for the magisterial curs they are. The whole of Shintallis will oppose them and further the strife."

Cahan stood in front of the Amalgam, numb, his mouth gaping at the round of fiery implications that he'd made. He could tell the magnate divulged this to him because he felt the Protosians would stay on their course, regardless of what he revealed to him. He also had a sense that he enjoyed his reaction.

"So your Presidium and the Ministry are linked," Cahan said. "That's why they didn't want me to interrogate you. They wanted to hide their involvement with Incendiaries." He watched the Magnate carefully to see if his statement would yield the expected reaction.

"Quell the thought, human!" he spewed bitterly. "The Presidium would never align with the Protosians."

"Explain it, then, you small-minded fool," Cahan said with clenched teeth. "You Incendiaries are perpetually offended. I'm sick of hearing about your plight and how 'magisterial' we are. You murder humans in their sleep, you cowards! And when we fight back, and your numbers are reduced, suddenly we're the heathens."

The fervor in the above decks had subsided, and Cahan heard the crewmen returning to their stations. He started for the door.

"Enjoy the citadel, magnate," Cahan spat, with his back to the Incendiary leader.

"Just as I expected," the Amalgam growled. "Humans and Protosians alike, always breaking accords."

Cahan turned to him and threw him the cell key, knowing that the magnate would be blamed for the unconscious guard. As Cahan departed, he heard the magnate in the distance, snarling about the keys to his chains.

Chapter 7
~ Protos and Her New Leader ~

Cahan lurked in the shadows as he spied on a conference in the Meeting Hall of the Protosian House of Magistrates. He studied the grand hall of perfectly sculpted, icy-gray stone as it vaulted upward into an apex met by an effigy of the Celestial Valese, who loomed, shapely and beautiful, with flowing hair. Valese peered down upon the procession contained in the towering, dark edifice. Cahan felt as though the effigy was looking directly at him. This representation was very lifelike and was garbed in the royal leather armor of a Protosian king. The powerful religious organization, the Seer Heritage, often depicted her this way, as if to revise history, branding the Celestial as a warrior sworn to the old monarchy. In less-public venues, Valese was depicted in a vaguely demonic form, engulfed in an aura of blazing light. Most scholars agreed with this depiction, as it was consistent with the early artwork originating in the pre-bygone era. It was common for the Seer Heritage to add on to existing buildings or monuments, as was evident in this hall, to leave their mark on the architecture. Shadowy gothic buttresses held the monuments of the Gargoyle architects that designed the hall, all grasping various masonry tools. These monuments were a later addition, after the Seer Heritage had profaned the grand hall, crafted as tribute to their brilliance by the Protosian artisans of Shirinisport. Just below the Gargoyle tribute, stones intermittently projected outward, forming the elaborate targe shield of the So'torish monastery. The So'torish monks had guarded the writings of the *Et dás Leiu*, the written philosophy of Valese, in the hand of Palibious, for hundreds of years.

Through Cahan's many studies, both abroad and in his homeland, he had learned about Palibious. Palibious was one of the three forms of Valese, the earth-bound presence of the grand Celestial. Palibious was given the name of the philosophical form. Valarious and Na'tesquieu, the two remaining forms, were so named the scions of rationality and ascension. The forms were representative of the gift the Grand Celestial gave to the world—the divinity of reason.

Cahan had studied Celestials incessantly at university, for they held many secrets. He often wondered if they existed before or after the cataclysm that spawned existence. Many thought that Celestials were responsible for the so-called "cataclysm" deep within the reaches of the infinite blackness, and existence was created due to a monumental battle between warring factions within the Celestial Augury, their grand domain.

Cahan knew that Celestial beings could only exist in the known world in one of two ways. According to scriptures, Celestials could choose forms that encapsulated their essence or they could forge mystical artifacts tethering them to physical existence. The former did not allow them to experience the physical realm firsthand, as each individual was simply representative of their attributes and possessed their own will, though a Celestial could guide and passively influence a form. A tether allowed a Celestial to grow in power and explore the infinite blackness beyond the world while maintaining a physical body. Some Celestials chose to remain with their kind, while most preferred a less passive experience of the outside world. A Grand Celestial, the most powerful of their kind, only experienced the physical realm sparingly, as they could shape reality with their minds. Cahan often pondered on how seductive that power would be, and he understood why it was kept from the populace.

Cahan honed in on a pewter-colored demon that stood stoically among the decadent tapestries and auburn runners lined with gold. He looked ostentatious amid the gathering of district governors and Gargoyle Priory denizens. His Shintallian name was A'uun, or The Hand of Valese, as he was sometimes called. Cahan knew a great deal about the Hand of Valese because he was well-known across the entire realm.

A'uun was a tall, lean, muscled creature with a gaunt face, well-defined jaw line, and raised cheekbones. His intense eyes held the intelligence of a perpetual being, unscathed by the ravages of time. Some of his physical characteristics resembled that of a spindly Gilpesh conjuror. His ears were each dual pointed, and his long hair was a typical mixture of white tinged with black. However, this was where the similarity to the Gilpesh ceased. His physical nature was of a warrior, tall and domineering. His bluish-gray armor was encrusted with cobalt-hued runic stones on his shoulders, chest, abdomen, shins, and gauntlets, with elliptical patterns circling outward from his bicep runes.

Cahan had heard the sigil-engraved stones moved about to different areas on the armor. His historical studies professor conjectured that the armor the herald donned was sentient, or even an extension of the herald's mind. Embossed on each pectoral was a long-forgotten runic script with an outlining of dark, hazy peaks that blazed upward.

Research spellcrafters based their entire careers on the runic script etched on A'uun's armor. The armor itself clung to the muscle tone of its wearer, with streaks of black lining the outer periphery of each muscle, which terminated in horizontal lines crossing over the dark spaces. The flexible armor was forged from the outer shell of a powerful antediluvian demon. A'uun's powers mystified some and frightened many more. According to *Et dás Leiu*, he was known across the lands and in other worlds by various different names, and had not been seen in Shintallis for many years, not since the reign of King Tharros.

Cahan turned his attention to the large dragonoid figure that faced A'uun. The immense Fenthom, Bloodbrand the Wise, was centered among the other dignitaries and had a forceful astuteness about him, apparent from the steadiness of his powerfully observant, sanguine eyes. It seemed nothing escaped his acute perception as he tacitly engaged the being across from him.

Bloodbrand was of a deep earthen color, with an angularly skeletal face, which culminated into two horns curving downward on either side of his chin. His humanlike nose retained some characteristics of his dragon ancestors. His nostrils flared, even when the rest of his body appeared relaxed, and there were two pits underneath them, an ancestral trait for detecting small prey. Two small fins splayed out on both sides of his head, covering his ear holes. Adorning his cranium were two rows of spikes, starting above his eyebrows, which formed an arc shape that delineated outward, almost like a natural crown of bone. Two large horns were affixed to the back of his head, protruding outward and then skyward to a sharp point, originating from the base of his skull.

His forearms and triceps bore a natural bone armor, which Cahan likened to rock formations. A tail jutted out from the base of his spine with several spikes at its end. His immense feet had a center toe with two splayed toes on both sides, and a raised ankle caused him to walk on the balls of his feet. Missing from his ancestry was any semblance of wings, save for a shortened, stubby bone extending out from his back, covered in earthen flesh, with outcroppings of natural armor around the base and pinnacle of the bone. His knight's armor was of grand Protosian caliber and closely matched the color of his skin, as well as his musculature.

Cahan was familiar with Bloodbrand Aldric of the High Valesian Mountains. Some referred to him as Bloodbrand the Wise or Bloodbrand the Cunning. He was the chief magistrate of Protos, the most zealous advocate of the separation of governmental powers. Bloodbrand was the key figure in the ouster of the bloody monarchy that had preceded him. He helped to create a new government that separated its powers in the form of the magistrate assembly, to protect Protosian citizens against the wrongdoings inherent within a monarchy.

"We have received word that the Incendiary Anaymous Nysrogh has made his way inland from the deserts of the serene to Protosian territory," Bloodbrand proclaimed to the group. "The Edelsen province claims they uncovered assassination plans in the hovel where he was secretly holed up."

"I thought you despised the Edelsen," a sour-faced Gargoyle said.

"I do, and I have not hidden my disdain for the province," Bloodbrand replied evenly. "But Anaymous has long been an agitator in the outer regions. We must put a stop to his long reign of Incendiary tactics and abductions."

"Edelsen is waist-deep in the work of the old regime, and the remaining pockets of N'dal loyalists that still infect your new government," A'uun said. He paused. "Can we trust the source? Is he actually near your border? Should we not focus on Elysium?" he added in rapid succession. "There have been sightings of winged Incendiaries in the region."

"When it comes to an Incendiary of Anaymous's caliber, we cannot afford to overlook it," Bloodbrand replied.

"Anaymous may have different aims," Cahan interjected as he stepped from the shadows to reveal his presence.

Cahan felt A'uun's eyes fix upon him. A'uun cocked an eyebrow and stared at him as if he could see into his thoughts. This frightened Cahan somewhat. He felt the tendrils of A'uun's mind entwine themselves amongst the outer reaches of his consciousness. It was as if A'uun had shared a thought with him. It was not in words, merely a feeling, similar to the communication he had with Bardon through the defero stone. A'uun also seemed perplexed by this bold interruption. Cahan found it striking that a Celestial herald decided to invade his mind before even speaking a word to him. He sensed from A'uun's mental grappling that he found something oddly familiar about his aura. Cahan snapped back to Bloodbrand's speech as his sonorous voice echoed off the magistrate assembly walls.

"Explain yourself, Ranger..." Bloodbrand allowed his words to trail off.

"Devlin, Chief Ranger Devlin of Verinda," Cahan answered. "I interrogated an Amalgam Incendiary leader close to the Presidium. He claims that Anaymous has defected and wishes membership to the Protosian Assembly of Districts." As soon as the words left his mouth, he realized they would sound ludicrous to anyone that heard them, especially dignitaries and leaders of this caliber.

The procession erupted into laughter, aside from A'uun, who continued to study Cahan thoughtfully, though he could no longer feel his mental interrogation.

"I realize my statements may seem out of the realm of—"

"Sanity?" the sour-faced Gargoyle chimed in.

Cahan turned to the Gargoyle and nodded his head in acknowledgement. "Yes, it may seem that way, but tell me this: Why would your Ministry of Information not want me to speak to this magnate? Why send an envoy to obstruct my interrogation?"

Cahan watched the frenzied faces as he heard a collection of gasps and hushed words mingle within the group of diplomats. Bloodbrand sharply waved his hand, quieting them.

"While it is true I do not trust the MOI, I can assure you, Chief Ranger, that Anaymous would do no such thing." Bloodbrand spoke with an air of finality. "He has been terrorizing our citizens and human colonists for almost a century. Now please excuse yourself from this chamber. We must continue."

Cahan turned away from the panel, ignoring any sort of foolish custom of bowing or other such nonsense. He searched his mind for a new strategy. He felt anxiety fueled by a quiet anger creep into his brain, scratching its surface mockingly. He started down a long, winding hall from the meeting chamber to a windswept courtyard of prodigious trees and chromatic-hued cobblestone walks. In the center of the courtyard, colorful shocks of Verindian paisleys extended upward and circled around a stone-lined bath of cerulean water. Cahan stared at his reflection for a long period of time, deep in thought. The sparkling water was somewhat hypnotic, so he broke his gaze and turned away from it to see a small, docile creature standing uncomfortably close to him. It was slumped and brown, with bulging, blister-like clusters protruding from its body. The bridge of its nose was wide and shot straight down, connecting to the top of its wide, stretching mouth. Its nose moved as it spoke.

"Chief Magistrate Bloodbrand was impressed with your courage in the meeting chamber. He asked that I give you this."

The creature handed Cahan a piece of parchment lined with emerald slash marks. Cahan grasped the paper on both sides and pored over it. The communication advised that he and his company were to assist the Protosian Cavalry in the apprehension of Anaymous and his Incendiary cohorts.

"The chief magistrate heard tell of your gallantry against the Amalgam and thinks your talents will be useful in this campaign," the diminutive creature said, as if trying to sell him a bill of goods. "The magistrate was, and is, quite the tactician himself."

Cahan narrowed his eyes and studied the pustule-ridden thing before him. His mind began to race, as he thought of the different outcomes that could branch from this offer. Cahan didn't stop until he saw, through the reflection in the docile creature's enormous black eyes, the anger in his own eyes. He never realized what he looked like in his natural state until that moment. It shocked him out of his rampant thoughts. To Cahan, it was like looking at another being.

"Very well, then, I will call my company to arms," Cahan said distractedly.

He called a meeting to inform his company of the mission that they were to embark upon. There was one notable absence in the meeting—Bardon. After the meeting, Cahan's cautious and somewhat paranoid mind began to overlay all the different scenarios as to why Bardon could have been missing. Some involved betrayal, while others involved abduction. Cahan had sent his men off to meet with the Protosian forces, while he darkly pondered what was to come. His thoughts were broken by a now-familiar voice.

"Sorry to have missed the meeting, sire," Bardon said. "I had to meet with my old precept. He said it was of dire circumstance."

A precept was the designation of teacher in most conjuring disciplines. Wealthy families generally had individual precepts in their employ for their magically gifted children or relatives. This gave Cahan some insight into the background of his mysteriously gifted charge, however marginal. Perhaps he was as powerful as he was due to all of the private tutoring he received, Cahan thought. He concluded there was more to the story.

"Understandable," Cahan said casually. "Go meet with Declan. He can give you the details of our next mission."

The surprised look on Bardon's face said that he wasn't expecting that sort of response. His robes billowed up as he dashed quickly to the rest of the group, as if Cahan might change his mind.

Cahan trained his eyes forward as Lieutenant General Graan surveyed the men that stood before him. His demeanor was different than it was at the Amalgam keep. The facial expression the large Fenthom donned was regal and purposeful.

"In mere moments, we will disembark to the last known province where the Incendiary known as Anaymous Nysrogh has been sighted," Graan said. "His capture is of the utmost importance. Now gather your supports and be ready to arrive in port within the hour."

Cahan's company rushed to their vessels. The Veldt district's port, their destination, was just beyond the Veldt Mountains. The Veldt Mountains, or the Shrieking Mountains, as some called them, had seen the massacre of dozens of humans and a royal constable in the neighboring village, just eighty years prior at the hands of a cultist group of Gilpesh conjurors known as "the Inherent."

Cahan had led several mock strategy sessions based on the Veldt Massacre in War College. He always found it odd the original mission's members were omitted from the mission codex. Some barristers of the time, notably those of the León'Velcrist district, blamed the soldiers, rather than the Inherent, for the infamous massacre. Cahan's studies revealed the Inherent as a fringe sect of Gilpesh, known for their dark-magic blood rites. Their prime aim was to raise the antediluvian "deities" driven away by the ancient dragons of Valese.

The encroachers, as Valesian adherents referred to them, tried to lay claim to Shintallis once Valese brought forth the orbiting Shintallian moons, which had the effect of stirring the primordial mire that made life possible. Once the building blocks of life began to resonate, Valese trifled with the natural formula to create the arcane dragons, the forbearers to the Fenthom. Valese's new weapons, though mighty, were not gifted with the divine ability of reason. They proved more than a match for the three off-world creatures and their sworn enemies, who would later make the claim they were deities to anyone who would hear their dark whispers of profane evil. At a much later date, the Fenthom would found Protos on the very ground where the three outworlders were defeated.

Cahan entered the alloy-and-brindle-lined quarters of Lieutenant General Graan aboard the Protosian flagship vessel. The office was littered with ancient relics and paintings of the ancient Valesian dragons. There were depictions of each known breed: mountain, marsh, plains, desert, and the rare hybrid plant-based dragon lining the walls. Old, dustless books lined the shelves behind him, even a few forbidden tomes, such as *The Dead Caller Testament* and *The Shabarian Chronicles*. The sight of these books did not set Cahan into any sort of alert, however. It was common practice for a Fenthom strategist to read about their enemies in great detail, even study their culture. The Fenthom created the curriculum at the War College in the heart of Protos and in Verinda, so forbidden tomes were part and parcel in military studies by design.

Cahan walked toward the creature's slumped figure leaning back in his chair. Graan looked up at the chief ranger austerely as he scratched together the talons of his thumb and index finger with an audible grinding noise. Cahan handed the regal Fenthom a piece of parchment. As Graan scanned the document, a book of note caught Cahan's eye: *The Ascension and Death of Forgatha*.

Forgatha was often referred to as the Dark Continent. It rested west of a broken and partially sunken land bridge near the Aundyre barrier that neighbored the Republic of Protos. This accursed land mass held the majority of the Shabarian dogmatists, including the Gilpesh Thaumaturgy. It was said that every wicked creature was born within its confines and that the continent itself was alive like the shrieking hills of Blasstock and Veldt Mountains, but far, far more potent.

The continent's nature was what gave its denizens their power. Shabaris the Dead Caller imbued the lands with evil that birthed the contrary side of luminous magic, or aphotic spellcraft. During the Grand Bygone War, the peaceful nations were said to have contained and trapped the continent's power—though its power was so great, it took the combined resolve of all lands to defeat it. As to where this power was trapped, many speculated, while others ceaselessly quested for it. If the continent was once again revived, the enemy would have gained a distinct advantage. Its evil nature would have spread to other lands and corrupted the whole of Shintallis. Forgatha, a charred corpse of what it once was, was said to stir and shriek every so often as it lay dormant in the sea.

"You wish the requisitioning of landships for you and your men?" Graan asked. "Three, to be exact…"

"Yes, Lieutenant General," Cahan replied. "I think much more ground could be covered this way."

"Granted. Once we have landed, see Brigadier Rigis. He will have the vessels waiting in the ship housing." He paused for a moment before he continued. "This is not one of your schemes the Rattock referred to, is it?"

"No, sire," Cahan lied.

Chapter 8
~ Sojourn of the Former Incendiary ~

Cahan dashed upward to the uppermost deck of *The Tumult*, one of the fastest ships in the Verindian armada. The wind bristled against his face and grit blew into his mouth as he emerged. He watched the forestry below blur past. He then shifted his eyes forward to the barely perceptible stone monoliths, which crept up upon the idyllic, cobbled homes, crowned by tottering rooftops against the backdrop of a dome-shaped, eldritch mountain. Cahan heard the faint sound of an energy chamber churning and grinding. He saw that the Protosians were pushing westward, away from the abandoned village, most likely the same route the alleged former Incendiary took in his quest to join the Protosians.

As the ship drew closer, he could see the domed, black husk of a mountain in greater detail. The craterous scars of something malevolent were branded upon the landscape. Obscene growth of blackish-green flowed out from the base of the mountain, like cannibalistic serpents gnawing away at each other. Just beyond the clutches of the hideous mountain growth, stood a manor, deep in the heart of a decayed vineyard.

The gray-and-white manor was at the centermost point of the grounds. Cahan thought that it seemed out of place with its surroundings. The architect of the home was clearly an adherent to a modernistic human approach to architecture. The ample use of glass cut across the simple but effective design, which naturally flowed with the elegant, rounded corners and bends of its anatomy. The manor conjured thoughts of the body of a curvaceous woman.

The manor had three stories. Each floor was smaller than the previous, and the structure was offset by curious symbols at each corner of the grounds. It was composed of a mixture of fine Protosian brindle wood and rough, gray stone.

The ponderous stone monoliths and the steep grade the village rested upon made a close landing nearly impossible. Cahan also did not want to alert the Protosians to this area by landing too close to it. He remembered that the

Amalgam magnate had said that Anaymous would be holed up in a manor of some kind. Cahan instructed his crew to follow the flagship vessel closely and to land near its location.

Once the entire fleet of landships reached their destination, Cahan made his way to the ship housing. Brigadier Rigis was a comparatively medium-sized Plains Fenthom. His grayish-white coloring revealed numerous battle scars on his forearms, chest, and tail. Cahan noticed that a small section of his tail had been hacked off, as the customary spikes did not protrude outward from the latter half of the appendage. The only scar missing was the hackneyed vertical eye scar so many told of in their lore about the noble warriors of old.

Cahan approached the battle-worn warrior to requisition his companies' land crafts. Cahan handed the Fenthom some parchment, which Rigis scanned thoroughly, grunting with noises of affirmation every so often.

"You may have use of the land crafts resting on the third platform," the warrior grunted. "Oh yes, I almost forgot. Present your piloting documents."

Cahan fumbled through the large satchel strapped over his shoulder and found the needed documentation. He handed the bent and tattered parchment to the brigadier, who closely matched the condition of his documents.

Cahan overheard the boisterous conversations of his militia as they stomped loudly up the ramp leading into the ship housing. Rigis surveyed the group and grunted prior to speaking.

"It would appear that you are not in need of three vessels, Chief Ranger," he said curiously. "I would also tell your men to shut their bleedin' mutters."

"Ah, you're from the East End, in Protos."

Rigis grunted as he nodded his head in the affirmative.

Cahan turned to his men and yelled, "You heard the brigadier!"

His men looked at him and snapped to attention.

Cahan refocused back on Rigis. "I just want to cover as much ground as possible, Brigadier Rigis. We may be spread a little thin, but our assignment is to simply alert your forces if we find anything."

The Fenthom hesitantly grunted and nodded his head, gesturing the way toward the third platform.

The three land crafts were well used, but still in working order. Cahan inspected the vessels closely. The lines of the vessels were similar to corbita boats, except for the leveled underbellies. The topsides of the crafts were flat and had small wooden housings located at the center. A long shaft of brindle stuck out diagonally from the housing. The brindle shaft controlled the direction of the ship, as it was directly linked to a clustering of propulsion ducts. Moving the shaft in a particular direction would change which duct would receive the swirling blue energy contained inside the topside housing. Just in front of the wooden housing was a recess the size of a Fenthom's foot. One was to step into this recess to release energies from the small chamber. Doing this fueled the aft-thrusting propulsion ducts. Cahan also noted with concern these vessels were barren of any weapon mountings.

Cahan stepped into one of the vessels solo, while the rest of the group divided between the remaining two vessels.

Just prior to the group's separation, Bardon approached Cahan. Far off, on the other side of the platform, Cahan noticed Declan's prying eyes from a recess within the smallest vessel.

"Why are you piloting a craft on your own, sire?" he said with his customary hint of cynicism and suspicion.

"Get in. I don't have time to argue with you, Bardon."

Bardon gave Cahan a peculiar look, but stepped inside the land craft without offering his usual fit of sarcasm, to which Cahan had become accustomed.

"You all know your positions," Cahan said to his men. "Circulate outward and meet at our mark at sunset."

Cahan stepped into the large recess in front of him, which vaulted the ship upward. He then dug the balls of his foot in and pushed. With a surge, the vessel shot forward, leaving crisp blue tides of energy streaming behind.

"What is it this time?" Bardon yelled over the whipping ash-filled air. "Planning to break the lawful accords once more? Maybe we can hatch a plot to steal money from old ladies."

"Nothing that sinister, Bardon," he shouted back. "I just plan to notify an enemy of the districts that the Protosians are closing in on him."

Bardon paused for a moment, mouth agape until soot flew in. He spat it out and wiped his mouth with his sleeve. "Do I even have to ask?"

Cahan explained to Bardon what the Amalgam magnate had told him. After much wringing of hands and angry posturing, Bardon conceded the argument to his superior officer.

"We are going to get killed, sneaking into a den of hissing Kalriss demons. Are you—?"

"You aren't going," Cahan said as he looked back at his compatriot. "I need you to keep watch." He looked forward again and gazed at death-shrouded Veldt on the horizon. "The Protosians will eventually check the village. I hope later rather than sooner."

"Do you still have the defero stone?"

"Yes."

"Very well, you will have to show me how to raise this heap to a higher elevation so I can get a better look," Bardon said.

51

Cahan looked back at him. He had a look of worry on his face as he thumbed his defero stone for a moment before looking up at Cahan. "Are you getting a sort of odd feeling from your defero?"

"Not at all."

Cahan and Bardon arrived at the field of bloodstained stone projecting upward in careful symmetry. Cahan quickly surveyed the area, checking for Protosians or enemies. If he wasn't careful, or if the Protosians caught wind of what he was doing, the former might become the latter, he thought. He shot a quick glance at the stone field; there were too many hiding spots to count. He figured that if someone were hiding, he would eventually hear them approach.

The symmetry and daunting height of the stones filled him with a sense of curiosity. He was near a monument of sorts—one that extended back untold epochs. A certain magnetism emanated from the cyclopean panorama of stone and blood, as if something from ages past pierced through the veil of time and spoke to him. He wondered darkly how many humans it took to paint the stones with their blood—but decided to ignore his instinctive draw to this area and focus on the vessel. They were safe enough—for now.

Cahan began to throw various levers and adjust the alloy piping leading into the small energy chamber of the land craft. The antiquated vessel sputtered and lurched. Cahan ripped off the gear system's outer shell, located near the bottom of the topside housing, as his thoughts became procedural and mechanized. He enjoyed working on air and land vessels; it tore him away from his anger. He kneeled down, drew his blade of illumed cobalt, and jammed it into the gear system. As he raised the sword upward, the craft rose several feet into the air. Still kneeling, Cahan shook his dagger at Bardon impatiently while he maintained his focus on the housing. A bit of blue energy trickled into his periphery from Bardon's direction, and he felt the energy seep into his weapon. Cahan jammed the dagger into the brindle wood housing beneath the sword to hold it in place.

"Don't touch anything," Cahan said.

"Your sword—"

"I'll be fine," Cahan said, tapping the crossbow holstered to his waist. "Just make sure nothing happens to the sword. It was a gift."

Cahan gave a final glance at Bardon and jumped to the ground below. He broke into a sprint.

He had almost made it to the abandoned manor of glass, brindle wood, and stone when the defero began to resonate with tremulous energy. Cahan grasped the stone tightly so the message would come into focus in his mind.

The mental markers came surging in.

"The Protosians are heading your way with mounted cannons at the ready."

"Already? But... how?"

"I don't know, but you had better make haste. I think they are simply going to decimate the manor with artillery fire. I can see the energy stirring within the cannons."

"Shit," he snapped.

Cahan sprinted even faster toward the wall in front of him. His stomach roiled and his bottom lip bounced to the rapid motion of his gait. He came to the towering wall of stone that surrounded the curvaceous manor. He easily bounded over the obstacle and landed on the other side—into a pit of roused Kalriss demons. Cahan reflexively drew his crossbow.

They all hissed at him in unison, which brought attention to the odd, conical muzzles with hideous, flaring V-shaped nostrils at the forefront of the creatures' faces. Large, glassy eyes were set on each side of the creatures' furry heads, which had small, pointed, ridge-lined ears. The mouths of the creatures tapered upward to their nostrils, revealing large, pointed incisors. Their brown, layered arms and legs were very different from the rest of their physiology. They were almost insect-like, with tiny hairs prickling outward. They were clad in leather armor—which only protected the areas their natural armor did not.

As one of the Kalriss approached Cahan, he noticed the odd nature of its torso. From a distance, the demons appeared to have a bony outer shell. Yet upon closer inspection, it looked like brownish, leathery skin stretched over plates of bone and arranged in a ring like pattern. The creature stepped closer with an outstretched hand, reaching out and curling its long, arachnid-like digits, preparing to pounce. The rest of the festering demons remained postured to attack. A chorus of gibbous, pestilent chatter filled Cahan's ears, like a swarm of insects greeting a rising moon.

Cahan grabbed the neck of the nearest creature and dug the bolt-loaded crossbow into its temple, or at least what he assumed was its temple. Cahan's mind raced, and his eyes darted to each of the demons in front of him. He could not think of anything but the tense situation. Protosian cannons were at his back, and demons ready to kill him were at his front. Cahan breathed in deeply and exhaled to clear his mind. He didn't have time for the anger that had been plaguing him.

"Take me to Anaymous now!" Cahan bellowed at the Kalriss demons. Cahan caught the anger creeping into his mind and consciously toned down his expression.

53

"Why would we?" came a hiss from the throng.

"Shut up!" Cahan interrupted out of necessity. "There are heavily armed Protosian land vessels on their way to kill you all. Take me to Anaymous now! We don't have time for your idiotic demonic posturing!"

"Why would you warn us, human—I hesitate to call you 'human'—about the Protosians?" The question came in a deep, guttural gnarl from an imposing figure that emerged from the dark doorway. Cahan instinctively knew that this was the demon he had been looking for.

Anaymous, also a Kalriss, was quite a bit larger than his fellow demons and seemingly much more intelligent. His eyes studied Cahan.

"They don't know you are attempting to negotiate peace. They are convinced that you're making a move either on the colonies or even the districts."

Anaymous chuckled. The shrieking outburst seemed to echo, with parts of it inaudible to Cahan's ears. He gave a long, assessing look at Cahan. "I would be at an impossible tactical disadvantage if I invaded Protos or her colonies. They must think me daft." Anaymous paused for a moment and continued. "How did you come to the conclusion I had abandoned the Parshist var' Crestis?"

"An Amalgam magnate minor told me of your 'change of lifestyle.' Is it true?"

"It is, Ranger. What is your name?"

"Cahan."

"If what you say is true, Cahan, it would seem that my quest to join the rest of the Valese-fearing world is intangible, a fool's errand."

"No, we simply need to prove to the Protosians that you have taken a new path."

"And how will we do that?"

"I have an idea, but we can't do it here."

Chapter 9
~ The Convert ~

Cahan and his newly acquired cohorts were at a distance, watching the energized cannons recoil as they cast spheres of devouring combustion, decimating the entirety of the abandoned Veldt village. Cahan watched as bursts of blue-and-crimson flames blanketed the hamlet. Chunks of stone were hurled about and collided with the rooftops of the once inhabited village.

"I think I know what's going on here," Cahan said as the display of artillery illumined his face. "The Ministry of Information fears you." Cahan shifted his focus from the destroyed village to Anaymous.

"Why would an arm of the Protosian government fear me? Have they grown corrupt?"

"They're the last loyalists of the old command, grasping onto their remaining power." Cahan paused for a moment—the surrealism of the situation was not lost on him. He was speaking to a scion of the Incendiary movement, the scourge of the deserts of the serene, about peace. Never in a million years. "If peace were achieved with you and the tribes that you could bring into the fold, they would be finished. They need chaos and tragedy to assume power. Otherwise, the neck of the beast would be cleaved."

"So they mean to diminish me and eliminate any parlance of peace between the tribes and Protos?"

"Yes. Someone close to you is in contact with the Ministry. Otherwise, they wouldn't be privy to your plans."

Anaymous suddenly slumped and put his clawed hand to his forehead. "We have a liaison to the Edelsen district governorship. It is he who must be in league with the Ministry. He goes by the name 'Valcroft.'"

Cahan felt a grim fear as he looked to Anaymous. "Is this Valcroft an Imbra?"

"Yes," Anaymous said with a reluctant nod.

"Valcroft isn't a liaison to the governorship," Cahan said. "He's the vassal to the premier of Dunnavisch Estuary."

"Premier Vashar N'dal," Anaymous whispered. "N'dal attempted to bargain with my organization. He inferred that we could sit on his court."

"What did you tell him?"

"No, of course." Anaymous wrinkled his brow at Cahan's implication. "I will not sit in the court of a country where all are made to suffer equally—a place where your path is preordained from birth to death in service of the state."

"This makes matters far worse than I'd thought," Cahan said bleakly. "Dunnavisch, Incendiaries, and the Ministry are linked. Dunnavisch has also been linked with the Dark Continent. N'dal must be attempting to revive the Dark Continent where his father failed eighty years ago."

"What was your 'idea'?" Anaymous said.

"You have the Tablature Oaths of the tribes in your community, right?"

"Yes, I was going to present them to the chief magistrate at the United Conclave. How did you know I would have them?"

"It's not important. I say we present the oaths as a peace declaration to Protos and attempt to salvage the treaty you wanted. However, first, I think we should go to Elysium en route."

"Why Elysium?"

"Something is about to happen there. I heard it directly from the mouth of Valese's herald."

"Herald A'uun? I owe much to him."

"You know him?"

"No. One of his former pupils is very close to me," he said. "Do you think I arrived at this conversion on my own?"

"If we can stop whatever is about to happen, it will be further evidence you've changed," Cahan said. His mind focused on the grand conspiracy that lurked over them. It seemed this task was too big, especially for a military deserter and a band of former Incendiaries.

Chapter 10
~ The City of the Stranded ~

Cahan moved toward Elysium with Anaymous and company, cautiously observing the grandiose, brown-hued cityscape and its sundry mixture of the huddling destitute and the thriving decadents. The permeation of earth tones came from the raw materials used in the city constructed of burnished stone.

The vast buildings that lined the normally busy thoroughfares loomed, waxing barren in the corrosive-smelling night air. The ample use of arched doorways and cupolas bemoaned the suggestion of a demon-and-human collaboration in the bronze, dim city. Shady ghouls skulked in the shadows, just beyond the reaches of the main thoroughfare that cut across the central point of the municipality. A protective stone wall of unusual proportions shielded Elysium from the many bloody raids that plagued the region—raids in the name of the former scion of the Incendiaries, known to his people as the tribes of the Deserts of the Serene.

Anaymous had warned them to tread carefully in the city. Cahan considered this to mean that his previous reputation was well known, and his new reputation had yet to be established.

For the most part, the nightlife of Elysium was said to consist of fiendish nocturnal ghouls, other scavenger breeds of demons, and fanatical, blood-drinking humans that were attempting to make the transformation to demonhood. The higher bred creatures, consisting of non-blood-drinking humans and the more sentient variety of demons, were relegated to their residences when the vagrant-filled night crested over the city. In most cases, even the criminal element of Elysium conducted their operations in the bright of the day. The night was for the mindless abominations that lurked without aim.

Cahan and his band of Kalriss waited at the heavily fortified front gates of the bulwarked city. The group, now cloaked from suspicion, was at the rear of a gathering line of refugees from the Incendiary-filled deserts. Lines of human and

57

demon migrants donned drab, threadbare clothing. The huddling masses protectively clutched their wooden drinking cups and scraps of food, waiting like orphaned children in the back alley of a dining house. Cahan scanned the faces of those around him and spied scars from old injuries, smelled fresh wounds and medicinal herbs, and witnessed the slightest glimmer of hope—a hope that was born of the escape from their respective homelands.

Cahan focused his attention back on Anaymous. "How will we get in? I didn't realize how heavily fortified Elysium is, nor the sheer number of refugees who seek asylum here."

"Luckily, we own most of the gate guards. They allowed the occasional raid in years past."

Cahan looked at Anaymous with repugnance.

"I know. It is something I am not proud of, but it does serve us well in this situation. We will have to tread carefully once inside. The inner sanctum guards could not be bought."

Cahan and the others easily passed the bribed gate guards. The shady, grizzled guards watched them casually, as if they had been permitted to enter dozens of times. Cahan noticed that after they passed, the guards resumed their checks of identifying documents and sponsored letters of political asylum.

"We should split up and scour the city," Cahan said.

"Very well," Anaymous said. "There is a former armory called the Brigand Arms where we can rendezvous. It is a safe house for syndicate members on the outskirts of the city. Just head northeast."

"Let's meet in three hours' time," Cahan replied.

"I will send Ose with you."

"No," he said flatly. "Not this time."

"Very well, then. We will be in Flat Seven."

Cahan started down the main thoroughfare as the night reached its neb and the presence of ghouls began to recede, though he could still hear their smacking and lapping echo about.

Cahan quietly stole across the cobbled, burnish street, closer to a sudden movement he had just witnessed. Several yards in front of him, a large, purplish demon haunted a dark alleyway.

Cahan picked the locked door at its northern entrance and let himself into the adjacent building. He climbed up a floor and peered out of a window partially concealed by a soaring black spire.

Spires were commonly used as energy sources. Cahan did not realize areas outside of Verinda and Protos used them. They were a luxurious spellcrafted item that drew in energy from the atmosphere much like airship energy chambers did.

The tall, looming spires supplied light to the orbs resting on the walls of various homes, as well as heat during the long, cold winter.

Through the partially concealed window, Cahan spied one of the gate guards approaching the purplish demon. He muttered something into its ear and furtively strode away. The demon began to move again, farther down the stretches of the alleyway and merged into a fork, bisected by an abandoned monastery that towered darkly over the thoroughfare.

Cahan inspected the outward appearance of the monastery and noticed something familiar to him. He saw the Divinity of the Bound sacrament carved into the stone work, represented by a pair of hands snapping its shackles. The Divinity of the Bound sect believed that the Valesian philosophies had been changed and misinterpreted by the Seer Heritage. Their founder, Elizabeth Cloister, a human woman, professed that Valese did not wish to be worshipped. She wished for her adherents' good works to be a beacon of all-consuming light, to quake evil to its core and tremble in their chaff. The mind, to Cloister, was the most sacred thing in existence, and the products of it should be exalted. Cahan had never seen a portrait of this woman, but he was well familiar with her harsh origins. Cloister began her existence as an indentured servant in Forgatha and worked her way up from poverty via the conjuring arts. She had discovered a new discipline of human magic as powerful as demonic spellcraft. Bound spellcraft, as it was called, named after her order, was very dangerous for most humans to wield and required a brilliance most lacked. Even if a human had the gift of magic, it was not certain if they possessed the will to employ Bound spellcraft.

All Bound monasteries were magically hewn by the hands of its adherents. Strict abolitionists comprised the order and would not allow any forced labor. One of the prime aims of the sect was to free slaves from their masters and to abolish the cruel practice.

Cloister often debated the established leaders of the Valesian philosophies, the members of the Seer Heritage, and made short work of their obsessive, ritualistic beliefs with logic and pragmatism. She proved the cryptically described events in the *Et dás Lieu* transpired in different locales and had divergent meanings from what the Seer Heritage professed. Their moderate view of slavery infuriated Cloister, who believed no being should be bound by another. Cloister's group believed a being should be bound only to one thing—individualism. For this idea, along with her other differences in philosophy, Cloister was deemed a heretic in the eyes of the establishment and forced her to flee her adopted homeland of Weshire and wander the countries and many deserts of Western Shintallis.

Cahan wondered how these demons could ouster conjurors as powerful as the Bound. The creature that had entered the monastery had no conjuring ability. He concluded the Bound likely abandoned the refuge.

He leaped down to the thoroughfare leading to the monastery where the demon had entered. He heard loud demoniac chortling in the front room. He instead investigated the rear of the stone structure. Scaffolding stretched across the building, but construction appeared to have abruptly ceased. Tools and magical implements were left behind. Another sacrament, half completed, boldly faced the large, flowing river adjacent to the refuge, most likely to call out to other Bound logicians and runaway slaves who traveled by boat. This river fed into the immense Icon Sea, which was both a route of trade and escape.

Cahan heard the venomous mutterings of the demon's language originating from the room at the pinnacle of the refuge. Once he climbed within earshot, he balanced himself on the scaffolding. Precariously stretched, he grasped planks with both hands and rested his feet on a half-decayed slab of wood. He could scarcely understand the dialect that the purplish pustule-ridden creatures were using, but he was somewhat familiar with it. The cadence of the speech seemed unnatural, and the hideous, hollow clicking sound resonated as he attempted to decipher the chatter. Cahan could understand a particular word that kept resurfacing throughout the rampant sounding conversation—docks—or that's what he thought the translation was when converted to base language.

The demon Cahan had tracked left the abandoned monastery and took a side thoroughfare that fed into subterranean tunnels, as if he were evading trackers.

By the time Cahan had made his way to the tunnels, he lost track of the rambling, violet creature. It was nowhere to be seen, and even its stench was masked by the stronger smell stemming from the surroundings. Cahan decided to meet up with Anaymous and report the information he had gathered.

* * * *

Cahan arrived at the rundown, tottering building of which Anaymous had spoken. All different manner of creatures filtered in and out of the tunnel-like entrance of the appropriately named "Brigand Arms." Cahan lurked down the main hallway of flyblown filth and decay. His stomach turned in disgust as the odors of the armory drifted into his nostrils. When he drew farther to the room where Anaymous said he would be, he began to cough uncontrollably from the burning miasmic gases that began to fill his lungs. Cahan reached Anaymous's room and pounded on the door. He covered up his outburst of coughing as best he could.

The door opened to the smell of fresh air, and Cahan immediately recovered.

"The miasma is only poisonous to one type of creature," said the demon that opened the door. "Did you hear coughing out there, human?" He cast a searching glance outside.

"Cahan, come in. We have been waiting for you," Anaymous's voice called from the adjoining room.

"We have to—" Cahan stopped mid-sentence as he entered the adjoining room, where Anaymous and his soldiers, including one new face, waited. To his shock, the demon that he had been following all morning was also there, accompanied by a group seemingly affiliated with him.

He looked at Anaymous for an explanation. Anaymous nodded his head in an attempt to tell him to play along. Awkward silence filled the room.

"You were saying?" Anaymous asked, breaking the silence.

"We have to leave soon. I wasn't aware you had guests. I apologize..." He trailed off.

"You 'apologize'?" the mysterious figure from the monastery asked rhetorically, turning his attention to Anaymous. "You have this human trained well, Anaymous. Though your vassal is quite bold, yelling out from the other room." He turned again to Cahan. "You would do well to learn your duty, human."

"Speaking of knowing your duty, you have yet to pay your tribute, Malphas," Anaymous said.

Malphas bowed to Anaymous and held a small satchel of Gilner coins in his outstretched hand. Anaymous used the opportunity to signal Cahan to leave.

Cahan left swiftly, closing his eyes and mouth as he sprinted down the poisonous hallway. He burst out the entrance into the peak of the afternoon. Waves of heat crested up from the bustling thoroughfare. Cahan noticed that he had drawn the attention of nearby sanctum guards.

The guards' looks of disbelief showed plainly on their faces, and they paused for a moment before they lunged forward in pursuit of Cahan. Cahan ran down the thoroughfare, attempting to avoid passersby until he was met by two sanctum guards squarely in front of him, crossbows at the ready. Cahan broke stride and came to a halt. He peered over his shoulder. The guards in pursuit had stopped just behind Cahan and fixed their crossbows on Cahan's back, panting loudly.

"Chief Ranger," the guard behind him called out as he tried to regain his breath. "You are being detained for abandoning your commission and for conspiratorial charges of being in league with known Incendiaries."

Cahan was dismayed by the latter half of the guard's statements. His mind searched for how they would know about Anaymous. Did Bardon betray him?

Cahan raised his arms up and clasped his hands in acquiescence of his detainment. The guards, in kind, sheathed their crossbows. The man who had declared Cahan's charges stepped forward to fit manacles to his wrists, but Cahan threw a punishing vertical elbow to his captor's jaw. There was a loud snap, and the guard collapsed in a heap.

Cahan heard the guard behind him draw a blade and felt the forward momentum of his pursuer as he lunged. Cahan turned and grabbed the guard's wrist mid-leap, guiding the curved, silver dagger into his enemy's Adam's apple. As the guard choked and gagged on his own blood, Cahan threw him into the guard standing in front of him.

The remaining guard, behind Cahan, wrapped his arm around Cahan's neck. Cahan lowered his center of gravity and maneuvered his left leg behind his assailant. The guard continued to hold onto Cahan's neck for dear life, though he could scarcely balance his own weight. Cahan lifted him off the ground by his legs before sending him downward, skull-first, knocking him unconscious. Cahan could hear the distant yells and chatter of a gathering crowd of civilians speaking of a peculiarly tall human fighting sanctum guards single-handedly.

Cahan got up and started for the guard that he had thrown the body at, when a piercing pain entered his arm. He turned around to see yet another guard lowering his crossbow from a distance. Without looking, Cahan pulled out the arrow—but blood didn't spill from his wound. The gathering crowd gasped. The malevolence began to take control. Rage brimmed just under the surface. Cahan's new attacker clumsily back-pedaled for a moment, a look of desperation erupted on the sanctum guard's face as he bollixed his crossbow about.

His tremulous hands reached for a bolt from his quiver as he worriedly glanced over at Cahan.

Cahan spied a loaded crossbow near the body of a dead sanctum guard and leapt toward the corpse, tucked his body, and rolled on his shoulder as he grabbed the weapon. He rose as the fumbling guard was about to unleash his weapon. Cahan squeezed the trigger of his pilfered weapon, and a slightly bent bolt soared across the domain of the cobbled thoroughfare. At the moment of impact, the sanctum guard turned his head, which caused the faulty projectile to miss and graze his sweaty forehead.

Cahan groaned and sprinted toward the guard, who was on his knees with his head down and arms flailing in a submissive posture. Cahan stopped short of the pathetic display. He piteously shook his head before driving a knee into the guard's skull. The guard crashed into the wall and bounced forward again into his original position.

Cahan chuckled at the guard's expense. He again began to make his way to the docks when he heard the rustling of a guard pinned under a dead body. His anger surged. The sounds of everything around him intensified. Footsteps echoed, breathing whistled, plates of armor softly ground against one another with his sweeping gait. Cahan went to the body and nudged it aside with the toe of his boot to reveal a shaken man with tears welling in his fear filled brown eyes. Cahan placed his boot on the guard's chin.

"Do you wish to join the others?" he demanded.

The man fearfully shook his head. Cahan, as fast as a whip's crack, struck the man squarely in the face, knocking him unconscious.

Chapter 11
~ The Winged Horrors ~

Cahan arrived at a sun-blistered dockyard, where several boats and air vessels rested. He looked up at the ominous sky. Dark clouds loomed, shrouded in black mist. A red energy storm collided against the mist, forcing it to yield, as it split the congregation of clouds and swirling, cerulean gales, in what resembled a bloody battle erupting in the heavens. A skyward brood of grotesque fowl bathed in the ethereal storm, as they cawed mockingly and lay in wait for fresh cadavers. This display made Cahan uneasy, as it might have portended to something dark—some sort of primal spellcraft.

Cahan surveyed the area and made a mental note of the dock master's hull and accompanying structures just beyond the privately moored vessels. A crackling gurgle erupted just to the west of him, and he tried to get a closer look at where the disquieting noise came from. He crept further westward, along the rearmost flank of the yard, and the gurgle became more potent, with an accompanying sulfur-like stench.

A large, gangrenous, wide-mouthed demon was heatedly frothing at a gate guard as it squeezed his frail human neck. The human could barely face the creature's hideous scowl as it chastised him beyond reckoning. The gaping demon slammed the human against a nearby ship and gestured eastward. The familiar gurgling crackle returned as sound slithered out of the demon's wide, cavernous mouth.

Unmoved by the display, Cahan began looking for a weakness in the boundary guard of the bleached, shipment-heavy waterfront. Cahan noticed an opening near a large argosy-class vessel. Only one guard, some kind of spiny, grayish creature, slovenly traipsed about on a raised platform. Cahan silently took cover behind some wooden crates—just out of the creature's line of sight.

Curiously, he heard a faint humming sound emitting from his cover. Cahan began to investigate the crates as inconspicuously as possible. He attempted to peer through a small hole, but could not get a good look at its contents. He jabbed his index finger through the opening and pulled a plank of wood from the box. Through the thin opening, he spied a case full of eluvium sheathed in clear cylindrical housings, which were set atop haphazardly customized shelves to accommodate the shape of the cylinders. Cahan pilfered several of the vials, wrapped them in cloth, and placed them in his duffle. Cahan heard footsteps behind him and braced himself for battle.

"Cahan!" Anaymous exclaimed in a loud whisper. "Were you planning to lay siege to the dockyard on your own?" He handed him a small axe.

Cahan took the axe and gestured to the box of eluvium. "I think they are going to destroy the entire dockyard with these. That would disrupt food and supply shipments to the colonies and even Protos."

"It is odd how they do not carry on like the evil that has arisen before," Anaymous commented. "In the bygone era and after, it was simply two sides gathering power and then all-out war erupted."

"They've learned," Cahan said.

Anaymous looked at Cahan with skepticism.

"They've become the body politic, as opposed to fighting it from the outside," Cahan explained. "They rot us from within." He left his statement as a cold punctuation and abruptly started for the argosy-class vessel with axe in hand. Cahan looked back at the group and signaled for them to stay put.

He remained concealed as the stout, spiny demon continued to mill about. The grayish, muscular creature had a menacing presence and appeared not to have a mouth. Four rows of three asymmetrically lined, sable eyes stared out from their deep sockets and rolled in different directions, surveying and assessing.

Cahan sneaked to the edge of the dock area and onto the pilings below to position himself behind the creature. He climbed toward his enemy as waves lapped against his legs, then rose behind the abnormally restless demon, lifting his head just above the wooden surface of the dock. Suddenly the demon became still. Its spikes wriggled excitedly, causing a chain reaction across its body as they drew in air, which caused a queer swooshing sound. Each spike rose prominently and then lay down as the next thicket of spikes shot up to draw in the surrounding smells. The creature, which still sniffed the air, shuddered for a moment. Then a purplish-red eyelid on the back of its head cracked open, and strains of red swelled as the eye gazed at Cahan. He raised his body and planted his feet on the wooden surface.

The four-legged beast aggressively bounded for him and lunged at Cahan, who rolled backward with the demon's forward momentum. Cahan kicked his legs up mid-roll and vaulted the creature into the air, breaking some of its spikes with his armored boots. It spun around midair and landed on its feet. Cahan continued his roll backward and rose to a fighting position, drawing his hand axe from his belt. His anger began to surge, but he knew that he had to be smart in this fight; this creature was heavily armored with potentially fatal spikes.

As the demon stared Cahan down, the spines on its body stretched out even farther, including newly emerged spikes on its elbows. It again bounded for him while simultaneously striking with its spiked elbow. Cahan swung his axe in an upward arching motion, implanting the blade into the underside of the beast's chin. Cahan let go of the axe and sprang away from the demon.

The creature paused for a moment and whirled to face Cahan. With a grunt, it pulled the axe out of its jaw and threw it to the ground with a clunk before charging once more. Cahan did not move to avoid it. Suddenly the creature combusted in a rain of crimson-and-gray pieces, sending smoldering organs across the platform.

Cahan retrieved his axe, which lay among the fuming innards. Anaymous and the others joined Cahan with questioning glances as he wiped smoky guts off his axe with his oft-used, moth-eaten rag.

"We have to move quickly," Cahan said. "Someone could've heard that. Apparently, this eluvium doesn't corrode—it explodes."

Cahan looked down at the eluvium he had stolen. Each vial had one of two color markings, red or green. He reasoned that the vials marked with green were probably the corrosive type and the ones with the red markings were the explosive formula.

Cahan looked at the Kalriss demons and wondered if they realized he had doused one of the creature's spines with the eluvium during the fight, which it in turn, absorbed. He didn't really care if they knew why. He just needed to keep moving.

Cahan leapt from the platform and climbed up the curved surface outer hull of the argosy-class vessel, looking for grip points as he ascended. Anaymous and the others were able to climb freely like the carnivorous arachnids of the Veldt Mountains. They easily reached the pinnacle before Cahan. The Kalriss looked down on him until he reached the deck of the ship. Normally, the sight of Kalriss demons lying in wait would be horrifying because they looked appallingly evil. In this case, it was inspiring. Anaymous extended his claw and helped Cahan aboard the vessel. That brief moment struck him. It was moving to Cahan that a former Incendiary, a scion no less, offered his help to a human who would have been his enemy not long ago.

Cahan and the others crept their way to the edge of the vessel. The dock master's quarters rested below between the argosy vessel and the beginning of several dry-docked air vessels. All of the ports contained in the yard had privately concealed tunnels that led to the dock master's quarters and fed into a large underground common room.

Cahan watched as Anaymous and his followers soundlessly jumped off the ship and gripped the side of the structure with their insect-like digits. Cahan sprinted toward the edge of the vessel and leapt. As he plummeted toward the roof, one of the Kalriss caught him with a prickly, insect-like arm. It was a weird sensation that Cahan didn't much like. He wanted to get out of the Kalriss's grasp as quickly as possible. It felt like the creature wanted to wrap him in a web, though he knew this was a ridiculous notion. At least the demon helped make the transition from ship to rooftop in silence.

Cahan looked at the cluster of Kalriss, already a good distance ahead. They reminded him of an insect swarm as they migrated to the center of the rooftop.

Cahan had finally reached the waiting Kalriss near the center of the roof and removed what he hoped was the corrosive eluvium from his satchel. His hands trembled slightly at the prospect that this concoction could combust and alert everyone to their whereabouts—or that he might well end up like the spiny demon he had just fought.

"You are sure this is the corrosive agent and not of the explosive variety?" Agares, Anaymous's second said.

"Positive," Cahan lied.

"Be solicitous, Ranger." Anaymous instructed. "I would guess this is a much purer extract of the formula and the entire roof and connecting parapet could be consumed if you use too much of it."

Cahan, annoyed, nodded his head. He poured a coin-sized droplet of the substance on the roof. A searing sound trickled out. Cahan and the others backed away, bracing themselves for an impact. Silence still dominated the area, as he and the group stared at the improvised entrance, arms still raised. The lack of explosion caused a collective breath to be released, and the group lowered their arms. A blackish corroded hole, big enough for the Kalriss demons to pass through, lay exposed. Heat rose from the chamber below.

Cahan plunged down into the structure. Four large climate pillars stood portentously in the room. Climate pillars were magically imbued masts that, when touched by spellcrafting beings, could change the ambient temperature of a room. Climate pillars were normally attuned to black-energy spires, from which they drew their power. Aside from the exorbitantly expensive pillars, the rest of the structure was substandard Forgathan wood and decaying, humidity-worn furniture.

Cahan and the others explored the dock master's hall and the connecting tunnels. They soon reached the main port, which was the central port of commerce. Several demons were pinning eluvium cylinders to critical support areas below. Cahan noticed an oddly constructed door that led into an elaborate stone structure. The door was white and had several protective runes encrusted upon its surface. Entwining gothic floral patterns surrounded a depiction of a spear-wielding Kharr'kari warrior slaying a Gilpesh conjurer, topped by a skyward Gargoyle. The wood was definitely prehistoric, possibly the ancestor of the brindle wood found in the many forests of Protos or even the ancient homeland of the Gargoyles, Ashwhend. Cahan was sure the door was of Gargoyle make and was reinforced with potent Gargoylian spellcraft. He had never encountered any such door or chamber in his studies, yet it was in the open for anyone to see. The thought troubled him.

"Why wasn't this documented in any history codex?" Cahan whispered to the concealed group as they spied on their enemies.

"To what are you referring?" Anaymous whispered back.

"Are you blind?" he whispered impatiently, gesturing toward his find. "That ancient Gargoyle egress."

The Kalriss looked at each other, befuddled. They looked at Cahan as if he had gone daft.

"I do not see a door, Cahan. Perhaps it is bewitched from our eyes?"

Cahan searched his mind for an answer. Rampant, paranoid thoughts filtered through his brain. He hoped that the malevolence had not finally driven him mad. Unable to come to a conclusion, he stifled his thinking and stowed his questions for the moment. "Regardless, we have to stop these damn demons from destroying the port."

A morose, flushed demon approached the Gargoyle door with several vials of eluvium in hand. Cahan shot an affirming glance to Anaymous. He and his men rose and darted for the vial-carrying demon. Cahan hurled his axe at its legs before it could reach the door. The axe sunk into the beast's calf muscle, causing it to falter and fall to the deck. The vials broke apart and seeped into its skin. The demon began to shriek and writhe in agony as it decomposed in mere moments. Its mouth gaped in torment, then faded to nothingness. Only a rancid mass of flesh remained.

* * * *

Anaymous assumed a defensive posture with his rubicund steel axe. A yellowish, horned demon charged at him. Anaymous set his eyes on its enchanted spear. As the creature drew into his radius, the crackling jade energy surrounding the spear grew in intensity. The yellow creature thrust its weapon toward his chest. Anaymous parried to the left with his gleaming red battle axe and latched on to the creature's throat with his right claw. Anaymous swept the demon to the ground as another approached him from behind. He whirled to his oncoming attacker and firmly clamped down with his powerful incisors, piercing his attacker's shoulder. Blood flowed from the bite wound, intermingled with a burning green venom. Gore poured from Anaymous's mouth in shafts of curdled fluid as he drew his head back. The demon clutched its throat and convulsed as it fell to the ground with eyes and veins bulging, and its sinews rose to the surface of its flesh. As Anaymous's opponent attempted to rise and rejoin the battle, Anaymous spun back toward him and cleaved its head open with his axe.

* * * *

Cahan spied a robed demonic sorcerer making its way to the Gargoylian door as he battled a pair of demons in front of him. Cahan continued to match the demons, blow-for-blow, as the sorcerer began to launch various obscure conjurations that traced the design of the door with a heliotrope incandescence. When the magic attempted to force the door to yield, the spell faded away in glimmering white, purifying the energy that was hurled at it. The creature signaled a few of its cohorts as the demon retreated from its apparent failure, evaporating from sight.

A yellowish-gray dappled creature began affixing large vials of combustion and corrosion eluvium to the arcane door. Cahan looked over to Anaymous, who was staring at the door. Cahan realized that the sorcerer had not failed at all. It had broken the spell that concealed the door from sight.

Once the demons had attached several vials to the door's surface, they rapidly shambled away. A succession of exploding and decaying agents thundered as they worked in unison. Cahan and the demons he was battling retreated and took cover behind some nearby crates. Charged, misty fog enveloped the door, and an unnatural wind brushed away the mist.

The arcane sorcerer once again approached the frail door. With one whirl of his hand, the egress splintered loudly with a preternatural crackle. The demon entered the room as if its life depended on it. Just as it cleared the threshold, rays of speckled white light filled the empty, broken doorway. Cahan suddenly felt connected to everyone around him, and fighting abruptly stopped. A soul-shaking stillness flushed through the bodies of each combatant with an otherworldly shudder.

Cahan forced himself to his feet. He felt a pain and anguish like no other throughout his entire body, prodding his flesh from the inside. The others were still under the overbearing power that permeated the harbor, and they all knelt in defeat as a primal force clutched at them. Cahan began trudging toward the speckled white light of the doorway and was finally able to pick up speed. His field of vision crumbled into flakes of charred embers as if in a dream. The light was the only thing he could grasp onto visually—the only thing that did not dissolve to black. He could no longer feel the malevolent anger. It was as though something had quieted the anger that burned inside of him.

Cahan finally reached the now-open chamber. His senses were suddenly stimulated beyond human, beyond demon. The dark creature that was pouring its seething blackness into the chamber it now haunted smelled of murder and dark, forbidden oaths. It reeked of decadent displays of human sacrifice at the behest of otherworldly beings, clattering and tittering to a demonic fervor. Beckoning, calling, screeching, and murmuring surrounded the esoteric figure as it darkly muttered its abnormal language of hissing and guttural contempt.

Cahan felt the clutches of insanity grip him tighter. He groaned aloud and pulled away, as if the insanity had manifested into the physical world and was attempting to drag him into a bleak abyss. He groped for the light and bathed his arms in the searing intensity of the doorway. His eyes and mind cleared, bereft of the clutching darkness. He could now see the sanctum of the Gargoylian chamber.

Hieroglyphs depicting ancient Gargoyles adorned the wall. One in particular caught his eye—a portrayal of a wise-looking, gaunt, winged creature with painted Gargoylian script beneath. The translated script read *Luttrel, the Sage of Ashwhend.*

The details of the rest of the room rushed into Cahan's mind, washing over him in a blanket of white. Runes offset a pedestal centered in the room, crowned by a glowing sphere of amethyst with clouds of red phosphorescence tapping and scratching its surface. It reminded him of the ethereal storm he had witnessed earlier.

Cahan opened his eyes and saw an empty room with no sphere, pedestal, or runes. Cahan closed his eyes again. The image of the pedestal and runes was seemingly only present in his mind. He wasn't sure what was real. He believed that madness had, in fact, overtaken him.

Cahan anguished as he attempted to cross the illuminated threshold. Again and again, it repelled him. Something was blocking his passage, as if he were not worthy of entrance. Cahan heard heavy breathing behind him. He opened his eyes and turned to see that Anaymous had emerged from the torturous, silent insanity that he had just endured.

"Something approaches, Cahan." Anaymous pulled him from the light-infused doorway. "Gargoyles," he added in a whisper.

Cahan looked up as the roof of the structure began to shudder. Burning red slashes appeared in the lines of the architecture and enveloped the roof in heat. Though they consumed the roof, the streaks of red remained for a few seconds. When the scarlet energy faded, sunlight poured in for a breathless moment, until four winged creatures tattooed with runes eclipsed the light with their outstretched wings. The metronomic sound of their flapping swooshed in an ominously synchronous tempo.

Cahan watched as the Gargoyles descended upon the throat-clutching creatures, succumbing to the hideous silence. These Gargoyles were different from the depictions in the chamber that bore the likeness of the Sage of Ashwhend. These creatures were more baneful and made Cahan feel empty. Through that hollowness, he felt as if his mind were surrendering to their minds as they drew closer. Whatever had connected him with the others now forged a gateway into the minds of these hideous creatures. Flashes of abominable acts deluged Cahan's mind. He could see the Dark Gargoyles in a grand hall of stone, sacrificing humans alongside the sorcerer that haunted the gargoylian chamber. An image of a Gargoyle writhing in agony flashed in Cahan's mind. Phosphorescent flecks of green swam in the Gargoyle's eyes as the creature threw its head back in pain. A searing red light shone brightly through the cracks and crevices of its cranial horns, and its skin smoldered to an ashen color.

Cahan witnessed a hideous, constantly phasing black wraith hand a large amulet to the Gargoyle. The blood-clouded amulet was octagonal and smelled of aphotic spellcraft. The amulet shimmered and began to phase, much like the wraith.

A piercing flare of the bloodstone temporarily sent a surge of pain through Cahan's body. As he recovered, he witnessed the four baneful Gargoyles easily pass the chamber's outer defenses. He struggled to move, but remained unable to do so. The Gargoyles were not swayed by the illuminated doorway.

Cahan watched the behavior of the group. They appeared to have a hierarchy. The creature that seemed to be the alpha held up its hand. The bloodstone around its neck shimmered as sanguine clouds swirled inside. Red energy wreathed around the Dark Gargoyle's raised hand. Cahan thought to himself that it was as if the Gargoyle had channeled the ambient delirium of the space and took hold of it. The Gargoyle's horns shone so brightly that Cahan turned away. Dark whispers filtered into the room.

Cahan faltered and fell to the ground. He looked over at Anaymous as he struggled to stand. The alpha Gargoyle glided to them, knelt down, and clutched their faces with his bloodstained, odorous talons.

"Stand!" he yelled as he maintained his grip on their faces.

They stood.

Cahan peered into the Gargoyle's eyes. The composition of red irises and green flecks appeared as the Dark Gargoyle muttered venomously. It revealed its sharp, earthen teeth as the incantation spilled from its mouth. A searing pain enveloped his mind. Cahan sensed the torturous grasp of the Gargoyle in Anaymous's mind as well.

Images of Cahan clutching a dagger with a gnarled handle invaded his consciousness. Suddenly, he was stabbed in the back.

The surroundings looked somehow familiar to him. Glass and stone encircled him on all sides. A wall of glass crumbled to dust before him.

Cahan shuddered as he realized he was now in Anaymous's mind. Anaymous's consciousness was full of dark wraiths, surrounding him in a cavernous chamber. The creatures wailed as they crept toward him, and Cahan screamed with panic. Anaymous seemed devoid of expression as the phasing wraith stood over him.

The pair snapped out of their visions. Cahan's mind whirled with anxiety and nothing made sense. He hit his face with his palm. Rapid, nonsensical thoughts streamed in. For a moment, he thought he was in Blasstock. He started yelling at the paramount Rattock officer. In the next moment, he was a stowaway on the Protosian airship.

"I have to be quiet," Cahan said with his index finger over his lips, feeling the insanity creep in.

Cahan heard wicked laughter, jolting him from his delusions. He could see that the alpha Gargoyle was amused. It smirked as it turned away. Cahan struggled to move again. This time, he was able to move just enough to see the Gargoyle chamber. The baneful Gargoyles came upon the hunched, dark wizard.

"I have prepared the ritual," the robed creature slurred as blood streaked from its forehead.

The alpha raised his hand dispassionately. Preternatural whispering rang in Cahan's ears. The dark spellcraft was aimed toward the wizard.

The wizard screamed in agony. Circles of blood began to dampen its clothing, and the lines of the spellcrafter's tormented face bent unnaturally. It looked down at its wounds and touched the blood-soaked circles before it collapsed to the ornate stone surface of the chamber.

Cahan, still afflicted by the Dark Gargoyle's spell, strained to push up onto his elbows. He watched the Gargoyles pick up the lifeless wizard and lay the creature at the feet of the alpha, whose amulet began to blaze. Strands of red energy connected with the downed wizard and metamorphosed into what looked like tendons dripping with red mucus. A surge of energy shot through the tendons, then spewed outward from the wizard, spattering the stone around them with blackened entrails. Out of the crimson haze of the amulet, an ethereal sword was forged. Once again, this set Cahan's mind back to the red storm. The battle between the elements and the emergence of the dark avian creatures swirled in his mind. The sword and the storm filled him with the same feeling of emptiness.

The alpha Gargoyle stepped forth. Its bloodstone flashed and shrouded its hand in red energy. The Dark Gargoyle brandished the sword with its illumined hand and sliced into the sphere that sat upon the pedestal, revealing a crystallized, pulsating cocoon that shimmered with light. The ethereal sword faded with a black energy that enveloped it.

Cahan's head was clearer now. He wondered if the sword had been destroyed or simply sent away to some nether region beyond imagination.

The baneful creature entrenched its claws into the cocoon's surface. The energy immersed itself into its skin, absorbing the glistening light. White spines pierced outward until the cocoon withered and folded into blackness. Its horns were no longer tinged with red, but with a waxing glimmer.

The four morose Gargoyles exited the chamber, wings folded around them. Cahan could move once more. He reasoned that the effects of the chamber had worn off with the absorption of its power. He felt a trembling beneath his feet and ran toward the dogmatic Gargoyles, who raised a wall of energy before him. Somehow, Cahan knew that he could pass through the spellcrafted wall, and he did. Coldness gripped him. He felt as though he were in a sphere composed of free-standing water. Several minutes seemed to slip by before he was able to work his way out of the sphere. However, once he was freed, Cahan realized only a few seconds had passed. They all still stood where they had been just moments ago.

The white-horned Gargoyle appeared surprised Cahan was able to escape, and it studied him for a few moments. The Gargoyle muttered something venomous to Cahan in an unfamiliar tongue. The four took to the air as waves of energy pooled around them.

The dock's structure began to fold, and something unnamable called out to Cahan. He felt an unnatural bleakness that he could not describe. Large hail began to pour in chunks. The stones of the chamber hauntingly clattered as if no mortar separated them. Soon the entire chamber began to resonate with blistering white energy. Then the stone edifice and water beneath crystallized. The sound of the chamber stopped to reveal an even more dangerous sound—a demon was shattering the vials of corrosive eluvium attached to the harbor pilings below. Yards ahead, Cahan saw Anaymous, lying inert on the ground. Panicked, Cahan darted to Anaymous and knelt by his side. He grasped his shoulders and shook him violently. Anaymous seemed lifeless and stiff. He put a hand on his leathery chest. He could not feel his heart beating. Cahan raised his fist and sent it crashing down against his comrade's chest. Anaymous sat up immediately and emitted a shrieking insect gasp. Cahan glanced up to see Agares looming over them.

"Get out now," Cahan yelled as he helped Agares get Anaymous to his feet.

The corrosive nature of the eluvium began to devour the harbor like a horde of mantis nymphs, consuming everything in its path. Once the swath of corrosion had eaten its way to the vials beneath, explosions occurred in rapid succession.

Walls of water and wood hurled upward in clouds of fire, interwoven with the corrosive element. Other portions of the harbor began to succumb to corrosion, and the chain reaction exploded outward.

Chapter 12
~ The Gilpesh, the Gargoyles, and the Dawn of the Fenthom ~

Cahan and the others cut through the thoroughfares, away from the violent uprising of fire and decay. When the chain of destruction had finally stopped, the only part of the harbor that still stood was the crystallized chamber. At once, the brood of grotesque birds swooped down from the ethereal winds that still blanketed the sky and clawed at the heads of Cahan and the others.

Feeling demoralized, Cahan pushed his way into a boardinghouse anteroom. They had failed their mission miserably. Darkness clouded his mind. He wondered what the long-term implications of their failure would be. He had to shake away his thoughts of defeat. His depression often led to the malevolent anger penned up within him, so he decided to focus instead on his cohorts. Cahan could not tell if they felt as he did, as their facial expressions were remarkably hard to read at the moment.

Cahan made his way to an old, rickety desk, harboring a shocked, vaguely human proprietor, who instinctively threw Cahan a key as he helped the almost unconscious Anaymous walk.

"It is the first room on the second floor," the man instructed.

He nodded his head at the proprietor, wondering why he threw them a key. Perhaps the sight of a human helping a Kalriss was what stunned the gray, spectacled man into relinquishing his room so quickly.

Cahan again thought to himself how odd the insect-like arms of the Kalriss felt. He hated abnormal patterns and textures. Deep down, it bothered him that there wasn't anything remotely human about the Kalriss.

As the group made their way to the room and got Anaymous settled comfortably, Cahan pondered the implications of the ancient door. He had known that Gargoyles were essentially the first architects of Shintallis, but he had never seen this offshoot of Gargoyle firsthand. The Gargoyle coteries were among the first sentient species. They even predated the Kharr'kari warrior clans and the

Gilpesh Thaumaturgy. The Kharr'kari and the Gargoyles both followed a common Celestial, Valese, while the Gilpesh worshiped the carrion-shrouded Shabaris, the Dead Caller. Cahan wondered who led these creatures. Why did the door depict a history lesson about Gargoyles, Gilpesh, and Kharr'kari?

The Kharr'kari gained their knowledge of combat and industry from the Gargoyles. The Gargoyles were also known for their conjuring skills and architectural prowess. The Kharr'kari could not wield spellcraft in the traditional sense by channeling the primal forces, so the Gargoyles built weapons for the Kharr'kari and other devices that could be used to slay the Gilpesh as portrayed on the arcane door. This exchange of knowledge led the Gilpesh to develop a seething hatred for both the Kharr'kari and Gargoyles.

The Kharr'kari further honed their knowledge of warfare, due to the many battles they had fought against the outlying rival Gilpesh tribes. Both nations grew in prosperity while the expansionist Gilpesh continued their dominance in their home continent of Forgatha.

Soon other Celestials encroached on the lands and birthed beings in their image. Some of these beings were just and good-willed, while others walked in the footsteps of the Gilpesh. Cahan figured these evil Gargoyles followed one of the other Celestials. Cahan thought about the other beings tied to the Celestial Augury. There were twelve known to the populace. Still, Shabaris appeared more likely to hold the oaths of these Gargoyles than a Celestial.

Cahan bit his lip as he continued to think. As the door depicted the origins of the three races, he continued down the roots of each civilization. He felt like the answer was scratching the surface—easily found if he just focused harder.

The Gargoyles openly sought out the good-willed nations and traded with them, fully knowing they needed allies against the growing Gilpesh scourge. The Gargoyles forged these alliances in earnestness, based on information passed on by a group of Gilpesh defectors. They warned the Gargoyles that the Thaumaturgy had their eye on the peaceful nations as they wished to have a southern route of expansion.

According to scripture, the Celestial Valese realized that the peaceful nations needed yet another strong race to ally with in order to deflect the imminent Gilpesh invasion. Thus, she willed that the dragons, her earlier conception, evolve into conscious beings—for in their current state, they were merely base creatures that only she could call upon. She dubbed this new race "Fenthom," which ultimately ushered in the extinction of the grand arcane dragons.

During this time of progress, a dissenting faction of Gargoyles, called the Malefic by some, sided with the Gilpesh and broke off from their brethren. Cahan reasoned that the Gargoyles at the docks must be this faction. The Malefic had never been physically described in any history codex, so this seemed like the best possible explanation. He realized the enemy had yet another ally. Not only must he fight against the Forgathans, Incendiaries, and Ministry of Information, he must also contend with an ancient sect of powerful Gargoyles. He wondered why the Forgathans would ally with the Malefic. This was not their first encounter.

The Malefic, at least the ones in the history books, did not believe in the exchange of knowledge with other nations and only gave their new allies lesser versions of their mystical sciences. Therefore, in essence, they could not be trusted. They used the Gilpesh to pursue their own ends by utilizing their rich raw materials, which ultimately led to Gilpesh defeat in the Great Bygone War. Their newly crafted weapons did not hold up to the other nations, and when forced to rely solely upon their skills of spellcraft, they were defeated.

Even in defeat, many Gilpesh agents infiltrated the peaceful nations. The thaumaturgy learned of the various groups of defectors and allowed them to escape. The Gilpesh realized if the defectors were able to form a bond, it would pave the way for future infiltration under the guise of desertion of country. So the Gilpesh arranged for other "defection" groups to seek asylum, which led to a time of betrayal and hostility.

Chapter 13
~ Reflections in the Forest ~

Cahan emerged from the lavatory room in their boarding house suite to see a waking Anaymous. Agares hurriedly pushed past Cahan in a desperate effort to relieve himself before he burst. Cahan realized it was an inappropriate time for humor, but he could not help but chuckle. He found it ridiculous that a Kalriss, "the curse of the deserts," used the facilities.

"Don't inhale too deeply," Cahan joked.

Anaymous and the others stared at him oddly for several seconds before erupting into abnormal, reedy laughter.

"So you do use lavatories. I wasn't even sure you had... you know... the equipment for it."

They laughed once more. Knowing that when evil is close at hand, one can only laugh in the face of it.

Agares once more joined the group, ignoring the laughter that had erupted.

"As we were leaving, I saw that the entire chamber was encrusted in some sort of crystallized material," Agares said aloud, addressing the group in a serious tone. "A spellcraft presumably, the likes of which I have never seen."

"It was of Gargoylian make, given the hieroglyphs within the sanctum of the chamber," Anaymous added.

Just then, a rap on the door sounded. Cahan cautiously approached. Agares elbowed his way past Cahan and opened the door to see that their food had arrived.

The food was a mixture of Kalriss delicacies, which mostly looked like insects in gray-colored sauces and white-hot stews, laced with tiny arachnid legs. Cahan could smell the stench of their food burn through his nostrils, and it made him nauseous. The Kalriss immediately began feasting. Cahan did not know if it was the proper time to eat, but then he concluded that now was just as good a time as any, since they had no idea where the Dark Gargoyles were.

"One thing we haven't discussed ... these Dark Gargoyles ..." Cahan trailed off.

"The Malefic?" Anaymous asked.

"So you already knew?"

"Yes. It was evident by the mark of the dark rites," Anaymous replied. "A normal Gargoyle would not have flecks of green in its irises." He took in a steaming spoonful of insect soup before he continued. Sauce dripped from the arachnid-like hair around his mouth. "One thing I did not know is the immense power they wield."

"Agreed. Those bloodstones may actually give them more power than a natural Gargoyle," Cahan stated.

"What of this chamber?" Agares inquired. "It seemed quite important to the Malefic."

"In the bygone era," Cahan began as the others continued to feast, "Gargoyles created a power source that linked to a corresponding wellspring of sorts, which essentially powered a barrier near Aundyre. The barrier is what keeps the remaining Forgathans at bay. I was never aware of the wellspring's location until now."

"That barrier has kept my kind"—Agares shifted his glance to Anaymous with sauce dripping from his mouth—"our kind from the mainland for centuries. If it has been damaged, let it fall."

"Can you blame them for protecting what is theirs?" Anaymous reasoned. "Given our history and that of the Forgathans? We have chosen to make amends. The Forgathans have not. The barrier must be upheld. Without the barrier, the human colonies would fall in short order with their western flank laid bare."

"The barrier hasn't fallen," Cahan said, pacing nervously and trying to disregard the disgusting odor of their food. "The chamber is inert at the moment. It protected itself from the explosion. However, the curate of the manor of Elrich still powers the western barrier, or I hope he does. Regardless, it'll be difficult for him to maintain it given he's no longer infused with the chamber's energies."

"Shall we go to the curate and see if the manor is still intact?" Anaymous asked.

"I think so. We could transport some of the attendants of the manor to the Chamber to see if they can awaken it."

"Transport? How?"

"I know where we can get an airship."

"There is also the issue of supply lines," Agares blurted, growing impatient. "This port, here in Elysium, is instrumental in supplying the Protosian military, yes?" He paused for a moment, seeming to assess the collective temperament in the room. "If you really want to prevent Protos from falling, you will need an alternate supply line . . ." He glanced around to see if anyone was taking his opportunistic bait.

"And you have the means to do this?" Cahan asked sternly, stopping in his tracks. "It's quite coincidental that the destruction of the harbor will line your pockets."

"I assure you, Cahan, this was not by design," Anaymous said. "I am not ashamed to admit that I look forward to the opportunity to trade with Protos and her districts. But let me make this perfectly conspicuous: we are not in league with any malevolent force that has an aversion to needless bloodshed or the destruction of trade."

Cahan nodded to Anaymous's claim.

"Agares, you will need to seek out Melcholm," Anaymous said. "He can arrange for the needed goods. Now the only thing we are lacking is transportation. You were saying?"

"We'll need a Protosian vessel," Cahan said thoughtfully. "Nothing else will pass the Aundyre barrier."

"What do you suggest?" Anaymous asked.

"There's a Protosian airship dock close to here. We'll have to acquire what we need from there."

"You are a fugitive, Cahan. They will not simply hand a vessel over to you."

"We aren't going to ask," he replied.

* * * *

After a few hours of travel by foot, Cahan and the group navigated the rough, wind-blistered landscape between Elysium and the airship field.

Cahan began plotting and planning as he stared at the airship field. The area had a vast basin that cut across the territory. Rivers from the Veldt and Valesia regions flowed into the sinking land mass, which eventually trailed off into the Dunnavisch Estuary, home of the indigenous and hated Marsh Fenthom.

An airship yard built upon a water source was customary. The intrinsic power contained in water was absorbed through the vessel's intake chamber during ascension, after which little energy was needed. The energy contained in the atmosphere could fuel the remainder of a voyage.

"So we all understand what we're doing?" Cahan asked.

"Yes, but I don't understand how you will be able to cross the body of water without being noticed," Anaymous balked.

Cahan and Anaymous halfheartedly argued for a moment before Anaymous acquiesced. He could tell that Anaymous still clung to some of his concerns, but he seemed to put them aside for the time being.

* * * *

Anaymous, trailed by the other Kalriss, stole their way into the neighboring forest across from the basin and came upon a circle of black-garbed conjurors gathered near the water separating the airfield and the forest. In unison, the spellcrafters focused on a single metallic staff centered amongst them. Light rose and cut through the air, resembling the shape of partisan spears with smoldering plumes of smoke left in their wake. The water bubbled to a frothy glow, which increased and expanded into distorted, surreal ripples that echoed harshly in one's ear, temporarily paralyzing to Anaymous and the others. Anaymous noticed that the mages seemed immune to this effect. They were so single-mindedly focused on the spell that they did not notice his group slip past them.

As the waterline preternaturally rose to replenish what had been taken by the constant barrage of outgoing air vessels, the Kalriss sank into the water and clutched the bottom of the conjuror's sloop boat.

Anaymous still pondered his argument with Cahan. His anxious mind homed in on Cahan's angry facial expression when he had said, "Don't worry about what I am doing. Focus on your part."

What was this abnormal human hiding?

* * * *

Cahan filtered through the trees of the black forest at a brisk pace. He had been through this particular wooded area many times prior, and knew the placement of the trees well, or so he thought. As he charged forward, he was barely able to stop himself from colliding into a dark husk of a tree near its death. Though he didn't remember the ancient tree's presence, he decided this was as good a place as any to change his armor.

He looked around cautiously, almost obsessively, to see if any onlookers were afoot. He sensed the creatures in the forest around him—but fortunately, those who dwelt in this forest were not often predatory.

Cahan could smell the musk of a Haitia, a beast that shared ancestry with Avarites and Simians. A crunching sound echoed as the creature gnawed on tree bark nearby. The thud of Heénd hoofs echoed near the Haitia. The deer-like Heénd would often eat the wood of the tree beneath the bark when there wasn't an abundant supply of sleeping hunters on which to feed. These creatures were often described as the hideous union of the slovenly tapir and the pestilent hart.

Nervousness shot through Cahan's brain like a million needle pricks. He felt overwrought as he furtively shrugged out of his armor, stripping down to a woven brown tunic and matching pants of the same material. He removed his pants first while looking around anxiously. Cahan felt haunted about the fact that someone might come upon him, but not because he was in his undergarments.

Cahan gazed at the fáyn'dear tree near him. Fáyn'dear wood was known for its reflective quality in both the bark and the heartwood. The sapwood in such a tree only mirrored back outlines and general shapes.

Within the surface of the wood, he saw the tired lines of a liar's face looking back at him. He could see the weight of everything that had been hefted upon him written in his black eyes. He longed for normalcy.

The distinct smell of fáyn'dear wood filled Cahan's nostrils. The smell reminded him of a cross between the Arcadian puff flower and the fragrant Protosian santalum tree. The scent burrowed into his mind and took him back to the airship compartment of his youth, which had been composed entirely of fáyn'dear wood. He saw reflected flashes of himself as he pounded the hold. He envisioned the gripping fear on his face. As he thought harder, he remembered a detail he had long forgotten—the roots of the malignant anger within him in the form of a horrific scowl. Did the anger take its grip all those years ago? Was it biding its time?

Cahan removed his shirt, exposing a muscular midsection that reflected off the trees. He closed his eyes and listened for a moment to his surroundings. He wanted to make sure nothing was approaching, at least not a human. Cahan heard nothing out of the ordinary.

He opened his eyes and they were again drawn to the reflective surface. He couldn't shake the feeling that the image before him was another person. The lines of his body were sharp and inhuman. His muscles were developed beyond what was natural. The sinews in his now-exposed areas were obvious and seemed exaggerated—something that Cahan found disgusting.

Within the reflection before him, he saw his image on the surface of the trees behind him, like a house of mirrors. Angular runic tattoos covered a significant part of his shoulders and upper back. He thought of the many hours it took to carve the enchanted ink into his flesh. Cahan turned to lay his shirt on the ground. He heard a loud crackle. His head snapped around and he crouched down behind a tree. His heart pounded, until he realized it was just the chewing of the Haitia. He lowered his head and exhaled deeply. As he looked up, still hunched over, he saw the reflection of a greenish, white outcropping of scales, which surrounded a set of large, undulating gills that rested on both sides of his body. He hated seeing this part of himself and turned away from the tree.

Cahan pulled some netting from his bag, flattened it on the ground, and placed some Gronxth hide atop the netting, due to its resilience to water. Cahan's thoughts shifted to water, which made him think about his secret abnormality. He reasoned that no one must know. Maybe the Kalriss wouldn't care, but they might tell others. No one would understand.

Cahan shook his head and chose to focus on the task at hand. He placed the armor and the shirt in the middle of the outstretched hide, then ground his teeth as he proceeded to tie the ends together in a ball. Rage began to burn within him.

Cahan's thoughts ran rampant, as anxiety-fueled doubt crept inside. He tried to occupy his mind with something else.

Stop. Just stop.

This was something he often told himself when he sensed he was about to lose it. His control began to fragment. He thought of it like fabric that was frayed at the edges, but would soon begin to tear across the middle and there was nothing he could do. Nothing could mend the breach. Tears welled in his eyes.

As he continued to chant the refrain quietly, he took out a rope, tied it to the top of the netting and fastened the other end to his belt. He peered up at a high-reaching tree branch and looked down at the rope still in his hand. He continued to stare for a time, assessing his life up unil this point. Should he just end this now? He chanted his refrain agan. He then picked up the ball of armor and clothes after putting his pack on his shoulder. He exhaled deeply once more. In his mind, that symbolized he was leaving his anxiety in this particular part of the forest, along with his hideous reflection.

Chapter 14
~ The Infiltration ~

Now that he was ready to take to the water, Cahan headed back to the edge of the forest, where a group of spellcrafters sat in an oblong circle bisected by a line of conjurors in the middle. This was a warlocks' circle. Cahan knew this was not the same group he had sneaked past earlier. The other group was arranged in a witch's circle. So if a new coven was on duty, the others were probably headed toward the compound at this very moment.

Cahan's mind went back to the convincing that had to take place—the convincing which allowed him to travel alone—and the lies he told to hide his secret.

"Stop," he continued to whisper to himself.

The mages were in a trancelike state, and Cahan vigilantly made his way past them. He heard one mage stir. Cahan dove behind a tree for a moment, watching the circle. The mage shuddered again and opened his eyes, breaking ranks with the others. The young spellcrafter was thin and had an emaciated face. He moved with an awkwardness of motion as he inelegantly plodded toward Cahan's general area. Cahan, still hidden behind the tree, was frozen in place. The mage looked around, biting his lip with anticipation. If the boy caused the others to break the spell, they would be there all night and into the morning, respelling the elaborate conjuration. He hoped the boy wouldn't stray too far. Since his entire coven would be at his throat if they had to put in those kinds of hours, he was sure that he wouldn't.

The mage raised his hands and murmured a few arcane words as a light came from his hand, spun toward Cahan, leaving a glowing trail of white behind it. Cahan sprinted deeper into the forest and took refuge behind a sturdy fáyn'dear. He would have preferred not to take refuge behind something that could cast his image, but his choices were limited. He hoped he was out of the tracer's range.

A buzzing sounded behind him and he whirled to the noise. The damn tracer caught wind of him. As the tracer neared Cahan, he snatched it out of the air and smashed it in his hand as if it were a bug. He hurled curses into the chilly night air. He was furious beyond his humanity that someone was tracking him and that he, might fail.

By that time, the mage had already found Cahan, and a look of astonishment was plastered on his homely face. The mage's eyes widened and the skin of his face grew tight. Cahan had seen this look before. He called it "the death stare." This was a man—a boy—prepared for his end.

Even in his anger, Cahan could not help but notice that his image was everywhere among the reflective surfaces of the forest. It was as if the trees were honing in on him. Cahan stared down the mage angrily as his frosty breath trickled out into the frigid night air. The fáyn'dear revealed his horrifying appearance, which did not please him.

With inhuman swiftness, Cahan palmed the mage's face and slammed his head into a tree. He looked up at his reflection and saw the horrific grimace on his face. He looked away and focused on the boy. The mage's gaunt, frail body was on the ground in a slump. The boy was not broken, but he looked as though he were a contortionist. His right arm was behind his head while his left arm was wrapped around his body with his hand under his waist. Cahan looked at the delicate twig of a conjuror and felt the pure venom of his anger and the need to kill course through his body. A chain reaction of shattering malevolence streamed through his brain, and he clenched his teeth and fists tightly.

He exhaled loudly. A cold breath escaped and floated upward between the reflected gaze of his sinister eyes. He looked again at the boy and thrust both of his fists on either side of his body. Part of him tried to stop what the other side longed to do—kill the insignificant conjuror. He grasped handfuls of dirt in both hands as he looked down at the boy. A strand of compassion fluttered into his consciousness at that moment. He muttered his refrain, trying to calm himself, and felt an inner warmth return. Cahan rested his mouth and then his clenched fists as he focused on the soothing cold of the night air caressing his face. He struggled to remind himself of who he was.

Cahan grabbed the mage around the waist and tucked him under his arm. He climbed a tree and placed him among the branches, out of reach of a Heénd that lurked nearby.

Cahan jumped down from the towering black tree and made his way to the water. The boat had already disembarked. Cahan dove, piercing through the water with the ease of a heavy spear thrust through flesh. Large shafts of light poured down into the water, revealing the various breeds of large fish that dwelt in the underwater domain. The fish scattered from the powerful white light as it raked across the water's surface. Cahan had to reach the cover of the boat, or he would be spotted by sentinel vessels.

He felt his gills perpetually in motion, undulating to produce the respiratory sustenance needed for his prolonged time underwater. The muscles in his body tensed; part of him felt as though he belonged in the water. Cahan caught up to the vessel and latched onto the trim that cut along the middle line of the boat, with his net of armor and clothes in tow. He heard the boat's energy chamber buzz and churn. Just over the hum of the chamber, he heard words of concern being voiced above.

"We forgot Crence," a mage cried. "Where is he?"

"He is probably investigating the forest because he 'felt' something. We all noticed he was missing. Are you saying you did not?"

"No."

"Let him figure a way back. He is a fuckin' idiot. If the other coven had not come when they did, we would have lost the spell."

Cahan remained submerged, waiting for the idiot mages to make a decision as the boat docked. His anger had not quite receded from before. Something must have kept it just below the surface. Was it the use of his gills?

Cahan's thoughts began a morbid spiral. He might well have to kill every one of them to save the mission. He readied himself for what he must do next. He would kill them all in the forest if he must and bury their bodies. Maybe ghouls would eat their remains. No one would suspect. Without bodies, they would think the mages abandoned their collective duty. The mission took precedence over human life.

"Very well," a mage said. "I will tell the next group to watch for him."

Cahan shook his head of the murky thoughts streaming to him. He reminded himself not to let the wickedness take control. He closed his eyes.

Stop. Stop.

Cahan turned and yanked on the rope pulling his belongings to him. Now the vessel had docked and the mages dispersed, he was free to surface and don his clothing and armor. He did so quickly, under the cover of a towering stone wall and shrubbery.

After he changed back into his armor, Cahan skirted the outer stone wall, edging against it as closely as possible. He heard combat boots scuff against the inner walkways as he crept closer to the meeting place. Pockets of ambient sound and chatter filled his ears. He hoped that the others had already made it. They could be dead or locked in battle for all he knew.

Finally, he had made it the rendezvous point, the western-facing wall of the airfield. When he arrived, a mixture of anxious faces greeted him—along with Anaymous, who wore an expression of indifference. His mouth, however, was twisted in a sour scowl. Cahan thought that these emotions were not actually that difficult to read, despite the difference in species. In a way, it gave them a human side.

Anaymous's eyes were an abyss of deep thought. "Cahan," he said with a nod, acknowledging his presence.

"We can't linger here," Cahan said. "We need to get started." He studied Anaymous's face. There was still a disparity about him. "Spill it, Anaymous."

Anaymous looked at him sternly. "If we are captured, the Protosians will never make an accord with my kind."

"It's kind of late to bring up your qualms now," Cahan replied. "We are already knee-deep in the shit."

"He is right, Anaymous," Agares agreed. "The only way out now is to proceed."

"Are you ready?" Cahan asked.

Anaymous's neck muscles expanded as he spat a searing globule of venom at the wooden fencing near the wall. In a smoky green burst, Anaymous's projectile enveloped and consumed the fence in rapid succession, leaving a foul smell behind. Cahan peered through the breech and saw a guard coming toward them. "He must've smelled the venom. Take cover."

As the guard neared, a violent flash of motion passed in front of Cahan's eyes. Anaymous seized the guard while clearing the venom-soaked breach through to the other side, landing on the airfield grounds. The others in the group quickly followed, as the black outlines of their bodies blurred through. Anaymous pressed his hand against the guard's mouth and shallowly bit the guard's wrist before casting the human aside. A trace of venom dripped from the guard's wrist.

"It is just enough to keep him at rest," Anaymous assured the others.

Cahan surveyed the airship dock. There were vessels of all makes and models. Several boat conversions lined the periphery. In the middle were military vessels. One vessel in particular caught Cahan's eye.

"That one," Cahan said, pointing to a triangular-shaped airship, reminiscent of ancient Gargoylian design. The vessel was mighty, clad in alloy armor, and ready for battle.

Once inside, Cahan began throwing levers at a feverish pace. He heard the vessel bellow. The heart of the ship made a sharp whistling noise. Cahan knew this type of vessel in and out. Now that he had shifted the core gear, he knew hundreds of swirling white staves of smoke permeated across the surface of the energy chamber of the ship, which would be expelled through an exhaust pipe. He hoped it wouldn't be too conspicuous.

Cahan waited for a moment until he heard what he was waiting for. Hollow echoes sounded throughout the body of the ship, which meant the pool of water beneath the vessel had expanded and contracted. He thought about what this display looked like when watching it firsthand. It made the water look as if it had lost its basic properties and had turned into some other viscous state. This would fuel the airship's takeoff.

The ship broke from the force that binds all things to earth, and heaved itself into the atmosphere as if escaping the clutches of an unseen hand. As it cleared the field and sailed over the basin, Cahan threw the intake lever and the ship absorbed another helping of water, which thrust the vessel even farther skyward.

Chapter 15
~ The Escape ~

As the airship absconded from its former sanctuary, Cahan left the controls to Anaymous's pilot. He felt a sense of pain and apprehension as he looked at the others.

"What is it?" Anaymous probed. "We made it without issue." His face showed relief.

Cahan noticed that the more time he spent with the Kalriss, the easier it was to discern their emotions and facial expressions. He thought that in some ways, they weren't all that different from humans. However, no one who knew his secret would think him a good judge of humanity.

Cahan shifted back to the overarching conspiracy and his increased episodes of bloodlust. He wondered if the malevolence would consume him. He had so much to do. If he could just hold it off a little longer.

"What did you do to these toggles?" the pilot bristled.

Cahan turned toward the cockpit and locked eyes with the pilot. The pilot quickly turned away and focused on flying the vessel, pulling levers and resetting the toggles, grumbling all the while.

Cahan's gaze wandered around the pilot's surroundings. The cockpit of the craft was an oval shape, cluttered with instruments. The instrument panel was constructed of finely polished brindle wood and the levers of a Gargoylian alloy. The propulsion controls consisted of a series of levers correlated to several groupings of ducts arranged at the stern, bow, and underbelly of the vessel. Most airships of this class, provided the ship was constructed of brindle wood and Gargoylian alloy, could make agile, pinpoint turns, without exertion.

Cahan surveyed the room, addressing everyone there. "There are many fronts happening all at once in this..."

Depression cast an empty feeling within him. Chaos beckoned, pulling at him, corrupting his mind. His thoughts returned to the wizards he was willing to kill without provocation. He pondered on the bent and contorted boy lying on the ground. It chilled him to the bone that the prospect of killing innocents secretly aroused delight in him.

"Cahan?" a voice said, interrupting his corrosive stream of introspection.

"We will have to fog the core," Cahan continued, recovering his train of thought, "for the ship to clear the naval blockade." He felt the warmth of normalcy begin to return.

At once, the Kalriss swarm looked at Cahan with questioning glances, their eyes red and narrowed.

"Why not circumvent the blockade completely?" Anaymous probed. "Should we not just fly over the eastern boarder or southern shoreline? We have a passage rune now that we have acquired a Verindian caliber vessel," he added.

"The eastern border and southern coast have barriers that aren't paired with any sort of passage runes. It permits no ship—in or out. Just think of them as spellcrafted walls." Cahan paused for a moment. "In all your years in the wastelands, did you notice any vessels passing back and forth from those areas?" he said.

"No, but we did not spend all waking hours watching the Protosians. I had a concern to run." The lines of Anaymous's face crinkled. He locked eyes with Cahan, his mouth pinched slightly. A sudden realization seemed to fire in his eyes. "So all airship traffic is filtered to an area where ship-busting cannons are at the ready. Will the rune alone not allow us to pass the blockade?"

"The rune gets us past the western barrier," Cahan said as he tapped his hand atop a strange, glowing rune embossed on the wall near him. "But the navy may soon be alerted to the theft of this vessel, or they could have an itinerary of travel on which we wouldn't be scheduled."

"So what will this 'fogging' do?" Agares asked.

"Not too many are aware of this tactic, as it has only recently been discovered," Cahan said, "but it's possible to create the cover of fog using the core of an airship. Doing this will also keep the barrier from flashing Verindian colors when we come through. That is just as important as the rest—we don't want to announce our arrival."

Anaymous nodded grudgingly.

"I'll go down to the core chamber straight away and make the adjustments." Cahan shifted his attention to the pilot. "You will shift all power to the bow propulsion ports and then immediately to the stern. After a count of thirty, you will repeat the process. Got it?"

"How will a traveling fog in the sky conceal us?" Anaymous asked.

"Through the prism of the barrier, which is very strong near Aundyre," Cahan answered. "With the cover of night, the navy will barely be able to see us at all. The barrier distorts eyesight. It will look vaguely like the aurora borealis in the night sky."

"How do you know all of this?" Agares asked.

"An enemy of Protos did this once, or at least his fleet did. Perhaps you have heard of him: Vashar N'dal."

The pilot looked at Cahan as if he had gone mad. The lines of his face turned sour.

"I... we have never heard of any such tactic, especially from the former king's son," Anaymous stated. "I hope we are not serving the whims of a mad man."

"Will that not tear the ship in two?" The pilot's eyes narrowed.

"There is no possibility of that, whatsoever," Cahan assured. "This ship is constructed of the finest brindle wood and alloy available. I know this vessel inside and out—I mean, this type of vessel."

"We will attempt your ploy. The only other alternative is to be blown to bits by the Allied Navy," Anaymous said, though his face still held traces of worry.

Cahan advanced aft to the ship's energy chamber. He proceeded to throw levers and adjust the leveling toggles with rapid precision. Cahan walked to the housing of the chamber. Its energy flow pulsated like a beating heart. He ripped off a cover from the housing and pulled out a stringy, half-solid strand, which bled a bluish green liquid. The engine moaned with a screeching, bewildering sound. The core turned black for a moment and returned to its normal color.

Cahan hurried up half the stairs toward the spar deck in view of Anaymous. Cahan signaled him and went back down below.

* * * *

Anaymous scrambled toward the cockpit. The pilot sat there, staring at the lever before him, as if he were not sure he should throw it. Anaymous hit the doorway to the pilot's chambers with the side of his hand, making some of the toggles and instrumentation rattle. The pilot recoiled and turned to face him, his ears glistening with sweat.

Anaymous nodded at the pilot, giving him the order to proceed. The nervous pilot turned around and looked at the instrument panel, then hesitantly threw the propulsion levers. The ship screeched from the strain on the core.

Silence surrounded Anaymous. He turned to check on the others. Agares's eyes were closed. Ose sat with his head slightly bowed, while Dzoavotis clutched the charm on his necklace. Another creak sounded, and the ship shifted violently. Anaymous remained silent as the chatter of his crew filled the cabin. He heard them muttering about listening to the stupid human.

After a moment, Anaymous realized the ship had not buckled. The others breathed a collective sigh of relief.

91

* * * *

Cahan proceeded to the absorption lever, which was used to take in the energy to power the engine, and yanked on it with the weight of his body. Cahan took in short, anxious breaths. He did not tell the others that the core could become corrupted and fail with this process. The blue energy turned a greenish color. Cahan immediately sprinted topside.

He jumped the last few steps and landed on the deck. A thick, misty fog had shrouded the ship, stemming from the propulsion ports, as it channeled upward in a black gaseous mass. Cahan ran to the ladder ascending to the crow's nest and climbed to the top. Atop the crow's nest was a telescope with metal footholds below it. Cahan was just above the fog that enveloped the ship under his feet. He peered into the telescope as he pointed it downward.

Down below, a vast array of naval ships rested just inside the barrier's limits. This blockade was a fail-safe, should the barrier falter. At the forefront, a clustering of alloy battleships called *The Crimson Runners* lined the seaway. Cahan had studied the history of this fleet in War College. These vessels were the scourge of the seas, as far as pirates were concerned. This fleet had driven many pirates, even the famed noble-born pirate, Baal Adramelech, from their plundering across the vast sea into the air. Pirates soon found they could not match or engineer the equivalent of such vessels, and it was nearly impossible to evade them on the open water. These seafaring marauders were hunted so effectively that they would often be forced into the corrupted waters of eastern Shintallis.

Before the inactivity of the living continent of Forgatha, the corruption had spread to the eastern and northern borders of Protos, not far off the coast. Vessels that navigated this area were torn to shreds and consumed by the black corruption called "The Quietus Sea." Cahan had always thought it ironic that the corruption of Forgatha protected eastern Protos from pirates. That corruption was also harnessed to power the eastern barrier, which protected against airship raids.

Cahan studied the ships of the blockade. Each battle vessel was topped by a flat surface, which housed a fair number of airships and three heavy-energy cannons, mounted on each side. The heavy cannons, or ship busters, were fed by an energy chamber in the deck below. Smaller pod mountings, fueled individually by spellcrafters, were located below the upper deck, on the curved outer hull of the ship. The crimson marauders were nearly unstoppable in terms of both speed and raw power. Behind the mighty battleships loomed traditional argosy-class vessels, constructed of brindle wood, as all of the allied districts had not yet caught up to Protos or even Verinda in naval construction.

* * * *

A deckhand aboard *The Specter*, a naval flagship, gazed at the stars near the general area of a fog-laden mass, but he shifted his focus to study the barrier's component parts, mostly out of boredom. Three prodigious black spires projected upward and curved slightly back to a point at their ends. Each spire emitted an elliptical energy pattern, similar to orbiting stars. The spires, strategically located at the boundary of Aundyre, were inscribed with Gargoylian runic symbols, which were revealed when energy coursed through the body of the monolithic structures. The space between the spires would also be set ablaze every so often, revealing a spellcrafted wall. Thick bands of onyx lined the ground, leading all the way back to the manor of the curate. It was through this connection that energy was transferred to the barrier. He wondered if the sea spires were also connected to Aundyre. They lined the seaway all the way to the corrupted waters of the north.

The deckhand again shifted his attention back to the stars and focused more intently on the mist through his gold-lined telescope, but he casually disregarded it. The haze of the barrier gleamed as its energy seemed drawn to the fog.

The deckhand below rushed to see his commanding officer.

"Yes, what is it?" the officer said.

"Sire, that light seems to be… moving."

The commanding officer studied the light and scowled. "Ready all cannons!" he yelled to his crew.

* * * *

Cahan slid down the crow's nest ladder and proceeded back to the energy chamber. "Get ready," he yelled to the others.

Needles shot through Cahan's mind. "Damn it. What's taking you so fucking long?" He threw the absorption gear and climbed topside. The rest was up to the pilot, but he hated the thought of leaving important things to others, especially something like this.

The fog was beginning to dissipate. Soon, the entire Allied Navy would see their vessel, naked and barren of any cover.

* * * *

"Ready the cannons!" the commander ordered once more. "Ensign… What is your name? Oh, who cares?" He laughed. "Do you want me to open fire on the sky?" the commander asked. "What the fuck did the sky ever do to you?"

An eruption of laughter spread across the deck.

The captain laughed so hard that tears welled up in his eyes. His alcoholic's nose shone an even brighter red. The ensign handed the telescope over after being prompted with a nudge by the commanding officer.

"Just the aurora borealis," the commander said, recovering some of his composure. "It is common in these parts, ensign."

A crew member was still looking around, clearly wondering what the blue hell was going on. "I was kidding," the commander said. "Belay the order."

As the deckhand walked off, he murmured, "Moving light fog is not common anywhere."

* * * *

Cahan sighed as the fog buoyed up once more. "Shit, that was close." The prospect of being caught excited and terrified him at the same time. Cahan looked curiously at the base of the crow's nest. It reminded him of another vessel in a different time in his life. It had remarkably similar battle scars, but with one absence—the hand-carved runic symbol of Valese. He decided to make this crow's nest bear the same symbol. With his dagger, he made a vertical line, a small arm that veered up at an angle connected to the vertical line, and a larger upward arm just below. Once he was done, he looked at the symbol and felt a deep sentimentality. It looked exactly like he remembered it.

Cahan headed below deck. As he passed the pilot's chamber, he said, "Could you have cut it any closer?" He walked a few more paces and murmured under his breath, "Fuckin' demons…"

"Fuckin' humans," the pilot's voice thundered from down below.

Chapter 16
~ Bloodshed at Manor of the Curate ~

Cahan stood topside as the airship landed with ease, just beyond the black, onyx metal gates at the entrance of Aundyre. Cahan's mind began to wander as he studied the black gate. This gate was revered because it was a replica of the gates of Gehínnda, and was a joint effort between the spellcrafting Gargoyles and the warrior Kharr'kari. It was not composed of the same metal as the fabled postern. In his youth, Cahan thought it odd that this joint effort resided on human lands. He always figured there was some sort of ulterior motive for the collaboration.

It was widely known the Gates of Gehínnda had stood for ages, even before the reign of Gargoyles, where the cavernous Úul and the lands of Shintallis intersected, guarding the world from wraiths and other such creatures that wallowed and wailed in its depths. Protosian and Valesian scholars still conjectured as to who constructed the gates. Cahan had often thought it was Valese herself. However, the only known fact about Gehínnda was the metal from which it was composed repelled otherworldly creatures and did not originate from Shintallis.

Cahan and the others swiftly filed out of the vessel, making their way into the city. Cahan could scarcely see the manor of the curate on the horizon of jutting stone. Something evil waxed dominant over the moonlight-tinged manor. He didn't know quite what it was, but it filled him with a deep hollowness and an abject feeling of sheer misery.

The city was hauntingly listless, but there was some commotion within the houses. Every once in a while, he would see furtive faces peering out of windows down upon the main city thoroughfare, gazing darkly at them. Cahan noticed that many of the homes were boarded up and fortified with metal coverings over the doorways.

Once they reached the manor's grounds, the group gasped with horror upon viewing the bloody carnage that must have ensued not long before their arrival. Cahan winced when he smelled the eroded flesh that filled the pungent air. Disfigured corpses, once animated by Shabaris, the King of Necrosis, lay limp and inert in the courtyard. Cahan looked closely at the creatures that haunted the area. Fixed upon the undead faces of the insect-like proselyte demons were masks of torment, disfigured by the hunger of unnatural cannibalism. Dried blood enshrouded the exquisite gardens and awe-inspiring craftsmanship of the architecture. Slender pillars capped by stone water nymphs loomed over the bloodstained courtyard. A procession of lion-headed waterspouts fed the now-tainted bath at the center of the open forum. A sense of anguish filled Cahan as he gazed upon the barbarism that mocked the moonlit heavens.

Cahan and the others cut through the piles of undead that blocked their path to the estate of the curate, the house of Elrich. The guard of the curate and a number of the curate's workmen lay among the nocturnal creatures.

Just outside the manor's eastern border, a witch battled a large regiment of Liche soldiers with a hefty, fully formed Gronxth sea spirit at her flank. As the group drew closer, they were astonished to see a grayish-blue being fighting alongside the witch.

"That is Herald A'uun," Anaymous said with reverence.

The entire group was awestruck at the sight of A'uun. It was somewhat rare to witness a herald of a Celestial in battle, though they often appeared to rulers and leaders.

"Move!" Cahan scolded as he brushed past the awestruck group.

Cahan studied the Liche soldiers. They resembled the undead the group had just encountered, but were more focused than most dead walkers. Some of them wielded swords, some magic. The sword wielders wore rusty, battle worn armor saturated in blood, tempered with arrow holes, and sword slashes. The spellcrafters wore wizard's armor, protected by runic carvings. It covered their shoulders, chests, and backs and tapered off into flowing robes from the waist down, lined with gold trim.

Cahan snapped his eyes to the strongest enemy—the Gronxth. The large, statuesque figure resembled a merman with green, scaly skin, gills located behind its ear holes, and a flat face with nasal slits. Its imposing hands were as large as kite shields, and its underbelly was the color of sulfur. The Gronxth bellowed, bearing its long, aciculate teeth, and turned toward the witch, revealing a dorsal fin on its back.

* * * *

The witch, Elizabeth Cloister, felt the shift in focus of the Gronxth and intuitively met its glare with one of her own. She pointed her small, gnarled staff of brindle wood at the colossal beast as it lumbered toward her. A reddish-black energy swirled around her staff that emanated from her eyes, blanketing the area. A spine-covered vine sprouted from the ground beneath the Gronxth and wrapped around its leg like a snake. As its spines grew longer and began uncoiling, it tore chunks of flesh from its thigh, which splattered to the ground. The Gronxth howled and tore the vine off.

The beast charged in a frenzy, as an otherworldly bluish-green light seeped from its bloody wounds. Cloister raised her staff to the sky. The ground beneath her became encrusted with glaring ice. All sound ceased at once. The Gronxth's face wore a look of bewilderment, which evaporated to rage. Nostrils flaring, it barreled toward her, grinding its teeth. It looked down at its spiritual form, flowing from its wounds in plumes of green. Using her staff, the witch directed the gaseous green spirit to the ice beneath her. She stepped briskly away from the ice as the spirit and the diamond-like crystal substance became one. The physical form of the Gronxth turned black and fell backwards with a loud thud that shook the ground.

* * * *

As Cahan moved toward the battle, he watched Lord A'uun with astonishment. Two Liche soldiers leapt toward the witch just after the exorcism of the Gronxth. A'uun quickly met the Liche with his sword. Unlike the Gates of Aundyre, A'uun's sleek, nimble blade was said to have been constructed of the same metal used to forge the Great Gates of Gehínnda. In essence, it was one of the deadliest weapons to wield against the undead. It had neither a guard nor pommel and required the best of swordsmen to wield it properly.

The herald's movements were so quick and decisive, it was as if he could anticipate the attacks of his foes. At times, it would seem as though he would be struck by his assailants—but at the last moment, his attack would fall into rhythm. The oncoming strike would be narrowly avoided, and he would cut through the undead creatures without effort. As A'uun sliced through the Liche soldiers, his sword left emerald lashes of energy trailing its movements. Soon Liche soldiers littered the ground, energy from the herald's sword seeping from their wounds.

Cahan's eyes shifted over to the witch. She jabbed her staff into the glistening crystal overlay. A painful moan echoed and abruptly stopped as the staff stood erect and absorbed the sea spirit completely. The Gronxth's physical form decayed rapidly as the ice outcropping melted.

Just then, another group of abnormally tall Liche soldiers slithered into the courtyard from the manor, their tongues hissing through their cracked and decrepit teeth. Cahan and the others had reached Lord A'uun and the human witch.

Cahan rampaged toward the Liche, roaring as he hoisted his axe overhead. In that moment, he felt as if he were the maligned horror that haunted the courtyard. The malevolent anger was coursing through him, though he did not mind it on the open battlefield. He let the wickedness overtake him, fueling his strength and speed, allowing him to react solely on his honed instincts. The raw power crept up through his body, extending to his fingertips, and Cahan let out an inhuman snarl as he sped forward.

Anaymous and the others pulled ahead of him, swarming the death-shrouded creatures in unison, furiously ripping them apart like ravenous beasts.

Cahan ducked under a sweeping sword swipe from his side while cleaving the legs off one of the shrouded creature's counterparts in front of him. He rose up and saw the point of a sword, aimed for his face. He slid to the ground and darted between the legs of the attacking creature. Once behind the Liche soldier, he jumped up and beheaded the towering specter with his hand axe. Cahan reveled in the death that surrounded him. He felt energized by the hateful creatures, knowing that they wished to kill him—however, he knew they were incapable of such a feat. That power was solely held by him, and it gave him a feeling of exultation.

A piercing heat grew against the back of his arms. He soon realized that a spellcrafting Liche was conjuring a fireball. Without looking, he threw his hand axe with all his might and splintered the creature's skull. He moved toward the slain Liche and pulled the axe from its rotting gray matter. The Kalriss, A'uun, and the human witch had already laid waste to their assailants.

Cahan walked toward the group, still surveying the battlefield. The surviving Liche whose legs he'd just amputated pawed and scratched at the ground, hopelessly trying to move. Cahan approached the creature and looked down at it. As it reared up, it gave a fork-tongued hiss. Cahan crushed the squirming Liche's head with a swift stomp, spilling its decayed brain from its splintered skull.

Now that the last of his enemies was defeated, Cahan felt the anger retreat from the forefront of his consciousness, and it once more began to skulk in the nether reaches of his brain.

The group met in the middle of the blood-soaked courtyard. The pungent odor of viscera and decapitation filled Cahan's nostrils.

"Lordship," Cahan acknowledged Lord A'uun sourly as he approached.

The others still looked at A'uun with awe and admiration. This embarrassed Cahan somewhat, but he understood their reactions—he was the most well-known being in all of Shintallis.

"Your reverence," Ose, one of Anaymous's guards, called out.

"I do not desire any form of worship," A'uun snapped, as if giving a theology lesson. "Any 'deity' or 'demigod' that requests such nonsense from those bound to the earth should be met with circumspection and distrust."

The human witch glared at A'uun as if to say, "Not now."

His solid white pupils contrasted with his black irises and flared with warmth. "Always remember, a true being of the light does not require the sanction of worship, just as you do not require the sanction of any other being to live," he intoned.

He began to walk briskly toward the manor. The group obediently followed, with Cahan trailing behind.

"We have pressing matters to which we must attend," A'uun said in a commanding tone.

"Do you know us?" Cahan asked, bewildered by the assumed familiarity of the bluish-gray herald.

"We have obviously met, and upon catching up with Elizabeth"—he nodded toward the witch—"I learned that your companion"—he gestured to Anaymous—"is the pupil of my counterpart here."

Cahan looked back over his shoulder at the woman the herald referred to as Elizabeth and Anaymous, who had slowed their pace. They spoke in emphatic tones while discussing the manor and the road that had led them here. The witch woman corrected the tall, looming Anaymous many times, as if rapping him on the knuckles like an ill-mannered student. Their friendly rapport was obviously that of precept and student, Cahan concluded.

As Cahan stepped into the manor, he took in the death-littered halls of the once venerated outpost. Decapitated heads, both Liche and human, choked the main hall. Bloody spears and refuse were strewn about, and the walls were caked with the stains of brains and blood. Wizards' staffs remained clutched in pale, lifeless hands, still carrying the energies of half-started spellcraft. Swords enchanted with fire and wind spells littered the ground, just out of the reach of the curate's guard. Cahan concluded the Liche spellcrafters must have disarmed the curate's guard by magic as they stormed the manor.

Cahan was somewhat shocked by A'uun's apparent disregard for the chaotic mess contained within the blood-dimmed manor. The others paused and took in the scene with astonishment and sorrow. Cahan dropped to one knee to behold a spellcrafter that was part of the progeny guard. His robes were tattered and threadbare, and his body was bent and broken. Several bite wounds seeped blood mixed with demonic ichor were concentrated around the stomach and ribcage. This particular guard piqued Cahan's curiosity because of the green flecks swimming in the spellcrafter's irises, even after death. He must have been desperate to the point of taking a dark oath, just to survive a while longer. He was willing to curse his soul to keep others safe. On his hand was a ring with the runic script for both marriage and fatherhood.

In a way, Cahan understood what the conjuror must have experienced and felt a bond of sorts. He faced something soul-clutching and eternally dark, but at the same time, his curse benefited him in the heat of battle.

Something stirred within the dead conjuror. Through the window of the spellcrafter's open and bleeding wounds, Cahan witnessed his intestines rapidly heal before his eyes. The cursed guard's hand twitched, and its face began a demonic metamorphosis, transforming into thick, insect-like dermis. The newly birthed proselyte lunged for Cahan. He grabbed its forehead and bent its head back, snapping the neck like a tree branch. Cahan placed the guard down with care, wishing, for a moment, that he was the one that lay lifeless upon the cold stone floor, free from the pain.

Cahan was so moved by the spellcrafter's plight that he had almost forgotten about the others. He looked up and saw A'uun watching him solemnly from the foot of a winding, granite staircase. In the next moment, he was standing before Cahan.

"There is something I need you to see." A'uun beckoned.

Cahan was somewhat taken aback by the herald's cavalier manner. It seemed as though he knew about the role he had been playing. Cahan looked at the herald thoughtfully and wondered if, perhaps, A'uun had been waiting for him at the manor.

The rest swiftly made their way up the stairs, including the witch. She moved inhumanly fast, but did not vanish and reappear like her cohort.

They found themselves before a gold-trimmed telescope.

"Look through the aperture," A'uun said.

Cahan hesitated.

"Go on," he urged, nodding his head in affirmation.

"This was one of your inventions when you were earthbound, wasn't it?" Cahan said.

A'uun nodded.

"I can't quite see beyond the meadow."

"Gaze upon the runic stone on the side of the device. Take note of it. Remember it."

Cahan looked at the red stone and studied the symbol grafted upon its surface. It was a grand slash with curved ends, bisected by a spiral pattern.

"Touch the rune and think beyond the meadow," A'uun calmly instructed.

Cahan did as he was told, and suddenly he could see well beyond the meadow. His gaze turned to a giant, menacing horde of all manner of creatures with Dark Gargoyles swarming overhead, near a corrupted cave mouth.

"You've improved your invention," Cahan said, turning to A'uun. "Anaymous, have a look." Cahan gestured toward the telescope. He turned back to A'uun. "That's the same breed of Gargoyle we encountered at the harbor."

Cahan, without waiting for an answer, began to explain to A'uun about the Malefic and their attack on the barrier room—the reason they were now in Aundyre.

"I assumed such was the case," A'uun said. "There is someone you need to meet."

Cahan was again suspicious of the herald, as if there was a hidden reason for pointing out the demons at the barrier. He also wondered if A'uun had wanted him to see some sort of connection or if he just merely wanted to show him how serious the situation was.

As Cahan and the others made their way down the hall, he could tell by their solemn expressions that everyone's thoughts were focused on the debasement of this once-grand outpost. Murderous thoughts entered Cahan's mind once more. Anger poured into his consciousness, telling him that the curate deserved a fate worse than death.

Stop, Stop. He repeated his refrain, clinging to a thread of humanity and hoping it would not snap.

With effort, Cahan turned his thoughts to the history of this place. The line of curates was something he studied almost as incessantly as Celestials. The House of Elrich was the domicile of the Progeny of Benevolence. There were several progenies in and near Protos. The Progeny of Spellcraft was the only other establishment as renowned as the place Cahan now walked. It was an educational institution for those gifted with conjuring abilities. Both demons and humans could be found in its halls. It also held the important task of maintaining the eastern-most barrier, which was constructed without Gargoyle support.

The Progeny of Benevolence had several members, chief of which was the curate of Elrich. The curate directly maintained the border of Shintallis in the form of a powerful barrier, which was supplemented by a blockade composed of The Protosian Naval Fleet and allied districts.

Both progenies often worked together, and the manor employed newly graduated students, but only those of the human and Venerite persuasions.

The curate, and likewise the progeny, was originally the healer that serviced the whole of Shintallis. The Celestial Valese bestowed certain humans and Venerites, the believed precursor to humans, with the gift of her light, which enabled them to heal others. The nations often bartered with services and coin in exchange for the progenies' curative powers. As a result, the Manor of Elrich grew over time, with many new structures engineered by the Gargoyles to harness more power for the progeny as they serviced a growing population.

These structures drew in the energies that fueled spellcraft and dispersed them to the progeny. Many saw this as a great spectacle of human and demon cohabitation, while others saw this as Valese's way to force humanity on to the whole of demonkind.

The house of Elrich dated back to the Great Bygone Era—an era that was fraught with civil war. Once the dark wizards, known as the Gilpesh, and the Forgathan military were driven out of the lands of Protos, the House of Elrich contracted the Gargoyles of the Arcadian Mountains to devise a barrier that would last through the ages.

The original curate, in collusion with its architect, decided that no other nation, Celestial, or herald should have access to the barrier's powers. The Gargoyles tailored the powers of the barrier to the characteristics of the curate and the progeny. Only the Gargoyle architects and the progeny could maintain its power, and only the energy that flowed from the curate could keep the barrier at full strength.

The Gargoyles created a supplemental fount of energy to control the barrier when a curate passed so that Protos would not be left unprotected while a new curate was called forth. Over time, the Forgathans grew stronger, and it became necessary for the fount to be used at all times to bolster the barrier's strength.

Cahan and the others had made their way down a long, winding hallway of gray speckled stone. Portraits of the various curates hung evenly on the walls. Cahan inspected the oil paintings as he passed. He had studied the various curates over the years, but had never been inside the manor or met the reigning curate, for that matter. The first painting depicted Curate Barstarnea Elrich, a bald and affable man, and the first bloodline named to the progeny. Barstarnea had two sons, Grethung and Scirii, who would eventually succeed him. The sons of Barstarnea were captured together on canvas. The pair managed to eclipse their father with many acts of honor and fortitude, which would eventually lead to their gruesome deaths at the hands of fanatics, in defense of Aundyre. Their heads were impaled on spikes and positioned as if they were kissing each other. Curate Therving the Handsome, the source of much controversy due to his many trysts, adorned the wall next to Grethung and Scirii. Therving had no legitimate sons or daughters, so his reign as curate faded into obscurity. Curate Crimear, the Silent One, as many referred to him, had a daughter, Herulinea. She had decided to join the Verindian army despite the opportunity of being the first female curate. Lastly, Curate Rugian the Bold, and some might say "the Obnoxious Curate," had two sons, Erepus and Adelrik. Neither Erepus nor Adelrik had been captured in portraiture since a masterful portrait was generally commissioned after a curate's death.

Cahan noticed that the room before them was made of an entirely different material than he had ever seen. The stone around the doorway of the room was greenish-blue, and looked smooth to the touch. It glimmered with resonance, reflecting the torchlight in the hallway as it cast a blue tinge on the faces of its occupants. It was almost as if the stone itself had an effect on the flames; at regular intervals, spears of flame would flare up, and then snap back to a normal teardrop shape.

The group came to a doorway that was tall—so tall, in fact, Cahan did not need to stoop down before entering. The door and frame looked to be of the same make as the barrier room's door in Elysium. Curiosity overcame Cahan. He reached to touch the stone. Each block was warm in the center and chillingly cold at its edges. He felt an energy pulsating within, as if some unseen entity was struggling to claw its way out. The stone blocks were cut to the size of one square human foot and had a sparkling gray sand bond, binding the stones between. He looked with awe at the remarkable artistry and the perfect uniformity of the staggered pattern of blocks. Once the door was open, he could see that the entire room was composed of these blocks.

Cahan noticed a brindle wood desk that stood straight across the threshold of the doorway. The desk looked as if a tree had grown into the shape it now held, as though no cutting tool had ever touched it. Branches pointed backward at the rear of the desk, and at its crown, two wooden limbs formed an outward arch with a light orb for reading suspended between. Just below the arch rested several small compartments containing scrolls. Papers and a writing quill were haphazardly strewn across the flat surface. The floor was composed of large rectangular quartzite, smoothly finished and scored at each corner without a single rough edge. When Cahan heard heavy, labored breathing, he shifted his attention to the center of the room.

Cahan's feeling of awe dissolved to terror when he saw what was now occupying the room of the curate.

A demon of Shabaris's ilk stood defiantly in the center of the room, a glaring paradox compared to its elegant surroundings. This beast was far more than a mere Liche soldier. It was a parasitic Nematraude, a creature that consumed everything in its path. Shabaris only bestowed this form on the most sycophantic of his followers.

Cahan's eyes raked over the creature's hideous form. Its gray outer shell was hard and layered like the covering of an insect. Its eyes, sunken into its skull, had two small red irises that darted irregularly. Its oval mouth housed several small rows of needlelike teeth. The creature bellowed intermittently and brandished its pincers.

Red anger stirred in Cahan, and his hand shook. Something within his mind shattered. He wanted to impale the creature with his blade and cast it into the moat below. However, he gasped in disbelief when he realized the creature was powering the barrier. Light permeated from the beast to the concentric circle upon which it stood, spreading outward to the bricks in the room. The light cascading off the creature bathed Cahan in heat. He realized this light warmed the bricks. So what caused the cold sensation? He decided to push that aside for the time being, because he stood face-to-face with a Nematraude, right in the house of Elrich.

How could this be? He turned to A'uun and opened his mouth to speak.

"You are thinking the circle only yields to familial blood and only the House of Elrich can be contained within its contents," A'uun said.

Cahan nodded slowly in acknowledgement.

"Meet Erepus, crown prince of the Commonwealth of Aundyre."

"But how?" Cahan hissed.

"As you witnessed earlier, the remaining Shabarian dogmatists attacked the manor. They had already claimed Erepus in an earlier battle and reformed him to his current state."

"So the energy of this room restored part of his humanity," Cahan guessed, focusing back on Erepus. "How did the Liche pass the barrier?"

"Liche are formed of human corpses and some spirits, like the Gronxth, can pass the barrier, as well. Once on the other side, they take physical form."

"Can that be?"

"Enough!" the creature rasped. "I will soon perish. The light that preserves my humanity is also killing the tainted part of me that keeps me alive," Erepus gasped in a sullen tone. "Let us not waste my brother's sacrifice."

Cahan looked at Erepus, now realizing his brother, the now former curate Adelrik, was dead because his brother now held the circle. Adelrik had sacrificed himself to get Erepus into this room to restore his humanity.

Erepus turned to A'uun. "Lord A'uun, you must find the next in line to lead the Progeny of Benevolence, even if it be a new bloodline."

At that moment, Elizabeth entered the room from the hallway, along with two attendants, who came to help the weakened Erepus to his quarters. Elizabeth bore an eccentric yet enrapturing presence about her.

"I will lead the Progeny. No one else has the ability," she said as the attendants helped the curate into the hallway.

"You are meant for a much higher calling, Elizabeth," A'uun said. "You will have to trust in this. I do not like to ask anyone to take charging leaps of faith, but I have seen this to be true."

When Herald A'uun called the witch "Elizabeth," something clicked in Cahan's mind. This was Elizabeth Cloister, the founder of the monastery in Elysium.

"I thought faith was at the center of what all religions are... or purport to be, Master Herald," Ose addressed A'uun.

"Faith without cause is the doctrine of the dead mystics," A'uun retorted. "Never mistake personal, or even communal, philosophy for religion."

The Kalriss nodded in agreement.

"What you are proposing, A'unn, is not akin to mysticism, and it is not without cause. I fully trust your judgment," Elizabeth conceded.

The room fell awkwardly silent, and Cahan knew why. A human had addressed A'uun without the title of "Lord" or "Herald."

A'uun stared at Elizabeth a moment. Everyone in the room braced themselves for the impending chastisement. Instead, the corners of A'uun's mouth curled into a smile.

"Very well, then," he replied calmly. "I have devised a temporary remedy to this unfortunate situation. We will need the prior curate's remains."

The group reacted with a mixture of astonishment and bewilderment at A'uun's statement. Amid the questioning glances, Cahan heard a hissing insect voice call to him from the hallway.

The group began a deep discussion of their next move. Cahan saw this as an opportunity not to participate in a useless debate because the group would follow A'uun's lead, regardless. He thought they should spare themselves the wasted time. A'uun always had the answer before anyone else.

Cahan stepped out to see the beleaguered prince, still accompanied by two progeny attendants.

"I see a commonality between us," the creature said. "The dualistic quandary in your heart is overwhelming."

It struck Cahan as odd that this abomination was able to simultaneously convey human emotion and wax poetic. He looked closer into the prince's red, darting eyes and saw the slightest hint of brown, most likely his human eye color. Cahan shifted his attention to the oval, gruesome mouth of the hateful-looking creature, as words once more forced their way out in a language unnatural to its physiology.

"Though I do not know your circumstances, I know the frail look of conflict in your eyes, Ranger. You feel as though one side of you is consuming the other."

Cahan wanted to speak, but thought better of it. This creature knew of the malevolency that stirred within him, because he, too, had evil clutching at his soul.

Erepus continued. "I will leave you with this. The root of the malevolence that stirs within you is not completely independent of your other side. Part of the wickedness stirs from your hatred and is rooted inside you. You give it strength. So I say to you, son, your battle is not a war between independent powers but a civil war that must be won within yourself."

Cahan stood, mouth open, as his eyes welled tears. A mixture of anxiety, embarrassment, and torment rushed through him. Defeat and hopelessness tore at him. His thoughts streamed in so quickly, he did not notice the prince take his leave.

The hissing voice of the retiring prince sounded once more from a distance. "Remember, you must rebel against it."

Chapter 17
~ The Imperfect Solution ~

Cahan and the group emerged from an airship to an island full of Kharr'karian ruins. Cahan was glad that Anaymous had the dubious task of carrying the large, ornate ossuary with the curate's remains. He heard the demon trudging and huffing behind him, and he did not envy him in the least. It reminded him of when he was a new ranger recruit—they were given all of the shitty chores. Carrying an ossuary was a kindness compared to mess duty.

Cahan studied his surroundings. The land mass they navigated was like a miniature tribute to ancient Kharr'karian lands. Giant copper-colored statues littered the landmass, all with one common element. All possessed large, bellowing mouths and sharp, protruding fangs. The statues' bodies had been carefully modeled in the tradition of the obelisks surrounding Shroud Lake in the northern provinces of Kharr'kari Island, one of the founding settlements of the proud warrior race.

Among the swaying tropical trees lay the corpse of an antique airship. Cahan could not believe his eyes. He felt an unnamable anxiety as he pored over the wreckage. The ship had taken heavy hull damage on its portside. Through the cracks and crevices, he could see the energy chamber of the ship. It was from the first generation of air vessels, created jointly between demons and humans, and its intake could only be powered by direct magic. In those days, wizards would have to chant and cast for long periods of time to ensure that the ship stayed airborne. In essence, the ship's main chamber fed from their energy, their life force. Once the convoluted transference conjuration was complete, the wizards were free to go to their quarters and rest. Performing a spell of this magnitude would require them to slumber for at least three days. There were some cases where wizards would fall somnolent, a kind of magically driven sleep, which caused the afflicted to think they were awake and going about their lives as normal, when they were withering away. Only spellcrafters were susceptible to somnolence. While in this state, specters were able to enter their bodies. Once possessed, it was very difficult to cast out the invading specter. Only a keen wizard willing to use all forms of magic, including the contrasting luminous and aphotic disciplines, could cure such an illness.

Cahan was still intent on the collective fossils that comprised the component parts of the airship. He felt an air of nostalgia as he entered the scarred remains of the vessel, and his eyes frantically glanced around the crew's quarters.

Cahan came to one room where he felt an even stronger sense of familiarity. He pictured the room in the past without damage when it was fresh out of the airship constructor's shop. He rapped his knuckles on a square-shaped piece of metal that was not quite flush with the wall. On command, the metal extended farther. The outstretched metal was met with Cahan's palm on its face, and the sides of the overlapping metal square bloomed outward with a click. Cahan braced himself for the pain that was coming as he grasped the newly exposed metal bloom. Another click sounded. Cahan drew his bloody hand back and a door creaked open. Cahan looked back at the group he had left standing before the decrepit airship. They looked at him with curiosity as they peered into the ship from a distance through the vessel's collective wounds.

Cahan turned away from the others and entered the hidden chamber. Once inside, he pulled out a small wooden box engraved with a sigil depicting an arcane dragon in lines of red from beneath a bed in the room. He clutched the box tightly and leapt from the chamber as the room collapsed behind him. Dust particles shifted upward and caked Cahan in century-old soot.

"We have to take this to a safe place now," he said as he brushed himself off.

"Well, what is it, then?" Cloister asked with a tinge of frustration.

A'uun studied Cahan intensely for a moment, as if he had just put the pieces of a century-old puzzle together. Cahan stared back at the piercing, otherworldly white of A'uun's pupils. He did not want to answer any questions right now, but just as he braced for the pain in the airship, he braced for the barrage of questions he would surely endure. The runic stone atop A'uun's gauntlet blazed red and traced the lines of his face as he stared blankly at Cahan.

An illumined compass with gold markings emerged out of thin air.

"Follow the compass," he said, handing him the object. "It will take you to where you need to go. Join us as soon as you are finished."

"How will I know where you are?"

"You have a compass, do you not?" A'uun said impatiently, as he gestured to the item. "Do not let it from your grasp. You never know when you will need to be pointed in the right direction."

Cahan nodded. "Say a grace for me."

"What does that mean?" Ose asked.

"It is just the way my people ask to say a prayer for those who are about to embark on a journey," A'uun solemnly replied.

Cahan watched the group as they looked to A'uun for answers, as if A'uun and he were colluding behind their backs in some way. Cahan took a last glance at the questioning faces that peered at him and sprinted off into the dense cover of jungle.

* * * *

Anaymous was filled with many questions. Part of him, however, thought it was not his place to question anything. He was new to their ranks and did not feel as though he had established his position among them. Part of him felt he was not worthy of his new companions.

A'uun turned to the group to address them. "Answers will come in due time. Even I have several questions. Now, unfortunately, is not the time for questions. Now, we must restore the manor as best we can or much will be lost, and then our questions will no longer matter."

As Anaymous continued to shoulder the ossuary, he looked upon the jungle with caution. The area was dense with monolithic trees, seemingly older than the rest of these wilds, whose eldritch shadows appeared to entrap darkness around them in an unnatural manner. Anaymous had never seen such a place. As they made their way deeper into the darkened swath of jungle, a large, oblong opalescent structure appeared before them, a structure that had not been visible just moments earlier.

It was as if an unseen hand pulled back a veil that had formerly blinded them to the presence of this odd formation. Anaymous looked for doors or windows, but saw none. It appeared the edifice was a large rock, forged into its oblong shape by some unknown, elder species.

A'uun strode toward the structure. The runic stone on A'uun's wrist shone with the same iridescence as the strange formation. A door cracked open, and a yellow light reached outward. The group was suddenly transported into A'uun's laboratory.

Anaymous marveled at his sudden change of surroundings, but also felt queasy. He looked to his old teacher, who continued to wear an abrasive expression. He could tell she did not like to be ignorant of details. Her mind was likely on Cahan and Herald A'uun. He had never seen this side of her. In their many lessons, she always had all of the facts. She seemed to know every detail about everything. He also found it odd that Herald A'uun called her Elizabeth. As long as he had known her, she had gone by her surname. She told him it dated back to her indentured servitude. Slavers never referred to anyone by their first name. It was considered an insult in Forgatha to call someone only by their surname. She decided to wear that as a badge of courage. It also reminded her of where her beliefs and ideals took root.

Anaymous studied Herald A'uun's laboratory. It was remarkable to him to walk these halls. He figured that few had set foot in these corridors, and that this was only one small part of the structure. Ornate, ancient artifacts, comprised of an ashen-colored Gargoyle wing, a gauntlet that moved of its own accord, various swords and shields from different time periods, and an odd fragment of cloth with frayed red gossamer edges, contained in a glowing, translucent prism decorated the south wall. Runic symbols were etched into the black granite walls in no discernible pattern at all, as if scribed by a mad demon. Various architectural sketches ranging from buildings to airships and other various war implements filled the north wall.

Below the designs were drawings of the basic physiologies of various demons, humans, and Venerites. Some of the flat, well-crafted tables were made of brindle wood, while others were carved of the same granite used for the walls. Spellcrafter's tools lay beside dissected wands, staffs, and large insects atop the tables. Dissected demon bodies were on tables at the rear of the room, their chest cavities held open by metal clamps. A set of telescopic spectacles lay beside one of them.

Anaymous and the group walked through the main room to the east wing. He set the ossuary down to observe his surroundings.

The east wing was large. Pillars of light shot down from the ceiling to reveal bodies suspended in midair. The ceiling held an elaborate carving of Kharr'kari men and women using the resources of the realm to create buildings, airships, and roads. On the horizon of the mural lay a grandiose city with airships hovering over its limits. The mural was a testament to a people who had mastered the resources of the world.

The group's focus lingered on the pillars of light and the humans trapped within them.

"These are neither slaves nor trapped humans," A'uun said with his usual academic exuberance. "Some refer to them as 'golems,' while others call them 'contivans.' These beings are made from the primordial materials of the ocean and the infinite blackness beyond Shintallis, bestowed life by spellcraft. They can think and feel if the caster wills it so. The human form is the only stock we are able to recreate through this process. These 'forms,' possess no consciousness."

Anaymous focused on two forms in particular near the center of the chamber. Suspended in light, were the forms of a man and a woman. These were the only ones with any sort of label. Etched on the wall near the man appeared runic symbols. He could tell there was more to the script, but it had worn over time. The script near the woman was indecipherable. Anaymous had never seen such lettering, though it was similar to the script on Herald A'uun's runic stones. He assumed it was an alphabet of A'uun's making.

"Anaymous." A'uun beckoned.

Anaymous lifted the ossuary and carefully placed it on a table near A'uun.

"Although we will be using the former curate's essence, I only create contivans with free will. There is a possibility he will not comply. Elizabeth, your assistance, please."

"I'm afraid I am somewhat lost," Anaymous said. "Herald A'uun, are you crafting a doppelganger of the curate?"

"Not in the strictest sense. The curate's spirit will become part of the 'form' before you. He will have certain attributes of the curate, but his body will harbor a different soul altogether. It is somewhat like the earthbound form of a Celestial."

A'uun made his way to a table with legs of granite and a brindle wood top, which stood near the pillar. Cloister walked to the fountainhead of the pillar and waited, as if it were her duty to assist him. Anaymous nervously watched as a piercing blue line shot out of the rune stone on A'uun's shoulder. The box evaporated from the table where he had laid the ossuary and materialized before the herald, who again tapped the runic jewel on his shoulder.

Circular light flowed in an orbital pattern, with the same luminescence as the pillar. Soon it engulfed the jewel on A'uun's shoulder. He grasped the light that spilled from the rune at its source. A large double-headed scythe appeared in his hand after the light dissolved with a final spark.

Anaymous studied the blades on each end of the scythe. A sharp clicking sound rang out before the blades retracted with an emerald swipe. What was left was an engraved, curved staff incised with the writings of the Gilpesh, called Gilsh. Anaymous often thought of Gilsh as a stylized form of writing with majestic strokes of curvy slashes, punctuated by concentric shapes. It looked more like art to him than inscription. He often wondered how something of such beauty could be born in such a callous country.

A'uun opened the ossuary. Anaymous could smell the pungent odor of the remains almost immediately. Cloister winced. Her hand latched onto her mouth. A'uun overturned the ornate box with a concentrated expression on his face, then splashed the remains of the curate upon the table. To Anaymous, he looked more like a scholar of science or an alchemist than a herald. Anaymous knew that normally only bones were contained in ossuaries, but then he remembered that the remains of a curate never decompose fully, due to the magical aspect of their being.

A'uun nodded to Cloister, who flourished her gnarled staff as A'uun raised his. The light of the pillar glowed even brighter, shifting to an indigo hue.

Anaymous's thoughts turned to his precept. He wondered what she thought of all this. This undertaking felt wrong to him. It seemed as though A'uun was toying with the fabric of creation. Should the herald wield a power just because he could?

Chapter 18
~ The Waking Golem ~

Out of the corner of his eye, A'uun noticed Cahan had joined them. Cahan stuffed the golden compass in his pocket and proceeded to watch the spectacle that had already started.

A'uun looked at the Kharr'kari mural. Previously hidden lines in the mural glimmered with a phosphorescent tone. A trickling of energy seeped down from the etchings like water from a dying stream, which revealed an energy field that pulsed steadily like a heartbeat. With a brisk crack, A'uun struck an etching on the granite wall, which gave off its own pulsating tone to offset the heartbeat. Each tonal energy field met in the middle of the room with a deep convulsion. A'uun felt everyone's consciousness at once as they lapsed into a meditative state brought on by the spellcraft. He sensed the reverberations of their minds, though he tried not to linger there. He experienced suggestions of their thoughts and desires, hunger pains, anxiety, awe, and anger. Amid the whirlwind of rampant thoughts, he identified the unmistakable feeling of doubt. A deep apprehension of his actions stretched out from Anaymous's mind, which he felt himself.

One particular reverberation struck a chord so sharply that A'uun had to turn away from Anaymous's misgivings. He intensely focused in on the vibration in an attempt to channel out the rest. The unique tone had come from the contivan.

A'uun looked on at the newly hewn being for signs of life. One of the contivan's eyes fluttered, and energy cascaded in waves toward him. Pulsating tones met the waves and absorbed some of the energy given off by the curate's remains, which in turn changed the color of the correlating energy fields to a brilliantly deep, penetrating green. Traces of natural energy flowed through the air, appearing intermittently, and fed the energy fields.

Loud cracking sounds filled the room. The reverberating heartbeats of the energy fields grew stronger. A'uun searched the flowing energy for a silver particle, which was the last tonal link to complete the spellcraft. Immense heat formed as the energy bent to his will and parted before him. In the nucleus of the stream of energy, he found what he sought.

As A'uun focused on the particle, a tonal echo stirred in his mind, interrupting the stream. The source had emanated from Cahan. This energy could throw the entire spell off, and have undesirable side effects. A'uun's mind instinctively merged with Cahan's consciousness. It was impossible to ignore. His mind was different than the others as he sensed in Protos on meeting the ranger. Rhythmic tones vibrated throughout Cahan's body, making the ranger's teeth clatter together with each pulse. A'uun sensed he was letting the melodic trance overtake him. A'uun focused on Cahan and sent a charge through his body to awaken him from his trance.

Cahan's eyes cracked open, and an angry expression washed over his face. A'uun experienced his disorientation and knew he was having trouble regaining his focus.

Blue energy engulfed A'uun's body as he teleported over to Cahan and put the end of his staff on his temple. The ancient Gilsh carvings illumined a bright white and then extended to his runic stones. He stretched his mind out to Cahan's through the direct bridge he had just created. This difference A'uun sensed in Cahan worried him. He instinctively knew he could not let the side effects of this spell take hold of him. The others would merely feel as though they were taking a nap. For Cahan, on the other hand, it was as though some sort of malevolent consciousness would be roused within him and overtake his mind, almost like a waking sleepwalker. He put a singular thought into Cahan's consciousness.

Do not let it overtake your mind.

He did not have long to save both the spell and Cahan. He had to finish things quickly or whatever horror lurked in Cahan's mind would be unleashed. He flashed over to a wall full of warlock inscriptions. That meant stepping over a line he did not want to cross. This action would mingle dark spellcraft into the conjuring and leave the golem open to possession. He decided to bury an imprint into the golem's energy signature. If he was possessed, A'uun would see a glimmer of red embedded in his aura. He reasoned that this course was the only way to save them both—a fail-safe of sorts. He struck a warlock etching, an outstretched hand holding a dagger surrounded by an octagonal shape.

Just then, a hollow sound slashed its way through the room and a sudden stillness fell. The remains were gone with nothing but a coal-gray burn in its place.

Elizabeth awoke before the others, and A'uun noticed that she had her faculties about her. She had grown quite powerful to be able to recover that quickly, A'uun thought.

The naked contivan placidly grabbed the robe that he was handed. His eyes looked bright with intelligence, but his body movements were slow and weary, which was normal. A'uun hoped what he raised was not evil. Moments from now, he thought, this golem might try to murder everyone.

The contivan wiped his dry mouth with his hand. He looked at his hand as if he had discovered something new. He beheld the rest of his body with the same look of discovery. A'uun had always empathized with how unsettling it would be to be born with the consciousness of an adult rather than a child.

A'uun watched his movements closely. He could not feel evil emanating from the golem. Cloister held a dish filled with water to the contivan's lips. He drank steadily until the dish was dry.

A'uun took a step closer to the contivan. The golem steadied himself as if he was about to experience a deep, contorted pain. The contivan's body convulsed and stretched outward. A'uun's eyes flared as he connected to the newly hewn being. He still felt uneasy about him, and he needed to be ready to strike him down if need be. The contivan's mind began filling rapidly with memories of the curate captured from the ether, tethered by the curate's essence.

After the transfer, A'uun severed his mental tie to the contivan with a mere thought. The contivan shuddered once more as the bridge between the two minds collapsed. A'uun hoped that the golem did not glimpse the darkness that was entwined to his life energy. A'uun had separated it from his consciousness as best he could for the time being, though he would have to devise a better way. He began brainstorming runic inscriptions that could stave off the darkness.

A'uun always severed his tie with contivans once they had gone through the process of gaining their basic knowledge. He disliked the fact that he had to force a particular consciousness onto the golem and that he did not have a choice. He reasoned to himself that the situation was dire enough to warrant it and that he would remove the curate's essence if the creature so desired, which was quite a risky undertaking for the both of them. However, A'uun still held a disdain for his compromise in principles, and he darkly pondered his actions.

This contivan was provided with the mental faculty to supplement the barrier, but it was still his decision as to whether he wanted to take up the mantle of the curate. In his mortal life, A'uun had acquired a vast wealth and had much to offer the contivan in return for his duties. A'uun proceeded to offer the contivan a home on his expanse of land in Kharr'kari and schooling beyond what he was provided in the mind bridge at the university located in his homeland.

The contivan agreed with a murmur. Though his body was somewhat disengaged at the moment, he had knowledge of the world and its workings. The newly hewn creature opened and closed his eyes often, filtering through the wealth of knowledge that was just passed to him.

The group disembarked once again for Aundyre after a quick detour to pick up several more of A'uun's creations from a neighboring island colony.

While in the air, A'uun and the group could see a large, uncontrolled throng of rumbling, feral demons, clawing and tearing at each other. The black mass of creatures was clearly cutting a path to the barrier. It was obvious to A'uun that they could hear and smell a weakness in the barrier's consistency.

Once the group landed, A'uun rushed to the barrier with the newly born contivan.

"What is your name?" A'uun inquired.

"Haran," the contivan said without emotion.

"You chose a Kharr'kari name. Why?"

"Part of your memories crossed in the transfer," he said. "I saw the reverence which you hold for your people. I saw the ingenuity in their architecture and their command over the resources of this earth. The Kharr'kari and the humans, from whom I am based, have much in common. I also saw how the Kharr'kari value the inner spirit and the spirit of the individual above all else. That is why I think Valese chose you as her herald." He glanced at A'uun. "You represent the values of why she shaped a world to be harnessed by the individual. Since I am not strictly human, in the natural sense, I chose a Kharr'kari name as something to aspire to."

A'uun nodded sentimentally, but a part of him still felt as though he had violated this creature's spirit—the same spirit that he so adamantly revered. A'uun, for the first time in centuries, felt like a hypocrite and wished events had not come to this. He wondered if he should have toiled with the formula of life in the first place. He had now perfected the creation of golems, but at what cost? His mind streamed to the past, to his earlier failures.

"Follow me, Haran," A'uun said as he walked to the barrier. "Energy fields exist in all places. All things around us give off energy. The energy that radiates from the star that lights our planet gives off a unique miasma, which staves off the engulfing cavities that appear and open up beyond our world into the far reaches of the stars. The energy that pulsates from all objects is an accumulation of what keeps this Celestial body we inhabit in alignment." He looked at Haran with intensity and studied his face for understanding. "More specifically, the energy fields created by these natural phenomena are what fuels the barrier and brings it life. It is also what fuels the spellcraft we wield."

A'uun reached out as if touching something invisible to the naked eye. The runic jewels encrusted upon his armor shone a bright orange. An energy field was exposed at the tip of his finger.

"This field is the form of the barrier—its shape, its essence, as it were." A'uun reached out again. This time, the jewel's light formed into a piercing red luminance. "This field is what gives the former its mass, its strength, so to speak. Barriers do not occur naturally on this world. You must bolster the red energy field so that the barrier has solvency. The curate's chamber in the manor will increase your power tenfold to aid you in this function.

"However, there is a catch. The chamber has a certain measure of sentience. It will figure out eventually that you are not fully human and jettison you as a foreign substance. You will not die from this, but you may have bought us time to name a new curate bloodline for the progeny and repair the Gargoylian chamber that supplements the barrier. As you can see, cracks are beginning to compromise the barrier's integrity." A'uun waved his hand. The runic stones on his gauntlets emitted a cuttingly bright, white cast, revealing gashes in the barrier.

It seemed to A'uun that the pieces of the jumbled-up information in Haran's brain were beginning to harmonize, forming into a melodic articulation of what was previously pushed into his mind.

"I understand," Haran said.

Upon entering the room of the curate, Haran took Erepus's place within the concentric circles at the epicenter of the chamber. From the doorway, A'uun watched the circles intently to see if his imperfect solution had worked. As the Nematraude left and the golem entered, the color of the circle shifted from white to blue. A'uun took solace in that for the slightest of moments, his compromise had worked. Erepus moaned in misery as he was helped out of the room by two progeny attendants.

A'uun nodded to Haran and said, "I will leave you to it."

A'uun trailed Erepus. He looked as though he was nearing death's door and was clinging to life solely for the purpose of restoring the progeny. The two attendants carefully laid Erepus down in a large bed of flowing white sheets. They closed the curtains attached to the frame of the bed so that Erepus could rest without the interruption of the beaming light that now engulfed the room.

"I say a grace for thee, Erepus," A'uun whispered.

Chapter 19
~ Bloodbrand the Wise ~

Cahan followed along as the group congregated in the energy chamber of the airship. The core's energy gathered and undulated wildly, as if it were reacting in unison to the emotions projected by the chamber's occupants. He sensed those emotions, too.

Lashes of blue energy snapped across the horizon of what looked like a miasma of gaseous clouds. At times, the energy would press up against the magically fabricated clear housing and cause a low rumble that rattled the chamber, then quickened and radiated into another color altogether, spiraling downward.

Cahan thought it was a sight to behold. However, no one else in the room seemed to be looking at the ebb and flow of the core. They sternly focused on one another.

Cloister looked to A'uun to start the procession. A'uun and Anaymous appeared to be lost in contemplation.

"At this point, we know that the Ministry of Information has had their hands in the past few days' events," Cahan began, deciding to ramp up the conference. "I say we infiltrate the MOI to see if we can figure out what they're planning."

Anaymous shook his head and ground his teeth. "If we storm the MOI, it will be over before we have even begun." Anaymous's expression changed to a look of concern.

"I know someone in the MOI," Cahan retorted. "For the most part, it will be safe."

"The first thing we must do is seek out Bloodbrand the Wise," Cloister interjected.

"The chief magistrate of the Protosian government?" Anaymous asked. "Why?"

"He will have resources and connections that will allow us to move about the city," Cloister stated matter-of-factly. "I also think it would be a good idea to seek his counsel. He did not earn his title out of inheritance," she added, knocking the former monarchy.

The airship cut a sharp path to the crystalline shores of Protos, just outside the unified districts. Many often journeyed to this area to take in the naturally occurring clindra rock that encrusted the coastland. During high tide, the sunlight beamed through the clindra outcroppings and reflected off the clear, cerulean water, creating a luminescent haze.

As the group made its way to the city, whispers of a magistrate assembly hearing fluttered among the discussions in the small shops and city thoroughfares in route. The focus of the hearing was Bloodbrand the Wise.

* * * *

Cloister pushed her way out of the double doors of the *Ye Old Weshire Cheese* pub. A green energy field surrounded her for a brief moment and dispersed as she cleansed herself of the cigar smell that saturated her clothing and hair.

She wanted to gather information about this so-called inquisition. The mere thought of it infuriated her. She briskly crossed the cobbled thoroughfare and joined the others on the corner of Abberville and Holly Springs.

The others looked at her with questioning glances—all except for Cahan. Cloister found him quite daft.

"Let us carry on, you lot of idlers," Cloister began as she ushered the others to make their way to the capital. "Bloodbrand is set to be the subject of an inquisition of disloyalty. Apparently, these 'disloyalty' charges rooted from an archaic law set forth by the Ministry to combat breaches of trust within the old monarchy."

"Ah, the Mullin accord…," A'uun said, trailing off.

"Yes, this law has led to many unjust executions in the bygone era," Cloister said, looking at Cahan and Anaymous. "Mullin was petty and rampantly wielded this law."

"What is the basis of the charge?" Anaymous asked, surveying the thoroughfare for guards.

"Bloodbrand the Wise is guilty, in the Ministry's eyes, of the unlawful abolishment of several branches of the old monarchy after relieving the deposed King Adar from his throne in the 'anti-monarchist' uprising," Cloister said.

"Did the monarchy not lose?" Anaymous asked. "How can those who lost now bring charges?"

"The Ministry of Information and the Seer Heritage contended that the chief magistrate is not divinely ordained to undertake such an act and that his actions were treasonous."

The cloaked Anaymous laughed loudly. "The Ministry thinks they are the arbiters of what Valese ordains?"

"Unfortunately for the chief magistrate, the Seer Heritage and the Ministry's ties ran far too deep in the grand restructuring from monarchy to republic to be annulled in one fell swoop," Cloister stated. "Instead, the Ministry continues to fester like a reanimated, rotting corpse waiting for its time to reclaim power." She turned to Cahan. "Cahan, you have stayed silent in this conversation. Your thoughts?"

"I wish Tharros had never selected Adar's house to reign. We wouldn't be in this mess if he hadn't."

"At the time, he had no reason to suspect that House N'dal was evil," Cloister said. "I am not defending Tharros in any way. In fact, I was also a detractor of his. Monarchies are inherently evil.

"The former king named the house of Adar N'dal to the throne because of their vast resources and long tradition of being a political family. No one knew that his homeland of Dunnavisch was full of such hatred. Adar's son, Vashar, was a decorated military leader, as well. He served in both the Protosian and Dunnavisch military forces, so Tharros thought it prudent to name someone whose respect extended to both the political and military realms. Unfortunately for Protos, Adar was merely feigning a belief of equal justice for all, to ascend the throne. Adar's rule allowed the whole of Shintallis to see the Marsh Fenthom for the maligned evil they truly are."

"Most monarchists name offspring as successors to the throne," Anaymous said. "Why did Tharros not name one of his own?"

"A large number of Fenthom males are born infertile, as was the case with Tharros, who had produced no offspring," Cloister said as the group continued for the capital.

"That is odd," Anaymous said. "There is generally good and bad in every race. Why is there no deviation with the dragons of the marsh? Were they not a Valesian creation?"

A'uun looked to Anaymous. "Yes, the Marsh Fenthom are a Valesian creation, but it is clear something has corrupted their bloodlines. I suspect Shabaris had something to do with it. His hatred for Valese and the Fenthom is well known."

"The evil of the marshes is also well known," Cloister pointed out. "While you were holed up in the Deserts of the Serene, you were shielded from the dragons of the marsh. They cannot stand desert climates."

"What did they do to gain such a reputation?" Anaymous asked.

"They were far worse than your organization ever was," Cloister said. "During Adar's rule, Marsh Fenthom often marched on cities abroad, burned them to the ground, and looted the citizenry blind. They earned the title of 'the Executioners of the South' during their many raids. Even the Incendiary syndicates within Protos steered clear of the dreaded Marsh Fenthom. Most of these creatures were of Adar's mind except, ironically enough, his daughter, Kasdeya. She was one of the few of the dark marshes that supported Tharros and how he governed the realms. Many conjectured she was of mixed blood, the product of one of Adar's many mistresses. Prior to Adar's reign, not much was known about them, save for Adar's well-known brood. It was as if they were waiting in the wings to gain power before they availed their true nature.

"Adar's first act as grand monarch was to execute Tharros, albeit secretly. The execution did not come to light until the siege of Valesia, the first target of Adar's occupation."

"Well, one thing you can say about Adar is that he unified the region," Ose stated nervously.

"You are right," Cloister said. "Together, Adar and Vashar extended the kingdom of Protos well beyond double of what it had been before."

"What made him so successful in that regard?" Ose asked.

"Adar would grant newly conquered 'districts' partial membership to the kingdom to start off, causing the districts to compete for full status rather than concocting revolts against the state. It was brilliant. It benefited districts a great deal to have full rights and status. Upon achieving full rights, a given district would receive committee representation and be allowed commerce privileges with neighboring districts. At the same time, Adar would line his pockets with the exorbitant district tax. This money went directly to his coffers."

"Adar must not have ruled for a long period of time, or else the Serene would have been affected," Anaymous said. "We knew of Adar, but never thought much of him. He was just another monarch."

"Adar's reign was relatively short lived compared to Tharros's 800-year reign," Cloister said. "An up-and-coming officer we all know as Bloodbrand Aldric led a revolt to remove Adar from his kingship. Bloodbrand's homeland in the high Valesian Mountains was one of the first areas conquered by the king, eight years prior. He was a fierce warrior on the battlefield and a brilliant military strategist. Many thought that had he led the fight against General Vashar, Valesia would have not fallen to the Protosians in the first place.

"Many called him the 'philosopher warrior.' Bloodbrand studied military strategy at university in Valesia, the city that stands at the foot of the Valesian Mountains. He felt that philosophy greatly increased his understanding of his enemies. It was because of this skill that during King Tharros's reign, Bloodbrand was often utilized for his ability to strategize and for his skill in peacekeeping negotiations.

"He studied the dragons of the marsh carefully. He knew how their minds worked and understood their reluctance to adapt in battle. He constantly changed his strategy and led his forces from the frontlines, rather than behind the battle like a king. He killed many of the marshes with clever ruses."

"Ruses?" Ose questioned.

"Yes, he became famous for them. Some suspected that these ruses amused him, but it is just how his mind works. Once, he had a smaller battalion engage Adar's troops, only to quickly retreat. When the Marsh Fenthom gave chase, a much larger battalion ambushed them. That day became known as the 'Dunnavisch Purge.' The enemy lost countless soldiers that day."

"How did the Magistrate Assembly come to pass?" Ose asked.

Cahan grumbled. "Do you really need to know that right now, Ose?"

"It is a long walk to the House of Elders," Cloister said. "We may as well speak of something constructive. The Kalriss are not current on Protosian history."

"It is very interesting, actually," Ose stated.

The rest of the Kalriss nodded in agreement.

"That was a good question, Ose," Cloister said. "Upon Adar's departure, Bloodbrand was named as the head counsel of the assembly that would establish a new government for Protos. Due to Tharros's death, Bloodbrand was the obvious choice. The first act of the assembly was to grant all districts full status or the ability to secede. Under this new government, no district chose to secede, though there were many trying times where districts considered it, due to their individual interests. Instead, each district immediately requested that they gain some of their identity back and rename their district after their original designations. Bloodbrand's home district was no longer District One—it was the District of Valesia. The other districts followed in kind.

"Bloodbrand and the council formed the Assembly of Magistrates, a group of non-military citizens voted from each of the eighteen districts of Protos. It was the assembly's charge to legislate, based on the interests of their constituency. It was also the decision of the council to create the position of head magistrate. The head magistrate would own the tie-breaking vote if the council were gridlocked in debate and would serve as the executor of the governmental body. The position was created only after much debate. Some in the assembly wanted to name another king. I remember Bloodbrand being emphatically opposed to this. Some of his greatest writings emerged from this debate. In an open letter to the Protosian Almanac, he wrote: 'We are free from the blood-stained bonds of entitled, despot kings. As long as a kingship exists in Protos, the individual is dead.'

"So Bloodbrand, being the clear favorite, at once forged his way into history and was elected into the office of chief magistrate. He eliminated most of what the corrupted Adar regime accrued during his scandalous reign.

"But as Bloodbrand grew in political stature, the Ministry broadened their base of power-corrupted, weak-minded politicians with bribes and threats. The Ministry wanted to reseat a king upon the throne—a king that would be their amiable servant.

"Bloodbrand often made statements that infuriated the Ministry. After receiving death threats in response to his first open letter, he wrote a follow up. Another noteworthy quote was, 'Freedom comes from neither mortals nor Celestials. It is innate, it is binding, and it is the only inviolable right born unto all sentient life from its inception.'

"Some would ask Chief Magistrate Bloodbrand why freedom is born unto all sentient life. He replied, 'It is innate because of one simple faculty—reason.'"

Chapter 20
~ The Inquisition of the Righteous Magistrate ~

Bloodbrand stood with determination and anger at a podium, not on a raised stage, but in a recess facing the grandstand in the magistrate assembly chamber, formerly the royal court. He kept his hatred of the MOI to himself as he observed the cortege of Ministry agents line the north and south walls amid foreboding stone pillars and black granite floors. The governing body of Protos occupied the right side of the court in a brindle wood inquisition box. The members of the MOI sat centered in the room on a grandstand of cold blue frost stone mined from the Permian Wilds of Forgatha. Bloodbrand gazed about the room from the podium. He clearly understood the MOI wanted to "lower" his gargantuan size to below their level. The political posturing never ended.

As Bloodbrand glanced around for familiar faces, he noticed that many citizens were in attendance, high up in a balcony overlooking the hearing. The citizens comprised not just a diverse mix of Protosians, but individuals from all districts, including humans from the island colony of Verinda. The Verindians held a special interest in the trial, as Bloodbrand had been pushing legislation to grant Verinda the right of districtship.

A movement in the balcony caught Bloodbrand's eye. He spied a cloaked A'uun slip into the tightly crowded area, just as the MOI agents in the grandstand rose.

One of the MOI ministers stood before a raised podium, making him slightly taller than Bloodbrand. The minister of the León'Velcrist district was a quasi-gelatinous thing. Most of the denizens of León'Velcrist were of this ghastly breed. Gill-like slits ran along the sides of its body, and its white robe with gold trim was tailored around it. Glowing subcutaneous ventricles shone phosphorescently through its viscid skin via its exposed arms, head, and hands. Its oval body shape and gaping mouth full of cartilage-like teeth were hideous.

Bloodbrand knew that the León'Velcrist district was wholly owned and subsidized by N'dal house during Adar's reign. This district swore allegiance to N'dal without bloodshed and was thusly given full citizenship to Protos, almost from the district's beginning. Due to its large size, it garnered more representation than the other districts, as well. It was said León'Velcrist representatives were part of a significant portion of the founding members of the MOI, and the entity was formed in league with Adar long before his reign during Tharros's kingship, under the guise of securing Protos' foreign and domestic interests. It was also said that it was because of the structure of the MOI that Adar was able to propel himself into power. Bloodbrand knew that the lot of them should be executed for treason, but the Justice House was still gathering evidence. He would be damned if he was going to behave like a monarchy and prosecute without evidence. That was the stuff of kings.

"This procession was called into order to examine the deeds—or misdeeds—of the chief magistrate, beginning with his rise to power." The creature lapped as his frothy mouth moved. "This court will also appraise the alleged illegal revolt against Monarch N'dal, led by the chief magistrate Bloodbrand Aldric of District One."

Bloodbrand cleared his throat. "Excuse me, Counsel, correction the District of Valesia is my homeland's rightful name. It is not the court's right to secularize something that was chosen by our forefathers and mothers." He looked up at the attendees of the hearing as they clapped loudly.

The counsel thundered his gavel against his block. The group's clapping receded after Bloodbrand raised his hand and encouraged the passionate group to allow the hearing to continue.

"We will also examine if the Articles of Natural Law, drafted by the 'chief magistrate' and the magistrate assembly, are legal and binding," the creature said.

The gelatinous form sauntered back to its seat and glopped down in a heap. The cortege of MOI agents kneeled as the lead counsel rose.

The lead counsel, a more fiercely repulsive gelatinous figure, began a vitriolic diatribe, abasing Bloodbrand in every conceivable way about a mission that happened decades before, back when Tharros was still grand monarch.

"On this mission, in the Veldt Territory, you unleashed two antediluvian monstrosities unto the Cordilleran Belt to lay waste to the village below," the lead counsel said. "Every living soul in the circumference of Veldt Mountain was slaughtered in the most ghastly fashion. Did you unleash these creatures purposefully by design? Probably not, but your carelessness led to the dismemberment of hundreds."

Bloodbrand remained unaffected by the minister's comments despite the knowledge that the villagers were slaughtered prior to his arrival and that an abstract sect of Gilpesh conjurors and a local human in the area had hailed the beasts forth.

The sharp vitriol of the lead counsel continued as his pustule-filled mouth parted threateningly. "Now let us examine the swaths of death Magnate Aldric bared upon the lands of Leon'Velcrist."

The minister's eyes gleamed with acidic overtones, and his wet, gelatinous lips smacked against his rubbery teeth until words formed in the green mucus that frothed in its gaping orifice.

"Does the grand magnate have any explanation as to why he tore asunder the lands and inhabitants of León'Velcrist during this supposed overthrow of a 'maligned' monarch?" The minister turned to Bloodbrand and stared at him, then refocused his attention to the council. "Was it merely war stratagem? Or was it a deep-seated hatred of the Velcristians? Our citizens were granted full citizenship to Protos magnanimously under the newly installed dynasty chosen by Monarch Tharros himself." He openly mocked and postulated down upon Bloodbrand before continuing. "I submit to you that Aldric, crestfallen in behest of this decision by the established government and body politic, seized the chance to take his aggressions on the innocent citizens of León'Velcrist. His crusade was not one of revolution or freedom. It was that of a creeping specter of death, bent on bloodshed." The minister stood abrasively with his attention back on Bloodbrand, pointing an accusing slimy digit in his direction.

"It is of the utmost importance that we banish this specter to eternally rot in the nether worldly auspices of decay," the lead counsel chortled.

Bloodbrand endured hours of testimony by supposed witnesses of heinous deeds he had committed. Time ticked endlessly away.

"The counsel rests," the lead counsel finally stated with a dramatic exhale.

Bloodbrand stood with an air of dignity and stern reverence. His hands were calmly folded atop the podium, and the fins on the sides of his head were flared neither in a dominant nor submissive fashion. With his head held high, he began. "The testimony you have just heard was that of a jumbled and hacked version of the events that transpired, bent and contorted to deliver vitriol and pure unabashed political posturing. To this, I will not respond. I will not respond to hopelessly inadequate thought. I will rely on your capability of abstraction to discern the reality of what actually came to pass."

The crowd applauded and bowed, which soon progressed into kneeling. Bloodbrand responded, "Do not kneel before me. Every manner of creature is sacred unto himself. Do not lower yourself so that you meet the unfounded whims of some despot or other irrelevance, or even someone of noble ambition. Only the dead mystics, barren of all reason, require such adoration bereft of mind and strength of body."

The crowd slowly rose.

"I did not always treat freedom with such a high level of importance," he continued. "After all, Tharros was a magnanimous and just leader. He did not tread heavily on our basic rights. It took a thoroughly corrupt autocrat for me to realize that power has to be balanced and weighed in favor of the citizenry, not a dynasty chosen singularly by one individual. For when you have an individual ruling, as opposed to governing, entities like the Ministry of Information can be created. Once such an entity is established, it is nearly impossible to repeal— especially if the entity has the support of the political organization known as the Seer Heritage."

A loud, crashing gavel rang out.

"This has nothing to do with the charges leveled against you, Chief Magistrate!" the lead counsel exclaimed. "You are simply trying to incite violence against the court. I will not stand by as you cast a grim shadow upon the Seer Heritage, an organization that has the good will of the districts!"

Bloodbrand glared directly at the chief counsel who was noticeably outraged at his bold implication that the Seer Heritage was a political organization, especially since the group represented themselves as a prophetic diocese of the Valesian Order. Guards rose to escort Bloodbrand from his recessed podium.

Bloodbrand focused in on the upper balcony just as A'uun cast aside his cloak. With a flash of blue-white light, A'uun transported himself to the lower floor, directly in front of the lead counsel. His eyes were filled with fury; lines of red flurried in his white pupils. His power and presence made the minister cower.

"You will let him continue," he said with a cold, echoing anger. A'uun's voice effortlessly filled the room in its deep, otherworldly baritone.

"You see, the chief magistrate wields the power of Celestial heralds to tread on our laws!" the chief counsel yelled. "Per scripture, heralds are not to countermand our written accords!"

"It is not necessary, noble one," Bloodbrand said to A'uun. "I have spoken of what I must."

A'uun glanced toward the satyr-like guards that were clutching at Bloodbrand's arms. They instantly dropped to the floor in slumber.

"The chief magistrate will retire to his manor," A'uun stated.

The viscid, jellied lump rose from his cowering position.

"Until a verdict can be reached, censure will be enacted on the chief magistrate. Therefore, all magistrate official duties will be vacated pending the outcome of this court."

* * * *

Cahan and the others were gathered in a large, open study in Bloodbrand's manor. The study had a loft area overhead, cluttered with books of war stratagem, ancient demons, philosophy, art, and music. Several unopened crates of non-canonical books, forbidden by the Seer Heritage, lay near the tall shelves of the library, waiting to be consumed by their owner. On a stand in the loft area, rested sheet music of Andreádé's nocturne of mourning, often referred to as the fall of virtue, near a proportionally sized violin, adequate for an individual large in stature, which stood upright on its stand.

Cahan was also familiar with the famous composer. Andreádé was one of the catalysts who sparked the creative fire of the enlightened age near the end of the Great Bygone Era. His music elegantly suggested the axioms of reason and free thought that Bloodbrand was known to hold sacred. This music, with its melodic overtures, passionate accelerandos, and oddly emotional cadences spoke to many and influenced Bloodbrand's academic studies.

The room itself was almost an extension of Andreádé's music. Cahan was fascinated by the regal curves of the architecture, which was of an ancient make, also from the Great Bygone Era. According to tradition, this home had been owned by Tharros for over a thousand years, and acquired by Bloodbrand after Tharros's untimely and "mysterious" death. The sturdy home was structurally reinforced with the nearly indestructible resilience of brindle wood, and the carpentry had vague undertones of exquisite organic Gargoylian artistry. The iron railing leading up to the loft had a gothic floral motif, punctuated by grand curvilinear forms. The rounded, oblong ceiling was comprised entirely of glass with square brindle wood seams continuing the motif of the railing. By the feel of this study, Cahan could tell it had been a place of creativity and intellectual respite for the gargantuan being that inhabited its halls.

"There is much to discuss, my friend," A'uun said calmly with his hand on Bloodbrand's shoulder. "Aside from the travesty we just witnessed at the hands of the MOI, a much darker scenario is festering beneath our noses."

A'uun explained to Bloodbrand the situation in its entirety and expressed the need for his assistance in their burgeoning revolution. He also explained Anaymous's intentions for peace and that he was in the process of attaining supplies for troops and citizens. Bloodbrand contemplated the grim circumstances that lay before him.

Chapter 21
~ Beneath the Remains ~

Agares's landship stopped short of a remote outpost in the Hydrian Desert, the southernmost desert in the barren lands of the Serene. Agares did not like traveling to this part of the map. The Hydrian Desert was known as the Unclaimed Lands, as it was generally patrolled by desert specters thirsting for life energy. Few knew how to ward off these creatures.

As Agares looked at his surroundings, he was reminded of Anaymous. It was in a place like this that he had sought asylum into Anaymous's organization. Agares had sworn allegiance to Anaymous at a young age, though he did not hail from Anaymous's lands.

The southern deserts were divided amongst three scions, which consisted of the White Moon, Naranth, and the Falarian deserts. Each desert housed a different tribe of the serene; Anaymous, Geryon, and Uvall, the scions of the south, ruled these deserts respectively.

Agares hailed from the Falarian Desert. He turned his back on Scion Uvall, who was responsible for the death of his father. He promised that one day, he would kill Uvall with his own hands. Agares had always questioned Uvall's ascension to scion, as he was nothing more than a displaced Forgathan. He was not born of the sands. Therefore he was not worthy to command those that were. Anaymous promised Agares's revenge, something he had not yet attained. He hoped to have Uvall's blood on his blade following the destruction of Protos's enemies.

This particular outpost Agares found himself in was allied with Anaymous's organization, dating back several decades. Melcholm, the leader of the Amalgam of the Hydrian Desert, was of the first of his kind to side with Anaymous and forsake the Amalgam Presidium. Melcholm fully realized Anaymous's potential as a leader straightaway, and they became fast allies. Anaymous had acquired much wealth and many resources in a relatively short amount of time, whereas

129

the Presidium was stagnant in growth, short on resources, and sapped its citizenry dry. The Presidium would routinely "acquire" much of the bounty Melcholm had amassed in their monthly raids—that was until he decided to ally himself with Anaymous's syndicate.

The building in which Melcholm resided had a bleak, gale scarred façade, indicative of underground Incendiary consortia. Its plain brown texture blended with the bristling sand storms that often surrounded the structure as a sort of camouflage. The building itself looked like a drab, cubic extension of the desert with a narrow rectangular door in front. It was common knowledge that this outpost was covered in cloaked runes to ward off desert specters. The runes did not have to be cloaked in order to work, but Melcholm did not want to give away his secret of how to ward off the creatures. He wanted no competition.

As Agares approached the door, a wave of sand cut across his path, blowing into his eyes and mouth. He shook the grit off his face and cautiously moved onward.

Agares put his hand on the spelled door, which freely opened to him. He crossed the threshold into the building and met familiar faces. Yet the faces seemed different somehow. They furtively gawked at Agares from the shabby table at which they sat.

"I seek Melcholm," Agares said. "Is he here?"

A large goat-like demon grunted and gestured to the back room. In its hand was a tooth, which accompanied a wooden game board. The demon snarled at the others and clutched its coin stack in front of him.

Agares found himself at a locked metal door. Embossed on the door were various ancient runes that formed into a spelled ingress. It was similar to the door that he passed through earlier, but he noticed it was far more fortified. A spellcrafted ingress was a means of keeping unwanted things from entering an enclosed area. It worked on the manipulation of sound. All objects gave off vibrations on their most basic level, which was an elementary principle of spellcraft. The ingress measured these vibrations against the occupier's preference of anyone who entered the room. The barrier near Aundyre also worked on a similar concept. If an unwanted or unworthy being should breech Melcholm's door in any way, even with a mere rap of the knuckles, an audible sound would call out specifically to him, giving him time to vacate through a hidden passageway. This door, though not tied to an energy barrier, was effective, nonetheless. Agares could hear the door's mechanical workings stirring within.

The spellcrafted door yielded to Agares and swiftly shut again behind him. Agares looked back at the now-blocked aperture and wondered what he had gotten himself into. Melcholm had never been so private as to even shut a door. He was loud, boisterous, and annoyingly accepting—even of humans.

As Agares found himself face-to-face with Melcholm, he methodically searched for the right words.

Melcholm approached Agares and grasped his forearm in a friendly embrace, dispelling the blatant tension in the room.

"Greetings to you, friend!" Melcholm drawled in his thick, whistling accent.

Melcholm was of Amalgam and Venerite descent. His large, incarnadine-tinted flat face was bisected by a wide, cracked viscous mouth, offset by large, bulbous, black eyes. Agares always thought of Melcholm as a deformed human. He looked as if someone had taken a human face and stretched it out like bread dough.

"I greet you with vigor, Agares, because allies are now few," Melcholm continued. "This part of your syndicate has almost been wholly consumed by a new organization—a nameless organization beholden to a nameless god."

"Is that why you have sealed your chamber?" Agares inquired.

"Were it not for the spellcrafted door, I would be murdered in the night by these creeping, furtive traitors." He paused for a moment. "Some here are still loyal, and I have managed to stockpile money and supplies. Yet more and more bow to the altar of this god they will not name. I fear I will have to leave soon."

"What would cause so many to betray Anaymous? What are they trading for? Allegiance? Money? What god do you speak of?"

"No, not just money, Agares—power! This nameless God and his disciples supposedly have influence in the Protosian government. They are offering representation, influence, and limitless riches. They are even offering Anaymous's Rynaut stronghold as a prize for loyalty. As for what god, my guess would be either something very new to Shintallis or something very, very old. Whatever, or whomever, this god is, it is very powerful."

Agares's mind was racing. He was afraid that Rynaut Keep would fall. The enemy was already offering it as some sort of prize for the traitors that had turned their backs on Anaymous.

"We need to gather the supplies and money you mentioned and depart for Partice. If Rynaut Keep is on the brink of being lost, I will also need warriors. Who is left?"

Chapter 22
~ The Ever-Divergent Paths ~

Cahan studied the serious expression on Cloister's face. He wondered exactly how old she was. Spellcrafters were often far older than they appeared to be. Many of them had perfected how to slow down the aging process over the centuries, and Cloister could be one of them. She could be 200 years old.

"You must let him know you have a contact in the MOI," Cloister whispered as she elbowed his ribs.

"It's not exactly an easy thing to explain, Cloister," Cahan whispered. "Protos doesn't know about her, and we're supposed to share information."

He took a brief moment to look around to ensure that no one had overheard their conversation. His eyes immediately went to the biggest creature in the room. The gargantuan Bloodbrand labored vigorously over his white, brindle wood architect's table. Spread out over half of the table was a map of Shintallis, while on the other half, Bloodbrand furiously scribbled notes on a fresh sheet of parchment. Anaymous peered curiously at Bloodbrand's work from behind. A'uun was in a trance-like state, murmuring words in a tongue he had not heard before. Cahan breathed a sigh of relief when he realized no one had heard his little outburst.

A'uun's eyelids split open from his trance, just before Bloodbrand rose from his desk to address the others.

"It is clear that the MOI is destabilizing the areas around Protos," Bloodbrand said. "They have wreaked havoc on trade routes and ports in the human colonies and have probably fostered alliances with the Amalgam Incendiary forces. I believe we must do our best to mend these riffs, where possible. A'uun and I will visit the Gargoyle Priory as a means to fully recondition the torn barrier."

Cahan turned to Bloodbrand and A'uun in preparation to speak.

Cloister gave him an encouraging shove. "You cannot hold back the information any longer," she whispered to Cahan.

"I know someone deep within the MOI," Cahan announced. "She's been secretly sabotaging the Ministry for the past ten years and passing information to Verinda. I think she can help us find out more about the MOI and their aims."

"Cloister will take you to the civil district," Bloodbrand commanded. "The pair of you will garner as much information as possible. I am sure Cloister can conjure some sort of disguise. Not many humans go in or near the Ministry's headquarters—so some sort of glamour will be necessary." He turned to Cahan after a pause. "For now, we will set aside the fact that Verinda did not share the fact that one of her agents is embedded within the MOI. This is something that should have been shared with the Protosian Assembly of Magistrates."

"I must return to Partíce and help Agares muster the supplies and warriors we need," Anaymous stated grimly. "My organization is likely under assault. If they have approached the Amalgam, then Rynaut Keep cannot be far behind."

* * * *

Bloodbrand instructed each group depart with one of his sea and land vessels from the hangar nestled in the mountain range behind his estate. Before Anaymous departed, he held up the Tablature Oaths before Bloodbrand, attesting to a treatise of peace from the tribes he commanded.

"This may not have meaning at the moment," Anaymous said, "but someday it will."

Bloodbrand looked at Anaymous earnestly. He felt the significance of this moment and hoped peace would someday be possible between Protos and the tribes of the Serene. "Keep it in your possession. One day you will present these oaths to me in the House of Magistrates."

Bloodbrand watched the land pass in a blur from the deck of his vessel and pondered on his vision of the future of Protos and her districts. Out of the corner of his eye, he could see the other vessels of his cohorts heading to their respective destinations. A scent jarred him out of his thoughts. He could smell the nearby forest and the creatures that lurked there in its borders. As the night sky began to overcome the dusk with a murky dimness, Bloodbrand grasped the railing on the deck with a quiet, focused anger. The Priory was just ahead. He took some solace in the fact that part of their problems could potentially be solved in a matter of days.

The Priory was contained within a hollowed mountain that housed a system of pathways leading to various parts of the municipality. Bloodbrand had studied maps of the Gargoyle's Priory and their native homeland of Ashwhend. His knowledge, however, was mostly academic. He looked forward to being among the proud race known as the arbiters of balance.

The Gargoyles were self-governed and not officially part of any kingdom or other republic, though they seemed to favor Verinda and Protos at times. They also traded with the nearby human colony, Weshire, just outside of the mountain.

Bloodbrand theorized that the Gargoyles were part of the first civilization, and that the birth of indigenous existence had begun with them and might well end with them. This theory seemed credible due to their advanced devices and construction techniques, which had been expertly honed over many generations. Their knowledge of the world and its secrets seemed eons ahead of every other known race born to Shintallis. The Gargoyles had extensively investigated the ruins of those not indigenous to Shintallis throughout the world, thus gaining the secrets of the so-called offworlders.

While at university, Bloodbrand conducted many interviews of various historical scholars. Many of these experts thought that the Celestial Valese in various times throughout history had walked among the Gargoyles and had even taken up residence in their native Ashwhend, and eventually the Priory. Some believed this notion to be heretical, as it would imply that Valese was a flesh-and-blood being.

Bloodbrand had requested extensive records on the Gargoyles and their elected leader that he had only just begun to examine. The elected leader of the Gargoyle government was Luttrel, the sage of Ashwhend, an ancient—and seemingly immortal—creature. According to Bloodbrand's archives, Luttrel was able to recollect the beginning of the Gargoyles and all manner of base creatures inhabiting the world, back when it had no name. In fact, most history books were based on the ancient Gargoyle's accounts. Though Bloodbrand was an admirer of Luttrel, he had always found this troubling. He preferred several corroborating accounts as opposed to the singular voice of one being.

One of Bloodbrand's most passionate pursuits was the history of early Shintallis. It was said that Luttrel knew a great deal about the dawning years and the encroachers from the infinite blackness that plagued this era. Due to Luttrel's knowledge of the distant past, it was widely believed among the human and demon populations that Gargoyles were immortal beings. Bloodbrand had read in the Gargoylian chronicles that Luttrel often dispelled this notion, stating that Gargoyles simply aged more slowly than humans and demons. They also had in their possession advanced medicines that could extend Gargoyle life on an almost eternal basis. However, Bloodbrand had a first-hand account that the Gargoyles had yet another method of retaining their youth, due to his access to Protosian governmental records. Gargoyles had developed mystical chambers that dramatically decreased the aging process that the general populace was not aware of. These chambers put Gargoyles in a dormant state for almost a century. Once a Gargoyle emerged from the chamber, the aging process was slowed tenfold. In addition to this, their physical healing capabilities were nearly unmatched, aside from possibly Bloodbrand's race.

According to an MOI codex, Bloodbrand had learned that Luttrel had two sisters of high stature in the Gargoylian commonwealth by the names of Blodwen and Amaranth.

Amaranth, the youngest of the line, was fond of humans. She often consulted the human colonies' governments. It was also well known that she had taken many human lovers over the centuries. Gargoyle females had soft, humanlike features, and it was not uncommon for them to become involved with Venerites or humans. Amaranth, like most of her kind, was a deeply sensual creature. Male Gargoyles were often more enamored with architecture or the invention of a new device to improve the livelihood of the commonwealth and their respective industry pursuits than their female counterparts. Male Gargoyles were not concerned by this because the human lifespan was fleeting by comparison.

By many accounts, both human and demon, Blodwen was known to be the polar opposite of her sister. She was a fierce warrior and served in the Gargoylian military. She led one of the biggest battles against the Gilpesh in the Great Bygone War. For almost six months after the war had ended, it was thought that she had perished in the battle, though her remains were never recovered. One day, she returned to the Priory with fragments of her memory. The one thing that she did remember was that she had been held captive and tortured by the Gilpesh.

Blodwen, like her brother, was ancient, though she did not look as though the years of her existence had affected her physical appearance. Blodwen was famous for being the first envoy to the Kharr'kari people, also an ancient founding race of Shintallis. She shared combat and military stratagem with the Kharr'kari, whose natural proclivity to combat took these skills to a new level. She mentored one Kharr'kari in particular above all others, who later became the leader of that nation. His name was A'uun.

Bloodbrand and A'uun arrived at the ashen, perfectly molded stone gate of the Priory, at the foot of the immense mountain the Gargoyle coteries inhabited, neighboring the human village of Weshire. Bloodbrand looked up at the sky. He heard the flapping wings of Gargoyle sentries overhead, who looked down upon them. Their eyes illumined their expressionless faces. One of them grabbed a crystal from a satchel tied to his waist. The crystal had an odd phosphorescent light emitting from it. Upon touching the shimmering object, the gates yawned to blackness, and a light gleamed in the distance.

Emerging from the blackness of the aperture strode the tall and gaunt Luttrel and the boldly provocative Amaranth. Both had their wings folded neatly behind them, and they looked exactly as they had been depicted in any history codex.

Bloodbrand could hardly believe that he was in the presence of a being whose accounts were the basis of most historical records. It was amazing to look upon a creature that had seen the dawning of Shintallis and had heard the Divine Anthem of Valese. The thought sent shivers down his spine.

Bloodbrand studied Luttrel, though he did not want to stare. His reddish skin stretched tightly over his sharp features, especially his cadaverous cheeks. His skull was somewhat elongated, with tiny spikes intermittently protruding outward, and his amber eyes appeared deeply intelligent. Luttrel wore a brown and white robe inscribed with runes in the customary heraldic embroidery of the Gargoyles. Despite his intimidating presence, Luttrel had an outwardly distinct, affable but wise energy about him.

A'uun nodded his head to the pair and headed inward to the Priory. Bloodbrand lingered for a moment in awe because neither he nor any other Fenthom had set foot within the Priory's limits.

A'uun also paused for a moment. "Welcome to the Gargoyle Commonwealth," he said.

"You stole the words from my lips, Lord A'uun," Luttrel said with a friendly smile.

"Bloodbrand the Wise, it is truly an honor. You have the respect of the Priory. Many here have followed both your military and political callings."

Bloodbrand felt astonished and bewildered. He had always thought of himself as a scholar of Gargoyles, not the other way around.

"Many of our citizens have read your written works," Luttrel praised him warmly. "Your philosophies are much like our own. You, however, have arrived at these ideals of your own accord. It is very impressive indeed."

Amaranth fully emerged from the hallway. Bloodbrand assumed she was allowing her brother to make the customary greetings before she joined them, and upon seeing her, he understood why. Her curvaceous hips and slim waistline were more than conspicuous in her form-fitting cool-blue dress. She donned a matching, finely woven tabard with heraldic embroidery over her shoulders. Her deep black hair was pulled back, which brought attention to her pleasingly symmetrical face and full, red lips. A barely perceptible glow shone from her light gray skin, as her thin tail moved back and forth seductively.

The group started toward the inner sanctum of the Priory.

"I assume you are here about the western barrier?" Luttrel asked.

"I am afraid so," A'uun confirmed grimly.

"Are you able to lend us the design schematics to repair the barrier?" Bloodbrand asked.

Luttrel looked as though he was about to answer until A'uun spoke.

"The architect who designed the barrier imprinted it to only respond to Gargoylekind and the Progeny."

"Why?"

"Because A'uun has far too much power at his beckoning, and power must be balanced at all costs," Blodwen said from a distance as she strode toward the group.

"Meet the architect of the barrier," A'uun said, smiling.

Blodwen acknowledged Bloodbrand as warmly as Luttrel. She shook his mammoth hand, which fully engulfed her own.

Bloodbrand looked to Luttrel. His forehead was crinkled, and he had the distinct look of apprehension etched on his face.

"I appreciate the heaviness of this matter, but as it stands now, we are in the midst of a civil war of sorts," Luttrel said. "An abstract sect of long-dead Gargoyles, or so we thought, has been laying siege to gain access to the Priory. Their numbers are great, which is unexpected. Even at their apex of power in the Great Bygone Era, they were a fairly minute force, negligible at best. We seem to be at somewhat of an impasse at the moment, as their activities have decreased, but we must remain heedful."

"I assume you are speaking of the Malefic?" Bloodbrand asked.

"Yes, how were you aware of that? This is a Gargoylian matter."

"There have been attacks engineered by the Malefic outside the Priory within the last few days," A'uun answered. "It would make sense that they would also destabilize the Gargoylian commonwealth."

"Destabilize?" Luttrel inquired.

"Correct," Bloodbrand said. "If the MOI is in league with some malevolent presence who wishes to overtake Protos and her neighbors, they would have to occupy the one group that could repair the crucial barrier separating the Forgathans from civilization."

* * * *

A'uun pondered what to say next. He wondered what he needed to do to convince Luttrel. There was silence for a few moments

"And we are following their manipulation to a fault," Amaranth said at last.

"So you're suggesting that Gargoyles are in league with the outside world?" Luttrel replied defensively. "Even for the Malefic, that is unprecedented."

"My unseating is the punctuation on this irreparably damaging crusade," Bloodbrand added. "It all fits together."

"I have heard of the attempted ouster of your command," Amaranth said. "If successful, dark times lay ahead for Protos and her districts."

Bloodbrand gave Amaranth a bleak, contemplative nod of agreement.

Luttrel turned to A'uun. "Any diversion of our forces may result in the loss of the Priory. Since the Malefic opened the catacombs, it has been a hard-fought battle."

"If A'uun and I assist you with this campaign, how many could you spare to fully repair the barrier?"

"A dozen or so?" Luttrel guessed.

A'uun grunted, as if to suggest that he alone could replace dozens of warriors. Luttrel smirked in response to A'uun's ego, despite his ascension to herald. "As fierce of a power you wield, Lord A'uun, you can still only be in one place at a time. In an open battlefield, you could replace entire battalions, but in the catacombs, that is a different story. There are countless, ghastly pits and baneful tunnels, shrouded with poisonous fumes, all of which are tightly spaced together like a hive. Not just the Malefic lurk its rigorous corridors," he continued in an advisory tone. "Base creatures that existed prior to all sentient life, said to be the children of the cosmic ones, infest the bowels of the mountain. We had them partitioned off until the Malefic intervened."

"I have already accounted for this, Luttrel," A'uun said in Luttrel's mind. "I am well aware of the creatures that inhabit this hollow, or have you forgotten?"

A'uun paused for a moment before speaking aloud and looked at Luttrel. "I assure you I do not speak out of turn or with over-boisterous egotism."

* * * *

It was curious to Bloodbrand that anyone would speak to A'uun as an equal because he was the herald of Valese. What was most intriguing was that A'uun did not seem to mind. It appeared as though Luttrel and A'uun shared a past that reached far beyond what was comprehensible to mere mortals. The knowledge between the two of them could fill volumes beyond imagination. Was it possible they were equals? The question echoed and faded in his mind, though he could scarcely envision such a thought.

"All right, I will send a complement of gifted architects," Luttrel acquiesced. "They are also fierce warriors. They will be missed on the battlefield."

"I wish to lead the repair of the barrier," Blodwen proclaimed. "I have some new ideas I wish to incorporate."

"Very well, then," Luttrel said with an odd hesitation. "You will select who will accompany you."

As they arrived at a central conference room near the smithies and the palace gate, Luttrel appeared troubled by Blodwen's decision to leave the Priory in such a time of need.

Although Bloodbrand was focused on the issue at hand, he felt a sense of wonderment about the inner workings of the Priory—it was a perfectly sculpted work of art. The system of tunnels leading to the metallurgy, residences, arcanums, and smithies were not just carved tunnels of earth. Rather, they were overlaid with molded stone slabs, smoothed to a luminescence, blanketing the Priory in a brilliant green. The Gargoyles were known for their molded stone process by which they melted large unrefined rock with a solvent they had cultivated over many years of experimentation. The final step of the process caused the material to harden into the smooth, even shape seen before them. No other civilization, human or demon, knew the solvent's properties, though others had attempted to develop it independently. The product of this duplication attempt unintentionally spawned the amber material, eluvium, which ended up not being a stone-working tool but a useful weapon in warfare.

The type of stone the Gargoyles used for these prodigious slabs were particularly amenable to their process. The chimera stone, as it was called, due to its diverse composition, was finished with a phosphorescent compound that allowed the Gargoyles to effortlessly move the several-ton monoliths when coupled with their energy staffs.

The staffs emitted radiant energy pulses, which made the stone seem as though it was as light as a bundle of wood. The phosphorescence in the stone also served as an ongoing and indefinite light source and could be brightened or dimmed with spellcraft. Gargoyles and spellcrafters alike were also able to change the color of the light with a thought. Certain color changes also meant that intruders were in their midst.

The walls and the foundation of the Priory were also lined with polished chimera stone and the occasional recess that contained stone murals depicting various events in Gargoylian history. Luttrel's founding of the Priory, the advent of metallurgy, and the development of arcanum workshops were among the prime murals of interest.

Bloodbrand studied these murals as best he could as they hastened through the halls. There were also depictions of the Gargoyles' previous homeland of the forested Ashwhend. Murals were a form of recordkeeping for the Gargoyles prior to the Great Bygone Era. During that time, the Gargoyles also developed a method to contain historical records within cylindrical pieces of crystal, which required a light-emitting cipher to view them. Gracian, owner of the first arcanum workshop, had developed the cipher.

As they neared the central artery of the Priory, Bloodbrand noticed several large arcanum workshops. He had studied what it meant to be an arcanist at university. However, the Gargoyles' knowledge in this area was unparalleled. Gargoyle arcanists enhanced weapons, masonry, and various other objects with special compounds. They refined various materials, which held powerful elements of spellcrafted energy, and then bonded the compound with an item that was to be enhanced. As Bloodbrand passed by Gracian's shop, he saw a large elemental spindle. At the center was a smooth, oval rock that lay on the ground, surrounded by a cubic metal structure made of cylinders.

Bloodbrand watched as the arcanist walked over to the cubic structure and placed several swords within. He then clutched the grip points on the outside of the cube. Immediately, the swords began to levitate, and the stone that was lying within the structure was set ablaze and began to float. Small particles channeled from the stone to each of the swords and orbited around the weapons. As the process went on, the swords began to smolder. This was not a process for a cheaply crafted weapon, Bloodbrand thought.

As the particles touched the surface of the sword, they were absorbed into the metal with concentric red markings. This told Bloodbrand that the arcanist was using ember borine to bond fire spellcraft to the weapon so its user could easily cast fire projectiles upon his enemy. Bloodbrand spied a curious substance he had only read about, pithitrine. Masonry blocks could be strengthened with this substance so they were nearly indestructible. Bloodbrand knew the Priory's chimera slabs had been reinforced with the rare ore.

As they moved past the arcanum, Bloodbrand saw a large brindle sign, *Ragnard's Metallurgies*. There were also various smithies on the east side, as well as tunnels that led to the decadent residences of the priories' denizens on the west side adjacent to the government palaces, which effectively sealed off the catacombs until recently.

In Ragnard's Smithy, a human, probably from Weshire, exchanged Gargoylian currency with one of the smiths for some swords. The Gargoyles would exchange their currency of gilt, a rare ore, between the workshops as payment for the completion of their weapons and building materials at various stages of development. These products were later sold to Protos, her districts, Weshire, and Verinda, the human colony. It was inspiring to see the process firsthand. Everyone was working in unison, but yet for their own personal interests.

"I think there is another underlying agenda to these attacks," Luttrel said to A'uun.

A'uun gestured to him to continue.

"Deep beneath the palaces lies a new, or rather, rediscovered, method of travel—the travel by which the Bridge and Time Celestials would sojourn effortlessly about the lands. We are just now beginning to understand its implications and the full scope of this forgotten bending of infinite blackness. It would seem that this particular fount was exclusively wielded by the Time Celestial, as it bears his crest. If this new discovery is forfeited to our aggressors, then needless to say, much will be lost. Imagine unyielding forces that can travel to any point in space instantaneously." For the first time, Luttrel looked bleak.

"Something tells me that we may also solve the mystery as to why the Bridge Celestial lost his ability to utilize his powers decades ago, and how Herald Mearain was killed at the hands of Shabaris," A'uun said. "Have you informed the Bridge Celestial of this discovery?"

"No, I have not. I will summon him as soon as we vanquish the Malefic. He does not like to involve himself in warfare."

Bloodbrand was familiar with Mearain—he was the herald of the Bridge Celestial. He was of Avaris descent, a broad winged, bird-like species believed to be relatives of the Gargoyle. He was also the first of his kind to be chosen as herald by a Celestial. No other herald had been recorded to have met death prior to, or after, Mearain. A'uun's commentary intrigued Bloodbrand. He did not know the Bridge Celestial had lost his powers.

"How did you not know about this chamber?" Bloodbrand asked. "You are as ancient as any being in Shintallis."

"Ancient?" he said with a smile. "I guess I am quite old, but not that old. The fount is far older than A'uun or me. I suspect this entire area used to be the domain of the Time Celestial. Perhaps this is why I felt as though this eldritch mountain called out to me just prior to our migration from Ashwhend."

"How does the fount work?" Bloodbrand asked after a moment's thought.

"I think this is something that has to be seen."

Chapter 23
~ The Veil Pulled Back, If Only Slightly ~

Cahan and Cloister arrived at the outskirts of the civil district, the Protosian legislative center, which was also the home of the MOI. Cahan gazed back at the sight of their land vessel. Plumes of smoke rose from the rusty corpse of metal. This landship was similar to the one that Cahan had acquired from the Protosians during his so-called defection. He thought to himself that its days were numbered. He hoped it would be able to make the journey back to the Priory, though he had doubts.

Cloister pushed Cahan behind the cover of a mammoth tree, whose trunk looked as though it were composed of fused cords branching outwardly with husky gray leaves. She studied him for a brief moment.

Cahan noticed that under her wild, curly hair and sarcastic exterior she was an attractive older woman.

He traced her frame and her soft, delicate, partially exposed shoulders with his eyes. Her lips were slightly dry, but full and seductive, nonetheless. She was thin, and her high cheekbones, sparsely located freckles, and ample bust rounded out her deeply feminine qualities. She wore a tan robe, similar to a wizard's robe, lined with cerulean heraldic embroidery that had obviously been tailored for a woman. She looked exceptionally beautiful without the aid of cosmetic dyes.

Cloister began to chant and flourish her staff in a counter-clockwise motion, creating an energy field that echoed and recoiled around her. In a flash, her face metamorphosed into the face of a frail Imbra demon. He was amazed to see a snout protruding out of her face and the overbite of triangular teeth covering a barely perceivable bottom jaw. Her skin was now an odd, ruddy color.

"Not much of a change," Cahan said with a grin. "Were you trying to conjure some sort of disguise?"

"Very funny, young man, but we both know what you were thinking just a moment ago."

142

Cahan was slightly embarrassed for a moment. "You read my mind?"

"Yes, but oddly enough, I could only skim the surface, and I did not like what I saw, anyway," she drawled with her pretentious accent. "Kind of murky in that noggin of yours."

"Well, just don't do it again." He touched Cloister's face in stunned curiosity. It felt human, not rough like leathery Imbra skin.

"I did not actually change physically," she said with a crooked smile. "Are you daft?" Her smile looked out of place on the face of an Imbra. "I simply changed your perception of my appearance." She jabbed her staff into the earth. "You and I will have to stay somewhat close to the staff. It is echoing an energy field that controls conscious thought."

"What type of demon do I get to be?"

"Wait a tick."

Cahan watched Cloister focus on her staff, which was still standing erect in the dirt. She temporarily dispelled the glamour creating the guise of an Imbra demon. The energy from the staff then poured upon him in a stream of white light. He heard snapping and hissing noises, as if trapped in a snake's coil. He wasn't sure if this was normal, but it was very uncomfortable. The light burned him every so often and it was difficult to see. Cloister's brow wrinkled, and her mouth was pinched tightly.

"So?"

"It did not work," she said. "That is odd."

"Did you do it right?"

Cloister looked at him as though that was the singularly most unintelligent comment he had ever made. "I have been able to craft this spell since I was but a wee yin. I do not think that it had anything to do with that spelled ink I sense grafted into your skin." She sighed for a moment and raised her head.

"I will try something else. The spell I am about to use does not last long and does not stand up to much scrutiny, so we will have to wait until the last possible moment to use it. I am going to bend the light around you, making you invisible, for the most part. We just need to test it first." Cloister seemed to be talking more to herself than to Cahan.

She drew her staff from the earth with a flourish—but the light around him didn't bend in any form or fashion. Cloister furrowed her brow, stroked her chin in contemplation, and muttered something underneath her breath. Previously invisible energy became visible in wisps of blue that began collecting in front of her. The collection of energy formed in an oddly shaped flaring ball, which slowly generated into a surreal globule of searing sparks. The sparks began to transmute into crackling embers.

"What are you doing?" Cahan said, nervous and eager.

143

The crackling embers formed into a purposeful circular pattern that gave way to a small flame. Cloister hurled the flame toward Cahan with a snap of her staff. The flame struck him and charred his skin about the arms and face.

"What's wrong with you?" he yelled. "Are you mad?"

"I needed to see if you were immune to all forms of spellcraft," she replied. "I can see now that you are not. Curious…" She trailed off.

"You know, you could've just asked me."

"Yes, I suppose so," she said. Her eyes narrowed. "What exactly are you, Cahan?"

"I don't follow."

"You speak in these odd abbreviations. For example, 'don't.' Who in Shintallis uses such gutter language?" She turned away from him, as if to help her think and carried on a conversation with herself. "You are immune to some magic, and you are ridiculously strong for a human. So again"—she turned back to Cahan and met his gaze—"What are you?"

"As for the 'odd abbreviations,' I'm from Silverstrine. You know, that tiny little island off the coast of Verinda? We use a little grammatical invention called contractions. I'm sure it will spread to this part of the world at some point, once you stop marrying your cousins and disposing of your shit by hurling it into the street."

"I am sure your 'invention' will spread like a festering disease," Cloister retorted. "It is as if you have taken base language and wiped it clean with a dirty rag." She paused. "What of this inhuman strength you possess?"

"I d-don't know where it comes from," Cahan stammered as he thought back to his weak "potions" argument with Bardon.

"You're…. Did I do that contraction thing right?" she said with a sarcastic smile. "You're lying, but that is fine. I am sure I will find out at some point."

"I'm," he said.

"What?"

"You said 'I am.' The contraction for that is 'I'm.'"

"Oh, sweet Valese. You are daft." Cloister reached inside her duffle, pulled out a cloak, and threw it at Cahan. She then respelled her Imbra glamour. "I guess this will have to do. You will have to stow that armor for now, and wear plain clothing. We do not want to draw the attention of the sanctum guards."

Cahan and Cloister arrived at a large, hoary building. Cahan knew the structure had been luxurious in times of antiquity, but its appearance was now marred by time and cruel demonic intentions. There were two idyllic pillars covered in plaster, as if covering some unseemly carvings on the corners of the cubic structure. Crumbling, muted white stairs led to a grandiose, Sylvanic door with tarnished gold circles for handles. Long ago Sylvanic doors were said to be portals that led to wish-granting forest spirits. Obviously this door was inert and likely purchased or stolen from an artifact merchant.

"I assume there will be some sort of violence involved when we enter this dreary thing that passes for a building, so be on your guard, creature," Cloister said.

"Creature?"

"Well, clearly, you are not human," she chortled.

"Let's just forget about your clear lack of tact for a moment and move to the part where, as I stated at the manor, I know someone here that we can talk to. We won't need to actually fight this time."

Cloister stopped and concentrated for a moment with her eyes closed. Cahan wondered what she was thinking. It troubled him that she might be close to unwinding his secret.

"Hello?" Cahan said, waving his hand in front of Cloister's face.

"I see. You have quite another form of aggression in mind." Her lips formed into a fiendish grin.

"What?"

Cahan chose to ignore Cloister's comment and led his traveling companion to the side of the decaying building to a stairway that led down to a subterranean doorway.

Cahan rapped his knuckles upon the nodule-ridden surface of the aged, rusted door. Moments later, a beautiful, pale-skinned firebrand answered the knock, a firebrand Cahan knew as Seara.

She carried a seductive air. The depth of her beauty belied her mixed heritage. She was half Venerite, a race closely related to human save for their unblinking eyes and dark temples. Venerites had one special gift that other races did not possess. They were not susceptible to any form of supernaturally fueled suggestion. They could see beyond the falseness of aphotic spellcraft. Venerites were often hired as negotiators of industry due to this special gift. Cahan realized Seara would see right through the façade Cloister was conjuring.

Seara led Cloister and Cahan down a long, narrow tunnel. The imbra glamour gradually flaked off of Cloister in flaring tufts of blackish-red energy that looked like simmering parchment at its edges.

"Who is this?" Seara demanded of Cahan with a tinge of jealousy.

"This is Elizabeth Cloister, known heretic," Cahan half-joked.

"The Witch of Weshire?" Seara said.

"One and the same. I often sacrifice Venerite women in my rituals," Cloister said mockingly. "You know, being a heretic and all—best to keep your distance."

"Now, ladies…"

"If you say 'don't fight over me,' I will slap you in the—"

Cahan turned to Seara, interrupting her. "Why are you always threatening to slap me in the face?" Cahan asked with a playful grin.

"Who said anything about the face?" Seara said warmly, her full lips returning his smile.

It felt good to flirt with Seara once more. It must have been dreadful for her being tethered to the ministries' inner workings.

"Immolate me now," Cloister muttered under her breath.

The group arrived in a large circular room of stone blocks. Cahan surveyed the room, looking for exit points. This was something that had become a habit over the years. Several tables rested diagonally with stacks of parchment neatly placed in the center of each table. He knew the neat stacks of paper were Seara's doing. She was always quite organized. A stone staircase coiled upward where a singular, Sylvanic door stood atop the higher imminence of the room.

"We need to find information on a particular insignia," Cloister stated curtly. "It is the mathematical sign of the infinite, but with one significant difference—it has two slashes through it."

"We also need to find out who the players are behind the MOI and exactly who this unnamed god they follow is," Cahan added.

"Can I speak to you a moment in private?" Seara said to Cahan. "Oh, and my name is Seara, by the way." Even though she was addressing Cloister in her last statement, her eyes remained glued on Cahan.

"I do not recall asking, but thank you for the extraneous information," Cloister quipped.

Seara grabbed Cahan by the hand and led him out of the circular area and upward through the coiling staircase, to reach the antique Sylvanic door. She placed her hand on the magically sealed door, and it yielded. The pair of them went down a narrow hall and to the right, to a private room she locked behind them once they entered.

"Have the fits of anger worsened?" Seara said as she stroked her hand against his arm.

"I wouldn't characterize them as fits anymore—more like blinding anger that results in bloody death," Cahan replied. His eyes followed his hand as he brushed hair from her face. He paused. "The lines are starting to blur."

"I can see a hollowness about you. You have to find a way to tell him. He has to strengthen the spell, or you'll be overtaken by it." She placed her hand over the one that rested on the side of her face, her eyes locked on his.

"I don't think he knows how at this point." Cahan returned her gaze unflinchingly, glad to be able to share his burden. "Can we focus on other things for now? I will do something about it, I promise." He drew her body closer to his.

"Okay, we can talk about other things, like the fact you still refuse to speak like the locals."

"It doesn't matter. They won't figure it out. You slipped up with Cloister. Don't you have to watch yourself, too?"

"You're right," she conceded. "It is difficult."

He slid his hands down her body, both hands coming to a rest on her hips. The olive-green fabric of her dress shifted between his fingers.

"I've missed you," Seara said in a soft tone as she embraced him.

Cahan pulled back slightly to look at her face. Her auburn hair flared outward like escaped bursts of flame from a burning hearth. The blue of her eyes bore wedges of cerulean light between locks of crimson. Every line that formed her full lips stood out expressively, as if all of her emotions were held around her mouth. He loved the femininity of her mouth punctuated by a slight gap between her front teeth. He never told her, but he thought the gap was adorable.

She pressed her lips against his in violent passion. Cahan grabbed her hips more firmly, causing her to groan with jubilant pain. She bit and pulled on his lip while she groped wildly for his clothing, pulling and tearing it off. When he was finally naked, she caught her breath and softly traced the outline of his chest.

She could clearly see his scale deformity but looked at it as if she had seen it hundreds of times. She pushed him down on the decadent davenport that sat ostentatiously in the middle of the room. She clutched his biceps tightly, pinning them back, kissing the scaled deformity to show him it did not matter to her.

Cahan shifted so that he was over her, and briskly relieved her of the rest of her clothing. The erotic lines of her naked body culminated in the epitome of feminine curves. The enticing fragrance of her skin filled his senses with a feeling of painful inebriation. She looked up at him with desire. He saw it in every line of her lips as her mouth formed into a sultry, anguished smile. He craved her soft skin in an unyielding, animalistic way and could not help himself as he passionately bit the flesh of her neck.

It was difficult for him, however, to be fully in the moment. He kept thinking of his cohorts in the back of his mind. Were they dying at the hands of the enemy while he enjoyed the company of this beautiful woman?

He continued to think he should stop and join Cloister, but Seara wrapped her legs around him, ending those thoughts. Cloister could wait.

Cahan could not help but look at how beautiful she was. He wanted to be inside of her, to extinguish the malevolence for just a moment. It was as if her Venerite side, the side that was impervious to the supernatural, extended out and quashed the anger within him. He just wanted the anger to stop for a while. He'd earned the right to be selfish for a few moments.

As he entered her, the contours of her face grew tense, holding down a feeling so intimate that it was not the sum of only one feeling. It was a feeling as indeterminate as the very definition of love. After a time, a feeling that could no longer be held within was borne upon the speckled translucent rays pouring across her angelic face in a moment of pure exultation. A climax beckoned forth across the whole of her body. Pulsating aftershocks permeated through to her core. Her release was a glimpse of beauty to him, a glimpse of her soul, a physical manifestation of happiness.

Silent moments lingered and lapsed. Thoughts gathered and dispersed. As the dampness of her brow moved away from his, a cold chill was left in its wake. Their lips parted, and her eyes suddenly looked distant, knowing that another life was beyond the threshold of that door. He thought of the disparate lives they led, and the critical state they found themselves in. The oneness of their interlinked bodies became two separate entities, drifting away in a form, just out of grasp— a painful reminder of the mediocrity by comparison that lay in wait just beyond—a mediocrity that was held as normalcy.

Chapter 24
~ The Dwellers ~

Anaymous paced the halls of his final stronghold, Rynaut Keep, which was on the brink of falling to the MOI'S agents, as the others had. A battle waged overhead, and combustion shocked the seams of the bunker they occupied. The thundering sounds of artillery fire jolted long-dead memories. He remembered back to his coup of the previous scion of the White Moon desert, Dasa.

The malicious Scion Dasa and his two sons, Ipos and Ipes, were pure evil. Dasa the Skinner, as he was called, would have decadent dinners among his peasants. If anyone committed a grievous act, such as coughing at an inappropriate time, he would fillet the wrongdoer of his or her skin. The following day, the surviving family members would receive the eyeballs and skin of the victim in an elaborate gift box.

Anaymous shifted his focus to Agares. He had just arrived from the Amalgam stronghold with the supplies and demons, narrowly escaping MOI agents at the base of their former allies. Agares looked at Anaymous with hesitation in his eyes.

"There are many things that can go awry with this plan of yours, Anaymous. Those creatures are unpredictable. Do you remember what happened last time?" Patches of earth fell from above as he spoke.

"Fault can be found with any campaign, but no battle is ever won without risk. It is not needless risk we take, Agares." Anaymous chose his next words carefully. "The Amalgam are holed up in a bunker in our lands. We can use this to our advantage. We know this realm better than the half-breeds,"

Anaymous reviewed the plan in his mind.

Agares looked down at a crystal in the palm of his hand. It briefly lit up with an orange radiance. "They are here, Anaymous," he said grimly.

Anaymous walked into an open room of hunching, earthen-toned beasts. The creatures shambled about the room, chests out, outward-arching tusks on full display. The creatures stared at each other noiselessly at regular intervals, and their black, oval eyes twitched back and forth in concert. This practice had always struck Anaymous as odd and made him feel uneasy every time he had witnessed it. These beasts were earth dwellers; at least, that was what most called them. Formerly slaves in the bygone era, at the hands of the MOI, the earth dwellers were used in large construction projects for their ability to burrow deep within the otherwise impenetrable layers of strata. The dwellers were responsible for creating the underground waterways that lay beneath Protos and Verinda.

Anaymous knew the dwellers had no written or spoken form of language. They were thought to communicate through a sort of telepathy, though the published works Anaymous had read were purely speculative and circumstantial. He made it a point to understand everyone with whom he did business, unlike Dasa, who preferred to bend everyone to his barbarous will.

Most Protosian studies concluded the earth dwellers would have to communicate in some way because of their highly synchronized and orchestrated digs. Rarely did earth dwellers cause any type of cave-in, unless it was by design.

From what Anaymous had learned, the dwellers' tusks had two uses: sensory and tunneling. Their long, shovel-shaped claws also assisted in penetrating the earth. Their long cylindrical bodies and their muscular, squat legs made it easier to squirm about beneath the surface, as well.

He clapped loudly to get the attention of the dwellers. Curiously, they had begun to focus on him before Anaymous's loud thundering clap sounded, which made him think the creatures were telepathic, or at least keenly sensitive.

Anaymous held a rolled-up map of the enemies' bunker location in his claw. He tapped the piece of rolled parchment against his palm with a nervous rapidity. He wondered how he would convey the location to the dwellers, as he had never tasked them in an undertaking like this before.

Searching the creatures' faces for any form of understanding, he unrolled the map and held it up before them. One of the larger dwellers shambled toward Anaymous. He studied the dweller as it moved with its peculiar gait. He had always thought that the creatures seemed unnatural when trying to move above ground.

As the dweller gazed up at him, Anaymous somehow knew the creatures understood. The telepathic conversation was two-way, as if the creature opened a door into his mind. Anaymous wondered if this form of communication could be used with demons other than dwellers. A vibration reverberated in his consciousness that answered his question. Any fluent demon could open the way to dweller speak, though it took some practice and a sharp mind. He also gathered humans could use this form of telepathy, but they could not open the way to it like demons could. This was all conveyed to Anaymous in mere seconds. The efficiency stunned him.

Anaymous signaled Agares to lead the dwellers to a tunnel where they could dig. Again, the dwellers accepted Anaymous's cue, and began to walk toward the door before Agares had taken a step.

Agares trotted behind the dwellers to a long, carved tunnel sparsely lit by illumine orbs. Once at the location, the dwellers plunged their claws into the earth, and in a moment, they disappeared into their domain. Grunts, digging noises, and groans echoed in the chamber.

Anaymous turned away from the tunnel and thought of his enemy and in particular the leader of his enemy. Like most Amalgam, their leader, Nerigaál, had oddly layered, peach-colored skin that resembled patchwork on a quilt, that is, if the quilt were composed of various patches of flesh. His face lacked, for the most part, any type of contour. It was peculiarly flat and slightly raised where his nose slits rested. His eyes were unleveled and misshapen, and the right eye socket was set slightly above the other. Both triangular sockets contained a damp, bulging yellow eye. The creature had a largely pronounced overbite of needle-like teeth, which infringed upon his speech.

Nerigaál wore scale armor composed of green lazren hide, reptiles indigenous to the Dunnavisch Estuary. His commanding corps and lieutenants also wore armor similar to his. Amalgam, for the most part, had to stay away from dragon-forged armor because it created an allergic reaction. Anaymous knew that Nerigaál was impatient, but also quick to react to dire situations. He pondered if Nerigaál would be susceptible to what lay ahead. Only time would tell.

* * * *

Nerigaál set base camp in an older part of Anaymous's stronghold from a time when Anaymous had a cause against the larger civilization, but was essentially too destitute to do anything about it. In that time, the Amalgam Presidium did not even view him as a threat, even though he had overthrown Dasa the Skinner. Nerigaál always wondered why this was the case. He had warned the Presidium directly how dangerous the up-and-coming scion was, but they did not pay attention until he brought Melcholm Moloch into his syndicate, something that greatly affected their flow of currency.

Nerigaál understood the history attached to this place. This area also served as an escape route in Anaymous's earlier days, from various factions of royal constables. He often tangled with the constables because he could not afford to bribe them. All that was long ago, and his enemy, the scion of the desert, was formidable these days and would resort to anything to win.

Nerigaál called a meeting of his lieutenants within an impromptu bunker that rested deep beneath the sand. Nerigaál felt vexed as he blustered at his lieutenants, who were collected in a semicircle around him. He had been expecting reinforcements from Dunnavisch Estuary long ago. Something seemed dreadfully amiss to him.

"Throngs from Dunnavisch should be here by now," he said. "Something is wrong. Has the Presidium been fully consumed, or do they leave us here to die?"

Nerigaál tried to steady himself as a deep, jarring rumble pervaded the makeshift bunker. Cracks in the earth projected upward, hurling earth violently in the rectangular space. A maddening wisp of ethereal utterances filled the bunker with an evil chill, filling Nerigaál with fright. He searched the bunker as mucus-like fluid seeped from his eyes—often caused when emotion overtook him.

"Wraiths," one of Nerigaál's lieutenants shouted.

"Cover your ears. Hearing their words will drive you mad," Nerigaál yelled over the unintelligible speech and loud seismic bustle.

As the ground shook, Nerigaál signaled his lieutenants to follow him and vacate the bunker. As he and the others approached the exit, a hideous wraith availed itself to the Amalgam.

Nerigaál could smell the wretched scent of carrion. The wraith had a putrid, yellowish tinge about it. Its face of rotting flesh appeared to shift in and out of reality, as if straddling the lines of the physical and the immaterial. When he looked into the creature's eyes, it was almost as if he was looking through a window into the distant grotesque plain of ghastly influence that some referred to as the bowels of Úul—a deep, black expanse of nothingness with spewing volcanic peaks in the distance. Glimmering pathways of red stretched out like bolts of lightning, and tortured screams rang out in the distance.

As the wraith emerged, it collected the madness of its world and unleashed its venomous reality upon Nerigaál's lieutenants. Nerigaál eyed the wraith's soiled garments as they changed from moment to moment, from different muted, macabre hues.

He froze in terror, and mucus poured from his eyes. He wiped the fluid on his sleeve, drew his sword, and swung violently at the wraith. Grasping the sword handle tightly, he continued to swing until he heard a snap. It felt as if he had broken one of his fingers because of his death grip on the sword. He gasped once he figured out the sword had no effect on the spectral wraith before him.

Turning, Nerigaál saw he had struck down and killed one of his lieutenants in his blind panic. The room turned cold and silent, so silent that he heard his slain lieutenant's blood dripping from his sword.

He turned to face the corpse-like presence, though it was the last thing he wanted to do. An outstretched, contorted hand appeared before him, phasing and shifting with swirling lines of gray and black.

The long fingers of the creature elongated even more and penetrated Nerigaál's pupils, twisting and turning its fingers inside his eye sockets. An erratic bone-cracking sound echoed into the space as its fingers grew. Nerigaál's teeth chattered in unison with the wraith's cracking bones. He did not know which was more terrifying—the painful movement of the wraith in his eye sockets or that he could still see. If he had to endure this, he could at least be blind. It was as if the wraith allowed him to see through spellcraft to add to the torture. He sensed this wraith had tortured many in the ghastly pits of Úul.

Through the eyes of one of his lieutenants, Nerigaál spied two other gaseous, phasing wraiths appear before him. He wondered why the wraiths were so bent on torturing him with these visions—then he realized it was to break his will. The wraiths wanted to control his body, and he had to be broken for them to achieve their aims.

For a split second, the wraiths ceased their constant phasing. Their hideous pink skin sprouted countless, impish eyes. Each eye focused on his lieutenants.

Nerigaál felt the unyielding pull of the wraiths as he gazed into the hypnotic eyes of the foul creatures. Black energy radiated from them, and the clutching darkness they gave off surrounded the lieutenants and pulled at their limbs, creeping hauntingly across their bodies. Strings of black tugged at their eyelids, mouths, and hair. The split second the tormenting wraiths remained corporeal seemed like an eternity to Nerigaál. He wanted desperately to give himself over. It was time. It was time to leave.

The wraiths' cavernous mouths opened. Rows of tiny pointed teeth sprouted up, encircled by bubbling white mucus. One of the wraiths lunged forward and enveloped the head of Lieutenant Deumus in its gaping mouth. Muffled screams sounded. Nerigaál wondered if he, or Lieutenant Beleth, the demon in whose consciousness he was trapped, was next. What would it feel like to be eaten? Through the extra senses Nerigaál had gained from the spellcraft, he heard and felt the crunching of the lieutenant's skull as the wraith consumed and digested him. He sensed the pointed teeth of the wraith extend deep into Deumus's head, as the Amalgam's limbs swung violently before falling limp to a suffocating death. Nerigaál looked at Deumus's hand. It would flutter every so often as he was being eaten.

Rage filled Nerigaál's consciousness. "Take me. Go ahead and take my body. I have nothing left—."

The other wraiths began digesting the remaining Amalgam, not only in a physical sense. Nerigaál knew that the wraiths destroyed their very existence.

There was a hollowness in the room. Memories tore their way from the minds of those who had crossed paths with his lieutenants, even across time. The memories somehow remained with him. Nerigaál supposed it was because the wraith was taking complete control of him and that he was shielded from the effect.

A tormenting darkness invaded his mind and he beheld Úul in all of its horror. Countless phasing wraiths festered in cavernous pits, intermittently lit by shades of orange and red. Energy beings of yellow continuously tried to escape their wraith captors. A snap followed by a silence erupted in Nerigaál's mind. The vision ended.

A dim emptiness brushed over him, his mouth gaped unnaturally as he traipsed out of the bunker to reach the battlefield. Nerigaál felt the slightest kernel of himself within the body, now owned by the wraith.

He still had his thoughts, but his senses were intensified. Every sound echoed with harshness. He heard a faint grunting in the distance, but knew that wraiths did not grunt. What was that noise?

He sensed the gripping darkness that cascaded from the wraiths in the network of catacombs below. Shrieking, humming, and disquieting vibrations trailed the creatures. He felt as though they were all staring at him through the spectral shadows. It sounded as if there were hundreds of them infesting the earth. He knew that the clay in these parts repelled them. How had this happened? He had not prepared for wraiths because he thought it impossible to be attacked by them here. He would have deployed wraith callers had he known. Again, a collection of grunts sounded, followed by claws scratching against clay. His mind sparked with the answer—dwellers also infested the earth. The dwellers must have bored the tunnels for the hideous wraiths, he thought.

Nerigaál felt as though he were fading. The tiny sliver of himself within the recess of the wraith's domain was dissolving into blackness. He felt the demonic mind of the wraith pulsating, pushing, and mocking. Its echoing screams were maddening, but it didn't matter—he only existed in a forgotten space of what used to be his mind.

Nerigaál remained an unwilling passenger as he finally surfaced to meet the ensuing battle. He stared at the commanding officers held up behind reinforced enclosures, out of harm's way. Seeing the world through the prism of a wraith was drastically different. He could see all of the energy that surrounded his officers—energy that appeared in speckles of white, silver, red, and orange. As his body drew near, the energy turned black. Some energy was absorbed while other speckles fluttered to the ground and disintegrated. He saw poltergeists stalk his men from the shadows. Demonic energy whirled in wisps of yellow. At that moment, he realized that he had never truly seen the world for what it was. Upon his unexpected arrival, he was met with the distressed faces of his trusted leaders.

"Magnate, why have you left your bunker?" the commander asked anxiously. "This battle is far from won." As he spoke, yellow, demonic energy passed in and out of his mouth. Silver speckles circulated around his body like swarming insects.

Nerigaál knew what the wraith wanted to do. He wanted to order his soldiers to leave this forsaken place of malady. The more he yearned to warn them, the more he felt as though he would fade away.

"If the Presidium hears of this, there will be a full inquiry as to why you were at risk," another commander suggested in frightened tones. Orange speckles enveloped the commander.

"That is why I am here, commanders." Nerigaál tried desperately to stop his mouth from moving. The echoes of the wraith grew louder than before. "I have received word that the Presidium has ordered our withdrawal," the wraith stated as the maddening whispers continued to cycle through his mind.

"This battle is within reach, Magnate."

"This is the decision of our Presidium. You will not question direct commands!" Nerigaál said with a wince of pain as the wraiths whispers became an unnatural, ghoulish shrieking. Amidst the voices, Nerigaál mustered every last bit of his consciousness. For a moment, the whispering and shrieking receded.

One of the commanders lit a nearby pyre, signaling retreat.

"Stop!" Nerigaál spat. Blood and mucus bubbled from his mouth and nose slits.

One of the commanders snapped to the sound of Nerigaál's plea. Nerigaál felt the warmth of the retreat pyre touch his face. He ground his teeth and bit his lip as he strained to move closer. The commander gazed with horror as Nerigaál drew near. He approached Nerigaál and looked into his eyes, widening Nerigaál's eyelids with his fingers. Nerigaál strained against the wraith to hold still so that the soldier could discover his secret. The hideous whispers permeated Nerigaál's mind once more, and the sounds of shrieking and chattering teeth echoed in his head. Nerigaál's arms groped wildly at the air around him as blood and mucus poured from his mouth, eyes, and nose slits.

The commander took two hesitant paces backward.

"Nerigaál has been bedeviled by wraiths," the commander said. "Rally the soldiers back to battle!"

Nerigaál, overtaken by the wraiths, produced a small blade from his belt and ripped open the commander's throat with a decisive swipe as the shrieking of the wraiths in his mind turned to loud contorting screams. Nerigaál stomped on the commander's face repeatedly until it was a bloody mass. The surviving commander had his lips upon the horn that re-summoned the Amalgam warriors to battle. The wraith clutched his weapon tightly as he spun the Amalgam commander around and plunged the blade deep into his spinal cord. The commander's body fell limp, but not before getting a brief horn blast off. Nerigaál sliced violently at the fallen commander's corpse until its skin was covered with bloody gashes.

Nerigaál looked on at the battlefield as the Amalgam soldiers seemed confused by the recanting of the withdrawal. The wraith shrieked through him as Anaymous's forces took full advantage of the confusion and crushed the Amalgam throngs, quickly dwindling their numbers.

Chapter 25
~ Woe to the Fallen ~

Anaymous stoically grasped his wrists behind his back as he surveyed the destruction before him. He contemplated the implications of this battle and the scope of what was happening in Protos. Anaymous felt battle-worn beyond what most could endure. He thought of what was at stake as far as his own interests.

Anaymous's plan was not to simply forsake the life of an Incendiary. It was also to cultivate the magical properties inherent in his desert realm. He knew that he could easily sell a compound that could repel wraiths on the open Protosian market. If he was able to help Protos overcome her enemies, he would become wealthy with the sale of his wraith compound.

Anaymous turned to the door when he heard frantic knocking. Anaymous opened the door to a frightened human sentry.

"Anaymous, the wraiths took one of the dwellers, probably bedeviled the creature. Some of them have returned. They are howling and clawing at everything in their path. They are forcing their thoughts..." he trailed off, horrified by what the dwellers must have forced into his mind.

"Sit down. Gather your senses, boy."

The sentry sat down and drew a deep breath. He expelled the air from his lungs forcefully, still shaking.

"We should have never commissioned the wraiths, sire."

"It would appear Count Raum's control of the wraiths is greatly exaggerated. He should not commission what he cannot command. Tell Agares to reach out to Raum. We may need him to track these things down."

The sentry drew in a few more frightened gasps of air.

"Where are the dwellers now?" Anaymous asked.

"Bunker Two," the sentry murmured.

Anaymous dashed toward the bunker with insect-like speed.

Upon entering the room of raging earth dwellers, their thoughts all at once poured into his mind, echoing in his skull. Anaymous let out a deep, guttural snarl that echoed in the room. The beasts snapped to attention.

A singular thought reigned into his mind—an acute intelligence was present. He felt the reverberations of the dwellers' mind, and he instantaneously understood. The dwellers not only feared for their compatriot, but also feared for the lands of Shintallis at large. If wraiths could travel underground at their choosing, even through the stretches that repelled them, they could feasibly destroy civilization at its core and eradicate the existence of whomever or whatever they wished.

The dweller suggested hunting down this group of wraiths before they gathered their numbers. Anaymous's thoughts flashed to the wraith compound that his colony manufactured. The dweller and Anaymous understood synchronously that it would be needed in their quest. Anaymous walked into the adjacent room that housed some of his troops.

"Gather all the troops we can spare for an away mission," he said. "We will also need large quantities of the wraith compound."

Chapter 26
~ The Beasts of Old ~

Cahan made his way down the long, brick-lined hall back to Cloister. He heard papers rustling in the distance. He looked back at Seara for the briefest of moments. Although she was not looking at him, he could tell she was still thinking about what had just happened by a slight smile upon her lips.

When Cahan and Seara arrived in the room, he saw Cloister riffling through various pieces of parchment at an inhuman speed. Piles upon piles of documents were stacked and strewn around her. Cloister shifted her attention to one stack in particular. She returned the parchment to its leather-bound encasement, which had militaristic Verindian symbols engraved on it. Cloister carefully placed the files in her satchel.

"Now that you are done with your depravity, would you care to find out what I have learned?" she asked in a matter-of-fact tone without looking at the pair.

Cahan stared at Cloister, thinking he should make some excuse or feign ignorance to her comment. He abandoned the notion and laughed aloud. Seara looked at Cahan with a small, embarrassed smile.

"The symbol of the infinite is not new," Cloister said. "The symbol itself originated from the ancient Lagios. It was from his writings that mathematics was born. Not to bore you with a history lesson—"

"We're aware, Cloister," Cahan interrupted. "He discovered the Time Celestial, and he and the other ancients were at odds with the mystics of that period. It was the era of reason versus mysticism."

"I was not sure whether or not you would need a refresher with all of the blood rushing out of your head—and into another one—for the past half-hour. Now that you have regained your faculties, shall we continue? There are more important things going on than having it off."

The pair nodded.

159

"You are correct, Cahan," Cloister said. "Lagios discovered an unknown Celestial through some cryptic perspicacity, through which he was acutely attuned. In other words, he could perceive the Celestial and received messages of mathematic knowledge from it. Thus, the concept of the infinite was born. According to the history codex, recorded by the MOI, a cult bent on unlocking the powers of the Time Celestial adopted the symbol and added two slashes through it. They believed that they could destroy the Time Celestial and attain his powers."

"What could possibly kill a Celestial, and where is this cult?"

"To answer the first part of your question, I do not know. To the second, a small sect of the cult inhabited the Veldt Mountains nearly eighty years ago. They were slain by a joint military mission between Protos and Dunnavisch Estuary, led by one Commander Bloodbrand Aldric."

* * * *

Bloodbrand and several Gargoylian sentries stood before the howling mouth of the heavily guarded catacombs, deep within the eldritch reaches of the Priory. A'uun lingered a good distance behind them, seemingly meditating. Bloodbrand looked on at the contivans that A'uun had summoned from their island refuge and noticed they were still, void of all expression. They looked like standing corpses. As Bloodbrand gazed into the abyss, he heard the insane laughter and heinous, blustering screams of the creatures that lurked in the hollow.

"We may need additional support. I was not expecting... so many," A'uun said as he opened his eyes.

The group went silent for a moment, expecting A'uun to say something else. Just as Bloodbrand was about to speak, an array of white particles charged downward and blanketed the space before the group. In its center, a phantasmal display of light swirled until something familiar began to form in the luminous center. Specter-like humanoid shapes stood, heads bowed, in four lines of three. The faces of the figures became clear to Bloodbrand, although they were made of light. An annular shaped florescence brushed softly at the apex of the spectacle and gave off burning trickles of a silver liquid. The forms began to outline the suggestion of flesh and bone until each was fully formed into corporeal, sentient life.

The beings that stood before Bloodbrand and the others were more contivans. These golems did not look as though they had taken up residence in an island refuge. They looked as if they had lived sheltered lives. They were pale and red-eyed, but shared the same secretive aspect of the island golems.

"These are my research assistants," A'uun said. "They are also gifted in spellcraft."

Bloodbrand was a bit taken back by the display. As he heard A'uun rattle off the names of each contivan, he considered the implications of the herald's powers. It was as if he were a Celestial and not the herald of one. He could summon a large number of beings deep within a mountain without a single utterance, incantation, or flourishing of his scythe. Thus, Bloodbrand fully realized the godlike power A'uun wielded. No other herald could equal the feat he had just witnessed.

An echo reverberated in Bloodbrand's mind. A'uun's consciousness was present. He asked Bloodbrand to lead the siege on which they embarked, pointing out it was his place as chief magistrate to lead. Bloodbrand sensed A'uun held a great deal of respect for the sovereignty of a nation and of one's self. He believed those tied to the Celestial augury, as he was, should not countermand the authority of naturally selected leadership.

After laying out a general plan, Bloodbrand signaled the Gargoyle sentries to follow A'uun, and the contivans to follow him. Each group took a different lane of the forking path in front of them inside the catacombs.

Long lines of decayed, furrowed pathways looped together in a complex labyrinth. Bloodbrand was amazed to see a purposeful system of walkways. This would suggest that, at one time, intelligent life shaped these horrifying edifices. As they moved closer to the center area of the walkways, a large corpse of a city lay entrenched between two deeply carved, barren ravines.

* * * *

A'uun walked through the pathways and by the decadently sculpted structures, feeling a keen familiarity. The musty smell of the hollow triggered an array of distant but fiercely lucid memories. His mind raced with images from the past, when these disturbing networks were filled with the reptilian dogmatists of the Antediluvian.

One of the "deities" was a grim amphibious creature, from which A'uun had forged his armor. The despotic amphibian had wielded its power thoughtlessly over the former denizens of this hollow. They always had their cave creatures in tow, baying and lapping. A'uun's mind shifted to a memory of walking down a thoroughfare such as this, with glassy-eyed heretics hissing down at him and screeching profanities. A refrain of "false herald" rang out from their balconies.

Before him lay the antediluvian monstrosity, menacing and bellowing, while it brandished its tentacles and glared balefully with its countless toad-like eyes. The core of the beast was an oval mass comprised of rubbery, noduled yellow skin, with thinly veiled, illumined blue strands swimming beneath the surface.

As the onyx metal-clad A'uun drew closer, the creature grew enraged. Iridescent clouds of cobalt stirred beneath its semi-transparent skin and rose to the surface in the shape of blue, prismatic rings that radiated outward. The creature turned cobalt after the anger-driven metamorphosis. A'uun stared, amazed that it had survived the great purge of the arcane dragons. Maybe the arcane beasts had not destroyed the encroachers fully. Maybe they had merely driven them off-world, only to return.

A'uun abruptly shifted to a Gilpesh named Mandra, a wizard whose fate was tied to the encroachers and his. A'uun had been many things in his long life—a warrior, a brigand, an architect of war machines, designer of weaponry, a leader of his people, and even a prolific painter—but he had most enjoyed his role of precept. A'uun did not take on that role until later in life after countless bloody disputes and dark times.

The Gilpesh and the Kharr'kari were warring tribes locked in a blood feud since the dawning years of recorded history. A'uun had been at the center of this feud since it began. The hostility came of nothing more than philosophical and theological differences among the ancient clans. Each clan commanded a fierce power and used it against the other.

The Gilpesh were wizards and witches of an ancient order, the first order. The Kharr'kari were fierce warriors steeped in the Gargoyle traditions of combat. The denizens of the Gilpesh Thaumaturgy were the sons and daughters of the great evil, Shabaris, creator of the living continent Forgatha. These pewter-toned menaces brought dark magic and conjuring to the masses. They learned their spellcraft and conjurations from the writings of the devils of old—the encroachers that had inhabited Shintallis before it was so named.

Gaunt, thin, and frail-looking with dual-pointed ears, these enchanters were often overlooked or underestimated, save for the Kharr'kari tribes. It was often said the Gilpesh were a powerful evil shrouded in false frailty.

The Kharr'kari were a people apparently akin to Venerites, aside from their much larger stature. They possessed a natural resistance to magic and gained unnatural strength from a dangerously lethal energy only they had the fortitude to survive, called the Rite of Strength. Their strength, coupled with their resistance to spellcraft, allowed them to defeat the Gilpesh time and time again, until a Gilpesh wizard of note appeared.

A'uun's eternal enemy, Mandra, was considered a vastly gifted prodigy by his people for good reason. He devised ways to overcome the Kharr'kari resistance to spellcraft by infusing weapons with the pure magic of the encroachers of antiquity, magic that was not watered down by the ages or by inaccurate translations of their antiqued tomes. He possessed an uncommon gift. He could commune with the dead and the fiends of ancient lore, reaching beyond unfathomed ages to a time when these creatures still haunted and festered in their dark towers, the time of the fiend Kneaar' and his morning star-wielding hunters known as "the Blood Legion."

Origin: The Nameless Celestial

In the age before the indigenous creatures of Shintallis gestated in the swirling vortex and Valese's divine anthem, otherworldly creatures inhabited the lands. They harvested minerals and ore for their homelands, deep in the infinite darkness. Each fiend constructed a black tower, similar to modern-day energy spires, from which they drew their arcane spellcraft. The Blood Legion was the enforcers of the seven slave nations, and its members served as vile taskmasters, ensuring that the lower-caste creatures, brought from their homeland, remained obedient. In those days, two warring factions were constantly at battle: the fiends, masters of the Blood Legion, and the antediluvian deities of old. In the modern era, the factions had been lumped together, simply referred to as "the encroachers." However, both meant to usurp the newly hewn world, and at the end of the conflict, there was a clear victor until the supreme Celestial interceded and her arcane dragons purged the faction left standing from the lands.

Both factions, prior to their undoing, had erected archaic temples. Some contained their secrets of mysticism and science. After many ages passed, the Gargoyles of Ashwhend, the ever-ebullient adventurers, often excavated these ruins and would eventually base their spellcraft, in part, from the ancient tomes and the inscribed sepulchers that lay hidden within.

As a youth of just fifteen fathoms, Mandra, the young prodigy, would often breach the ruins, which were under Gargoyle control, in pursuit of his antiquarian interests. It was on those unhallowed grounds that he first discovered his gift to communicate with the spirit world.

At first, the young wizard feared the spirits that haunted him. Then, after a time, he began his long tutelage under their guidance and eventually swore many dark oaths. As he made each oath, a fleck of green appeared in his irises until his eyes appeared wholly emerald. His own people dubbed him "the Emerald Abomination." After taking his vows, a runic branding of each fiend's crest appeared on his skin.

Mandra rose in power quickly, far surpassing his teachers and the other masters of his community. Even with all the power he amassed, he hungered for still more as had the dark, evil Shabaris that had risen before him. He sought the opposing faction of the antediluvian spirits to gain their secrets. For a time he was able to deceive both sides. Mandra founded religious sects in the names of each faction, and diabolically kept them at odds.

Once the opposing spirits learned of Mandra's misdeeds, they began to torture him and slowly stripped away his powers. While searching for a solution to retain his powers, he came upon an ancient tome that detailed the spellcraft of possession located deep in a newly discovered ruin. Through this magic, many disciplines of spellcraft were born. However, Mandra's prime focus was on the root spell. That did not stop him from creating the genocidal spellcraft responsible for the deaths of thousands of Kharr'kari. With this rediscovered knowledge, Mandra created energy staffs, master stones, and portals to different parts of the world to ambush his enemies and many other cleverly diabolical ways to kill. A'uun knew of these spellcrafted inventions well because he had lost his father to them.

Mandra soon realized this spellcraft could help him evade the archaic horrors that pursued him so fervently. At first, he possessed others in his community. Each time he possessed a new body, the spirits would leave him alone, unable to find him for a time. Mandra soon realized he needed a stronger body to wield the spellcraft needed to stave off their respective attacks permanently.

On the sixty-first day of the second epoch, Mandra created his greatest conjuration. He devised a way to alter the spell found in the ruin and possess the resistant Kharr'kari warriors in a ritual similar to the Kharr'kari Rite of Strength ceremony. Possessing a Kharr'kari would have the effect of wielding both physical strength and spellcraft in tandem. He would be able to sustain his new spellcraft for long periods of time—long enough to steal the spirits' remaining power and extinguish them for good.

The newly augmented spellcraft of possession was in its early stages of development. Mandra was the only Gilpesh strong enough at that time to perform it. Determined and impatient, Mandra wanted to use his creation immediately. His target would be A'uun, who had just attained the title of Kharr'kari sovereign.

The Kharr'kari Rite of Strength ceremonies were held the sixty-fifth day of the second epoch, only a few agonizing days away. Mandra had disguised himself through spellcraft to look like his enemy so that he could infiltrate the territory of Kharr'kari proper. In theory, Mandra would be able to use the energy of the Rite of Strength ceremony to perform the possession, and he knew A'uun would be in attendance, as it was customary for sovereigns to attend Rites of Strength ceremonies. Siphoning power from a powerful existing spell was an old wizard's trick that Mandra utilized very well. This served him in two ways: he would be able to use less of his own power, and be able to link into the only spellcraft that affected resilient Kharr'kari warriors.

* * * *

A Rite of Strength ceremony was a magnificent and elaborate display of the Kharr'kari people. A'uun had always held the celebration of the soon-to-be-venerated Kharr'kari warrior in high regard. Tournaments were held of both the Kharr'kari hand-to-hand combat art called Pan'craish, which incorporated joint manipulation techniques in tandem with punching and kicking, as well as their art of sword wielding.

The Kharr'karian art of sword wielding was founded on principles similar to spellcraft. It developed using the techniques Gargoyles attempted to teach the Kharr'kari when they discovered the proud warriors could not wield spellcraft in the traditional sense.

The Kharr'kari adapted what they learned from the Gargoyles and applied it to their combat. A long-held axiom of spellcraft stated that all objects gave off an innate vibration on a basic level, as if a string were snapped and never ceased its movements. This yielded a unique energy. This energy would fluctuate constantly, based on motion. The Kharr'kari had an unrivaled ability to sense these vibrations and anticipate their opponent's next move based on the tonal differences emanating from their body in motion. To the Kharr'kari, a sword battle was a sophisticated and strategic orchestral symphony of tones and cadence, cunningly discerned by its practitioners.

Crafty wizards and well-practiced Kharr'kari had the ability to mask or manipulate the vibrations for brief periods of time, thus shrouding their true tactics. Only the keenest of minds could survive a swordfight with a Kharr'kari. The Kharr'kari became so adept at this skill that a high-ranking warrior in the Kharr'karian Army, named Har'rayition, created Pan'craish, which emphasized close quarters combat.

Har'rayition had noticed that while in close quarters, it was difficult to get a reading on tonal vibrations. He spent many years developing grappling and joint manipulation techniques for this purpose. A'uun was an early adopter of this fighting style and excelled in it naturally.

During this particular ceremony, two Pan'craish experts faced off in a harrowing battle that became legend. A student named Ty'dest faced his master, Ker'yon. After hours of grueling combat, Ty'dest defeated him. The resounding crack of Ker'yon's arm breaking decided the battle. The epic fight became so engrained in Kharr'kari culture that the finishing move Ty'dest Kyo'ke utilized was renamed "Kyo'ke'" after the victor. Before every Rite of Strength ceremony began, participants performed a brief reenactment of the final moments of that fight accompanied by music and all the pageantry of such a celebration.

Once the battle of Ty'dest and Ker'yon ended, the Rite of Strength ceremony began. A pale-yellow energy portal, tied to a master stone in Mandra's laboratory, formed in circles beneath the wizard. Mandra shielded the energy signature with his magic, hiding it from the keen senses of the Kharr'kari warriors. He conjured the portal so his body would safely transfer back to the Gilpesh homeland after the possession. Once the elaborate display of energy from the ceremony spooled to a climax, Mandra performed his spellcraft. With clocklike precision, the newly inducted Kharr'kari warrior received his strength infusion, and Mandra's consciousness transferred to A'uun. His former body fell through the portal, back to his homeland, where it was most likely preserved.

No one was the wiser, aside from A'uun trapped inside the wizard's consciousness. He was an observer of all of Mandra's misdeeds. He even had access to the legendary spellcrafter's past. Over time, he learned many little known secrets of spellcraft, as Mandra wore the guise of A'uun.

Mandra ruled as the Kharr'kari sovereign for decades, allowing his countrymen to survive and thrive. The Kharr'kari were deeply dissatisfied with what they thought was A'uun's new governing doctrine. As years passed, Mandra's deception had one unforeseen side effect. A'uun's body began to take on the features of his possessor. His skin pigment changed, and his ears achieved the conspicuous dual point of the Gilpesh, though he still retained the muscular Kharr'kari physique. One of the more easily hidden features left A'uun capable of wielding spellcraft, a feat no other Kharr'kari could do.

Once the ruse was discovered, Luttrel of Ashwhend helped the Kharr'kari expel Mandra from A'uun's body, which earned him the title of "The Sage of Ashwhend." Much damage was done in the name of A'uun, but word had spread about the possession, and through time, much was forgiven.

A'uun retained Mandra's powers by design. Luttrel had intimated to A'uun that if he was able to leave Mandra's spellcraft and the part of his consciousness that contained the breadth of his arcane knowledge inside him, the wizard would not be able to return his consciousness to this body and would, perhaps, fade into the ether of nonexistence. By doing so, Luttrel created an abnormally powered being. A'uun had the brutal strength of a Kharr'kari and the wizardly know-how of a potent Gilpesh conjuror. Blodwen of the Gargoyles, A'uun's former combat teacher, was one of the chief objectors to this unnatural union of powers. She was doubly outraged when A'uun was gifted with even more power as the Supreme Celestial's herald. Valese had her own reason behind A'uun's selection, the motive of which the radiant Celestial would bring to light in time.

Chapter 27
~ The Lungs of the Beast ~

Cahan searched his mind for answers. He was not particularly shocked by the implications of Bloodbrand's involvement in the Veldt mission, often referred to as "the Veldt Massacre." This was mentioned in his inquisition by that gelatinous lump of a counselor. He did find it striking that Dunnavisch was involved. It was obviously before the dragons of the south had become so reviled.

That party also contained one other notable figure. Vashar N'dal. The former king's son's involvement piqued Cahan's interest. As he started to probe further, he heard echoing footsteps in the hallway.

"Take everything you need," Seara said. "Our time is now short."

Cahan haphazardly stuffed pieces of parchment into his and Cloister's bag. Cahan came across the Verindian-branded encasement. He paused for a moment and considered. He wanted to take a peek inside. What could Cloister possibly want with a Verindian military record? His paranoid mind continued churning.

"Hurry," Cloister demanded.

Cloister's scathing voice pulled Cahan away from his rampant thoughts. He gathered the rest of the documents and placed them in the duffle.

Seara led Cloister and Cahan into the adjacent hallway from a hidden side door. Seara grabbed Cahan by the back of the neck and kissed him softly. Cahan brushed his hand against her cheek.

"Take this hall all the way down, where there is an exit northward," Seara said. "Be cautious. There are inquisition rooms south of the exit." She paused solemnly. "Goodbye, Cahan."

"I'll see you soon," he said with a reverent sincerity.

"I know."

Cloister and Cahan started down the hallway. Cloister flourished her staff. Charged energy surrounded her and blurred, rendering her virtually invisible.

"Got any tricks for me?" Cahan asked.

"Actually, no. Shall we be off, then?"

Cahan made it to the end of the hallway. Doors leading to the outside world stood before him. He heard the faint footsteps of Cloister trailing closely behind. He was about to reach for the door when he heard the inquisition room door across from the exit swing clumsily open. Cold air filtered out of the room. In his bones, Cahan felt there was something wrong. He turned and heard a familiar breathing pattern. He had become especially sensitive to this since his affliction began to change him physically. Cahan had learned that everyone had their own specific pattern, and this one was glaringly obvious to him.

Cloister forcefully pushed Cahan's shoulders down so he would assume a kneeling position and pressed her body against him, concealing as much of him to the naked eye as possible. Cahan knew Cloister's invisibility was merely a distortion of the energy around her, not true invisibility, so standing in front of an object would render it wholly shrouded.

Cahan heard another familiar breathing pattern and then two voices. He stretched his neck slightly away from Cloister's bosom to see Declan and Bardon stridently conversing just prior to the door's closure.

A ghoulish demon ambled out of the room and leered in the direction of Cloister and Cahan, its black pupils dilated as its squeamish-looking face tensed up. After a moment, the creature pressed on. Bardon and Declan poked their heads out of the room to see what the demon was leering at before they returned to their argument. Cloister stood up, still cloaked and blocking Cahan from Declan and Bardon's fields of vision.

"Did you enjoy that?" she whispered sarcastically.

Cahan felt hollow and sickly until anger began to course through his heaving chest.

"What is wrong?" she demanded sharply.

Cahan started for the room. The dark malevolence stirred in his mind as though his entire body shook with adrenalin-fueled rage. He thought of nothing more than squeezing the life from both of them. His teeth ground together as he considered killing them and staring upon their lifeless bodies with satisfaction.

"No," Cloister whispered fiercely. She erected a sound barrier.

The door behind Cahan swung open as Cloister pushed a wave of air toward him, sweeping him outside. He crashed noiselessly against the wall behind him. Cahan's head was swimming. When he looked up, he saw her disapproving face. Her eyebrows furrowed. With a wave of her hand, the door closed behind them. The pair found themselves in a system of alleyways far from the main thoroughfares. Cloister continued to push Cahan away from the MOI with her spellcraft.

Once they were safely away, Cloister spirited toward Cahan in a flash of inhuman quickness. Green energy flooded from her eyes as she shoved him with a magical zeal, knocking him on his ass. Cahan stood up. Red anger filled every fiber of his being.

"Have you grown mad?" she yelled.

Cahan started for the MOI building once again. Cloister reached out with her spellcraft. Branches of blue energy clutched Cahan's arms and legs, holding him in check. He struggled angrily. The energy felt hot and cold at once, and twisted around his arms, cutting off his circulation.

"Look at yourself," Cloister commanded as a cluster of energy appeared before his face and shot his reflection back at him.

His red eyes resembled the color of a scheming fire nymph. His bloody bottom lip came from the pressure of his teeth.

"I served with both of those men," Cahan interjected.

"They're fuckin' traitors."

Cloister raised her hand, and a blue mass of energy, equal parts cold and warm, surrounded Cahan's head. It calmed him. Eyes half closed, he took deep breaths. His anger began to recede. Now that the malevolence had faded somewhat, his mind churned with implications.

"Why did Declan try to cast doubt on Bardon during our mission if they were both working for the Ministry?" Cahan demanded.

"One of the chief rules of deception is to not do anything outside of character," Cloister replied. "Would it have been curious to you if he were not suspicious of a new member of your company?"

Cahan did not answer. Being deceived raised a different kind of anger. He continued ranting about the two men and heatedly informed Cloister about Bardon's possible betrayal in Veldt.

"Listen, Cahan," she interrupted. "We have to get back to Bloodbrand and report our findings. We will sort this out when we can. There are greater things at stake here. We must not focus on irrelevant distractions."

"Irrelevant?" He bristled.

"For now, yes, it is irrelevant. Now we have to focus on the social and political uprising of the MOI and its attacks. You know I am right, Cahan."

Cahan's anger waned. "Let's get to the Priory," he conceded dejectedly.

Chapter 28
~ The Bloody Catacombs ~

Bloodbrand studied the underground city. It had several mysteriously constructed buildings, which were not made from brindle wood or any building stone he recognized. They appeared as an extension of the catacombs themselves as if some unknown race had wielded the acid rains that formed the caves into hauntingly precise structures of calcite. Inside the buildings, Bloodbrand spied a subtle remaining impression of life in the form of pottery, art, and decayed furniture. He wondered if this was the stronghold of Gargoyles prior to their settling in the Priory. It did not seem at all like anything of Gargoyle make. It seemed far older and looked alien to his eyes.

The golems followed Bloodbrand listlessly. They were furtive, vagrant things with chillingly dim expressions. Bloodbrand thought it odd these golems, or contivans, as A'uun called them, had no interest in these cryptic ruins. He thought they might be the first of the outside world to view these arcane remains, which likely dated back to before the Great Bygone Era.

Bloodbrand set his academic curiosity aside for the time being. He could now smell the base creatures that Luttrel spoke of, though they were a great distance off. An ambush was in order.

* * * *

A'uun's attention came sharply to the present. He could sense the Malefic just ahead.

"Lord A'uun, I hope I am not speaking out of turn," a Gargoyle sentry said.

"Go on."

"Would it not be possible for you to transfer our enemies somewhere else, as you did with the golem creatures?"

A'uun gave the sentry a genuine grin and clapped him on the shoulder. The Gargoyle sentries appeared somewhat bewildered by his reaction. They had probably never seen a Celestial herald act so friendly.

"The Malefic are far too clever for that. They guard themselves against such spellcraft. Besides, the conditions needed for such a feat are hard to duplicate outside of my laboratory."

A'uun felt energized by his interaction with the Gargoyles, chiefly from the standpoint of the exchange of knowledge. He very much enjoyed the role of teacher.

"Our foes are just ahead," A'uun continued in a serious tone. "Mind your anger and think clearly."

The group emerged from an ancient, sculpted tunnel. Just below them, a sharp precipice tapered off and led to another tunnel. A'uun studied a large oval mouth of calcite that lay agape to dark silence. A'uun figured that the Malefic must have sensed their presence at this point, because the resonance of their energy was softened down to a grim lull.

Suddenly, a chorus of writhing agony rung out from some unknown source and cut through the dankness. The sound was familiar to A'uun, though he could not quite place it. Mixed within the chorus was a single sinister snarl.

A'uun walked to the sheer edge of the precipice and looked down. He touched the smooth cobalt rune on his left gauntlet above his wrist. It morphed into a deep sapphire hue, which travelled to and engulfed his palm. A'uun clenched his fist tightly and formed the energy into a malleable state. He silently commanded the others to hold their positions.

He knelt down, placed his glowing palm on the vertical rock formation, and leapt downward. The blue energy gripped the rock wall tightly, allowing A'uun to descend quietly to the small valley below.

Once A'uun touched down in the crag-pitted vale, he pressed the runic stone on his gauntlet again, returning it to cold, cobalt blue and tapped another rune on his living armor, affixed to his triceps area. A dull, muted energy surrounded him for a brief moment before it vanished with a nearly soundless timbre. A'uun calmly walked to the far side of the canyon-like area to reach the yawning mouth of the cave.

He looked up at the Gargoyle sentries. One of the Gargoyle sentries, Renu, watched him intently. A'uun could hear them, even from this distance.

Renu turned to his brother, Draven. "I cannot hear even the slightest of sounds coming from Herald A'uun," Renu whispered.

"We could use him in the stealth games on Shroud Mountain." Draven chuckled.

A'uun tapped the runic stone on the side of his wrist and at once the Gargoyles were silenced, unable to speak. A'uun sent a message to them through dweller speak, telling them to remain still.

He made his approach to the opening, still concealed from sight, just to the side of the tunnel's mouth. He placed his hand on the smooth calcite surface. A dull flicker of light in the runic stone in his hand pulsated, causing the calcite to move to his will like fresh clay that moved of its own volition.

A small opening parted so that A'uun could peer through. His eyes began to adjust to the darkness, which meant that the red lines in his white pupils were rising to the surface and branching outward beyond his onyx-colored sclera and around his eye sockets. Every time this happened, he felt an intense heat. His vision came into focus and pierced the veil of blackness that shrouded the room. He noted in his mind, as well as those of Draven and Renu, the locations of the Malefic dogmatists, seething angrily in the shadows.

A'uun gestured toward the sentries, and they were at once engulfed in the muted white cast of a sound barrier. Draven tested the sound barrier, swiping at the cave wall repeatedly. He looked at the indent of his claw for a moment and picked at it with his talon. A'uun focused and sent them a message to hurry along. The sentries ripped downward, eyes ablaze like beasts, casting away calcite as they descended. The pair pushed off the cave wall and soared over to A'uun.

A'uun could sense that the Malefic knew they were coming, but they did not know how close they were.

A'uun again placed his hands upon the calcite, and the rune stone atop his hand dispersed a muted resonance once more. Renu and Draven readied themselves for combat.

All at once, in the twitch of an eyelid, two large rectangles of calcite, which was formerly A'uun and the sentries' cover, were flung at the two largest Malefic Gargoyles in a skull-crushing blow. An intense light erupted in the room. A'uun and the sentries filed into the cavernous space through the newly opened rectangular passageways. The Malefic looked like bats roused from their sleep as they shrieked and flapped their wings at their attackers.

The next strongest Malefic Gargoyle began a low, frantic chant in a desperate attempt to erect a barrier against magic. Its cranial horns blazed red, as did its bloodstone. As the barrier began to form, A'uun hurled a large, black lightning-infused projectile at it, which sent the Gargoyle whirling toward the rock wall behind. After the thunderous crash, the now charred and smoldering Malefic tried to rise. A'uun had already covered the distance between them, with a spear drawn from the runic stone on his bicep.

The Dark Gargoyle found itself on the receiving end of A'uun's spear, driven entirely through it into the wall behind. Another Malefic swooped behind A'uun. He abandoned the spear. In one smooth motion, A'uun drew his cutlass of onyx metal from the runic stone on the side of his wrist and separated the leg of the hovering Malefic from its body. The Gargoyle shrieked, grasping for the leg that was no longer there, and its wings ceased to move. In a cobalt blur, A'uun repositioned himself beneath the plummeting Malefic. He decisively drove the onyx blade through the Gargoyle's shrieking mouth, ending the horrific noise.

A'uun looked upward when he heard another Gargoyle's guttural growls. The Malefic flapped its wings and maneuvered behind Renu, slicing off Renu's wing with its rubicund claymore. As Renu careened downward, the Malefic warrior followed head-first and delivered a fatal, bone-cracking thrust to its enemy's ribcage. The Malefic smugly stared down at its fallen foe and flapped its way back to the pinnacle of the cave ceiling. Draven took to the air, as a war cry blasted from his vocal cords. He soared toward the Malefic killer with rage emanating from his body in waves of clear energy dimmed with blackness.

The Malefic, wearing a smug grin, raced toward its new rival and struck with the same thrusting technique that killed Draven's brother. The strike pierced his shoulder, sending blood shooting out the wound. Just as the Malefic was about to finish the remaining brother, A'uun intervened and assailed the Malefic with a blinding burst of light, accompanied by an earsplitting sound. The sentry used the opportunity to slice its foe's stomach, spilling its innards. The Malefic and its organs plummeted into the dusty hollow below.

A'uun knew the tide had turned. He focused on one of the three remaining Dark Gargoyles as it latched onto an oddly glowing amulet with artery-like ventricles that carried a glowing fluid. It looked akin to bloodstone, but within it was a greater power—the power to transport its wearer to a master stone. Upon grasping the strange amulet, the remaining Malefic Gargoyles vanished in an emerald wisp of light. A'uun gestured with his hand. Every runic stone on his armor blazed with a brilliant white light. Mere seconds lapsed, and one of the disappearing Gargoyles reappeared, lying in a smoldering heap before them. The emerald energy that surrounded it prior to its vanishing spilled into the air in incandescent globules.

A'uun stretched out his arm, palm outward. Blue energy surrounded the Gargoyle and it began to levitate horizontally above the ground. The blue energy cleansed the area of the green emission, counteracting its dark and profane aura.

"We have matters to discuss," A'uun said mockingly to the struggling Gargoyle.

A'uun knelt down, put his elbows on his knees, and stared piercingly at the Dark Gargoyle. His branded, dark oath symbols were revealed on the surface of the creature's skin. A'uun wondered if he would fall so low to let in evil as this creature did. Black anger rifled though his thoughts.

"All these sigils that you bear…" Bone-deep rage stopped him. "None of these wicked seals will save you now." A'uun clenched his fist, forcing the protective runic inscriptions to dissipate. Fright took the dark creature as it frantically clawed at the energy surrounding it.

A'uun started back to the Priory with the remaining sentries. Their newly captured prisoner lagged behind, floating in the air.

* * * *

From a lofty, natural overhang, Bloodbrand surveyed a throng of base creatures who tore and clawed at each other, like the rabid Raík hounds from the depths of Úul. The creatures were single-minded and fierce. The four-legged, cylindrical-shaped horrors had small disk-shaped, dripping eyes, well-muscled squat legs, and expansive mouths that housed several rows of hideous, wedge-shaped teeth. They reminded Bloodbrand of modern-day amphibious predators often sighted off the coast of Arcadia. Their pigment matched that of the yellow-tinged caves, and their faces had abrupt flatness. The creatures wore long, haggard whiskers, which indicated to Bloodbrand they were at least partially blind and relied heavily on their other senses.

As Bloodbrand made mental notes of the creatures' behavior, he witnessed a wingless hulk of a Gargoyle avail itself to the beasts. They ceased movement obediently at its behest and shrieked as if affirming its superiority. The grand Gargoyle snapped at one of the creatures, which rolled to its back in submission. The familiar sign of the infinite bisected by a slash had been branded into the thick, porous skin of the Gargoyle's arm.

The Gargoyle was not of the avian variety. It was of a different phylum, and probably too large to take to the winds, even if it had wings. It had a massively strong jaw, indicative of a meat-eating predator, and sinewy, dense muscle mass. Despite the appearance of being a base creature on the surface, the preternatural-looking beast had a keen intelligence to it, as demonstrated by its telepathic control of the cave creatures. Bloodbrand instantly knew that this Gargoyle would be a challenge in battle, even for him.

The brooding Gargoyle sniffed the musty cave air, then closed its eyes and massive mouth, as if meditating. It must have smelled something in the air, because a mixture of anger and worry erupted as it cracked open its red, venomous eyes. It shrieked, piercing the ears of the senseless creatures at his feet, which caused them to shriek in response as the Gargoyle bellowed in a deeper, huskier snarl.

* * * *

A'uun could now place the shriek he had heard earlier as it once more rang in his ears. The shrill sound came from the colossus known as Stryge of the Old.

Stryge, now one of the chief leaders of the Malefic, was part of a dying genus of the Gargoyle race. It was one of the same unholy terrors Luttrel had spent thousands of years trying to eradicate. Only a dozen or so of these remaining creatures sought respite in the hidden caves and decaying landscapes of the dead continent, Forgatha.

Stryge, and others of his ilk, were blood drinkers, though many also fed on flesh. These seemingly unquenchable parasites routinely consumed seventy times their body weight in a given cycle. Entire civilizations were lost at the hands of these gluttonous savages. The Vampiric Gargoyles did not consume blood for any supernatural sensation or as a means to attain the myth of preternatural immortality. They drank because of the ample sustenance within the blood of their victims. It was simply a biological need. Their mouths secreted agents into their victim's bloodstream to keep it from curdling, enabling them to feed until the victim's veins were empty. They were designed by their creator for the act of genocide.

A'uun had always contended that these Gargoyles were the creation of Shabaris, the Dead Caller, as a means of striking at the proud sensibilities of Luttrel. Shabaris's hatred of Luttrel was well known. He had come close to killing him on many occasions, as the feuding factions of the Dead Callers' carrion-shrouded disciples and Luttrel's Gargoyle warriors often tangled in battle. It was said that the first Vampiric Gargoyle was the result of Shabaris fusing the bloodlines of Gargoyle and some unknown, extinct parasitic creature. With the joining of the two races, a larger, wingless tainting of a noble species occurred. Many theorized that Stryge was the first of his brood.

Upon hearing the Stryge's shrill wail, A'uun whirled to his captive, his eyes burning brightly. Instantly, the Malefic was catapulted and splayed out, suspended by force against a cave wall. The venomous Gargoyle squawked and hissed as a thin layer of what looked like white tree bark began to encase it. Moon-shaped emerald discs sprouted from its eyes and encapsulated its eye sockets. At once, the beast was at rest, as if a sculpture of the Malefic had naturally occurred in the growth of a tree trunk.

A'uun and the Gargoylian sentries began hurriedly for the epicenter of the Stryge's chilling howl.

Chapter 29
~ Dragon's Flame in the Catacombs ~

The golems were standing apathetically against the back drop of the yellow arcane catacombs. Bloodbrand was formulating a strategy, when suddenly he heard the familiar vibrations of A'uun's thoughts forcing a fervent discourse into his mind in the form of dweller language. A'uun abruptly informed Bloodbrand about Stryge and the details surrounding the creature. Bloodbrand sent a mental message back to A'uun, asking for a favor.

* * * *

Down below, where Stryge and the hideous creatures stirred, an eruption of earth shifted beneath their collective feet. Stryge followed the cracks in the mantle to a corridor of crystalline formations, just south of them. Stryge beckoned the yellow cylindrical creatures with his mind, which obediently followed. He sensed the one-sidedness of their consciousness. It was clear to him that the creatures responded to nothing but stimuli. When his voice came through to their minds, it gave them a focus—and they were able to shut everything else out. Stryge began to hunger for blood, and for a brief moment, he considered taking it from the cave creatures.

Stryge withdrew into the crystalline hallway, curious about the unnatural eruption of earth. He felt a splintering in the cave creatures' thoughts. They were drawn to their reflections in their surroundings. They began to sniff and tear at the crystalline formations, looking at deformed images of themselves and growling at the reflections.

It was difficult for them to gain a footing on the smooth, translucent surface. He was suddenly hit with a shocking notion. He charged out of the space, using the sharp edges of his feet for balance. Stryge compelled the cave creatures to follow, though he could tell their minds were overstimulated. Stryge smelled the distinct, smoky smell of spellcraft above him and looked back to see the cave creatures wearily making their way toward him, pushing and sliding.

Stryge focused ahead and found the source of the spellcraft. What looked like mere humans to Stryge began to rain fire down upon the cave-dwelling creatures from an elevated area just above. The beasts were unable to move quickly, so Stryge saw them immolated, one by one. Charred remains began to fill the area with a putrid stench.

Stryge sprinted away from the clutches of the ambush, digging his right claw into the cave wall. He flexed his arm and made the sharp turn into the adjoining cave. As Stryge rounded the corner, a pair of red eyes met his own. The Mountain Fenthom thrust its powerful Gargoylian blade in a flash of black energy, piercing Stryge's shoulder. He let out an unearthly series of guttural moans. The Fenthom landed a kick in Stryge's chest with a deep thud that slid the Gargoyle off his sword and into a heap on the ground.

Stryge felt as though his chest cavity had caved in, and he could hardly breathe. He then realized that the creature he was fighting was none other than Bloodbrand the Wise.

Stryge glared up at Bloodbrand with venom. With a guttural growl, Stryge lunged at him. Bloodbrand threw his sword down, leaving it impaled in the cave floor. Its black energy swirled around it. A familiar, sculpted Gargoyle head rested at the sword's hilt. The mouth of the fierce-looking Gargoyle surged with a red flare, much like a Fenthom's flame. It was as if the blade could sense the intensity of the moment and reacted to the events that were now transpiring. Stryge knew this blade well.

As Stryge closed the distance between them, Bloodbrand shot low to Stryge's knees. He felt Bloodbrand's amazingly strong grip as he wrapped his arms around his legs, making the bones in his knees crack. Bloodbrand hoisted him upward before he drove him into the earth with a spine-cracking crash. Stryge hissed and kicked away from Bloodbrand. As he kicked, he felt an immense pain in his knees.

Bloodbrand reached for a mineral-rich rock in the satchel tied to his waist. He bit into the rock and swallowed it, causing tufts of ember to flutter out of Bloodbrand's nostrils. Stryge leapt to his feet, and Bloodbrand exhaled a blistering wave of fire, blanketing half of the beast in a spiral of red-and-blue flame.

Stryge fell to his knees. The flames penetrated like hot daggers into his skin. The only thing he could think of is that he must live. This type of flame would not consume him. It was not as potent as dragon's flame. Yet he could smell his own burning flesh and knew he would need a lot of blood to recover. He gathered the strength to move away from the radius of Bloodbrand's flame, knees cracking loudly as he moved.

Stryge desperately grabbed an item from a satchel tied around his upper bicep. It was an odd, heart-like pulsating globule. Stryge crushed it in his hand; a red-brown viscous liquid spilled out so horridly pungent it masked the odor of the smoldering cave creatures.

* * * *

A'uun and the others in his group arrived at the crystalline hall. As Bloodbrand turned to A'uun, the burned, defeated Stryge slipped away.

"Stryge has alerted his comrades," A'uun cautioned.

"How so?" Bloodbrand asked. "Through that odorous stench?"

A'uun nodded.

"We will have to make a stand here in the catacombs," Bloodbrand said. "Stryge wants us to call on Luttrel's forces to leave the Priory unguarded."

"Yes, it all hinges on us now," A'uun agreed.

"How powerful are the golems? Can we rely on them?"

"The wheels are always churning in that mind of yours," A'uun said with a smile. "Their power is just beyond that of a master human wizard. I would say the contivan would be equivalent to a fairly experienced Gilpesh conjuror, or even a Bound logician. Yes, they are worthy of our confidence."

"I think Stryge will strike back soon," Bloodbrand said. "I am also convinced he was not fully exploiting his abilities in our brief encounter."

"Agreed. Had he been, you would have some battle scars of your own. He was buying time. He will, however, heal quickly from the flame you assailed upon him. You will need fire of a different sort to have any lasting effect." A'uun handed Bloodbrand a mineral-rich rock similar to his own, but speckled with emerald deposits.

"What is this?"

"Berylocite. I have used it in many experiments and researched its properties for the better part of a century now. I have found the Fenthom can use it with great effect. Use caution. It will increase the boundary of your flame tenfold and burn much hotter than anything you have ever ingested. You will not need a great deal of the mineral to do a considerable amount of damage. One ingestion will allow you several flame bursts."

"Is this what the arcane dragons ingested to achieve the all-consuming fires spoken of in the great dragon lore?"

"Yes, and only the Mountain Fenthom can handle its raw power. No other breed of Fenthom is to use this mineral. Only the physical makeup of your ilk can bear the fierceness of its properties."

"What would be its effect if others…?"

"Death," A'uun answered.

"How do you…?"

178

A'uun spoke to Bloodbrand in dweller speak for the purposes of brevity, given the nature of the situation they found themselves in. "Long ago, I witnessed a Plains Fenthom attempt to consume the substance and exhale dragon's fire. It burned his body from the inside out. This is how I came to know the mineral. I have since studied it incessantly, referencing it with various oral traditions and written lore about the pre-bygone dragons that roamed the hillsides and mountains of Valesia. This mineral was always present in trace amounts around or near the remains of your distant ancestors. The mountains they often would nest in were once rich with berylocite, but the grand beasts consumed most of the resource, leaving the lands virtually barren of the element. I have a small cache of it in my laboratory, and I have a trusted contivan understudy laboring to remake it by artificial means, though he is currently on another errand of high importance."

With the rotting smell of Stryge's beacon still looming in the air, A'uun, Bloodbrand, the sentries, and golems gathered to strategize.

"We must cut off the main access into the Priory, near the old palaces," Bloodbrand said. "We cannot allow the enemy a means of escape, nor allow them to reach the interior of the Priory. Ideas on how to do this?"

"If we cut off avenues of escape, then we will also be trapped," a golem said.

"We will win," Bloodbrand said. "We will fight with much more urgency when our backs are against the wall and choices are few."

"We can cut off the passage through means of spellcraft," A'uun suggested.

"Then the board is set," Bloodbrand said. "I have a plan that should work."

* * * *

A'uun honed in on a distant mass rumbling that shook the catacombs. He noticed a mass of energy traced the path that the brutish Gargoyle had taken. A'uun and the others quietly followed the pathway. Soon they were upon the place where Stryge and his brood of demonic followers had congregated. A'uun spied a large cluster of the putrid, yellowish cave creatures and a sizable group of Malefic Gargoyles gathered in a shallow chasm. A large, cubic master stone, the size of a horse-drawn wagon, loomed amid the throng of creatures. It enabled the teleportation of the Malefic within the cave and also counter-spelled other forms of teleportation not tied to the stone within the hollow. Thick ropes of energy radiated from the emerald stone, which spiraled and brushed across the periphery of the chasm. It was here where they would be spirited away to, should they use the strange, almost lifelike bloodstones that most wizards referred to as "slave stones." Each Gargoyle also had one of the more common varieties of bloodstone amulets A'uun had seen earlier.

"Those amulets, what are they?" Bloodbrand asked.

179

"The Malefic need them for the more elaborate conjurations they cast."

"They cannot wield spellcraft naturally?" Bloodbrand asked, somewhat surprised.

"As punishment for their attempted coup before their sect split from the established Gargoylian culture, Luttrel stripped the Malefic of the bulk of their power. They reattained their abilities through the infused might of the amulets they wear, although the amulet's energy wanes more quickly than natural magic."

Bloodbrand looked at A'uun as if he uncovered some grand revelation. "I think an added tier in our strategy is in order. Can you create lifelike automatons with your spellcraft, Lord A'uun? They do not have to be elaborate."

A'uun nodded, sensing Bloodbrand's intent. He reached out with his mind to the contivans to see that the sentries had sealed off the entrance to the Priory. Strategically, they were in a better position to undertake Bloodbrand's plan. He had to do more than reach out with his mind for what was to come. He needed to possess the consciousness of the contivan at the closed cave mouth and conduct the conjuration through his body. Possession was the only way. If he traveled in his physical body, the master stone would detect him and alert their enemies, and this spellcraft was also well beyond what his charge was capable of independently.

He sent out a mental communiqué to the golem, asking for his permission to take his consciousness under control. A'uun could sense that the golem was puzzled by this request. He replied to A'uun in a scathing tone that he knew he was not capable of the spellcraft that he had in mind, and that possessing his consciousness was the only logical solution. A'uun was instantly reminded that not all golems shared his beliefs of the sanctity of the individual. He realized he had asked permission more for his own sake than the golem's.

A'uun prepared himself for the transfer of his essence and inhaled and exhaled at regular intervals. He concentrated on the journey his energy must take to reach its destination. The path to the golem flashed past as various rock formations and locales ignited in his mind. Now he had plotted his path, a swirling vortex of energy started to swell around A'uun until it fully shrouded him in a protective energy cocoon. In a cobalt blur, the energy funneled out of the chrysalis. Disjointed particles floated about and turned to whirling lashes of blazing red as he spirited past.

A'uun's consciousness weaved among rock formations, caves, and even through walls. Suddenly, he could see the listless contivan before him, and just as the force of his mind met the golem's consciousness, he turned toward the unseen presence of A'uun's astral self. Abruptly, the expressionless contivan's eyes blazed.

In control of the golem's body, he raised his head and assessed his surroundings in the briefest of moments. Lines of cobalt trailed behind as he ran forward and stopped without effort before a narrow, musky cavern. He was well ahead of the venomous brood that stirred just beyond the hollows of vast chaparral rock formations.

A'uun raised the golem's hand and the cave molded to his will. The vague shape of Gargoyle warriors rose from the auspices of the cavern, smelted from the calcite-rich deposits of the passageway. The faux warriors gave off a slight shimmer, as if the inanimate cave sculptures contained the faint glimmer of life.

Through the golem's eyes, A'uun turned to the Gargoyle sentry. "Do you see the life glimmer?"

"Do you not see it? It blazes before my eyes—almost too brightly!"

A'uun focused in on the formations and reduced the glimmer slightly. He needed to attune it to a Gargoyle's sensitivity and not his own. "Does it seem more realistic now?"

The Gargoyle nodded its head as it still gazed upon the formations. "They still look like rock soldiers and not real Gargoyles."

"Be prepared to move quickly," A'uun said through the golem's mouth.

A'uun flashed over to his cave creations and summoned a dark granule of electrified energy surrounded by a black-tinged, translucent sphere. When the granule flashed within the sphere, the yellowish walls of the cave achromatized into a pallid affectation, as though his conjuration was sapping the energy out of its surroundings. A'uun transmogrified the granule into a shadowy, electrified sphere between his hands. As he forced the energy to expand with his mind, he shrieked in pain and writhed in agony. He began to feel the limitations of the contivan's body, but knew he needed to push a little farther. He had not felt the constraints mortals must endure for quite some time. He had forgotten them. He did not like the feeling of impatience it gave him.

The sphere began to pulsate, which made the golem's body enter into a deep, magically-driven convulsion. He could feel the spellcraft begin to overcome the contivan's mind. The magic was tearing and shredding the contivan internally. The contivan's brain felt as if it were on fire. A'uun simultaneously healed the contivan while focusing on the spell.

He cast the conjuration with his last bit of the contivan's strength in the direction of the grisly cluster of demons. As it surged forward, planes of energy were exposed in the form of barely distinguishable walls of light. The farther the energy traveled, the more it seemed to grow and metamorphose. The spellcraft dualistically combined aphotic and luminous spellcraft, both to destroy and feign signs of living creatures. A'uun felt a hollowness as he once again compromised and wielded aphotic spellcraft. He also profaned the contivan by using the dark

181

arts within his body, but he could not cast aphotic spellcraft while in a spiritual form. He would have had to swear to a dark oath to do so.

A'uun broke from his host. The contivan fell to its knees, chest heaving. A'uun raised his hand and focused a luminous burst at the contivan, which blanketed it in white light. The contivan began to breathe at a normal pace and rose to its feet. He looked up at A'uun and nodded.

Before returning to his body, A'uun surged toward the enemies' base camp. As he sped forward, he cloaked himself from prying eyes. He watched from above as the energy collided into the middle of the encampment. The spellcraft commanded the unseen force that binds all mortals and used that force to decimate the creatures within its all-consuming radius. As the spheroid crashed into its target, the master stone shattered into shards, impaling some of the cave creatures and Malefic. Other Malefic that were directly in line with the sphere were ground into a pulp of bloody gore and bone fragments. The base of the master stone was cracked and seeped green venom.

The surviving collective of monsters rose from the calamity with a black, simmering hatred and focused on the origin of the spellcraft. However, A'uun knew their perception was not reality. The creatures did not see inanimate cave sculptures. They instead saw a horde of Priory sentries through a veil of white energy fields.

The energy veils continued to latch on to the life glimmers A'uun had created as the Malefic raged closer. From a distance, the Malefic rained dark spellcraft down upon the cave sculptures through the intensified strength of their amulets. They climbed the cave walls quickly like savage Forgathan Nematraudes, hungry for meat. The contivan did as was instructed and sent ripples through the energy fields so that their adversaries saw the faux Gargoyles casting protective barriers to block their attacks. This caused the attacking Malefic to beckon their comrades from the adjoining passages. The Malefic mass moved in unison to torch their enemies into a red oblivion.

The body of monstrosities joined together in a spell to hurl their energy in a concordant strain of howling wickedness. Winds gathered and transfigured into a tempest of gray-and-white whirling plumes. The power cascaded in a radial pattern and seared into the seams and curvature of the hollow. Its brilliance changed the landscape of the cave. For a moment, time seemed to creep slowly, and for that instant, the whole space seemed bereft of pigment and light. The ensuing collision decimated the entire façade of false sentries. A'uun could not help but smile.

The Malefic amulets suddenly seemed to be beleaguered beyond capacity. He sent a mental message to Bloodbrand, which was his signal to lead a contivan-backed charge on the east side of the enemy. A'uun surged forward to his body so that he could lead an assault from the west side.

A'uun knew that even with the Malefic's impairment, he and his group of aviary comrades must be cautious. His enemy was still trained in the Gargoylian ways of combat. A'uun at once summoned his scythe from the runic stone ensconced in his shoulder. Upon this summoning, the scythe transformed from its prior appearance to a double-bladed weapon, with each end pointing in opposite directions. He gripped tightly the curved arc of brindle wood, which had archaic engravings etched upon its surface. The piece of wood looked fragile, but was virtually indestructible due to the potent spellcraft A'uun had bonded to it.

A'uun signaled his cohorts to follow him and moved on the enemy in a pincer-like movement, forming a partial circle. The bulk of enemies on the west side of the hollow were Malefic, with a few stray slobbering cave creatures. A'uun advised the sentries telepathically to focus on using magic—something that their enemies could not match.

The Malefic took to the cave floor and migrated in wailing unison like a plague of ravaging locusts.

A'uun surged to a cave wall while he simultaneously told his group to hold their position. His hand was set ablaze in a white-hot smolder as it penetrated the cave wall, almost as if it had merged with the cavernous body. Blades of calcite erupted from beneath the horde of Malefic. Their bestial shrieks rang out as they were skewered by the calcite formations.

At that precise moment, A'uun mentally signaled the Gargoyles to blast waves of thunder-filled spellcraft as the Malefic attempted to dart away from the magically influenced stalactites. Those who had not been consumed by the double-sided trap of spikes and spellcraft took to the cave wall.

A'uun held his double-sided scythe aloft, horizontally at shoulder level. Blue energy flowed through the weapon as it became two. With a blade in each hand, A'uun led a charge through the heart of the throng of Malefic before him, cutting through swaths of evil Gargoyles as they peeled from the side of the cavernous hollow. Though he searched, he did not see Stryge in the thick of it.

One Malefic lunged for A'uun as he moved to the northern edge of the battle. A'uun vaulted off the cave wall and landed behind his assailant. He lifted his blades to each side of the Malefic's neck and sliced through flesh and vertebrae, cleanly cleaving the attacker's head off. Blood sprayed onto A'uun's face and armor.

An energy overcame the runic stones attached to the inner forearm area of A'uun's gauntlets. The miniature scythes retired to the stones while A'uun produced a gray metallic-looking bow and a quiver of arrows. As the bow began to materialize, A'uun already had its taut string pulled back. He loosed an arrow, which sailed toward a Malefic that was advancing on the cave ceiling, hitting him squarely through the side of the head. The Gargoyle plummeted to a broken stalagmite's sharp edge.

Suddenly, A'uun felt a presence behind him. As he spun around, the bow evaporated to a rune on the underside of his wrist, replaced with his nimble sword of black metal. As A'uun completed his spin, he sliced into the forearm of the muscular mass known as Stryge.

The brooding Gargoyle drew back its bloody forearm and produced a glimmering dagger covered in odd characters. Stryge lunged at A'uun with the small blade. A'uun parried his attack and struck Stryge's shoulder. Blood began seeping from its newly inflicted wound, but Stryge seemed unaffected. Stryge lunged once more with the mass of its body led by the glowing dagger. A'uun, unable to parry this attack, was struck in the upper pectoral region of his chest, near his collarbone. The blade miraculously penetrated A'uun's living armor, which was able to adapt to any weapon, protecting the herald from virtually any attack. A'uun's eyes widened in surprise, but he showed no other signs of shock.

As he stared down the monster, the battle around them was cresting. A burst of light emanated from his wound. The armor and his skin were restored. A'uun telepathically taunted Stryge, inviting the hulking ghoul to charge again. Stryge accommodated his request and raised the dagger overhead. A'uun touched the rune on the inner forearm of his gauntlet. The dagger Stryge was holding evaporated into a yellow light. Just as Stryge was about to reach A'uun, two massive earthen red hands grabbed both sides of Stryge's head. The gargantuan fingers of the unseen figure pierced the skull of the hulking creature as they cranked the Gargoyle's neck, forcing a loud snap. The figure dropped the Gargoyle to the ground in a heap, revealing Bloodbrand's massive presence.

Bloodbrand looked at A'uun thoughtfully. "I am glad you were able to relieve it of that weapon."

"I was not able to in time," A'uun said hesitantly.

"I saw it fade with the yellow light."

"That was not my doing. No conjuration of mine ends in yellow light. Only one I know of..." He trailed off.

"By what sort of spellcraft was that weapon forged?" Bloodbrand spoke, curious.

"That was a weapon of the mystics and not ancient. It was a newly forged weapon, not more than a human lifespan in age."

"I have suspected for a number of years that the dead continent was on the path of being inspirited to its former evil."

"It is no longer a matter of traveling a path, Bloodbrand, when it has already arrived at its destination and eclipsed its former power," A'uun stated grimly.

"What do you mean?"

"That dagger was just a token of what they have achieved, a surface yet to be scratched. The Forgathans now have the ability to harm or possibly kill Celestials. If such a weapon can pierce my armor, then it is a certainty they possess this ability."

"So they wanted us to find out that Forgatha is once more reborn? Who are they, and to what end?" Bloodbrand stared fixedly at the fallen corpse of Stryge.

"Whoever this nameless Celestial is and its servant, Mandra. The infection of Forgatha is thankfully still contained. Yet how long will that last?"

When Bloodbrand knelt down beside the fallen Gargoyle, A'uun saw dead, bloodied cave creatures strewn across the massive xanthous expanse. Lingering black energy from Bloodbrand's sword trickled from their wounds. A few Gargoylian sentries roamed the bloodstained battlefield, giving a quick end to the remaining beasts that crept and slithered about, punctuating a fleeting victory.

Chapter 30
~ The Viscount Erelding ~

Cahan and Cloister's landship plodded forward at an ever-slower pace as they headed for the Gargoyle Priory. Cahan cussed flagrantly as the landship sputtered.

"Oh, do shut up!"

"It's not going to make it to the Priory," Cahan said. "We will have to stop."

"I have a friend who now resides in these parts from my days in Weshire."

"Isn't this Viscount Erelding's ward?" Cahan said. "Hasn't he been ousted yet?"

"No, though he has been brought up on charges by the Assembly of Magistrates on suspicion of slavery. However, upon inspection, he was acquitted of those charges."

"Shouldn't we steer clear of the viscount? He must have some power. He is the only remaining member or the Royal Peerage."

"He held on to his title because he swore to abandon slavery and he committed troops to overthrow Monarch N'dal."

"I still think it is a bad idea, Cloister."

"We will be in and out in short order."

Cahan scanned the township of Falkeland. It looked as if this ward had been plucked from the Great Bygone Era. Within the castle walls, many of the houses were made of sillian stone, an ample resource in the area, while others in the poorer areas had thatched roofs with clay and timber walls. Cahan wasn't merely scanning the architecture. He had his eyes open for bandits. In the back of his mind, however, he felt reasonably safe. It was common knowledge that this was a human ward. So, if he did have to fight, it would be a nice change of pace to face off with a human.

Cahan wondered where he would get the needed components to fix the landship, as most in this ward still made use of horse-drawn carriages.

186

"Do not worry, creature," Cloister said. "We will have the necessary parts. There is a blacksmith here with first-rate skill."

"Really? Can you quit scanning my mind, Cloister?"

"I see you have accepted the moniker of 'creature.' How does it feel to be the only non-human in these parts?"

"I am human. I've just learned to quit arguing with you. By the way, I don't think we should have someone else fix the landship."

"Cahan, you need to learn to relax. You are wound up like a child's toy. There." She pointed ahead at a sign. "There is the blacksmith."

Cahan looked at the sign, but could not believe what it said: *Baldemar Smithy.*

"Impressed yet?"

"Yeah. What is Baldemar doing here in the midst of dung and thatched roofs?"

Cahan had only heard stories of the grand smith Baldemar. He had trained many of the Protosian smiths before becoming a monk. Evidently, he had turned his back on the cloth—though Cahan didn't blame him. The Seer Heritage had become corrupt. Even still, something compelling must have pulled Baldemar from his calling. He was the type of man that would try to change the corruption around him, not simply turn his back. Cahan thought it was a good thing that he did. He was sure that Baldemar would be up to the task of fabricating a few landship components.

Cahan and Cloister walked into the smithy. The first thing that caught Cahan's eye was an enormous forge sitting at the back of the shop. It was connected to a spellcrafted heat source, which were cylinders that drew in energy and converted that energy into fire spellcraft. The forge itself looked like a large tube composed of Protosian steel with a yawning chamber opening.

As Baldemar trudged toward them, Cahan spied a flicker of cobalt. The hammer that rested on the smith's shoulder had a similar spellcraft bonded to it as his sword that now resided with Bardon, the traitor. Baldemar reminded Cahan of a smith's hammer. He was short, but broad-shouldered, and had large, muscular arms and leathery skin. Gray hair with tufts of black crowned his head, and his heavily scarred hands were immense for a human.

"Cahan, this is Baldemar."

"Valese to you," Baldemar said as he shook Cahan's hand tightly. "Quite a stout lad. You should be a smith. Cahan, is it?"

"You are from the Éire Cape," Cahan deduced.

"What gave me away?"

"You shook my hand instead of my forearm. I thought the famous Baldemar of the Black hailed from Dranda."

"No, lad, 'tis a common misconception. Éire Cape, born and raised. I hail from a family of smiths in the cape. It was published that my roots were in Dranda because every Tom out there would be after an enchanted weapon from my family. Cahan? That is an Éire name. What is your surname?"

Cahan felt paralyzed as he stood before the revered smithy.

"It is Devlin, is it not?" Cloister said.

"Yes. Definitely an Éire name. The Devlins are a well-known clan. According to local tradition, it is said the Devlins are direct descendants of the original tribe of humans from the shores of Arcadia. The rest of us are just run-of-the-mill descendants of humans that came hundreds of years later. It is also said that Valese herself had something special in mind for the first tribe, and she did not create the rest of us as equals."

"That is quite interesting," Cloister drawled. "I thought you were from Silverstrine, Cahan."

"My family was originally from the Éire Cape, but we moved to Silverstrine long ago. As for the tribe thing, that's just an old wives' tale."

"Well, you definitely do not speak like an Éire born! Are you kin to Cathal Devlin?"

Cahan focused on remaining calm. He didn't want to react to that name. "Possibly, he could be a relative. Not sure. We really need some parts fabricated for our landship."

Baldemar laughed aloud as he threw his head back. "What did you do, Cloister? Did you damage your ship to get him to stop here?"

Cahan looked at Cloister as anger boiled within him. She laid her hand upon his temple, which both chilled and calmed him.

"Now, Cahan, you need to settle yourself," Cloister said. "We are here for a different reason. While I did damage the vessel to get you to stop, I made sure that I did not do any real or lasting harm. I knew you would not stop otherwise. I could have done this in a more... ugly way... with the use of spellcraft. I could have willed your compliance. Consider yourself lucky."

"Why are we here?" Cahan demanded, annoyed.

"The suspicion of slavery charges against the viscount are quite real. Erelding is somehow hiding his operation. Baldemar alerted me to this after the battle at the manor. Baldemar is a strict abolitionist, as am I. In fact, that is why he left the Seer Heritage. The organization that started out as just and forthright is now corrupt. Publicly, they are centrists on the issue; privately, they support those who willingly participate in the cruel practice. They are in league with the viscount. We are here to stop them."

"That's great. Slavers are evil, but we don't have time for this now. We can come back and handle this. We could even bring Bloodbrand and A'uun along."

"This is my duty, Cahan. It cannot wait. I founded the Divinity of the Bound as an abolitionist movement. The roots of this cause grew long before I took up arms against the Nameless One. I was sold into indentured servitude in the scum pits of Forgatha for years. Only once I had served my term, my master did not let me go. I swore at that moment that I would not allow anyone to be bound by another."

"All right. What do we need to do?"

Chapter 31
~ The Path to Spectral Death ~

Anaymous and his caravan of landships had been searching for signs of wraiths and the wayward dweller for hours, with no luck. Anaymous knew that wraiths always left some sort of telltale sign of their presence. Sometimes a surrealistic bending of reality occurred, with muted colors taking the place of their proper counterparts, while in some cases, wraiths would leave an obscure abnormality in their wake, something that looked normal from all outward appearances—but when the object was touched or handled, it crumbled to dust.

Anaymous called for the group of vessels to stop so they might organize and come to a consensus on how to proceed. The vessels formed a circle around the meeting, which consisted of Anaymous, Agares, Raum, the wraith master, and three leaders of their partisan units, Ayperos, Nybbas, and Thamuz, the weapons master. The questing dwellers were impatiently shambling about the outward periphery of the resting landships.

"Why would our enemy, whoever he is, need dwellers and wraiths?" Anaymous asked.

"There are many ruins that could be proliferated with the tandem of these creatures. Wraiths can unlock the hidden secrets of religious iconography and relics," the reptilian Nybbas conjectured.

"Relics are one thing, and they do hold power, but what is worth the effort and risk of usurping such vile creatures away from a wraith caller?" Anaymous asked.

* * * *

Raum grimaced as he asked the question. He had firsthand experience with the usurping of a wraith. Wraiths frequently turned on a new caller because it took many weeks to control the specter fully. A link had to be established that only time could produce. There were few callers, as the wraith being broken must

190

be contained underground in a chamber composed of soil indicative of Anaymous's stronghold. Not many had access to such places.

"Well, the Gargoyle Priory holds many powerful secrets," Thamuz grimly mused. "Their mountain stronghold is composed of a similar mixture of elements repellent to the wraiths, akin to the makings of our desert lands. They would need a dweller to enter."

"You would have to be mad to lead an invasion into the priories' depths," Raum stated. "Gargoyles are not to be trifled with."

"Anyone who can usurp a wraith from its caller and wield the creature has immense power," Thamuz replied.

"Agreed. Either way, it would be a bloody battle, to say the least."

"One item still leaves me in a state of uneasiness," Anaymous said. "How are the wraiths controlling the dwellers? They are immune to each other's gifts. That is why I chose them for the battle against the half-breeds."

"I think our enemy is controlling both the wraiths and the dwellers," Agares explained.

"It is clear where we must go," Anaymous said after a brooding, long pause.

Chapter 32
~ Ghosts of Another Kind ~

Cahan watched as Cloister scoured an open, grassy field.

"What are you looking for, Cloister?"

"Something feels off. I am sure that it has something to do with that mine." She pointed to a far-off mountain.

"Over here!" Baldemar yelled.

Cahan followed Cloister as she went to inspect Baldemar's discovery. Baldemar knelt down in the tall grass next to a large patch of dirt. In fact, it was the only grassless area that Cahan had seen. Baldemar brushed away the dirt with his massive, callused hands.

Beneath the dirt was a large white circle that looked smooth to the touch. Cahan knelt down next to Baldemar and placed his palm on the white surface. It felt like a mixture of warm and cool with a dull resonance about it, making his hand vibrate.

"It feels almost like a climate pillar."

"That is no climate pillar, Cahan. That is a cresentia pillar."

"What the hell is that?"

"It augments a spellcrafter's power. They were only used in Forgatha. My former task master had one, but it did not work. I have never seen a working cresentia. They have not been used since Shabaris walked Shintallis."

Cahan touched the soil near the pillar.

"Careful, this soil is corrupted. These pillars only work in shrieking lands."

"I have some experience with corrupted lands. Blasstock soil actually drinks blood. This land doesn't seem the same."

Cloister waved her hand. Runic markings on the soil appeared on the patch of dirt, and dispersed at once. The soil now looked dark and gritty.

"'Tis only this patch of dirt," Baldemar said.

"Quite clever," Cloister said as she knelt down. "Look at this ring of soil surrounding the corruption. It is slightly different. It is mineral-rich, full of rocks and lava ash. It was brought here from the Gargoyle Priory and keeps the corruption from spreading. If it spread, it would be obvious and the Protosians would have uncovered it."

Cloister stood and flashed a good distance across the field.

"I love it when she does that," Cahan said with a smile.

"Hurry up, then, slow coach." Cloister yelled from a distance.

Cahan sprinted toward her. He heard the old blacksmith grumbling as he trailed behind him.

"You all right, old man?"

"You just keep a-runnin'."

Cahan looked forward to the impatient Cloister. She flashed to two more points in the field before they reached her.

"Look," Cloister commanded.

Cahan brushed away some dirt and saw another large oval.

"Why not bury the whole thing? It would be easier to hide that way."

"The corruption must feed off the energy contained in the air to keep the buried soil alive. In a way, it is almost like a plant."

"There are two more in this field. The pillars must stem from an underground chamber directly beneath. I would assume the chamber is accessible through that mine. Shall we be off, then?"

The entrance to the mine was like no other Cahan had seen. A glistening, black surface stretched arcoss the slope of the moutain and around the cave mouth. As Cahan moved closer to the entrance, he noticed a prismatic color change refract in the gleam of the sunlight. Over time, the black rock had formed into a vaguely rectangular shape with rough, irregular stones wedged between each piece. It looked as if the wedged rocks were spikes or a natural armor for the mountainside.

As Cahan entered the cave, air surged around him. Something brushed into him, pushing his shoulder back. He looked at Cloister. "Something just pushed me out of thin air."

"I know," she said. "I felt it as well. I do not know what it is. Let us keep moving."

"Is it some sort of spirit?" Baldemar said.

"Possibly," Cloister replied.

This troubled Cahan. Cloister usually had an answer for everything.

Cahan saw a blue gleam in the distance. The gleam was part of a spellcraft-influenced lift that sent miners downward.

When they reached the lift, Cahan and the others stepped onto the flat rectangle made of steel with handle grips welded to it by means of spellcraft. The grips were three simple arches attached to a short metal post, centered on the steel, and could accommodate several pairs of hands. Near the backside of the rectangle, a pillar of blue energy was attached by a steel bond. This bond, specially made to merge with all sorts of spellcraft, was the only thing that held the lift in place.

As they traveled down, Cahan saw a vast open chamber supported by brindle wood around the perimeter. Noises echoed upward, along with the suggestion of chatter as the wind whipped around them.

"Cloister…"

"Cahan, I do not know what is down here."

The lift thudded against the chamber floor and started to rise. The three quickly leaped off.

Cahan went to the lever mounted in the wall to recall the steel platform. He could vaguely hear what sounded like yelling high above.

"Cloister?"

"Cahan, I am at just as much of a loss as you."

"That is it. It has to be spirits," Baldemar yelled.

"Keep it down, or you could cause a cave in," Cahan whispered. "Yes, we get it. You are from the Éire Cape, you loud, drunken bastard."

"I have not had a drop since taking my vows, laddie."

"Both of you, hush," Cloister whispered loudly. She paused for a moment before continuing. "Think about it. This cave is full of precious ore. It has to be worth ten fortunes. Yet, the viscount is not mining it."

Cahan ambled to the wall of the chamber and saw pickaxe marks along with subtle traces of black spellcraft mingled into the mineral-rich ore. "An enchanted pickaxe was recently used here. There are still traces of its energy in the wall."

"That means it was just used moments ago," Baldemar said.

"I think I might know what is going on here," Cloister replied. "We need to keep moving toward the pillared chamber."

As Cahan and the others pressed toward the chamber, they experienced fewer encounters with unseen things knocking into them.

Cahan saw nothing when they reached the chamber, except the pillars. A dull rumble echoed in his ear. The wall of the chamber folded open and two Gilpesh conjurors appeared. Cahan drew his hand axe and lunged for the wizards. The tall, lanky spellcrafters grasped hands and launched a fire projectile at Cahan. Cahan was thrown backward and landed on his back with a grating thud. He did not feel as though he was burned, although it was much hotter inside his armor.

Baldemar drew his hammer and surged toward the wizards. The Gilpesh volleyed the same fire spell at Baldemar. He held up his hammer, and at the moment of impact, a protective barrier stemmed from the cobalt energy and coursed through it. Baldemar swung his weapon in a circular motion. Waves of clear energy erupted from it, pushing the Gilpesh back.

Cahan scrambled to his feet. He circled around the spellcrafters and approached them from their side, slicing cleanly through the leg of his opponent. Blood gushed from the Gilpesh's stub as he fell to the ground and grasped what was left of his leg. Black energy folded from his hands and the bleeding stopped. That same black energy molded into the shape of a leg. Once again, the Gilpesh was on his feet. The black energy that now composed its right leg surged with red granules. The Gilpesh grimaced and formed a barrier as he focused on a spell.

Cahan looked to Cloister as all of the sound in the room had ceased. Her eyes turned a searing white with a pallid smolder. The light was so intense he had to cover his eyes with his forearms for a moment.

Cahan turned to the Gilpesh. One of the wizards cowered behind his cohort's barrier. Runic brandings appeared on the Gilpesh's skin and dispersed. Cloister moved closer, stalking the grayish-blue wizard. The Gilpesh threw large projectiles of black energy from behind the barrier, one after another. Blood streamed from his nose. By the sight of the blood, Cahan realized the Gilpesh was using more spellcraft than he could handle.

Cloister whirled her staff, and the black projectiles the Gilpesh had cast began to orbit around her and turn a bright orange. Cahan had to shield his eyes once more. She continued to push toward the frightened Gilpesh as he feverishly projected fireballs toward her. The fireballs were wholly absorbed by the orbiting orange globes. Her eyes phased to orange as the orbiting globes merged in front of her. Four pillars of energy surged toward the Gilpesh wizard, pushing him back until he had nowhere to go. When the energy in front of Cloister dispersed, nothing was left of the wizard except a permanent shadow on the cave wall and the charcoal smell of his cremation.

Cloister approached the other wizard cowering behind his barrier. She stared into the Gilpesh's eyes and then turned back to Baldemar and Cahan.

"Go on, have at it, then."

Baldemar and Cahan roared toward the Gilpesh, who had a curious look on his face. He put his hand against the barrier, and his fingers went right through his creation. The wizard cursed in Gilsh and turned to flee.

"Let him be," Cloister said. "We have larger concerns." She placed her hand on one of the pillars. "We do not have a ghost infestation in the mine. It is simply this thing hiding slaves with its spellcraft."

A mass of porous, red flesh and tentacles materialized before them in a shroud of refracted light. Its tentacles were wrapped tightly around the pillars.

"It was using the cresentia to cloak the slaves and control their minds. Those Gilpesh must have been controlling the creature for the viscount. Well, go ahead. Try not to splatter any monster guck my way." Cloister stepped back. "You should hurry, or it will try to control your minds. It is no longer under the control of the Gilpesh."

Cahan and Baldemar hacked and splattered the creature's guts about the room. The chamber walls were coated in gelatinous flesh.

"I think we got the raw end of the deal, Cloister."

"I defeated the Gilpesh. Had I let you fight them, it would have been long and drawn out."

A mass rumbling of echoing voices poured in from the main chamber. Cahan headed toward the source. Hundreds of former slaves were rubbing their heads and talking with one another. Lines of them were heading for the lift.

Cahan heard Cloister approaching from behind. "We may have freed them, but we still need to take care of the viscount."

As Cahan and his cohorts rode the lift up, he heard someone yelling. When they reached the surface, there were several of the viscount's guards attempting to corral the former slaves.

"These men and women are no longer bound by you!" Cloister yelled.

"By whose authority?" Viscount Erelding asked as he pushed his way past his men.

"Using the offspring of the off-worlders in tandem with Gilpesh wizards?" Cloister yelled. "You will be brought up on charges of treason, along with your entire guard."

"Do you really think Protos will take notice and enforce treason charges when the world is in such upheaval and in the midst of ratifying a new government? They need my money."

Cahan looked at the soldiers the viscount commanded. He knew their dogged expressions all too well. These were the faces of men who had lost their morale over a long time. Undoubtedly they carried out many misdeeds in the name of the viscount, which made him feel a deep surge of anger.

"He's right. Protos is far too tied up with the recent revolution. By the time all of this comes to light, all of the evidence will be gone," Cahan said as he secretly pulled a small knife from his belt and concealed it in his hand. He turned away from the viscount.

"Many of you," Cahan said as he pointed at the demoralized soldiers, "hate this man for what he has made you do, and you hate yourselves for following orders. You wish you could have a just leader, someone that would not make you conceal slavery. I can tell by some of the seals you bear you were once noble knights and honor guard. You probably wish you would not have taken your oaths with this man. Did he promise you a fortune? That money was earned from the sweat of their forced labor—"

"Kill this man," Erelding ordered as he placed his hand on the shoulder of a man wearing the Verindian honor guard insignia.

The man backed away from Erelding.

Cahan placed his hand upon Baldemar's shoulder. "This is your new viscount, Viscount Baldemar."

Many of the men agreed with him, but there were still some loyal to Erelding. The malevolent anger swelled in his mind. He could not believe some would still be loyal to such a man.

Turning toward Erelding, Cahan locked eyes with him and smiled wickedly. In a flash, he grabbed the back of Erelding's neck and slit his throat. "Does this make your decision easier?" Cahan said as Erelding choked on his own blood.

Chapter 33
~ Shape of Things to Come ~

Bloodbrand was sitting down near a dormant fireplace in a circular room lit by the incandescent gleaming of the chimera stone. The room was a cozy place for thought and respite. From what Bloodbrand gathered, Luttrel and Blodwen often used this room for study, writing, or just to be alone in their thoughts. Their personal belongings were all over the room. Bloodbrand glanced over several of Blodwen's and Luttrel's various journals, stacked up on the reading room tables. These books contained their insights on spellcraft, lore of the off-worlders, science, and the dead mystics. Bloodbrand turned his focus to others texts within the library. The room was lined with circular-shaped bookshelves, flush with the walls. The carefully preserved tomes contained in the study were ancient and worth a fortune. Many of the books were written in the hands of the three forms of Valese.

Though this library was intended for times of personal reflection, this was not one of those times. Bloodbrand was accompanied by Lord A'uun, Luttrel, and Amaranth. Luttrel was deep in conversation with Herald A'uun, vicariously reliving the tale of what they had just endured.

"What a spectacular display of strategy and wit," Luttrel said with reverence for Bloodbrand and Herald A'uun.

"Lord Luttrel, I think it is time for me to depart for the curate's manor," Blodwen interrupted.

"You seem eager to mend the barrier," A'uun said.

"I have many augmentations I wish to impose on the barrier," Blodwen said casually to A'uun. "I will also need one of your runic stones."

"Impose? Interesting word choice..." A'uun's eyes narrowed as the words left his mouth.

"It is just her way—forceful and assured," Luttrel interjected diplomatically.

"Yes, I once knew another who was forceful and assured," A'uun said, eyes trained on Blodwen. "His stain branded the districts with bloody feuds."

"You are now the herald of the most powerful Celestial, and yet you bicker like a frigid female." Blodwen turned her back to A'uun and left the room.

"The two of you will never mend your bond, will you?" Luttrel asked.

"Let us hope she is more adept at mending barriers," A'uun said as he handed a runic stone to Luttrel.

* * * *

Assembled before Blodwen in the Priory airship chamber were her most trusted of allies. Chief among her strongest of supporters was Acantha, a striking, ivory-haired beauty who had frequented Blodwen's bed many times over the centuries. Blodwen studied the lines of Acantha's body. She was fond of her, but did not share the love she knew her partner felt. To Blodwen, love was a warrior's biggest weakness, so she did not revel in such nonsense.

Standing next to Blodwen was the imposing figure of Drusus, the largest of the Arcadian Gargoyles. Blodwen considered Drusus her fiercest pupil, aside from her former pupil, A'uun. When training Drusus, it was Blodwen's focus to forge a warrior that could surpass A'uun, at least in combat. It was doubtful that anyone would attain the level of spellcraft that A'uun had. It angered Blodwen that he had even surpassed her brother, Luttrel. Besting A'uun was something she thought of daily. This yearning caused her to be cruel to Drusus in their training sessions, as she expected nothing but perfection. Every time she looked at him, she felt anger, as if every single movement was somehow wrong. Even at this moment, she wanted to strike him to see how he would react.

Rounding out Blodwen's inner circle was Crow the Tracker. Crow, though young by Gargoyle standards, was well known for his tracking skills, far eclipsing many of even the Ashwhend Gargoyles. Crow had been born in the Priory and possessed no sentimentality toward their old homeland. Blodwen discovered Crow during a search for a tree nymph who had stolen a precious artifact from a Gargoylian ruin. Crow was the only one of a large search party who had been able to track and capture the creature—and capturing a tree nymph in a forest was no small feat. Blodwen watched Crow as he gathered his implements. She wanted to make sure he brought the proper tools. Outside of tracking, he needed much supervision.

Each member of Blodwen's inner circle was accompanied by the small throngs each of them led respectively. Every throng was a reflection of their leader and held similar skills and physical characteristics.

As the group prepared to disembark, Blodwen noticed that Luttrel and Bloodbrand were hurriedly making their way toward them. Luttrel handed her the runic stone A'uun had given to him.

"Why do you need this, Blodwen?"

"To reestablish the link between the barrier and the wellspring," she said in a formal tone as she grabbed the stone, still focused on her crew.

Blodwen shot a final glance at Luttrel before heading toward her vessel, *The Amodai*. She had felt distant from her brother in recent years. She wondered why he had changed so much over time. She hated how open he was to all sorts of demons and humans.

Blodwen longed for the years of the Gargoyles past. Her ship was a reflection of that feeling. The finely constructed vessel's architecture harkened back to the more combative times of the Gargoyles, when most of their air vessels were triangular, metallic battleships fitted with heavy, spellcraft-infused artillery cannons.

Blodwen and the others boarded *The Amodai*. She took her spot on the ship's deck and signaled the pilot to depart. As she turned her back on her brother, her thoughts shifted to her work at the curate's manor. She was ready to make her improvements. Did her brother actually expect her to embrace him and say farewell?

* * * *

The fins on the sides of Bloodbrand's ears twitched. He heard the sound of flapping wings in the distance. As the sound grew louder, he spied a Gargoyle flying toward him. The sentry swooped and landed, bearing a piece of parchment. Bloodbrand sensed everyone's eyes on him as the sentry handed him the message.

"Chief Magistrate," the sentry said.

Bloodbrand studied the envelope. It was embossed with a circle and two thinly curved shapes on opposite sides, bisected by a crude slash. It was the MOI crest.

Bloodbrand broke the seal with a pinch of his fingers and read the message. "It appears the council has reached a verdict, and I am to be summoned to the Chamber of Elders," he said. "It also appears as though the navy and the air fleet have been recalled and disbanded, pending the proclamation of my verdict."

"What will you do?" A'uun said.

"Though this is dire news, I cannot take my leave now. We must question your prisoner first and deal with the obligation at hand."

Bloodbrand and A'uun returned to the spot where the Gargoyle was frozen upon the cave's wall. A'uun touched the wood encasing softly, and the shell began to dissipate. The three-toed, taloned feet were uncovered first as a wave of bark began to evaporate. The arms were revealed next. As the midsection covering dissolved, a gaping cavity in the creature's chest appeared. The Dark

Gargoyle had been relieved of its organs in a grotesque fashion. Bloodbrand thought it looked as if it had been burned from the inside.

"I assume this is not a side effect for this type of spellcraft?"

"No.. Someone cast this upon him. No small feat, I assure you. And curiously, there is no lingering trace of the spellcraft that was used or the caster's magical signature." He continued investigating the hollowed-out Gargoyle until it fell to the ground. A'uun made a gesture with his hand, and the creature was consumed by blue fire.

"I should have been able to feel a spell that could overcome one of my own as the spell was cast," A'uun said. "The Gargoyle should have been protected in that encasing. I have seen giants unable to breech that spell's fortification."

"Chief Magistrate and Lord A'uun, landships approach the Priory," a sentry informed from the darkness.

The shrill humming of an antiquated landship filled the air. From high atop the stone perch where Bloodbrand and A'uun stood, they spotted a landship leading an entire procession of modern landships equivalent to those found in Protos or Verinda. The pair made their way to a magically powered lift near them to meet the landship voyagers at the front gate.

The landship's cylindrical energy ducts retracted as the low-hovering vessels landed at the foot of the Priory, kicking up dust as they came to rest. Bloodbrand nodded at Cahan and Cloister as they filed out of their antiquated airship. Anaymous and his followers emerged from the well-crafted and armed landships from Rynaut Keep.

Anaymous and Agares made haste past Cloister and Cahan to the Priory gate, where Bloodbrand and A'uun stood.

"Lordship, wraiths are making their way to the Priory for a full-scale incursion. We also witnessed a flock of Gargoyles bearing the mark of the Malefic soaring this way as we traveled here," Anaymous reported to Bloodbrand.

Just then, a group of contivans emerged from the shadowy mouth of Priory gates. A'uun instructed one of the contivans to summon Luttrel.

Chapter 34
~ The Grand Misdirection ~

Blodwen and her trusted cohorts arrived at the Manor of the curate to find Haran, the golem A'uun had left behind, busily working on a system of gears and pulleys on the west wall. Blue energy flowed from him, indicative of progeny members who had just been in the chamber of the curate. Blodwen approached the hard-at-work contivan.

"What are you doing, you aberrant thing?" Blodwen fumed with teeth-grinding hatred.

"I am trying to reverse an obvious error in the manor's fortification," Haran said, surprised at Blodwen's anger.

Blodwen reached into a satchel and produced a red-and-black bloodstone amulet similar to what the Malefic wielded, but much smaller. She pressed the phasing stone against Haran's chest. With a flutter of gray energy, the golem ceased movement and fell to the ground, inert and barren of the energy that had animated him. Thick, bluish fumes filtered into Blodwen's amulet and flowed through its ventricles. It pleased her to see something of A'uun's come undone. She felt as if she was setting a great misdeed on a righteous path.

"Begin working on the barrier's fortifications," she said to her cohorts with a sneer. "The true curate must be limited in his access to the energies of this monstrosity. He will awaken now that this creature is inert. He still has some life left in that husk of his. I can still smell his stench."

Blodwen handed Drusus, Crow, and Acantha pieces of parchment detailing the barrier's design, as well as the modifications that would have to be made to limit the curate and the progeny from its powers. Blodwen knew the fortifications would be easily repurposed, something the golem had just been trying to change. Blodwen snapped out of her hatred of the golem's toiling when she heard a faint noise. She clenched her jaw with a new anger as she glared upward at a stirring

202

in the balcony above, a noise so minute that it would have likely not been heard by any other ear, save for the Gargoyles.

Blodwen scaled the wall, ferociously impaling her sharp talons into its surface, casting away clumps of brick as she surmounted the edifice. With each impalement of stone, she grew angrier still. Blodwen arose to see a beguiled progeny caretaker, hunched in the concealed balcony. The woman's face was flush with fright and tears were streaming down her face.

Blodwen grabbed her hair and pulled her up to a standing position. The woman wrapped her arms around herself defensively. Blodwen snarled at the woman, hoping she would react—but the caretaker's face just looked barren, wet, and helpless. Not wanting to waste any more time than was necessary, Blodwen sliced across the caretaker's exposed veined neck with her talons, severing her ability to scream. She clutched the woman's face. Her blood-soaked claws sunk into the caretaker as she hoisted the woman up off the ground. The caretaker mouthed silent, choking prayers that Blodwen could feel damply against her palm. Anger erupted in Blodwen's mind. She hated the feel of the human's damp mouth against her skin.

Blodwen flung the caretaker down below to a bone-cracking landing—she always found a certain joy in the sound of cracking bones. She leapt down and knelt over the woman to make sure the body was, in fact, now a corpse. Caretakers were far more resilient than they appeared, she reasoned to herself, though they were still stinking humans. Not wanting to leave anything up to chance, Blodwen thrust her talons through the caretaker's chest and ripped out her heart. She placed the bloody heart on the caretakers face, over her eyes. She did not like the woman's eyes. It felt as though the human was staring at her. She gestured the other Gargoyles to come forth.

"Put her in the forest. Something will devour her. Rub the heart's blood all over her to attract predators." In the back of her mind, she half-wished she had a wraith at her disposal so the creature could fully erase the caretaker's existence. No one would even remember the sobbing whore.

Blodwen set her mind to find the curate—the real curate, not A'uun's poor excuse of a creation. If the curate did not perish, the changes that were made to the manor would not fully take hold. She would, however, have to be much more tactful in this undertaking, she thought.

Blodwen picked up the lifeless golem under her arm and went to the balcony where the caretaker had been spying on her. Once she reached the pinnacle, she set Haran down carefully, propping the inert golem against the wall. She held her amulet aloft and uttered an incantation in the tongue of the bygone archfiends. The gray energy contained in her amulet coursed through the veins of the stone, refracting a dismal black glow. The stone began to seep with a dark mucus from its outer reaches. Blodwen held the stone above the contivan's mouth, forcing it open with her hand. The viscous sludge slid down the throat of A'uun's creation. In a fit of impatient anger, she bashed the stone against the creature's mouth and broke its front teeth. After a moment, the contivan was animate, but at Blodwen's behest.

Blodwen turned to her new servant and moved closer to his ear. "Where are the progeny caretakers and the curate?" she whispered in the language of the wraiths of Úul. "I cannot sense them. Why can I not sense them?"

The contivan sent a mental image to Blodwen of the chamber the curate inhabited. However, there were many such chambers in the manor. A vibration resonated in her mind.

Why are you siding with the Malefic? Was it really necessary to bash in my teeth?

Blodwen guessed the inquisitiveness A'uun instilled in some of the golems was still present in this one. This mental bridge she created with the contivan was two-way. He could also use it to peer into her consciousness.

* * * *

The golem saw flashes of memories and haunting, vague outlines of demons and humans spiraling in an surrealistic tempest of morose colors. One flash focused in with clarity for a brief moment. It was Blodwen arguing with Luttrel about A'uun:

We have to dispel Mandra's powers from A'uun. Kharr'kari are not meant to call upon spellcraft—they are already too physically powerful. You have to balance this… or… will… someone…

The memory became indistinguishable as floods of hazy fog decayed the vision, as if Blodwen closed the memory off to her new disciple, but another one came flooding in. The golem saw Blodwen colluding with a gaunt, darkly pigmented Gargoyle. Haran could also identify another in this meeting from his base knowledge transferred from A'uun. The hulking Stryge loomed behind the Dark Gargoyle. The memory came into sharp focus.

"It is true that Luttrel has lost his way. I am giving you fair warning, he means to banish you from the Priory."

"What do you plan to do?" A younger Blodwen said.

"The plan still remains the same. N'dal house has..."

The Dark Gargoyle trailed off. Its mouth still appeared to be moving, but the contivan could no longer identify what was being said. A Marsh Fenthom entered the room just before the vision cut off to a loud thunderous clap.

Blodwen expunged the contivan from her mind. "Enough, creature, we must find the curate," she said, shaken.

"You do not fear A'uun because his power must be balanced. You fear him because he is better than you. He is what you wish you could be. It is awfully human of you to be so jealous." Haran forced a smile upon his controlled, bloodied lips.

Blodwen clutched Haran's throat. She wanted to squeeze with everything she had and feel the blood drip down to her talons. She yearned to extinguish all that he represented to her. Yet she realized that was exactly what he wanted. He would not have to help her if he died.

"Nice try, creature."

Blodwen and the golem started for the wing of the manor that housed most of the living quarters. The pair passed by a few caretakers who assumed that Blodwen was just there to mend the barrier. The chaste caretakers bowed slightly as she passed. Blodwen was well known to the progeny as the architect of the barrier. She hated their impudent bowing and customs. The caretakers' eyes were drawn to Haran's bloody mouth and broken teeth—and she wanted to behead every last one of them.

As they walked, she reflected on what had transpired. She realized that she should not have risked a mental link with the contivan. She could have just asked one of the amiable caretakers where the curate was. Even now, she felt the contivan attempting to riffle through her memories in its inquisitive way. She thought of the repercussions of A'uun regaining control of his artificially created creature. She concluded that it would not matter once she accomplished her mission. She was even glad that she had sullied one of the herald's works.

Blodwen and the golem came to the curate's communal chamber on their way to the living quarters. From the hallway, Blodwen could see the reflection of several caretakers through one of the many mirrors resting on the walls of the chamber. The blue energy gleamed off the mirrors as they were receiving energy for their healing spells from a light fount, but the curate was not present.

"Caretakers, where is the curate?" Blodwen asked assertively.

"He is resting in his quarters. He is . . . not well."

"Please summon him at once. I must speak to him." Blodwen knew that she had to spill the curate's blood in the chamber or the mantle of the progeny would not be passed to her.

She studied the caretakers' expressions, one by one. They had stunned looks scrawled upon their faces, and no one made a move to accommodate her demand.

Blodwen could see the reflected anger overcome the lines of her face as she grew increasingly impatient. She wanted to shatter each of the mirrors in the room. Her lip curled and she tightened her jaw, but she tried to tone down her expression. Her hatred for humans was setting her internal scale off-balance, and it was difficult to remain calm. She knew what was to come of Protos and her districts. Why continue to accommodate these dirty insects? She hated that the humans were standing in her way. All of the repressed anger that she had held back over the centuries ascended to the surface. Venomous rage began to permeate the whole of her body unquenchably, and her fingers began to twitch.

"The curate could be in any number of rooms," she muttered on the brink of madness. "I built this barrier for the humans, and they just stand there like dazed cattle with their stupid, questioning faces when I ask... when I request..."

"You will do as I say now, you scabrous roaches," she screamed at them.

The caretakers twitched nervously at the sound of her shrill, primal scream. They could see that she was overtaken with rage and madness.

Blodwen drew a dagger from her belt, grasping the handle of her weapon so tightly that her fingers felt bloodless. One woman attempted to dart out the outer door, but Blodwen easily caught up to her. She dug into her shoulder with her claw and threw her to the ground.

"Stand up," she yelled, leaning over the woman.

The woman did not move.

"Stand, you infection!" she spat.

The woman stood. Her shoulder seeped with blood, and she wept profusely.

Blodwen extended her hand out, still holding the dagger, and stared blankly at the woman.

"Grab my wrist."

The woman's shaking hand stretched outward. She groped for Blodwen's cold flesh. Blodwen looked at her as she felt red violence stir in her mind. She saw herself stabbing the caretaker repeatedly and felt a smile tugging at the edges of her mouth. The other caretakers huddled together, shivering in the corner.

"Where...did the...curate...go?" She used a restrained tone.

"South wing healing chamber..."

"Pull the knife into your stomach."

The woman cowered as if she had shut down. Blodwen reveled in her response. Suicide was antithetical to everything the progeny stood for.

"Pull the knife into your stomach, or I will kill every one of these whores." She pointed at the huddling mass of weeping women.

The threat seemed to convulse the caretaker back into reality. The huddling women protested bleakly and sobbed, begging for their colleague not to comply.

"Do not do it, canoness," a few of them pleaded.

Blodwen turned to the huddling mass and screamed, "Shut up!"

The woman weakly pulled the knife in as Blodwen finished the job. She plunged the dagger deep into the caretaker's stomach, smiling as she twisted the dagger even deeper into the woman's abdomen. She wrenched the dagger from the woman's body and raised it to her lips, licking the woman's blood from the blade.

She set her sights on the remaining caretakers. Blodwen hacked and slashed her way through the huddling mass of women until vertebrae and organs were disseminated about the room. She reveled for a moment in the orgiastic satisfaction derived from the carnage she had created.

Chapter 35
~ Blood, the Dead, and the Victors ~

Luttrel stood, attentively listening among comrades, new and old. After profuse reasoning, bargaining, and citing of good deeds recently done at the hands of Anaymous, Luttrel finally acquiesced in favor of allowing the former Incendiary leader into the Priory. Luttrel also realized that they would have to unite together to properly defend the stronghold, due to the recent multitudes of Malefic Gargoyles migrating toward them.

One thought held him immovably, however. Would the barrier be okay in the hands of Blodwen? Luttrel had found subtle evidences of resentment toward humans in the preceding weeks. Luttrel pushed the thought from his mind. If the enemy gained the secrets of the Priory, all would be lost. Existence itself would be in peril—and that was not a thought he could entertain.

As the group of allies gathered in a large, circular room, the chimera stone gleamed warmly with a green light. Luttrel pondered while they waited for Agares to bring this wraith repellent that Anaymous had spoken of. In the back of his mind, he still felt uneasy about exposing secrets to an Incendiary Scion, former or not. He remembered back to another uneasy alliance with a Celestial, who turned out to be overcome by dark rites and aphotic spellcraft. This event led to the destruction of Ashwhend. This ally also claimed to be above board and wished to eradicate Forgatha from the map. Luttrel decided that he would err on the side of caution with this Anaymous. The only reason he decided to proceed was that he doubted he could deceive both Cloister and A'uun.

"What do you think their target might be, Luttrel?" Anaymous asked.

"I would venture to say that this nameless force seeks out the light founts of the Time Celestial. The only way to open the fount is to straddle realities, a characteristic all Celestials possess."

"All Celestials, and to a lesser degree the wraiths of Úul," A'uun added. "The wraith creatures wield enough power to at least gain entry into the Time

Celestial's domain. Upon entry, one can gain the power of a Celestial. In this case, the power of bending the cosmos to the will of its possessor."

"Can a wraith realize such a power even if it has access?" Anaymous asked.

"No, the creature will open the portal for another, someone steeped in powerful spellcraft," Cloister answered.

"Could the Time Celestial not simply stop whoever enters his domain?" Anaymous further questioned.

"No one has seen the Time Celestial in a millennia," A'uun said. "Many have deduced that he is exploring the infinite blackness beyond. His chamber, however, still holds great power."

Luttrell studied Agares as he trudged his way into the room and set three large burlap bags before the group. He still felt perplexed that Kalriss demons had access to the Priory. He hoped he was not repeating history.

"This will repel the wraiths indefinitely," Anaymous said. "They cannot endure the inherent qualities within it. Its composition is fiercer to the wraiths than the minerals natural to the Priory. I am sure we can use it in some way."

* * * *

Cahan decided to break away from Cloister and the others for a moment. He strolled to the Gargoylian dig site so he could have a few quiet moments. Quiet moments were few and far between these days. Being alone in his thoughts sometimes frightened him as of late, but he was tired of Cloister's glaring eyes.

She had chastised him all the way back to the Priory for the way he handled the viscount. He felt as though she should understand on some basic level why he had taken the action he did. An uprising was likely while Erelding still drew breath. Even Baldemar scolded him and said that he should be brought up on charges. Though ultimately, Cahan thought he backed off because he lessened the risk of rebellion. He told himself that one man died so that many would live. It did scare him that a part of him enjoyed ripping that bastard ear-to-ear.

Cahan decided that being alone in his thoughts was not helping, as he tended to dwell on things for abnormally long periods of time. His biggest problem, he was often told, was his unwillingness to let go of things. He wished that actually was his biggest problem.

Shaking it off, he buckled down and helped make preparations for the oncoming battle. The flashes of blood pouring out of the viscount's neck, however, would not leave his mind. He could still smell blood on his boots. Overcome, he ran to catch up with the others.

As burlap bags of the wraith compound were brought in, Cahan took a long look at the Time Celestial's doorway. The fount chamber was composed of oblong, turquoise bricks. Cahan touched the glimmering bricks. They were hot, similar to the curate's chamber. The floor was composed of carved and flattened earth, with sunken bas-reliefs intermittently bearing the plasticine effigy of the glowing Time Celestial. It looked as if there were an anthropoidal figure in the midst of a glowing orb. The luminescent Celestial fount was encapsulated by finely molded stone in a circular aspect, punctuated by whirling energy in orbit above the molded stone.

Cahan watched as A'uun focused on the ground for a moment. The ground began to tremble, and a rounded trench formed around the fountainhead. Anaymous's compound began to flow from the large bags, as if a miniature sand storm stirred within the space. The compound at once changed direction, filling the trench A'uun had just created.

A'uun summoned his one-bladed scythe from the runic stone on his hip, spinning the scythe in a whirling, vertical blur before him. An ice-like material began to crust over the blade of the Gilpesh armament—the same material encasing the compound that lay in the trench. A'uun repeated the same process in the ceiling, but this time, a circular swath was cut into the glowing turquoise bricks.

Once the compound was encased in the ceiling, a crystalline light emanated from it. The light soon met the same limpid glow originating from the trench, forming a phosphorescent link between the two sources. A'uun touched the runic stone on his gauntlet. A reverberating energy poured out and affixed to the mountainous part of the room and directed itself toward the crystalline light, supplementing its power with the intrinsic qualities of the mountain and the Celestial chamber.

"After only moments, you have already improved the compound beyond my comprehension," Anaymous said to A'uun.

"I will show the process after the battle," A'uun said. "It is something you should easily be able to duplicate, if you are as clever as I think you are."

Cahan was still trying to avoid conversation with Cloister. They were both in their spot at the forefront of the cavern. Before them were tunnels that led to a large, open area, riddled with stalactites and small canyons. Cahan was also still trying to shake his mind of the situation in Falkeland, so he decided to watch the different groups disperse in the hollow. A'uun seemed to be giving his usual exuberant directions, based on his hand gestures and facial expressions. He had gathered his golems to set a line of defense in the tunnels leading to the light fount. Gargoyle sentries were on their way to the cavern in front of Cloister and Cahan.

According to Bloodbrand's battle plan, they were to gather in strategic places where they would be able to attack the Malefic's usual oblique formation with several multi-tiered flanking maneuvers. The battle plan all hinged on A'uun. If he could get to the wraiths during combat, the battle would be over and the gateway to the Celestial realm would be lost to the enemy. A'uun had said that he half-wished that heralds could open founts to the Celestial Realm. He could simply close off this gateway from the inside, though he would need a Celestial tether to re-enter the physical realm because his body would be destroyed in the process. A'uun also explained why heralds could not enter the Celestial Realm—they would be a threat to its inhabitants. Celestials had a fear that heralds could attempt to usurp their power and claim the realm for themselves.

"You cannot avoid talking to me indefinitely, Cahan," Cloister said, interrupting his thoughts. "You must answer for what you did. I understand why you did it, but what bothered me most was your facial expression during Erelding's execution."

"What do you mean?" he said scathingly.

"You... smiled."

Cahan looked at Cloister. She was genuinely hurt and frightened.

"Clois... Cloister... I take no enjoyment in killing," Cahan stammered. "I just did what I had to do."

"That is the problem, Cahan. You always do what you have to do with no regard for the rule of law, or morality. That is the code the enemy lives by. This is wrong, Cahan." She locked her unblinking eyes to his. "There is a right way and a wrong way to do things. You need to stop living in your bleak, gray world. There are absolute truths in this world, whether you like it or not."

Cahan exhaled deeply and touched Cloister's face, making her facial expression soften a bit. He could tell Cloister thought he was about to agree with her. "There is no right or wrong when you are at war. There's just blood, the dead, and the victors. I had the opportunity to secure victory with these hands." He placed his other hand on her face.

Cloister pried both his hands away. "If you stain your hands enough times, then the blood can never be washed away."

Chapter 36
~ The Insurrection Is At Hand ~

Draven was lined up with his Gargoyle brothers in their place among the stalagmites of the hollow. He studied the dripping, musty cave and wondered what eldritch horrors the stalagmites had seen. He gazed upward at the stalactites that covered the cave ceiling. They appeared to be leaking teardrops that had suddenly frozen in stone.

He sensed the enemy was close, and he listened intently. Every solitary noise jumped out at him. Trying to quiet his mind was not working. His thoughts were still on his brother, Renu, who was killed at the hands of a Malefic just hours ago. Thoughts of revenge poured into his mind. He hoped that he would be facing that Malefic's brothers in this battle, so he could kill as many of them as possible. Chief Magistrate Bloodbrand had told them what to expect from these creatures after consulting Lord Luttrel's books—and he knew they were ready.

A'uun had asked that some of the soldiers allow him to view the battle through their eyes so he could see from multiple fronts. Draven had volunteered without a moment's thought. It was of the utmost importance that the wraiths be spotted quickly, so he took this burden directly in his hands. This important task could save countless lives.

Draven heard a subtle sound, like flint striking steel. The clinking noise began to sound more and more cadenced, and Draven felt ashamed that he did not place the noise earlier. It was the sound of talons against stone. He would get his wish—moments from now, he would be facing the Malefic.

A sea of shields and spears emerged from the darkness. Bloodbrand was right. They were in their oblique formation, just as he had surmised. When Draven saw the formation with his own eyes, it looked far more intimidating than he had imagined. The Malefic were well-guarded as they marched elbow-to-elbow, shield-to-shield. Draven spied the incandescent gleam of bloodstones peering around the periphery of their shields. This sent chills through Draven, as that same gleam may have been the last thing his brother had seen.

The Malefic charged forward. Waves of swords and shields clanged together. Blood spurted around Draven, and cleaved tails, talons, and heads fell to the ground. He began swinging his sword into the chaos. It was horrifying. Out of the corner of his eye, he saw a sword swing his way. He turned to block the attack and launched a fireball from his hand into the Malefic's chest. The scorched Malefic flew backward. Right at that moment, he sensed a spear thrust and immediately turned and parried. Draven wondered when he would not be quick enough to meet the next attack. He could smell the pungent odor of aphotic spellcraft all around him. Many of his brothers were dying. Their wounds seeped with dark energy and gushed blood. Blistering screams and growls echoed in the hollow from Draven's right side. He turned to look.

A flank of sentries stormed in, as well as a staggered line behind them. Many of the Malefic on that side of the throng were left no choice but to break from their formation to meet their attackers. When the Malefic broke their formation to meet the first-line attacks, the staggered sentries marched on them and surrounded them. Draven's attention snapped back directly in front of him when an enemy charged forward with an illumined spear. He side-stepped the attack and sliced through a Malefic's shoulder, down to his navel.

As the growling and moans receded, Draven sensed the intensity of the battle dying down. He looked around as a deep rumbling shook the hollow. A hole in the cave's side wall crumbled open. The Malefic's reserve forces had arrived. Draven knew the tunnel must have been dug by dwellers.

From the newly bored tunnel, Draven witnessed the hulking Stryge surface, apparently brought back from the clutches of death with several Gilpesh conjurors in tow. The Gilpesh shadowed forth, slinking to inconspicuous areas as energy radiated from their staffs and eyes, linking together in galvanized strands of blue. Draven sensed A'uun's presence in his mind. He could tell that the arrival of these particular enemies was keenly important to him.

* * * *

A feeling of stimulation ignited in Raum's mind as a message from A'uun resonated within him. It was not in the form of words, but in images that were easily understood in an instantaneous manner. Raum lit his signal fire for Ayperos, Nybbas, and Thamuz and charged ahead.

Raum focused in on their assignment. Still feeling the raw reverberation of A'uun's mind, he knew that his group was to eradicate the small Malefic force tasked with shielding the Gilpesh as they conjured their spellcraft. Raum normally summoned wraiths in battle, but thought better of it this time. He still felt a deep anxiety as he thought about summoning the creatures. He reasoned that it was too risky, as the wraith usurper might well be lurking amongst the enemies' forces. He decided that he would make use of creatures called graylings, so named because of the gray energy that discharged intermittently from their eyes. Graylings were wizards overcome by dark rites, transitioning to becoming a wraith. While in the process of change, graylings appeared sickly and often vomited ectoplasm. They drank the magically potent blood of living spellcrafters, which temporarily staved off the coming metamorphosis. Some would even enter somnolence of their own will, as an alternative to becoming trammeled in the ghastly pits of Úul. Callers often summoned graylings because they were far more amiable, though less powerful than what they would ultimately become.

Raum sprinkled Mydian salt on the ground and extended his hand. The salt began to circulate within gray tempest winds and formed into a warlock's circle with Execurian stars situated north, south, and east. On the west side of the circle, a line of salt forged its way between the southern and eastern points. The moment the line was completed, three hunched creatures began to claw their way out of the ground, as if this very ground were their burial site. Raum knew, in fact, the graylings came through a portal that stemmed from a bridge between worlds—more specifically, the space that lay between Shintallis and Úul.

The hunched and cloaked graylings began a haunting chant. Their whispers were carried on preternatural winds. Each grayling sliced into their forearms with their long, black nails. As blood flowed from their newly opened wounds, they chanted their preternatural whispers once more. The blood suddenly metamorphosed into a raw bloodstone. Raum focused his concentration even harder on his new disciples. Each creature clutched onto their newly forged amulets, and their black claws sank into the stones. Raum's eyes flared while controlling them.

Raum and the graylings pressed closer to the Malefic. They situated themselves on an overhang just above the Dark Gargoyles. The graylings began raining down fire upon the Malefic as their eyes shone gray. One Dark Gargoyle was burnt severely about its shoulder and back, while another in the group was seared horrifically on its face, almost making its race indistinguishable. The other four were able to erect a quick barrier before the blast did any real damage.

The Gargoyles responded with a volley of their own, as black energy burst forth from their amulets. Four large blasts shook the overhang and incinerated a good chunk of Raum's cover. He sensed that A'uun had signaled Ayperos, Nybbas, and Thamuz to attack each side of the Malefic from down below.

Raum watched intently from atop the overhang as two Malefic converged on Thamuz, one from the front and one from the rear. Raum tried to time another volley of fire at the precise moment his cohorts would need it. He had to wait until the Gargoyles were slightly distracted so they would not be able to shield themselves. He could sense the impatience of the graylings. They wanted to kill. Their wicked thoughts extended to Raum's mind, scratching beneath his skull. Their sullen eyes were trained on him, waiting. Raum's hand shook as he raised it, and the ghastly graylings snapped to focus. The gray energy from their eyes flared as they lay in wait. Raum could tell that the graylings sensed his nervousness. He hoped they would not turn on him as a wraith would in this situation.

Thamuz skillfully thrust his spear into the necks of the two Malefic concurrently with his double-sided weapon. Raum admired the skillful move, but continued to focus nervously on his cohorts. Nybbas was in the process of being overcome by a Malefic chanter as he hurled his venomous spellcraft at him. Dark strands of energy wrapped around Nybbas's body like a sea serpent weakening its prey.

Raum signaled the graylings. Three fireballs shot from the overhang and merged into one singular mass of fire. The Malefic chanter erected a barrier, taking his focus off Nybbas, which was exactly what Raum had planned. A piercing red illuminated Ayperos's eyes. He cast away the strands strangling Nybbas with an emerald swipe of his hand. Nybbas turned to the Malefic chanter and thrust his claw into the Dark Gargoyle's chest, relieving it of its heart. Raum signaled the graylings once more as additional Malefic formed around them.

* * * *

A'uun levitated above the calamity of the battle. He closed his eyes, and the runes on his armor gleamed cobalt. When he opened his eyes, blue fire flared outward in a brief, luminescent burst. He could see every angle of the battle— Raum's unit, the Gargoyle sentries, and Cloister. One sentry was staring at him, as he could see the black veins on his own face had risen to the surface. He no longer looked like himself, but an evil Gilpesh wizard, leering coldly at the battle below. He looked a little more like Mandra than he liked.

A'uun extended both arms, his fingers were outstretched. Blue flames surrounded his hands. From the north and south of the hollow, Gargoyles stared at the blue fireballs that had just materialized. The Gargoyles dove for the ground as the cobalt fireballs multiplied, spread out, and hunted their prey, never failing to find their Malefic targets.

Amid the flare of the raw power A'uun projected upon his enemies, he spied, through the window of Raum's eyes, the attack on the Gilpesh protectors and realized Nybbas and the others needed help. He mentally summoned a contivan, Cloister, Bloodbrand, and Cahan from their secondary positions. A'uun knew that the powerful Gilpesh wizards could turn the tide if left to their own devices. Gilpesh were experts at supplementing the power of their troops through their aphotic spellcraft. The existing force would feel like double the number if the pewter-hued demons were allowed to wield their conjurations.

Chapter 37
~ The Impossible Choice ~

Cahan ran side-by-side with Cloister to the forefront of the battle. He thought that Cloister was moving amazingly fast due to her spellcraft-influenced strides. He had wondered why she had changed into a formfitting spellcrafter's foundation garment. Now he had his answer.

He pushed a little harder to keep up with her. "That chasm the Gilpesh passed through might contain the wraiths," Cahan yelled. "They could be hiding in there to keep from being exposed."

"We will have to fight our way to the chasm and trap the creatures long enough for A'uun to silence them," Cloister shouted back.

Cahan felt immense heat emanating above him. When he looked up, he saw a line of several golems on a small ridge above. They were feverishly rending spell casts, one after another, down upon the Malefic forces to open a way for Cloister and him.

A deep, guttural growl blasted out over the calamity of the battle. It was Bloodbrand, singularly focused on extinguishing as many enemy lives as possible. He was in rare form, even for him. He crushed, maimed, and leapt while slashing through Malefic and Gilpesh alike. It was almost as if he were in some sort of battle trance. It was amazing to Cahan how agile he was. Bloodbrand was suddenly surrounded by a horde of enemies. Cahan started to break away from his path when he felt a hand grab his forearm.

"He will be quite all right," Cloister said.

* * * *

Bloodbrand reached for the Berylocite that A'uun had given him. He ingested the substance and felt a surge unlike any other—a surge so powerful that he felt compelled to disgorge the flame lest he be consumed by it himself. Bloodbrand unleashed the dragon's fire upon the Malefic in a wave of all-enveloping blue flame. He could smell burnt flesh around him. Faces once bound by skin crumbled to bone, then ash. The enemy was consumed in what seemed like an instant. The area around him was charred black, and the dark outlines of their bodies still hauntingly remained in shapes of fleeting agony.

* * * *

A'uun's eyes glowed with piercing cobalt once again, as he conjured a spell of prodigious magnitude. The energy around him grew and his voice echoed preternaturally in a tongue foreign to Shintallians. The conjuration was a whirling dark sphere of energy with tides of blue-and-white waves that crested and ebbed within the heart of the spell. Sparks of electricity crackled and illuminated the cave intermittently.

A'uun saw a large group of Gilpesh was fervently attempting to counter his spell. He sent a telepathic message into Cloister's mind with a profound resonance.

* * * *

Cloister stopped her long, sinuous strides and gasped from the force of A'uun's thoughts. She bent at the waist and grasped her knees tightly. A'uun instructed her to cast a spell at the countering Gilpesh and the surrounding Malefic forces.

She rose up and tightened her fists. Charged energy began emitting from her hands as she focused. She felt a power that she had never felt before, a byproduct, she surmised, of A'uun's telepathy. Cloister summoned forth a white-hot fireball and cast it toward the Gilpesh throng of wizards and their cohorts. As the whirling projectile hurled toward its target, she could see a broader spectrum of light. Everything in the cave was a different color. The cave walls were a mixture of white and red. The awestruck faces of the enemy looked green around the edges and yellow in the center. Purple particles flowed from their mouths as they screamed. An ominously hollow, cracking sound was emitted from the spellcraft.

Cloister watched a light-infused reflection of the Gilpesh and Malefic alike as they sent waves of phosphorescent shields toward the fireball. The spells were also not their normal hue. As they drew closer to the fireball, shimmering white gave way to blue. Her fireball easily punctured through their desperate counter spells. The ensuing explosion erupted upward and folded outward at its apex. Half of the group of beleaguered conjurors and Gargoyles were obliterated. All that remained of the fallen creatures were crackling embers that sparked from bluish-gray flesh in the spell's wake. The remainder of Gilpesh spellcrafters could not hope to counter A'uun's spell now. She felt vibrations beneath the enemies' feet as if she were there, a lingering effect of her spell. Clumps of earth projected upward, and the earthen hands of dwellers thrust up above the strata and pulled the dark wizards into the folding earth to meet a suffocating death.

Cloister could still feel the power infused to her from A'uun, as if it were now a part of her. As she looked down, hissing white energy pervaded from her hands. When she exhaled, deeply charged flecks of energy mingled with her breath. She saw a vision of A'uun. His eyes were ablaze with lines of red that intermingled at the center of his white pupils. She felt that he was about to cast a spell of a magnitude that she had never experienced.

* * * *

A'uun centered his focus on the spellcraft, and his mind. A cone-shaped light shone so intensely that nearby combatants had to shield their eyes. Time seemed to pass more slowly as different languages of many worlds permeated his mind. Preternatural hisses tugged at the edges of his skull. For this spell, A'uun had to weave in a dark element, while he simultaneously countered the dark side effects with luminous spellcraft. He was determined not to swear a dark oath he would later be beholden to. The spellcraft had many different layers, and he felt splintered beyond his limits.

A'uun heaved the mighty conjuration toward the enemy. For a moment, time once again lapsed and the colors of the cavern whirled together in a cyclone of abnormality. For several moments afterward, darkness blanketed the space. Once the spell had climaxed, reality snapped back. The linear aspect of reality was restored and general cognizance relapsed into focus. A significant portion of the enemy forces were decimated and some sentry casualties also added to the death count. The power he had given to Cloister had gone to good use. She had shielded herself and Cahan from the raw cosmic power of the spell.

* * * *

Blackness faded into focus, as Stryge opened his eyes. He saw several sentries lying in the hollow near him, not yet conscious. This was a unique opportunity. Stryge hastened toward the small chasm. Just inside the rim of the shallow crater, lay a defenseless sentry. He raised his massive leg and stomped on his enemy, smashing helm and skull. The others began to stir. He quickly plunged his taloned hand into a nearby sentry's chest. Another young Gargoyle slowly rose, rubbing his head. Stryge grabbed his cranial horns and twisted violently. The neck cracking sound jolted a hollow memory loose. It roused something in him, but he could not place it.

Stryge smelled the smoke of dragon's fire and knew a Fenthom was near. He surveyed the musty landscape. There was a small cave near where he had entered the hollow. He knew he would not be able to withstand dragon's flame. He retreated to the safety of the black cave mouth.

* * * *

Cahan focused his attention on the deep chasm before him. Amid the countless bloody casualties of the explosion lay a clear pathway before them. He

219

sprinted along with Cloister to the opening, avoiding charred body parts along the way. As they drew closer, the sounds of battle began once more.

As Cahan reached the fissure, he caught wind of the snapping sounds of Cloister's spellcraft-influenced strides behind him. The mouth of the chasm contained a frightful aura and noxious, miasmal gases that burned his eyes and throat. The awful stench seemed as though it had bonded with his armor and he felt its oily residue spread to his skin.

His mind shifted to his academy lessons on wraiths. He wanted to ensure this actually was the hiding place of the creatures. They had little time for error and could not check multiple caves. He also knew that this could be an elaborate ruse, designed to throw them off target. He ran his hand over the opening of the cave, which appeared natural. As he investigated a little more, he sensed something off. While he kept his head clear of the cave, he reached in, hoping to find a clue. Upon touching the wall just inside the opening, the calcite crumbled to dust in his hand—a sure sign of wraith abnormality.

"The wraiths are here," Cahan said to Cloister. "Can you do anything about the gas?" He made a sour face as the acidic fumes made his eyes water.

Cahan noticed Cloister's eyes seemed distant. He waved his hand in front of her before she snapped back to him.

"Sorry, I just received word from A'uun," she said. "Yes, I can clear the miasma." With a deep breath, Cloister held her gnarled, accursed staff upright. She brandished the staff overhead, standing at the threshold of the yawning mouth of the tunnel, her eyes closed tightly.

Cahan scanned the area. He felt nervous for Cloister. She was vulnerable at the moment. He would have to protect her, but he hoped they would not be noticed. A small group could get to her, and there would be nothing he could do about it. Breathless moments passed. Cahan's eyes anxiously darted around the immediate area for enemies. He still heard clanging swords in the distance.

"Cloister, pick it up," he said nervously.

She summoned the energies floating about, barely visible yet unyielding. The tiny particles began to flutter and disperse in rhythmical aspect, like that of a beating heart. Finally, one intense palpitation coalesced the particles in grand unison. The particles turned a dark charcoal color and began absorbing the putrid miasmal gases.

Upon clearing the venomous fog, the particles migrated in a cylindrical formation to Cloister's staff. The staff, for a moment, burned with intensity upon the arrival of the decaying energy she had channeled into it.

Cahan winced with sympathetic pain and grasped his own hand. He could only imagine how painful that must have been.

Once the staff cooled, Cloister grasped it with the opposite hand. Her hand was red and horribly burnt from the quelling of the gas. However, in a mere moment, her scorched palm healed before his eyes.

"We have only a limited time to find the wraiths and silence them," she said.

"What? We're silencing them? Why not A'uun?"

"We do not have time to argue, Cahan. The gases will return and the corrupted energy in this staff will soon discharge." She paused for a moment. "We may both perish."

Cahan nodded. They wouldn't die—not here, anyway. Not by the hands of these damned wraiths.

They started down the long, burrowed tunnel. A rancid odor still saturated the air Cahan breathed, and his throat and lungs felt like they were burning, making it difficult to keep up the pace. A dark, baneful feeling filled him as he ran toward the source of the malignant horror that drenched the tunnel with blackness.

Cloister cut through the blackness with a luminous beacon that emitted from her waning staff. The light brought into full view the commanding corps of the Amalgam army. It was apparent to Cahan that the half-demon soldiers were not whole. Their rotting faces of bone and insects indicated that they were now owned by some unknown Shabarian dogmatist via the Wraiths of Úul. Cahan heard a chewing and slurping sound emanating behind the unwhole Amalgam. A dark figure pushed its way past the others with a severed Amalgam arm in its hand. Once Cahan got a good look at the figure, he knew who it was. Before them was Nerigaál, ghoulish and cannibalistic.

Nerigaál lunged, mouth open, at Cahan, with flesh-eating intent. As Cahan dodged Nerigaál's advance, he noticed that the ghoul moved with precision and there seemed to be no degradation of its mental faculty. Nerigaál's eyes burned with a sentient intelligence, not the dim, carrion-shrouded apathy indicative of most Shabarian acolytes. It seemed to Cahan that the fresher the body, the fresher the mind of the servant.

Cloister flourished her staff at one of the Amalgam lieutenants. This took Nerigaál's focus away from Cahan. A wave of flame enveloped the lieutenant, burning away the lower portion of its body. As the burned corpse drew nearer by way of its groping arms, Cloister severed the head from the torso with an authoritative downward strike of her staff.

Cahan saw this as an opportunity to go straight for Nerigaál. He charged and sliced off Nerigaál's right arm with his Gargoylian blade, then spun around and thrust his sword deep into Nerigaál's chest. As Cahan retracted his blade from Nerigaál, it fell to the ground.

Nerigaál looked up at Cahan and muttered, "Nelás veris."

Compelled to lock eyes with Nerigaál, Cahan saw them begin to blaze an intense yellow, revealing a runic slash on its forehead. The spell stifled Cahan and arrested his movement. He felt something stream from his eyes and mouth. Blood dripped down to his boots.

Cahan struggled to look over to Cloister. A distraught look overcame her, and she feverishly began to counter the incantation.

He sensed a transformation coming on. He was turning into one of the carrion-shrouded things he was fighting. Cahan felt his mind begin to give way to madness, and his thoughts did not feel like his own. He heard preternatural whispering in his mind, and feared he would lose himself at any moment. Just as his thoughts were in a total state of decay, he heard another voice in his mind telling him to fight. Then the whispers receded and faded. As he fell to the ground, he saw black energy flowing into Cloister's staff.

Cahan opened his eyes and felt a burning sensation on his chest. He moved his armor slightly to take a peek. Under his armor, he could see the top portion of a runic symbol that had been branded onto his skin. He looked over to see that Nerigaál had been incapacitated. He searched for the other creatures. He tried to rise, but could not will it. He anxiously wondered where Cloister was. Nerigaál's lieutenants were at a distance, just barely out of the reach of Cloister's luminous beacon.

A voice from behind him called out. "That will prevent further transformations. I am a little surprised it worked. You have been resistant to other spellcraft. We must make haste, as the miasma will return. Come on, up you go."

Now clear of the Nerigaál's influence, Cahan's vision came back into focus. He no longer felt as though he was being drawn into a marsh of black, haunting solitude full of whispering wraiths. He quickly rose.

Cahan heard a groaning noise. Nerigaál leapt up in a fit of cannibalistic anger as its slobbering mouth smacked. Its lieutenants snapped out of their dormant state, eyes glaring red. Cloister threw a dagger in Cahan's general direction, but the decayed Nerigaál leaped for it. Cloister willed the small blade to vanish midair and reappear in Cahan's hands. Cahan plunged the dagger into the base of Nerigaál's skull as it lunged for him. The former leader wavered and fell to its knees. Its rotting corpse fell into a state of uncommon degradation. Just before the creature decomposed entirely, its neck twisted and cracked, and a demonic slime spewed from its wounds and mouth.

The two remaining corpses disappeared into the spectral shadows of the hollow. A resonant rumbling shook the ground that Cahan stood on. Sounds of heavy mouth breathing began to creep and echo into the chasm until the glaring forehead of Stryge reflected off Cloister's luminous beacon. Stryge lumbered forward, his glistening, blood-soaked mouth churning.

Cahan felt an intrusion scratch the surface of his mind. He feared that it was a Shabarian acolyte, once again leveling mental warfare against him. He felt warmth and knew it was Cloister's doing. She telepathically communicated that they did not have time to deal with the creature and that he needed to leap back with all his might on her mark.

Stryge sprang forward and took a rending swipe at Cahan. He connected across Cahan's jaw line, sending him reeling against the side wall and then fell to the ground of the dusty hollow. Cahan stood up. Stryge appeared confused by this, and the ancient lines of his face contorted. Cahan once again felt the warmth of Cloister's presence in his mind. He leapt backward as the tunnel collapsed atop the hulking parasite. Cahan met Cloister's eyes. This had bought them only a little time.

Cahan and Cloister hurled themselves into a frightened pace. They flashed by the two retreating Amalgam corpses, who swiped and groaned at them as they ran by. Finally, they reached a piece of earth that was somehow wrong. Everything seemed out of phase with reality—in a state of constant flux.

Cloister swung her staff horizontally, and the space around them metamorphosed into a waxing distillation of clear but perceptible energy. The wraiths shrieked and appeared before them. Their rank odor cascaded into otherworldly emerald gases, folding and curling around them. Their constant phasing began to cease, and for once, Cahan could see the true faces of the horrors that crawled from the depths of the ichor-saturated bowels of Úul.

Cahan wondered if what he saw could actually be called a face, for in the middle of where a face should be was a gaping pinkish hole of poking triangular teeth, punctuated by leaking pustules of viscid fluid. The creature's long, gnarled fingers were tipped with wicked-looking, curved black nails, most likely broken and bent due to the fabled abyss they'd slithered out of to gain their freedom. What looked like soiled clothing while the creatures were in their phasing state was actually charred, tainted flesh.

The wraith at the forefront of the group leered at Cloister hatefully. Hidden amongst the pulsating mass of teeth and pustules emerged eyes at the surface of its rotten dermis. The leering wraith slinked queerly toward Cloister. Her irises turned black with red lines, similar to A'uun's. Circular echoes of luminous energy assailed the creature as it struggled to shriek. Gelatinous muck spilled from its gaping mouth and porous extremities. Filled with malevolent anger at the sight of the creature, Cahan stabbed the now-corporeal thing repeatedly.

Cahan woke from his bloody rage to see that Cloister's next conjuration was much larger. He knew that her silencing spell needed to affect the two remaining wraiths that haunted the hollow. Cloister amassed the energy needed and hurled it upon the legless, floating masses of tainted flesh. Just as the spell had started to take effect, Stryge emerged from the long stretch of darkness. The floating wraiths sprouted branch-like extremities that rooted them to the ground.

Cahan watched the phantasmal energy closely as it unspooled and dispersed, vanishing from sight. He could tell that Cloister was recanting her spell and possibly repurposing it—but for what?

The dispersed energies reemerged and metamorphosed into a darker swath of blanketed energy. Immediately, the naked, aberrant wraiths responded to the black hex that was now dispersing in the hollow. Their heads jerked unnaturally backward, and their eyes burned with sanguine evil and honed in on the brutish hulk, Stryge. The wraiths uprooted their hideous, branch-like extremities. As the pair of drifting ghouls raced for Stryge, countless impish eyes emerged betwixt the pulsating flesh and clattering teeth of the charnel terrors.

"We have to leave, now," Cloister said emphatically.

"What about the wraiths? We can't let them live."

"If Stryge does not kill them, we will. Trust me."

Cloister took the lead this time and ventured further down the tunnel. She was leading him somewhere important, he figured. Cloister would not simply leave the wraiths if it were not of the utmost importance. She stopped at a column of light pouring down from an open sore in the earth, from which the wraiths must have come. A dead and mangled dweller lay bloody, bathed in the light with outstretched arms, apparently attempting to flee after he had bored the tunnel.

"We have a decision to make, although it is one-sided. I bring it up because I want you to know what we are doing. In this staff are the collected energies of a wraith and Shabarian dogmatists. If the malignancy contained in this staff is released through that shaft of light, the village nearby will succumb to evil and enter a metamorphosis."

"What kind of metamorphosis?" Cahan asked, horrified.

"They will become disciples of Shabaris—proselytes—the product of which you witnessed at the manor."

"Why don't we just dispel the energy here in the hollow?"

"The malignancy will not disperse into the soil. It has to be propelled to a large, open space, otherwise it will fester and grow stronger and eventually become an entity all its own. This is how all creatures of pure evil are forged." She sighed, her face sullen.

"If it is turned back into the tunnel, the evil will make its way back to the wraiths and revive them, even if Stryge has killed them by now. My staff cannot hold the demonic influence of the wraith much longer. I have to dispel the energies. If this is undertaken improperly, the enemy will have a chance at the Time Celestial's domain once more. Even worse, the wraiths will not only be bolstered by the energy of the proselytes, but also by the Gronxth spirit that is trapped in my staff. With that much power, they may be able to force their way past a weakened A'uun."

"Can't you just make the staff disappear like the dagger?" Cahan said, exasperated.

"Cahan, I have limits. A vanishing spell can only carry an object a small distance. I am not A'uun. I cannot simply spirit the staff away to the stars. Believe me, Cahan, I do not enter this lightly. The village above is Weshire, a place I called home once."

A beating of gargantuan footsteps echoed in the hollow, escalating rapidly. Cahan knew it was Stryge coming for them.

"Stryge has finished the wraiths. I must draw any lingering energy," Cloister said, as a lone tear traced a path down her cheek.

Cahan was angry at the entire prospect. Tears of rage freely flowed down his cheeks.

Cloister drew in the remaining energy. After one last hesitation, she solemnly dispelled it outward toward the shaft of light. The light was engulfed by the darkness. A black pillar of noxious miasma snaked its way out of the sore in the earth, leaching the life out of its surroundings.

Silent moments passed as Cloister and Cahan stared at each other in surreal disbelief. Screaming echoed from the nearby town. Cahan shuddered. Above, the newly released Gronxth beast bellowed. Anger and sorrow assailed Cahan to the core. He fell to his knees.

Cloister sealed off the tunnel to prevent Stryge from reaching them as she collapsed to the ground in horror. Cahan heard several more sets of footsteps gathering near Stryge's grumblings.

Cloister solemnly grasped Cahan's hands. She wept as she rubbed the top of his hand with her thumbs. "Now both our hands are stained."

"What do we do now?" Loss assailed Cahan as he listened to the rancorous sounds of carnage pouring from the small town. His mind shut down.

Chapter 38
~ Aftermath ~

Bloodbrand felt some measure of relief. The diverse group of warriors, aided by Gargoyle sentries, had held off the Malefic and the Gilpesh encroachers. He decided to form a search party and find Cloister and Cahan. Then they would set their sights on the barrier.

He had explained to the group that if the barrier fell, it would be catastrophic for Protos and the human colonies, as the naval blockade and the airship contingency had been disbanded and withdrawn. This fact alone told Bloodbrand that Protos might well fall back into the clutches of despots. They were setting the board for a complete overthrow. What the MOI did not realize was they would be consumed by the Forgathans once this coup ended. Bloodbrand knew firsthand the Forgathans did not take half-measures like the Ministry did. Zealots always consumed those who dealt in approximations. If they failed, they would become slaves to the Forgathans. The barrier was the only thing standing in their way. By setting the destruction of the barrier in motion, Bloodbrand knew the MOI had dug their own graves. Should the barrier be breached, there would be no back-up forces to stop the onslaught of the dead continent's displaced inhabitants, all amassed at the barrier's threshold.

Bloodbrand led the expedition to find his two lost compatriots. He knew the general area the pair had gone off to. He had spied them as he was in the field of battle. Bloodbrand had tracked their scent just short of the now-closed fissure. With a glance from A'uun, the chasm cracked open. Trapped, hideous odors drafted upward, making the group cover their faces. Bloodbrand caught the scent of wraiths and the stagnant odor of undead corpses. As they started down the miasma-eroded tunnel, Bloodbrand caught wind of the demonic Stryge. He looked down to see his colossal, cloven prints embedded in the earth.

"How does Stryge still walk among the living?" Bloodbrand asked A'uun in shock. "I felt his neck give way in my hands."

"He was likely rejuvenated by a particular Gilpesh wizard of note," A'uun replied.

"Who? The wizard you had mentioned in the catacombs?"

"Mandra... I do not yet know how," A'uun said in a tone that halted any further questioning. "The signature of his spellcraft permeates this space." His eyes narrowed. "They are here."

The group came upon the burnt, ravaged corpses of the wraiths. The creatures' branch-like extremities were twisted and broken, and their bodies were covered in claw and bite marks. It looked to Bloodbrand as if their jaws, or what would pass as jaws, had been stretched beyond what was natural, and the creatures lay there with their mouths bizarrely agape.

"It looks as though Cloister was successful in making the immaterial material," A'uun observed. "Though these bites and claw marks were obviously not left by humans."

"Why would Stryge attack wraiths that were fighting on his behalf?" Bloodbrand asked.

"Cloister probably turned the wraiths on him. If I were a human with limited means, I would do the same. Very clever. She is more powerful than I had thought."

The group came to a cave-in. Once again, A'uun pushed aside the refuse effortlessly with his mind, without even a hint of incantation, though by the tired lines of his face, Bloodbrand could see that Herald A'uun was quickly approaching his limits.

An awestruck silence came over Bloodbrand as he witnessed both Cloister and Cahan in a state of all-encompassing horror. A dead body was placed to the side, shrouded by Cloister's cloak. By the scent of the corpse, Bloodbrand could tell it was a dweller.

"You had to dispel the corruption toward the town. Move!" A'uun yelled.

Bloodbrand moved aside as A'uun pushed past Anaymous. He evaporated from sight and then emerged at the light shaft's depths. He leapt upward in a flash. Bloodbrand wondered how A'uun had immediately picked up on the cause of Cloister and Cahan's distress.

Bloodbrand leaped up through the hole in the earth. He absorbed the destruction of Weshire with a gasp. Bloodbrand turned to see Cloister had emerged as well.

"I had to release the energy. We had no choice."

Bloodbrand saw permanent damage had been wrought in the moments after Cloister's expulsion of energy. He saw and smelled hundreds of proselytized creatures that quested through the town's thoroughfares for flesh. A'uun could at least put the bedlam to a halt. Bloodbrand took solace that he might be able to save a few lives in the process.

* * * *

A'uun saw the profusion of energy lingering above the city as he stood amongst the dark calamity of a broken and bloody cityscape. The creatures running rampant could not see him because A'uun had hidden his presence from them with spellcraft. The Gronxth and several proselytes flashed past him as they fought each other. He summoned his scythe from the middle of a cobbled thoroughfare and blanketed the entire area in a cerulean curtain of brilliant light. The black, murky ichor started to buoy upward and churn with the blue aura.

A'uun evaporated and reappeared as he made his way to several points in the city. He wanted to ensure his spell was taking effect. He saw that the glassy-blue, unblinking eyes of the proselyte scourge that littered the cobbled street begin to metamorphose back into their former humanity, even the dead.

The former proselytes looked dazed for a moment after their return to humanity. One human nearby looked down with horror to see others torn to pieces at his feet. A'uun sensed a familial bond between the living human and the dead ones around him. When the human looked at his blood-caked hands, he fell to the ground and wept uncontrollably. He pitied the human. Wailing and sorrowful cries filled the bloodied thoroughfares. Sadness welled in A'uun.

Once the township was fully cleansed, A'uun hurled the energy toward the stars, where it erupted into a luminescent horizon in the blackness beyond.

Chapter 39
~ Betrayal at the Gate ~

Cahan stood in silence with the others in front of the oval aperture of Luttrel's metallic airship. With the feeling of defeat still lingering, Cahan mustered the energy to board. Despite what happened, Cahan knew that he must move forward—and moving forward at this time meant checking on Blodwen's progress at the manor. He hoped that she had not also faced an attack.

Cahan grabbed the railing mounted around the periphery of the topside deck when he felt the rumbling of the energy chamber below. Columns of blue energy pulsated and then at once thrust at full power. He closed his eyes and felt the effects of liftoff in the pit of his stomach. A poisonous despair lurked in the recesses of his mind. It worried him that what he felt was not anger. He realized the emotion he was now feeling was wholly his own—only darker and more ominous.

* * * *

Bloodbrand stood silently near an outside window in the ship's common chamber. His mind raced with grim outcomes in a whirl of anxiety. He felt a deep sense of guilt, guilt for the many lives lost in the human town of Weshire. He pondered what would happen if the die had been cast—if the MOI had made their irreparable mark. Surely all of the denizens of Shintallis would be safe. The architect of the barrier would be able to mend the life-granting invention to full capacity.

He smelled the smoky plumes of blue propulsion begin to recede as the airship started its descent. He raised his head from his introspective haze.

229

As he looked through the nearby window, he surveyed the area and noticed that there was no contingent of Gargoyle architects or progeny workmen overhauling the outer workings of the barrier's energy chambers. No caretakers were tending to the landscape. There were, however, all manner of demonic creatures clamoring at the barrier's border. Bloodbrand was somewhat relieved the barrier appeared to be intact, impeding the gnawing Forgathans.

"I have some information to discuss with you, Chief Magistrate," Cloister said in a hushed tone, as she emerged from the doorway. "I will make it as brief as the subject matter allows."

"You attained the information? Why did you not come to me sooner?"

"You were deep in thought, and I did not wish to disturb you, and the loss at Weshire has affected me greatly." She paused to clear her throat. "The information I am about to impart will be disturbing and perplexing."

Bloodbrand gestured Cloister to the nearby study and advised a crewman that he would be back in a few moments.

"While we were at the MOI, I did what you asked." She paused as she scanned his face for a moment. "As you know, the Ministry has detailed records of all human colonists. Without deviation, all humans are accounted for, even me. I destroyed many of them. Anyway, as I was saying, all humans have a full life record from infancy to death, save for one."

"Cahan," Bloodbrand said.

"Oddly enough, there is a partial record of Cahan, going back ten years. His acceptance declaration into the Verindian Rangers," Cloister said. "There's no birth record, no record of parentage or anything else. It is as if he did not exist prior to ten years ago." Cloister's misgivings showed plainly on her face.

"How did this escape the attention of the all-seeing MOI?" Bloodbrand looked dumbfounded. "Why would they allow him to roam free of any scrutiny? I would think he would be locked away in the Verindian Bastille. Do you think…"

"I do not think he is an agent of the MOI, if that is what you mean, but we cannot be certain. At the least, he has assistance at a level in the hierarchy eclipsing a mere clerk." Cloister looked at him with a sense of indignation.

"What is it?"

"Yes, he has support at the highest levels of the Protosian government. His Verindian citizenship bears your seal and your coat of arms, something that is almost impossible to forge." She took the Verindian leather-bound case from her satchel and laid it on the desk before Bloodbrand. "I found it strange that you would send me to find information you already knew," Cloister added with a tinge of anger.

"It has to be a forgery, Cloister," Bloodbrand said in an abrasive tone. "I did not give my sanction to Cahan's citizenship, nor did I allow his entry into the Verindian army." He looked down at the document. "Yet that crest is genuine, and the writing seems to be by my hand—"

"Then I do not know what to gather from this information." Cloister sat down in a chair and sank back for a moment.

Bloodbrand studied her, not knowing what to say.

"Why were you suspicious of the boy in the first place?"

"Just a vague, gut-wrenching feeling," Bloodbrand said. "He looks very much like a human with whom I had often gone on missions and into battle."

"Was he significant?"

"Yes, he was the only human I know of to survive the Rite of Strength ritual of the Kharr'kari."

"A human was infused with Kharr'kari strength? Odd indeed..." She trailed off in thought. "There may be a connection there. He is strong. What was this human's name?"

"Cathal Blake. He was from Dranda."

"The surname does not sound familiar, but Baldemar mentioned a Cathal Devlin while we were in Falkeland. There must be some connection."

"I have a lot of fond memories of Cathal. He always wore a warlock's gauntlet in battle. He was a great warrior..." He trailed off. "Keep a close watch on him—but for now, we have to ensure the barrier is still standing at day's end. We shall address this tomorrow, should there be one."

"There is one other matter, Bloodbrand. On our way back to the Priory, I stopped to investigate a claim that Viscount Erelding was participating in human subjugation."

"He was cleared of all subjugation charges . . ." Bloodbrand thought for a moment and realized that there must be something more to the story. "What happened?"

"As it turns out, the viscount was using an antediluvian spawn to cloak mining slaves from sight. This is why Protosian constables turned up nothing."

"Did you inform the Protosian Constable's office?"

"No. We decided that the constable's forces would be needed if Protosian defenses were breached. We knew they were already spread thin."

"So you jailed the viscount—"

"Not exactly. Baldemar the monk is now the acting viscount. Cahan carried out a wartime execution."

"There is no declaration of war, and Falkeland is a Protosian territory. Erelding should have stood before a tribunal. If we carry out executions without due process, we are no different than the Forgathans. The both of you have much to answer for."

* * * *

A'uun started up the stairs leading topside. He had felt the vessel enter into another level of descent, which meant they were close. It felt odd to him to be riding in an air vessel. He had not needed the aid of such a craft in a long time. It was much quicker for him to travel through means of spellcraft. He was a passenger of the craft as a showing of solidarity with the others.

As he stepped on deck, he saw Cahan holding onto the railing, staring off into the distance. A'uun decided to leave Cahan with his thoughts and walked to the other side of the deck. He had overheard what Cahan had done in Falkeland and figured that his mind was no doubt on the execution he had carried out. A'uun studied the barrier as the vessel neared it and waved his hand. The rune on his wrist shined a bright white. As the light from A'uun's rune intersected with the barrier, he could see its consistency and color. It appeared a light orange, meaning it had been weakened.

The nose of the mighty Gargoylian vessel freely passed through the luminous barrier. As it passed through the midsection, everything the barrier touched appeared to be orange. Around the edges of the vessel was a sparkling barrage of energy being displaced.

A'uun grabbed the railing instinctively as the ship touched down just outside the grounds of the manor. He was again reminded of the length of time since he had been on an airship. The landings used to be rough. A'uun's rune stones began to illumine as his body rose above the deck. He touched the rune on his chest and made his way to the ground below, waiting as the others exited the craft. Bloodbrand was the first out of the ship, followed by Cahan, who brandished a mace acquired from the airship. Anaymous and the golems made their way out.

As A'uun looked around inquisitively at his surroundings, he noticed a small airship had landed just outside the barrier's reach upon a small raised land mass, peeking above the surrounding water. A Gargoyle emerged from the swift, triangular-shaped vessel and flew rapidly toward the shore.

"Amaranth!" A'uun yelled as the striking creature settled to the earth.

Amaranth folded her wings behind her. She had a look of morbid distress. Out of the corner of his eye, he saw Cloister join them.

"Something is wrong, Lord A'uun," Amaranth said. "Blodwen has done something to the barrier. My ship would not pass through the barrier's ingress protocol. My ship's rune has been dispelled."

"I am sure there is some mechanical or spellcasting explanation for this, my dear," A'uun said soothingly.

"Full of accusations as always, sister," Blodwen said, emerging from the dark drum tower that overlooked the courtyard of the manor. She had Haran in tow.

A'uun caught a glimpse of Haran's aura. There was a red shimmer amid the other colors. Anger instantly erupted within A'uun. As he focused his energy, all of his runes shone in a spectral gray. A version of A'uun, made of pure cobalt energy emerged from the runes. His vision of the landscape blurred past. He appeared to Blodwen on her perch within the tower. He erected a sound barrier in the shape of a globe around them so no one else would hear.

"What have you done to Haran?" A'uun's voice rang out, deep and supernatural. "He has the stench and aura of a proselyte possession."

"I thought I had shielded his metamorphosis from prying eyes," Blodwen said lackadaisically.

"What have you done?" A'uun demanded angrily.

"Take a glimpse yourself," Blodwen said with a contemptuous smile. She raised her outstretched and still-bloody index talon and touched the spectral A'uun. In his mind, he witnessed Blodwen wearing a bloodstone amulet deep within the recesses of the catacombs. She strode toward the prisoner encrusted in A'uun's spell. With a gleam of the amulet, her right talon was set ablaze in blue flames. She ripped right through the spell's fortification and thrust her smoldering hand into the Gargoyle's chest.

Why reveal your intentions now? A'uun responded.

She did not answer, but A'uun sensed she had accomplished her mission at the manor.

Haran managed to send A'uun a mental image of the energy chamber churning and grinding in an evil fervor. At its inner sanctum, a pedestal appeared, bearing the familiar sign of the infinite with intersecting slashes, freshly carved upon a runic stone, his runic stone. The chorus of gears and phosphorescent conjuration beckoned mockingly. This abomination was designed with mechanical ingenuity and spellcraft, specifically engineered to work against A'uun's influence.

A'uun felt the permeation of dark spellcraft amidst the ever-churning gears and pulleys. He could not put his finger on what Blodwen was trying to accomplish. The only thing he gleaned from this display of dark wizardry was that it summoned something to the manor, something from deep within the bowels of Úul. At present, he could not sense it directly. A'uun reasoned Blodwen was trying to shut the barrier down, though something did not fit. Instead of diverting power, the manor was summoning more. The fount that was destroyed in Elysium had several protective fail-safes should someone usurp the power of the Progeny.

A'uun was sure whatever Blodwen was attempting to do revolved around the elemental fount. He also realized the framework for her plan, whatever it might be, must have been in place since the invention's inception. That was why she had been so bent on his absence from the construction of the barrier from the beginning. It had nothing to do with balancing powers. Blodwen knew his philosophies about power, and she played on his long-held ideals, knowing he would agree. She was merely waiting for the right moment when the Forgathans, the Malefic, and the MOI would ally.

"How long have you been Malefic?" A'uun growled furiously. "What is the true nature of this perversion?"

"To your first question, since Luttrel's ostracizing, betrayal, and wrongful banishment of our brothers and sisters," Blodwen yelled. "As to the second, you will see soon enough."

In a phosphorescent blur, A'uun returned to his body and started to feel Valese's influence fading from him. A'uun pressed on his temple as he faltered. The barrier apparently served that purpose, as well. However, A'uun sensed he still possessed his other gifts prior to becoming a Celestial herald.

A'uun explained the circumstances now underway through dweller speak to the group, for purposes of instantaneous understanding.

Amaranth, visibly angry toward her sister, hurled Gargoylian curses at the dark tower.

"Amaranth, you will stay with your vessel," A'uun said. "Should we not make it out, you will relate what happened here to your brother. Blodwen may have engineered a way for you to be trapped here once her evil takes full effect. You must leave while you can."

* * * *

A sudden coldness chilled Cahan to the core. Abnormality filled the air. The further clutches of the manor portended the musk of dark rites. Malevolence hovered in the back of his mind, as if it took comfort in its current surroundings.

As Cahan and the others reached the twilit entrance of the brooding edifice, they came to a choked archway of stone and mashed corpses. Cahan looked to A'uun as he parted the obstacle with a flare from the runic stone atop his shoulder. Once the refuse was clear, Cahan led the way into the reaches of the dank structure. Evil blanketed the crimson-stained place with even more saturation than the courtyard. Cahan smelled the putrid odor of evil stronger now. Among the smell of aphotic spellcraft, a new smell lurked and wafted about, though he could not quite place it.

Cahan caught a flash of movement. A lapping noise accompanied by gruesome glopping sounds echoed in the murky darkness. He surmised this new odor was attached to creatures likely loosed by Blodwen.

The group drew nearer to the curate's chamber. As A'uun lit the room with a dim white light, Cahan gasped at the butchery that had transpired here.

Cast about the room were the corpses of the curate's caretakers. Several lay in silence without heads, while others had been relieved of their skin. Emotion overcame him. He had seen innumerable battles, bloody ones at that, but this was perhaps the most gruesome display he had ever seen.

One particular caretaker drew Cahan's eye. She lay there, slightly propped up against the wall as if she'd been posed, with the permanent look of oncoming death branded onto her contorted face. He knew that the last thing she saw was a menacing Blodwen rending her talons into her flesh. Cahan also noticed that all of them were stripped nude. Only a soulless creature was capable of this. Cahan's mind shifted to Falkeland, and he wondered if he was on the same path. As he shook the thoughts from his head, he noticed another woman, pale and bloodless, lying in the corner. Had Blodwen resorted to vampirism like Stryge?

Cahan strayed over to a desk nearby, similar to the tree-like one in the curate's chamber. Crumbling arcane books were opened to barbarous, ancient rites. Cahan caught a scratching sound. He once again heard the creatures that stirred just beyond the room, skulking in the dark.

"I know the odor of these creatures. I have fought them before," Bloodbrand whispered to the others. "They are called 'collectors' by the conjurors that use them."

From his studies, Cahan knew that collectors were creatures of a fetching kind that served the maligned purposes of evil wizards. Many profane rites or rituals of the bygone era and pre-bygone era required that organs be brought forth to summon the likes of Shabaris the Dead Caller and other ancient fiends.

Cave writings went as far back as the first Kharr'kari scrawling upon the cavernous walls of antiquity, depicting the creatures bringing body parts and organs to pewter-colored demons with dual-pointed ears. Cahan had read about the numerous ancient tomes that displayed illustrations of the beasts, beckoning the call of the Carthen reptilians and their onerous acts of genocide, as they commanded the creatures to kill humans and their precursors, the Venerites, while they slumbered.

No historian, not even the immortal chronicler, Sut'aict, could pinpoint the emergence of these creatures in the murky Shintallian timeline. It was said that since the dawning of thinking beings, these creatures had been servants of torture and pestilence during the nameless spans of time before the written word.

The collectors' pungent odor increased, and Cahan knew they were getting closer. He watched Bloodbrand and waited for him to give an order. Bloodbrand signaled Cloister through the arched opening to the adjacent room. A'uun crept northward, whilst Anaymous circled around to the opposite of Cloister. Each of the golems waited, huddled at the southern side of the room occupied by the beasts.

Cahan found it odd that Bloodbrand did not give him a direction. He decided to trail behind Anaymous. Cahan witnessed one of the creatures in full view. The creature appeared to be scavenging for organs as it sniffed the air and scented with its tongue. It had long, thick, and hairy forelimbs and skeletal protrusions extended out of its elbows. The creature moved with a preternatural quickness. It was roughly the size of a tall human. Its body was thin but densely packed with muscle, dually combining the nature of reptilian scales and simian structure. Its neck had a path of greenish-white scales leading up to a cone-shaped snout of sharp, trilateral teeth with slit-like serpent nostrils resting atop. Its wet, sunken eyes were framed by a reptilian ridged brow. Its long, floppy ears were thin and semitransparent. On top of its head was a crown of needle-like thorns that swept back beyond the head.

Cahan's eyes darted over to the southern entrance of the room, where eight more of the creatures entered. He noticed there was some deviation in the placement of bone protrusions amongst the group of deviant beasts. Some had coral-like bones projecting out of their distinctly developed trapezius area, while others had layers of bone crusting over their knees. He noted where they were naturally armored in an effort to find and exploit any weaknesses.

Cahan watched in silence as he noticed a quick flurry of movement from A'uun, who was the first to strike. He called his dual-bladed scythe from a rune stone on his shoulder. He separated the weapon in the middle. A collector sprang forward, mouth gaping. A'uun turned the blades so that the top of each weapon touched. He hooked the blades into the creature's upper and lower jaws, and with a circular outward motion, broke the jaws and heaved the beast over his shoulder into another oncoming, snarling collector.

The six remaining creatures all merged toward A'uun. Anaymous charged into the room and flanked the creatures, with Cahan following behind him.

As Anaymous approached a collector, it turned on him with its preternatural quickness. The collector wrapped its cavernous mouth around Anaymous's thigh, shaking its head and tearing his flesh. Blood spilled, staining the collector's clump of fur branching around its neck, as it fixed its eyes upon Anaymous.

Cahan bolted toward Anaymous just as he tore the creature off him with his immense claws. Anaymous sliced through its exposed neck until it fell limp, blood gushing from the wound.

Another collector bounded for Anaymous and tore into his upper arm. Anaymous twisted and broke free, then drew a dagger from his belt and flung it at the foul thing. The dagger plunged into its collarbone, making the collector shriek. It paused before it continued its charge.

Cahan's anger bubbled to the surface. He needed to kill something. He bore down on the beast with his mace and summarily crushed the degenerate quasi-reptile's skull.

While Cahan stood over the collector he had just slain, its cohort crept atop his back and dug its claws into his flesh, sinking its teeth into his ribcage through a crease in his armor. The stinging sensation of the claws made Cahan respond in anger. As the collector's powerful jaws clamped down, a shrill grating of metal and fang sounded. A piece of Cahan's armor and underclothes dangled from the collector's teeth.

Cahan felt the air meet the scaly section of his body, and a deep anxiety overcame him. He did not want anyone to spy his secret. As he struggled to keep the abnormal dermis concealed with his hands, his chest pounded even harder. He had that familiar feeling of sharp pain in his mind. This time it didn't feel like needles, but like spears.

He wasn't sure what to do—he could not reach the damn collector on his back. Cahan had become so accustomed to lying, but lying would not help him now. The cold truth was moments away from being exposed.

The creature moved away from his ribcage and attempted to clamp down on his head. He heard its snapping jaws and moved to avoid them. He looked in front of him to see Anaymous wearing an expression of shock.

Cahan stared hollowly at him, waiting for him to react. Cahan prepared himself for a fight as Anaymous moved closer. The malevolence in Cahan's brain started to rise to the surface as it battled the anxiety within him. Just as Cahan readied himself to strike, Anaymous snatched the creature off Cahan's back and bit into its neck, spitting out a significant mouthful of reptile flesh, then dropped the collector to the ground. It convulsed for a moment before losing its grasp on life. Its skin turned noticeably dark from Anaymous's poisonous bite.

Cahan covered his scales with his hands, looking around the room to see if anyone was nearby. Then he looked at Anaymous, not knowing what he might do. Anaymous stood before him, expressionless. Cahan thought that he probably used this expressionless look on the members of his syndicate and in his dealings. It was a great tool for building up anxiety, because he had no clue if Anaymous would report this to the others. Something inside told him to kill Anaymous and blame it on the collectors. Cahan closed his mouth and gestured to Anaymous to speak, choosing to ignore the dark thoughts—but Anaymous said nothing.

Cahan looked again nervously around the room. Downed enemies lay in piles before the others, with various wounds inflicted by spellcraft and weapons. In the distance he saw Cloister, who'd been bitten on the leg. She busily tended to her wound with a curative spell. A'uun's resounding voice called out to Cahan and Anaymous, asking them to come over to meet the group. Cahan, still consumed by anxiety, stared at Anaymous, hoping to get a read from his monstrous face. His hands were shaking as he approached.

Chapter 40
~ Secrets ~

Cahan looked down at his right hand and watched it shake. He gripped his fists tightly to stop the tremor in his hands. Anaymous looked at him questioningly at first, and then hardened his eyes until they looked like the shiny surface of an onyx metal shield. The pair shared a gaze for what seemed like eons to Cahan. He saw himself in the scion's glassy eyes. The voices of the others continued to ring out in the background, beckoning them, as they continued to share a disquieting silence. Cahan thought of the argument they had before "acquiring" the vessel at the airship field. He figured that was what Anaymous must be thinking about—he was piecing together the lies.

"This is what you were hiding," Anaymous finally said. "This is why you are so strong and could easily subdue one of my own. You are not human—or not fully human." Anger washed over Anaymous's face. His insect features now seemed more baneful, as if a creature inside of him took hold and pushed out all reason from his consciousness.

Thoughts came streaming into Cahan's mind.

Will he attack? How can I explain this to the others?

Cahan rapidly concocted lies in his mind. He looked at his cohort once more, pleadingly. The creature in front of him held all of the cards.

Anaymous threw him a large red cloth from a satchel on his belt. "Talk to me when you are ready to explain whatever this is." He gestured toward Cahan's deformity.

Cahan opened the broken armor as the remaining torn buckle dangled uselessly. He wrapped the red cloth around the scale outcropping, once again concealing his secret.

"Let's hurry to the curate's chamber," Cahan said awkwardly, in a shallow attempt to be friendly, as they sprinted toward the group. He turned to Anaymous, who followed at a distance. He knew full well that he had lost his trust.

The group rushed to the chamber, filled with what Cahan would describe as a spectacle of pure, contemptible madness. All manner of foreign implements were assembled in the chamber. The hairs on Cahan's neck stood as he viewed looming circles of magnetic stone with strands of blue energy branching out between them. Blood spattered the rock in odd circular patterns. Effigies of Shabaris and Ulian, the apparition of the abysms of Úul, gleamed atop pedestals of a black, sand-like substance. Cahan's gaze moved to a rectangular onyx stone. What he saw filled him with horror. Pinned to the large onyx was the head of the curate, returned to his human form.

It looked like an ancient rite torn from a black, superstitious era long forgotten. Blodwen was at the center of the spectacle, seemingly mad and muttering darkly into an unseen, fetching abyss. It was clear she had taken a forbidden oath as flecks of green gleamed brightly from her irises.

The group tried to move toward the unseen demonic presence holding Blodwen in its clutches, but they were repelled. Cahan noticed even A'uun was thrown.

A deviant piping of bizarre rhythm whistled outward. A yellow, curling, supernatural fog emerged from the howling darkness.

"We are too late!" A'uun yelled over the tempestuous reverberation.

A'uun raised his hand and a shaft of light reached upward. The beam of light bored through the stone ceiling. A searing white light woefully illumined the space.

* * * *

Pulsating beats echoed in the room. Then feeling arose once more in Cloister's fingertips, and she sensed the cold alloy beneath her hands. When the whirling stopped, everything fell jarringly into its place. She looked around and found herself in Amaranth's vessel. Amaranth knelt beside her, with her hand on her back.

"Where are the others?" Amaranth said.

"I do not know. There was a white light... That is the last thing I remember."

Amaranth left her side and headed for the cockpit.

Cloister put her hands to her face, summoning a cooling blue energy, hoping it would refresh her. She heard the buzzing of propulsion ports ringing in her ears. As the ship lifted off the ground, her stomach jolted.

"You will still be blocked by the barrier," Cloister said, lifting her face from her hands.

There was a loud rumbling. Cloister flashed over to an outside window to get a glimpse. The manor of the curate crumbled inward, and a black energy mass darted out of it and whisked away. The barrier began to crackle and lose its integrity in place of the newly realized barrier. It was composed entirely of aphotic spellcraft, black and morose, with red strands snaking through it and tufts of smoke trailing behind.

"Amaranth… Blodwen was not simply summoning evil," Cloister said. "She has changed the barrier to allow the demons ingress—and trap humans within. Humans will not be able to get in or out."

Anxiety washed over Cloister. She pressed her finger against the window of the vessel, and a light emanated from her fingertip. Blue beads of energy trailed her finger as she drew a small rectangle. Through the blue rectangle, she was able to view the Forgathans clamoring at the barrier's boundary as if she were just yards away. There were so many demons that she did not bother counting. She had never seen such a gluttonous assortment of demonic creatures, all scratching and tearing at the barrier. Some she recognized, while others looked foreign to her. By the size of the creatures, her intuition told her that quite a few of them dated back to Valese's divine anthem. One creature in particular was singularly vicious. It was at least twelve stones tall and had a horn-like fin atop its head and a yellow underbelly. It stood on its hind legs at the moment, but seemed as though it belonged on all fours. It knelt down and began feeding on another demon's intestines. Cloister realized the creature was feared as the demon herd kept their distance from it.

The red demon's head jerked up when the mass of creatures stampeded for the barrier. A resonant snap sounded from her blue rectangle. By doing so, Cloister discerned the new barrier had almost overtaken the old one. The red demon rampaged for the barrier, casting the smaller demons aside, and rammed into it with its horn, leaving a large crack through which glowed an orange light. The other creatures howled maniacally and slammed their bodies against the gash. As the Forgathans broke through, the pulsating orange barrier shattered like glass. The hue of the barrier turned black and freely allowed the rampaging creatures entry. As more and more of the blasphemous horde filtered through, the remaining energies dissipated with a loud, otherworldly crackle in a puff of orange smoke. In that instant, the barrier returned to a fully transparent state.

* * * *

Cahan opened his eyes and felt woefully drowsy. Lines blurred in front of him and slowly came into focus. He saw a waking Bloodbrand, the golems, and Anaymous, just inside the barrier's reaches at the edge of town by a sheer cliff.

He figured that A'uun's white light teleported them to this place. He felt a quake beneath his feet and ran several yards back toward the city. What he saw next stopped him in horror; his arms fell limply to his sides. A herd of demons rampaged through the city. It looked like a giant mass of red, black, and gray, and he could barely distinguish the individual creatures in the herd. Cahan ran back to the others.

"Bloodbrand, we have to move now," Cahan yelled as the seismic stampeding of demons shook the ground. "There are hundreds of thousands of Forgathans." Cahan caught a glimpse of Amaranth's vessel, floating near the cliff in front of them. "Look."

Cahan spied Cloister on the topside deck next to Amaranth.

The ground beneath his feet began to crack.

Cahan started toward the vessel while Cloister yelled frantically, waving her arms. The howling wind carried human screams to Cahan's ears.

"I cannot tell what Cloister is trying to say," Bloodbrand yelled over the calamity. "We must hurry and board the vessel."

Giant fissures opened near them. Cahan ran toward the crumbling cliff, shoulder-to-shoulder with the others. Cloister, just ahead, was still screaming. Cahan looked back at the demon herd as they stampeded toward them.

Cahan and the others jumped almost simultaneously. As he approached the apex of his leap, he noticed a black energy surrounded him, though he passed through it. Anaymous and Bloodbrand landed on each side of Cahan. He looked at both of them to see if they were okay.

Where were the golems? He looked around frantically.

"Shit," he yelled. He whirled back toward the cliff and caught a blue gleam that peeked up above and reflected off the railing of the vessel. He ran to the railing.

Below, he saw the golems suspended by energy strands that rooted from their outstretched arms. One strand gripped the side of the cliff while the other latched onto an unseen source.

"Can you make your way back to the ship?" Cahan yelled.

"No," Cloister said abrasively from behind him. "How did you clear the barrier? It was specifically attuned to reject humans. Apparently, golems are more human than you. Amaranth, pull the vessel away from the cliff. Demons can pass in or out of the barrier now." She glared at Cahan. "I would not want them to board the ship."

Cahan jumped a little as the vessel lurched away from its hovering point, a good distance to the other side of the chasm. Cahan turned toward the golems. The blue energy strands holding the golems crawled upward like spider legs. Cahan knew, deep down, they did not stand a chance. The town and what was left of the manor were overrun, and there was nothing he could do. He also knew his friends were moments away from discovering his secret. Anxiety clawed in his chest, and his breathing became heavy. His heart pounded as sweat poured from his brow.

"Why would a demon-attuned barrier reject a golem egress, but readily accept you?" Cloister said to Cahan.

Cahan noticed she was eyeing the red cloth covering his body. He closed his eyes for a second, then decided he should simply accept his fate. His mission had failed. He opened his eyes again to see Cloister still staring at him. With a flip of her wrist, Cahan's armor opened and the cloth fluttered away, revealing the patch of greenish scales.

"What are you?" she demanded in shock.

Bloodbrand stared at him rigidly, and Amaranth walked toward Cahan. He flinched as she drew near. He looked her in the eyes, which had a sweet softness to them.

"It is okay, Cahan. Let me see," she said soothingly, studying the deformity. She softly ran her hand over it.

"This is Marsh Fenthom flesh," she said in a higher pitch than usual.

Cahan looked at the group in stunned silence, not able to find words. They knew. Darkness overrode his senses as he lost consciousness.

Chapter 41
~ The Jade Fenthom ~

Lord Bael lit a candle. The light from the tongue of flame crept along the decrepit wooden floor and made its way into an adjoining room that was part of a broken and worm-eaten hovel in the depths of one of the many swamps contained in the Dunnavisch Estuary, home of the maligned Marsh Fenthom. One such Marsh Fenthom, Vashar N'dal, sat smugly in the next room. He stared at Lord Bael through the large open doorway. Bael walked into the room. He considered Vashar an annoyance.

"Must we be here in this ramshackle of refuse and worms?" Vashar demanded impatiently.

When he leaned forward, a coral-like natural armor covering his chest gleamed with the touch of light that had taken residence in the room. Vashar had three pointed fins protruding from his head. One of the fins radiated squarely from the top of his cranium while the others swept back to a sharp point terminating from the crown of his skull. Folded scales circled underneath both of his scheming, wedge-shaped eyes. As he shifted back, the light drew attention to the deep yellow of his irises.

"There is a balancing act at play here, Vashar," Bael said as he walked over to the windows, swiping the curtains aside. "I cannot be seen colluding with one side more than the other. Our biggest hurdle has been overcome." Bael looked at his grayish, thin, and disproportionately large hands through the reflection of the window. Long white nails protruded from his fingers.

"Starting to feel the touch of age?" Vashar prodded.

Bael touched his face, almost reflexively. Every wrinkle in his face was getting deeper. Vashar was right. Age was creeping up on him, but that would be alleviated soon.

"Are you sure the herald perished?" Vashar said.

"All that remained was the carcass of his living armor, still smoldering from Blodwen's spellcraft."

"Were any of the runic stones recovered from the armor?" Vashar pursued with cautious optimism.

"I am afraid the stones melted away with the rest of him, but that does not change anything. The manor has fallen, quite literally. Most of it fell into the Icon Sea. When will Protos fall?"

"Days. They are spread far too thin to last any longer than that. What of the chief magistrate?"

"If he is not dead, he soon will be. It can be by your hand, if you like. I know of the bad blood that exists between you."

"Bloodbrand is as big a threat as the herald was," Vashar said.

"He should not be taken frivolously."

Anger spiked in Bael. He grew tired of this glorified marsh lizard. Fenthom? Hardly.

"I have business at the Priory," Bael said abruptly. "I have been summoned. Go to the capital. I want you to command the remainder of the siege."

He could tell the glorified lizard was angered by the fact that he was addressing orders to him. Bael knew he needed to put him in his place. He had heard of Vashar's unquenchable hatred for him. He had also heard Vashar secretly plotted against him.

Bael turned to Vashar and wrapped his now-illumined hand around his neck. "You understand very little, you glorified lizard. Do not presume you know what is at work here, or what is a threat and what is not."

Vashar's eyes began to roll backwards. His skin grew darker, almost to an onyx hue. Bael threw Vashar back to his chair, and the color in his scales began to return.

"I am tied to Celestial augury. Do not forget that."

"Yes, Lord Bael," Vashar said, capturing his breath.

Chapter 42
~ The Aver ~

Cahan awoke to the muted gray of a small, dusty stone cell with no windows or doors. His head throbbed with agonizing pain, the likes of which seemed magically influenced. He looked around hastily, out of breath and panic-stricken. The lack of windows or a door made him feel intensely claustrophobic. The malignant anger began to well up inside his mind, desperately trying to burst out at the seams like a thousand contusions, breaking the unseen wall of his sanity.

He clenched his teeth as he tried to fend off the fury, then loosed a wordless scream. The blood rushed to his face and he pounded the wall, though he did not remember standing up or how he got there. As the wall shook from his might, he thought back to the cursed progeny wizard at the manor, though he envisioned something far different than reality. He saw the guard laying him down on the stone carefully, his neck badly broken. He wished desperately for the peace the progeny guard now possessed and focused on Erepus's words. He needed to rebel against the hatefulness within him.

"You have to go back to the island." Tears welled as a shriek blasted from his vocal cords.

A familiar voice poured into his mind and calmed his rage.

What island?

Cloister?

Yes, Cahan. What island, and why do we need to go there?

The wooden box I found in that old airship. He didn't tell me why. He said it was important, very important. You have to get it. It's in his laboratory.

Who told you it was important?

A'uun.

When did he tell you of this? Is he still alive?

He told me years and years… Not your A'uun. Trust me, you have to get it.

246

* * * *

Cloister thought for a moment. Something stirred within her. Clearly, he was in some sort of delusional state, but A'uun had reacted oddly when Cahan retrieved the box from the antique airship. If she were to go to the island, she must hurry. Somehow, she accepted she must go. It rang true to her. Bloodbrand was rallying the Gargoyles to fight the Forgathans in the capital soon.

Where did you leave it?
I'm going with you.
Cahan, you are in a cell I cannot reach. Your cell is of Luttrel's making. I do not know where you are. I am only able to speak to you telepathically. I cannot physically come to you.

She paused for a moment, remembering he was in a fragile state.

Do you understand?
Just get it. A'uun said I would need it after I was imprisoned. It's coming back to me... Hurry. Show it to Luttrel. No, wait... he won't be able... I think you will be able to figure out what it is. Maybe Seara can help.

Cloister didn't know what to make of Cahan's orders. She wanted to dwell on his words for a moment, but she didn't have time.

She made her way to the entrance of the Priory air vessel chamber. The chamber was immense and covered with rune-inscribed molded stone, supplemented by supports of Gargoylian alloy. The luminescent quality of the room was a deep rust pigment. Cloister had thought the odd light made her skin look much like a pumpkin. There were a variety of ships resting in the space— battleships, sentinel vessels, guns ships, mineral transports, archeological rigs, passenger, and pirate-buster ships. All fully implemented with metallic battering rams that would shred most other vessels.

Two young guards were posted near the ships. Cloister considered herself lucky there were only two, since most of them were with Bloodbrand and Luttrel. She shut her eyes for a moment, still concealed behind a wall away from the sentries. As she focused, wisps of blue spiraled upward next to her and formed into a glamour of Luttrel. The illusion seemed exactly like the Gargoyle leader with all of his mannerisms, down to the specific way he breathed. The glamour looked at Cloister, as it possessed some intelligence.

"Go on," she said with a wave of her hand.

It shook its head and walked to the sentries. Upon seeing their revered leader, they snapped to attention.

"You are needed in the strategy chamber immediately," the glamour said. "We need all available sentries."

"Yes, sire," they responded.

Clear energy pulsated around Cloister, shrouding her in invisibility. As the sentries dashed past her, Cloister thought of what the glamour had just said. It did not sound at all like Luttrel. Idiot glamour. Once the sentries were safely away, she lifted the invisibility spell and made her way to a small vessel. She had no time to explain or endure formalities to justify the theft. A part of her also knew if anyone were to catch wind of this undertaking, they would think her mad. She figured she had some time because Luttrel was about to commune with the Bridge Celestial.

She fumbled with the piloting instruments at first, but quickly became accustomed to them. Gargoyle vessels were different from those of the human and demon variety. She looked to her side to see her spell was eagerly awaiting her next command like a loyal puppy.

"Oh, shut up," she said with a wave of her hand that dispersed the energy of the glamour. As the energy dispersed, the glamour had a look of disappointment on its face before it evaporated into nothingness.

She throttled the small vessel and blazed a tide of blue tracers encapsulated by the orange glow of the chamber. As she sped away, she noticed the night sky loomed unnaturally overhead. She again fixed her gaze in front of her, hurling away from the mountain.

She traced the route to A'uun's island in her mind. The coordinates slowly came back to her. She set motion to the aft propulsion ports and imbued them with a little of her own spellcraft.

Cloister made good time to the island and navigated her way to the general area of the laboratory, where she found two confounded figures inspecting the expanse of the obelisk-riddled jungle.

"Show yourself," Cloister yelled with black energy surging up in her hand.

The two figures revealed themselves to Cloister. She recognized them immediately. One was Seara and the other was the man Cahan had identified as a traitor at the MOI archive. Cloister sensed powerful magic within him.

"Cloister. We need your help," Seara cried. She turned to the man. "Oh, this is—"

"A traitor that is in league with the MOI," she interrupted.

"Well, I actually go by Bardon. It is a little shorter than—"

"Shut up. What are you doing here?"

"He is not a traitor, Cloister. He is one of A'uun's pupils. He was investigating the MOI, just as I was."

"He warned the Protosians of Cahan's plans in Veldt, when Cahan was seeking to bring Anaymous together with Bloodbrand."

Bardon tossed a defero stone in Cloister's direction, which she snatched out of the air. She sensed something odd about it.

"It is muted now," Bardon said. "Declan—or someone helping Declan—listened to Cahan and me through the stone. They were eavesdropping. That is how they knew what he was doing. Something seemed off about the stone, but it did not take long to figure it out. Afterward, I had to spin a few lies to the Ministry to justify some of my actions."

Cloister's eyes narrowed. She was still not sure if she could trust them.

"The other man I was with when you were at the MOI is the traitor."

"You knew we were there?" Cloister furrowed her brow.

"That invisibility spell may have fooled Declan, but come now. Would a pupil of the—"

"You did not answer my question," she interrupted again. "What are you doing here?"

"We are here searching for signs of A'uun. What are you doing here?"

"I am here to…" She paused, still not convinced she could trust the pair. "I am here for the same reason. He will be needed in the battle against the Forgathans."

"Where is Cahan?" Seara said.

Cloister paused for a moment. "You have wanted to ask that since you arrived, have you not? He is at the Priory with the others. He needed to be there."

Seara, noticeably disappointed, nodded.

Cloister knew that the passage to A'uun's laboratory was always difficult to find, even for his pupils. The passage changed over time to protect the many secrets and forbidden truths that rested within its boundaries.

After a time, Cloister was able to find the passage near a rock formation that overlooked a small lake. She debated as to whether or not she should let her newfound companions enter, then she had an idea.

Cloister rested her hand over the subterranean stone entrance switch. She brushed her hand against the cold chimera stone, feeling for pock marks. She closed her eyes and connected her mind to an unseen force. The door yielded to her request.

"Over here, you two!" she yelled impatiently. "Get over here, you dozy sods."

Seara arrived first, followed by Bardon, who gasped desperately for breath.

"Go on," Cloister said to Bardon. "A little exercise would not hurt. Maybe a little sun, too. Never seen someone so pale."

Bardon and Seara looked at her questioningly for a moment.

"I have to hold it open while you go in. Now, go on."

Cloister watched as the pair descended the steep stone stairway that stretched out in a straight line for a bit, then curved awkwardly westward before descending to its lowermost point. Bardon and Seara studied their surroundings. Green torches provided light as they drew closer.

Cloister winced and braced herself, listening as if something explosive were about to happen. Silence still pervaded, save for their echoing footsteps.

A look of recognition crossed Bardon's face, and he looked back at Cloister with a tight smile. "Ah, you told the Eidolon that guards the laboratory to destroy us if we had malicious intentions. Well, we are still here. Trust us now?"

Cloister nodded.

Seara glared at her bitterly.

"I had to be sure," she said. "Too much hinges on what rests here."

Seara scoffed.

"Take the path as it is intended," Cloister said. "Shortcuts like jumping over the stair railing can set off a series of traps."

"Do I look like someone who jumps over stair railings?" Bardon said. "Yes, we understand." Bardon looked at Seara, who was still perturbed. "I mean, I understand," he corrected.

* * * *

Luttrel made his typical friendly eye contact as Lord Bael entered the Gargoyle Priory. He noticed Lord Bael paid special attention to the rousing of sentries by the ever-charismatic Bloodbrand and his newly acquired ally, Anaymous, who were gathered in the reaches of the air vessel chamber. Lord Bael shifted his attention to the upper hollow, in his methodically uneasy way, to see even more sentries gathering weapons along with dwellers shambling tensely to and fro.

"Master Celestial," Luttrel called out in his warm and respectful tone.

"Do you think it wise to have all of your forces concentrated in one area with no one to defend the outer reaches of the mountain?" Lord Bael said with his typical pretentiousness as he studied the glowing slabs of stone that lined the hallways.

"We will be fine, Master Bael. No one knows of our troop movements outside the Priory."

Bael turned to Luttrel and fixed his eyes on him. Luttrel always thought Bael had the shrewd demeanor of a vastly wealthy merchant. Now that he thought of it, it had only been in relatively recent years that Bael had seemed so self-assured. He had grown accustomed to Bael's self-important manner, though he had not seen him for many decades. He had had no need to summon him until now. Those tied to the Celestial Augury could not set foot in the Priory unless called upon because of a sacred rite sworn years ago. Luttrel had lost contact with many of the Celestials.

"As I am sure you already know, the Priory came under attack recently," Luttrel said.

"Yes, I had heard." Bael's voice seemed to caress the air ominously.

"We think forces are mustering their power to gain entry to an archeological discovery recently found in the Priory."

"And what discovery would that be, Luttrel?" He turned to him as his eyes narrowed.

* * * *

Cloister came to a fork of pathways in A'uun's laboratory. Something called her. It was the Eidolon. A blanketing cold around her seemed to latch onto the fibers of her clothing. She continued to walk ahead and grew even colder. She began to shiver fiercely as the penetrating cold revealed puffs of her breath.

"See? I knew she was frigid," Bardon's voice called out behind her.

Cloister rolled her eyes at the comment, then stepped back for a moment and became warmer. She realized the Eidolon was playing the child's game of hide-and-seek with her. As she stepped back again, she felt even warmer. She looked toward the large stone staircase encased in blackness and began to feel cold once again. She rotated her vantage point slightly to the east and felt warmth saturate her clothing. As she moved, the warmth grew around her, kissing the surface of her skin.

She found herself standing squarely in front of a stone wall. Shadows danced around one specific area on its surface. She touched the wall, revealing a runic stone. Cloister hesitantly reached for the runic stone. Nothing happened. Cloister placed her palm fully on the stone. A wooden box, painted with a red dragon sigil—surrounded by light—emerged from the stone. The light then dimmed and flickered away.

Cloister opened the box to find a dagger with a handle of gnarled wood. Rock deposits lined the inner walls of the box. The box smelled like the Priory. Bardon and Seara's footsteps sounded behind her. As she picked up the dagger and thumbed the wood, she sensed something familiar about it.

"I do not understand. He said it would help. Tis just a dagger."

251

Cloister's mind raced back to Cahan's exact words. He had said Seara might be able to help. She smiled and placed the dagger back in the box.

"What are you doing?" Seara looked puzzled.

"You have to draw the blade from the box," Cloister said. "I know what this is."

Bardon appeared to understand immediately Cloister's train of thought. "Go ahead. It has to be you. Odd though, the dagger does not feel like a simple glamour."

Seara looked curiously at the pair before she reached for the dagger. She felt the surface of the odd mineral deposits before she drew the dagger out by its gnarled handle. She held it for a few seconds of breathless silence. The dagger began to change. The gnarled handle stretched and coursed like a rolling brook. At the edge of the flowing wood, straight corners formed until it took an oblong shape. The blade folded toward the handle and pages of parchment sprouted from the center and fluttered for a moment before resting on the gnarled cover.

"But why?" Seara said in a state of befuddlement.

"It was a spell," Cloister said. "Cahan had a conjuror bewitch the dagger to not reveal its true shape until the one he loved lay her hand upon it. May I?"

Seara looked up at Cloister, glassy-eyed, and handed the book to her.

"That is a powerful spell, Seara," Cloister said with a warm smile tugging at the corners of her mouth. "The love must be absolute for it to work."

Cloister began to examine the book. Her feeling of vicarious happiness evaporated into fear.

"What is it?" Bardon demanded.

"See for yourself."

Bardon took the book and concentrated on it for a moment.

"It is a Celestial tether," Cloister said aloud. "The Bridge Celestial's."

"What is a Celestial tether?" Seara stared blankly.

"It is a spellcrafted object that keeps a Celestial bound to this realm," Cloister answered, shaken. "Without it, they would not be able to maintain a physical presence."

"So if it is here, and not in the Bridge Celestial's possession…" Bardon trailed off.

"Then who is really at the Priory with Luttrel?" Cloister muttered.

* * * *

Luttrel faced Bael, the Bridge Celestial, Master of Corridors and traveler of alternate realms. "Forgive me, Master Bael. It sometimes slips my mind the Priory conceals power both within and without. You would not have felt its discovery concealed within the mountain." He paused, looking at him. "You see, the Priory—"

"I understand the inherent qualities of the Priory, Luttrel," Bael interrupted. "What did you find?"

"We found one of the light founts of the Time Celestial. As you know, his power is closely related to yours. Just recently, A'uun and I postulated you may be able to regain your command of gateways, should you enter the light fount." Luttrel refocused on Bael. "Did you ever find the cause as to why your powers were lost?"

"No. I suspect Shabaris had a hand in it, somehow. He claimed the life of my herald."

"I have always wondered why you did not call for a replacement."

"Still searching. Mearain will be very, very difficult to replace. Let us go to the light fount, so I may regain my calling to the augury."

* * * *

Cloister, Bardon, and Seara raced toward the Priory in the small vessel, with no plan of what to do once they reached Luttrel. Cloister looked back at the ghost-white faces of Bardon and Seara. Her mind was tormented by the catastrophic scenarios streaming in. She supplemented the propulsion ports to increase their speed. The vessel stretched itself beyond capacity like rubber tie-offs ready to snap. She heard an eerie bending sound of tensely stretched wood over the hum of the central energy chamber. Was Luttrel already dead?

* * * *

Luttrel and Lord Bael made it to the light fount dig site. A few pieces of scaffolding and digging implements still littered the area outside the fount.

A crooked smile crossed Bael's face. "Why did you not tell me of this, Luttrel? I had to get this information from Blodwen, of all things."

"W-what?" Luttrel stuttered. A shock erupted through to his core. Fear and anxiety, things he had not felt in quite some time, coursed through him. He painfully recalled Bloodbrand telling him of Blodwen's betrayal upon their return from Aundyre. Was Bael a traitor? Had he taken some sort of dark oath?

Bael pulled a runic stone from a pocket in his sleeve and held it between his thumb and forefinger. The stone blazed with black resonating energy as a wraith of Úul began to emerge.

In horror, Luttrel remembered Blodwen's insistence that she attain a runic stone for the barrier. Bael now held that stone.

"Finally, something of Herald A'uun's has proved useful," Bael said. "Blodwen convinced you easily before she went to destroy the barrier."

"You took the wraiths from their caller." Luttrel summoned a spear from a stone embedded in the entryway of the dig site, but before he could wield it, Bael shot a black energy surge at his chest. Luttrel collapsed to the floor.

* * * *

Raum emerged from the tunnel leading to the dig site; a grayling trailed behind him. He had sensed the presence of one of his wraiths. Raum's eyes widened as he tried to stretch his influence to the constantly phasing creature. He could not hear its inner mind of contemptuous whispers. For a wraith caller to call the creature, the caller had to link himself indirectly to it using its own tactic of preternatural suggestion. It had been shielded from control, a spellcraft only a very powerful being could wield. The wraith leered at Raum as if it recognized him, turning its head unnaturally. At once, the wraith charged him, dark energy laced with bright red tracers spilling from its many emerging eyes.

Raum sent forth the grayling in desperation. He had felt fear like this before. As a youth, he was tasked with controlling the beasts for his father's maligned purposes. Once, a wraith would have consumed him had his father not interceded and risked a direct bridge with the creature's mind to save him. Raum's father did not have the luxury of time the power of suggestion required because Raum was being consumed before his father's eyes. A mind bridge was simply a test of wills. The wraith caller risked falling somnolent within such a union, as Raum's father did, though he managed to silence the wraith in the process. Raum spent many years attempting to wake his father from his magically driven sleep, until ultimately, his heart gave out. The specter that had invaded his body in the ensuing years had taken too much of his life force.

The grayling hurled blue-and-white projectiles at the creature, to no avail. The energy simply traced the gruesome figure of the wraith and evaporated. The wraith stopped just short of the grayling and stretching its gnarled fingers, penetrated the grayling's eye sockets. The grayling transitioned into a state of black, contorting metamorphosis, a metamorphosis that completed its transition to a wraith. Then the two wraiths shifted their countless red eyes threateningly on him.

He desperately tried to control the wraith that had just transitioned. He could not gain full control, but he slowed down the creature. Just as the newly formed wraith was about to follow Raum's command and attack the other creature, he felt a sharp pain in his abdomen. The other wraith was ripping at his flesh with each swipe of its grisly, gnarled fingers. The wraith that was nearly controlled by Raum broke loose of his suggestion, and in unison, the two wraiths digested him, starting with his legs. All Raum could do was watch as the wraiths feasted.

* * * *

A barely cognizant Luttrel awoke to Bael's gesture, meant to counter A'uun's earlier fortification of the light fount. The wraith compound turned to ash and dissolved upward.

"Open the fount."

The wraiths floated to the cylindrical fount that spewed blazing particles. As they held up their phasing hands, light instantly bathed the room, which dispelled a glamour around Bael, revealing another form. Luttrel forced himself up as he coughed blood.

"Mearain?"

Mearain, the herald of the Bridge Celestial, called the wraiths back to the runic stone and entered the chamber. The light receded and the chamber closed.

* * * *

Cloister and the others made it to the Priory at last. As they were about to land, several airships emerged from the cover of fog with turrets fixed on the Gargoyle Priory. Immediately, the gun turrets began to glow, leeching charged energy fragments from the air. The energy contained inside the clear housings of the airship fleet expanded and contracted. At the climax of the contraction, blue-white bursts of energy discharged in procession from their bellies into the Priory's exterior. A brief moment of nothingness swept over the mountain. It seemed to be drawn within itself for the span of a heartbeat before it expanded outward in a violent, fiery concussion of ruination.

The group gasped.

Shock struck Cloister as she looked at her companions. "They are all dead."

* * * *

Cahan woke as his cell shook violently. He studied the cell walls. Several deep cracks appeared and a brilliant red light shone through them. He shielded his eyes with his forearm as he approached the cell wall.

He heard a hissing noise the closer he advanced. When he touched the wall, it crumbled to dust. He was not sure what lay before him. He saw a black and twisted nightmare, devoid of anything natural or living. It looked like a vast, open expanse with pathways made of energy particles. He got down on all fours and looked over the precipice. A red pathway lay below him. He sensed something oddly familiar about the pathway. He thought this familiarity might be tied to something he had read, but it seemed deeper than that to him. The answer was at the edge of his thoughts, just out of grasp.

Cahan made out the figure of a man running down the passage, with waves of red cresting outward behind him. He heard the hissing again, but this time the noise surrounded him on all sides. He realized the rest of the cell was about to crumble to dust. He jumped down to the pathway.

As Cahan landed, he collided with the man he had seen running moments before. The man stumbled a good distance backward and landed on his back. As the man raised his head, Cahan realized he was of Venerite descent. He wore an old overcoat with soiled garments a few sizes too large underneath. The man hopped up.

"Where are we?" Cahan said.

"Run," the man yelled. "The Vaa'corthra is coming."

In horror, Cahan suddenly realized he had traded one cell for another. He was now imprisoned in the domain of Úul.

The End... but More to Come

About the Author

Aaron R. Allen, an online professor and part-time elementary teacher, developed a passion for writing at a very young age. Like many writers, he spent quite a few years in the realm of academia. While working toward his bachelor's degree, the sparks for his current book began to ignite and continued through grad school. Aaron lives in San Tan Valley, Arizona, along with his two kids, Keltyn and Abigail.

facebook.com/originsaga
www.aaronrallen.com